The Last Suppers

Also by Diane Mott Davidson

Catering to Nobody

Dying for Chocolate

The Cereal Murders

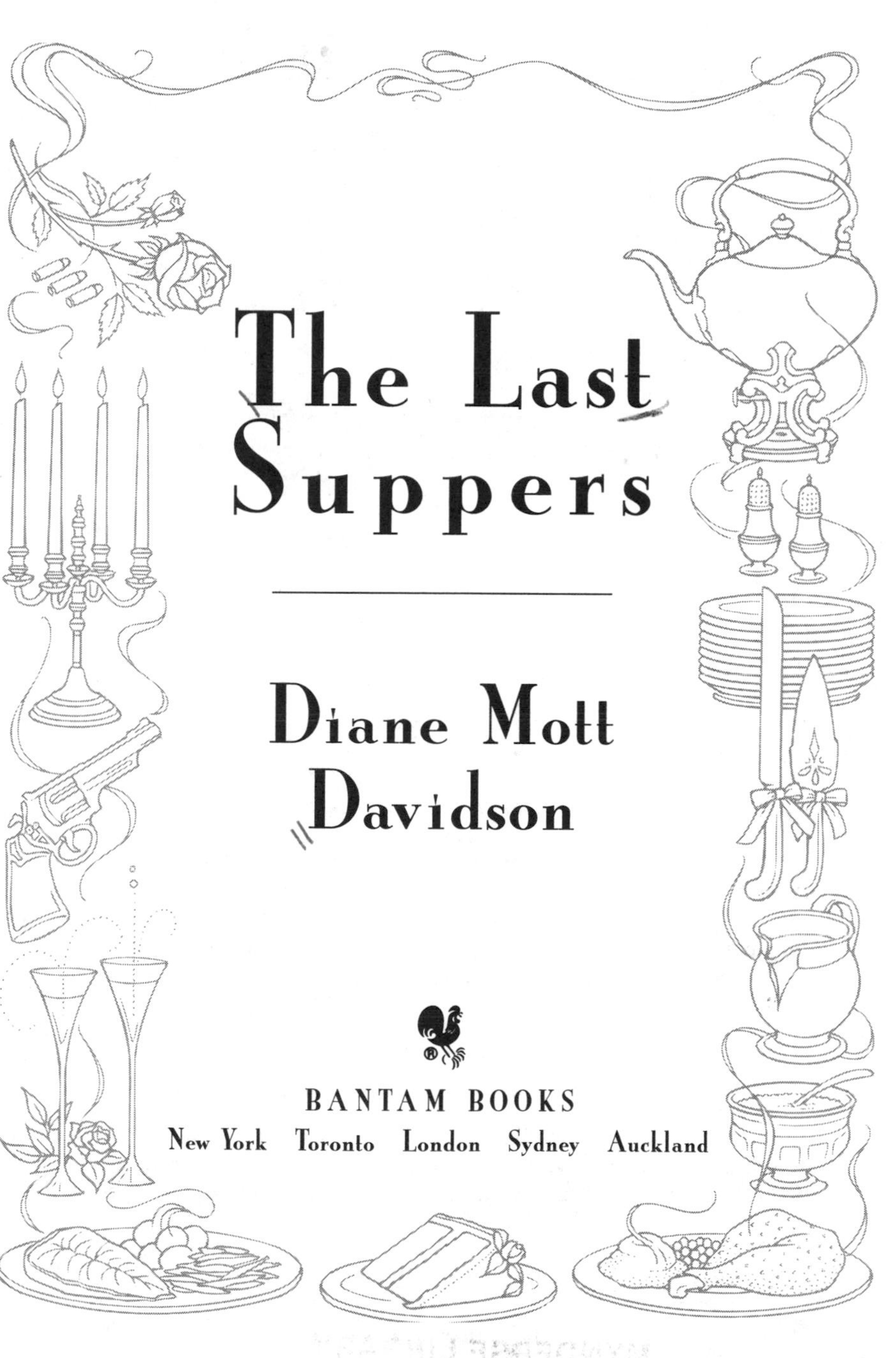

The Last Suppers

Diane Mott Davidson

BANTAM BOOKS
New York Toronto London Sydney Auckland

For the Reverend Constance Delzell

The Lord rebuilds Jerusalem; he gathers the exiles of Israel.
He heals the brokenhearted and binds up their wounds.

—PSALM 147:2–3

Interior illustrations by Jackie Aher

ISBN 0-553-09587-0

Published simultaneously in the United States and Canada

Bantam Books are published by Bantam Books, a division of Bantam Doubleday Dell Publishing Group, Inc. Its trademark, consisting of the words "Bantam Books" and the portrayal of a rooster, is Registered in U.S. Patent and Trademark Office and in other countries. Marca Registrada. Bantam Books, 1540 Broadway, New York, New York 10036.

PRINTED IN THE UNITED STATES OF AMERICA

Acknowledgments

The author wishes to thank the following people: Jim Davidson, Jeffrey Davidson, J. Z. Davidson, and Joseph Davidson, for their unceasing love and support; Sandra Dijkstra, for being an unflaggingly enthusiastic agent; Kate Miciak, for being the outstanding and thoughtful editor she is; Katherine Goodwin Saideman, Deidre Elliott, Dorie Ann Stapleton, and the Reverends Jack Stapleton, Larry Donoghue, and Constance Delzell, for their meticulous and insightful reading of the manuscript and their helpful suggestions; Lee Karr and the group that assembles at her home, for their excellent comments; Carol Devine Rusley, for wisdom and inspiration; Karen Johnson and John Schenk of J. William's Catering, Bergen Park, Colorado, for teaching the author how to cater awedding reception; Emerson Harvey, M.D., for his medical expertise and insights; Steve Wormald of Guarantee Upholstery in Denver, for his professional expertise; the B-10-D Evergreen Stingers soccer team, for tasting and commenting on Chocolate Truffle Cheesecake ten weeks in a row; and as always, Investigator Richard Millsapps of the Jefferson County Sheriff's Department, for providing superb expertise, assistance, ideas, and insights.

Prayer book quotations are from *The Book of Common Prayer,* published by the Church Pension Fund.

Without having seen him you love him;
though you do not now see him you believe
in him and rejoice with unutterable
and exalted joy.

—I Peter 1:8

There's nothing wrong with this parish that a
few well-placed funerals wouldn't fix.

—Popular saying among Episcopal priests

Wedding Reception Menu

Smoked Trout with Cream Cheese, Vegetable Terrines, Water Crackers

Spinach Phyllo Triangles

Bacon-Wrapped Artichoke Hearts

Portobello Mushrooms Stuffed with Grilled Chicken, Pesto, and Sun-Dried Tomatoes

Salad of Field Greens with Balsamic Vinaigrette

Fusilli in Parmesan Cream Sauce

Sliced Roast Tenderloin

Fruit Cup of Fresh Strawberries, Black Grapes, and Kiwi

Heated Sourdough and Parkerhouse Rolls

Dark Chocolate Wedding Cake with White Peppermint Frosting

1

Never cater your own wedding reception. It's bad luck, sort of like the groom seeing the bride before the service. Death or destruction could result. Not to mention ruined cake.

Thirty minutes before I was due to get married for the second—and last, I'd sworn—time, I was trying to check on stuffed mushrooms as I listened to directions from Lucille Boatwright, head of the Altar Guild, about how to walk. Sixtyish, with an aristocratically wide, high-cheekboned face framed by silver hair curled into neat rows, Lucille made the decisions about how the weddings were run at St. Luke's Episcopal Church, no matter what you read in the prayer book. *Sway and pause, sway and pause. Goldy, are you paying attention to me?*

At that moment, I would have given anything to see Tom Schulz, bad luck or no. But the groom-to-be was not around. Perhaps he'd had a call on his beeper. The Sheriff's Department of Furman County, Colorado, put great stock in Tom; he was their top homicide investigator. Still, it was hard to believe the Sheriff's Department would call on him on this of all days. While Lucille yammered on, I longed for a comforting Schulz embrace before the ceremony. Suddenly our parish's newly hired organist sounded the opening notes of the first piece of prelude music: Jeremiah Clarke's *Trumpet Voluntary.* Lucille Boatwright stopped swaying and pausing, whisked the platter of mushrooms out of my hands, and bustled me out of the church kitchen.

In the hall, Lucille crisply ordered a group of whispering women back to work in the kitchen. Then she scurried to retrieve my garment bag from the church nursery. The Sunday School rooms had no privacy, she informed me briskly, and the bride traditionally dressed in the church office building, even if that antiquated edifice was undergoing a *horrid* renovation. And speaking of *horrid:* I asked if anyone had been able to get into Hymnal House, another church-owned building, where Tom's and my wedding reception was supposed to be held. Unfortunately, the old house across the street was locked up tight. Lucille's stalwart body bristled inside her scarlet suit. She shook the perfect rows of silver hair and announced that Father Olson was *supposed* to have opened Hymnal House this morning. She herself had had to open the priest's office building when she'd arrived. Imperiously, she pointed to the empty, unlocked office building, ten yards from the side door of St. Luke's. *Goldy! Pay attention! Twenty-seven-and-a-half minutes.*

Great. No groom, no historic Hymnal House dining room, no food being set up. And no caterer; I was trying to be the bride. Clutching my garment bag, I hopped gingerly across the walkway. Gray flagstones and buckled wooden steps led to the St. Luke's office, a squat century-old building that originally had served as a stagecoach way station between Denver, forty miles to the east, and points west. Small squares of thick-glassed windows peeked out from the thick paneling of vertical unpeeled pine logs. Now the office building formed part of a national historic district along with the buildings from the once-famous Aspen Meadow Episcopal Conference Center across the street: rustic, log-built Hymnal House and cavernous Brio Barn. I glanced at the higgledy-piggledy boarding-up job that was the only indication of the pipes that had exploded in the office during a hard freeze this February. At the old conference center, Brio Barn was also falling apart, but the office emergency and its renovation had taken priority. Our parish priest, Father Olson, had told me historic districts ate money the way catering clients gobbled hors d'oeuvre.

Once I'd pushed through the door to the office, I couldn't see or hear a soul, much less catch the strains of prelude music, all of which had undergone the required approval of Father "Please-call-me-Ted" Olson. The only noise reaching my ears as I hastily wriggled into my new beige silk suit was from a family of raccoons scratching in the attic over the office.

I concentrated on a dozen tiny pearl buttons that made me wonder if I should be serving smoked oysters instead of smoked trout. From a purple satin bag looped around the suit's hanger, I carefully removed and then snapped on a stunning double-strand pearl choker on loan from an upcoming Episcopal Church Women's fund-raiser. Marla Korman, my best friend and matron of honor, had somehow convinced the churchwomen that letting me wear the two-thousand-dollar bauble would be great advertising for their upcoming jewelry raffle. When she'd proffered the necklace, Marla had waved a plump, bejeweled hand and boasted to me about the unique advantages of her fund-raiser: easier than a bake sale, and a thousand times more profitable.

I looked around for a mirror. Where *was* Marla, anyway? I sighed; there wasn't time to worry about what was out of my control. My mind raced over post-wedding details that would have to be altered if no one could find the keys to Hymnal House. If we had the receiving line and photographs at the church, that would still give my helpers enough time to set up the food in the Hymnal House dining room—once they forced their way in.

Poking a pearl-topped pin to secure a brimmed hat to my unruly blond hair, I imagined parishioners' comments on my bridal appearance: *Shirley Temple dressing up as Princess Di.* I shuddered and visualized the reception food. All the lovely platters and heavy chafing dishes had been hastily left in the church kitchen when the helpers couldn't get into Hymnal House. Whether the hotel pans would survive the transport across the bumpy ice and gravel of the church parking lot, across the bridge over Cottonwood Creek and Main Street, and up the walkway to the conference center was questionable. One unexpected bump on the gravel, and the smoked trout with cream cheese could spew everywhere. An inept move could send a layer of the carefully constructed cake on a slide into the frigid creek. And if Father Olson droned on about the loveliness of marriage—about which he knew nothing—the Portobello mushrooms would be history.

The low door into the slope-ceilinged office building bumped open.

"As *usual,* Father Olson is *late,*" Lucille Boatwright declared, her ice-blue eyes ablaze. "We can't keep you over here any longer. If Olson wants to give you the premarital blessing, he'll have to do it in the sacristy." She looked me up and down. "Father *Pinckney* never would have been late. Never in *fifteen years* was Father Pinckney late for *one* wedding." Blandly conservative Father Pinckney, now retired and living in his native South Carolina, had attained hero status among the older generation in our parish. Despite the fact that the charismatic Father Olson had become our new rector three years ago, Lucille and her cohorts had, for the most part, managed to ignore him.

She lifted her chin. It was wide and dauntingly sharp, and boasted a shuddering dimple. "The bridal bouquets have arrived." She narrowed her eyes at the pearl choker. "Did Olson say he was picking up the groom? It looks as if they are *both* late."

Oh, for heaven's sake. I bit my lip, then stopped when I realized I was wearing lipstick, not my custom. "I don't know their transportation arrangements, sorry. I haven't seen either since last night. We had a small supper after the rehearsal here at the church. . . ." I did not mention to Lucille that after that supper, Tom Schulz and I had undergone our last premarital counseling session with Father Olson. The session had not gone well, which I put down to nerves. But telling anyone in our church a tidbit of personal information was tantamount to publishing it in the local newspaper. This was especially true if you prefaced your comments with, *This is confidential.*

Lucille groaned at my lack of information and told me to put on my beige wedding shoes. I did; they were even more uncomfortable than I remembered. Then, dutifully, I followed Lucille's dumpling-shaped body as it swiftly marched back across the ice- and mud-crusted walkway between the old office and the contemporary-style St. Luke's building. The air was cold; thin sheets of cloud filmed the sky overhead. Rising haze from melting snow formed a pale curtain between the soaring A-shape of the church roof and the ridge of distant mountains. I dodged across the flagstones to avoid the mud. Flickers flitted between the lodgepole pines and the construction trenches of the incomplete St. Luke's columbarium near the parking lot. Farther down, chickadees twittered and dove between the bare-branched aspens and the banks of icy, swollen Cottonwood Creek.

The high, dramatic strains of the trumpet voluntary reached my ears. *This is it; everything's going to be okay.* At that moment, in spite of the awful shoes, the locked Hymnal House, and the too-typical lateness of both priest and groom, excitement zinged up my spine. *I'm getting married.* Our wedding was going to happen despite the threat of April snow here at eight thousand feet above sea level. Despite the fact that it was a Saturday in Lent, when Father Olson said weddings were not traditionally performed. On that subject, Olson had laughingly informed me, the Altar Guild was having a fit about the luxuriant flower arrangements I'd ordered for the altar during this traditionally penitential season. Unfortunately for church procedure, the last Saturday in Lent was the only time Tom Schulz and I could fit getting married into our zany work schedules. We both had to be back in Aspen Meadow by Tuesday so Tom could testify in court and I could cater a three-day meeting of the diocesan Board of Theological Examiners, a church committee to which I'd recently been appointed. Our three-day honeymoon at the Beaver Creek Lodge would be short, sweet, and unencumbered by telephones and food processors.

I hopped gracelessly across the last mud puddle and onto the sidewalk. Actually, the most astonishing fact was that I was getting married at all. *In spite of everything.* For seven years I had been the wife of an abusive doctor. I'd left the disastrous marriage with a wonderful son, Arch, now twelve; the ability to cook; and an emotional scar the size of Pike's Peak. I had thrown myself into developing a catering business and sworn off marriage forever and ever. But then Investigator Tom Schulz had appeared and refused to leave. Tom had convinced me of his kindness and durability, even if we had argued last night. About the afterlife, of all things. Facing marriage for a lifetime, I'd asked at our last premarital counseling session, who cared about Pie in the Sky By-and-By? At the mention of the hereafter, Father Olson had rolled his eyes and murmured, "Ah, eschatology," as if it were a truffle. My stint as a third-grade Sunday School teacher hadn't covered " 'til death do us part." Father Olson had said we would have a *very* long time to discuss it.

"Hurry along now," chided Louise as she pulled open the side door to St. Luke's. From inside the church, the high peals of organ music mingled with the buzz and shuffling of arriving guests. Lucille shooed me into the sacristy, the tiny room adjoining the sanctuary where the priest and acolytes put on their vestments before each service. On the counter next to the parish register lay two bouquets of the same type as the disputed altar flowers: luscious spills of creamy white stock and fragrant freesia, tiny pink carnations and white and pink sweetheart roses. There was one for me and one for Marla, who in addition to being best friend and matron of honor, was the other ex-wife of my first husband. Lucille informed me Marla was out in the narthex, "giggling wildly with that jewelry raffle committee, but what else would you expect?" She would send her back. Lucille's tone signaled her opinion of both the raffle committee and Marla, its chairwoman. Giving me another of her razor-edged glances, she commanded me to stay put.

Arch craned his neck around the door to the sacristy. He pushed his glasses up his freckled nose and said, "I know. You're nervous, right?"

"Remember your first day of seventh grade?"

"I'd rather not." He scooted through the door and closed it softly behind him. "Hate to tell you, Mom, but your hat's on crooked."

I smiled. Thin-shouldered and narrow-chested, Arch had clearly taken great pains with his own scrubbed and buttoned-up appearance. But the kid-size tuxedo only emphasized all the growing up he'd had to do in the last five years. First he had escaped into fantasy role-playing games. Then he'd endured harrassment at a new school. Only in the last few months had Arch found a sense of family support from two people—Julian Teller, our nineteen-year-old live-in boarder, and of course, Tom Schulz. For the first time in years, my son seemed genuinely, if precariously, happy.

Reluctantly, I turned to look at the crooked headgear in the long mirror behind the sacristy door. As I feared, the glass reflected a short, thirty-one-year-old female with blond corkscrews of hair protruding from a cockeyed hat that looked too sophisticated for her slightly rounded, slightly freckled face. I removed the odious beige silk thing, reseated it, and stabbed ferociously with the hat pin. I loathe hats. Even when catering the most elegant dinners, I never wear a chef's cap. But Father Olson had suggested my wearing a hat would appease the Altar Guild, whose many rules I was shattering by getting married in Lent, for the second time, with lots of flowers. Arch, on tiptoe behind me, frowned as he adjusted his black-and-silver-striped cravat. The tuxedo was a little big. Nevertheless, he looked absolutely dashing. I turned and gave him an impulsive hug.

"You know, Mom, it's not as if you haven't done this before." He pulled away from me and reddened to the roots of his straw-brown hair. "I mean, not just when you married Dad. But all those wedding receptions you've catered. They came out okay, even when things went wrong."

"I know, I know." I glanced at the empty ring finger of my left hand. Fifteen minutes. "Arch. You don't know if they got into Hymnal House, do you?"

He grinned gleefully. "Julian broke a window."

"Oh, please."

"It doesn't look that bad! Julian and the helpers swept up the glass. Now they're setting up the tables and chafing dishes and everything. He said to tell you."

"They haven't started transporting the vegetable terrines, have they?" I asked desperately. "Did Julian drive over with the cake or is he going to try to wheel it across the parking lot? He'll have to avoid the construction . . . and did the oven in Hymnal House work?" Under my barrage of questions, Arch shrugged and fiddled with matches for the candle lighters. "Arch," I pleaded, "could you go ask Marla to come back? I'm sorry, I'm just nervous about getting started." I strained to hear. "How're the musicians holding up?"

"Handel's *Water Music* is next," he announced. "I have the whole program memorized. I like the Jeremiah Clarke, because they play it before that TV show, *Stories of the Weird.*" When I sighed, he touched his cravat and added hastily, "You know that lady who dresses like an Indian? Agatha Preston? Anyway, she got out the terrines. The other women haven't moved them yet. I don't know about the cake or the construction or the oven. I'll get Marla, but then one of the church ladies or Father Olson is supposed to tell me when to bring Grandma down the aisle." He opened the door of the sacristy and peered out. "Man, it looks like a priest convention out there. Did you invite that whole committee you're on?"

"Honey, I had to. And all the parishioners, too. I've been in this church since before you were born. I had to invite everybody or risk offending someone. But I can't look, it's bad luck. Is he here yet?"

Arch torqued his head back. "Who?"

"Tom Schulz, silly. Please come back in here." I grimaced at my reflection in the mirror. My hat was undeniably still crooked.

"All I can see is some guys Tom introduced me to from the SWAT team," Arch answered. "And back in the open area where you first come into the church? What did you say that was, the columbarium? I think it's going to be on my confirmation test."

"Arch, please. A columbarium is a place where they put the ashes of cremated dead people. We're building one next to St. Luke's now. The open area in the back of the church is called the narthex. Confuse them and you will have a mess on your hands, not to mention probably flunk the confirmation test."

"Yeah, okay, well, back in the *narthex,* Marla and her friends are yakking away. And there are thousands of guests, it looks like. Uh-oh, here comes that mean lady from that committee that takes care of the altar linens and money and bread and wine and stuff."

"The Altar Guild? Who is it?"

He quickly slunk out the door without answering. I wanted to tell him that someone should load the cake in the van and drive it over to Hymnal House. Filled with resolve to check on doings in the kitchen, I reseated the hat, stalked after Arch, and promptly collided with Lucille Boatwright.

She glared up at me. "Goldy! Where do you think you're going? Your hat isn't even on straight. And your hair is a disaster."

"I'm going to check on the cake and—"

"You are doing nothing of the sort—" The pealing of the church phone cut short her scolding. "Oh, *why* hasn't someone turned on that fool answering machine? Contraptions! Father *Pinckney* never even would have *allowed* . . ." Lucille stormed off, muttering.

I nipped down the hall, past the Sunday School rooms and the oil portrait of the greatly missed former rector, and finally slipped into the kitchen. Any haven in a storm. Besides, if the churchwomen dropped the hotel pans of pasta or scorched the beef, they'd have to wait until the Apocalypse before I catered another of their luncheon meetings.

Happily, the volunteer servers were doing a superb job. Two women pushed carefully out the kitchen's side door carrying bacon-wrapped, brown sugar–crusted artichoke hearts. Another team picked up the pans of creamy Parmesan-sauced fusilli and flaky phyllo-wrapped spinach turnovers. Crystal bowls brimming with jewellike slices of kiwi, fat strawberries, and thick bunches of black grapes would be next. The smooth, layered terrines, all six of them, were snuggled into coolers and set on wheeled tables next to the juicy tenderloin and sherry-soaked Portobello mushrooms.

Come to think of it, I was kind of hungry. No time for breakfast, so much to do, and . . . where was the cake? It was supposed to be set up on a special wheeled table already. . . .

"*What* are you doing here?" gasped a shocked voice. Arch was right: Agatha Preston did look like an Episcopal Pocahantas. Her beaded, sheath-style salmon-colored dress boasted a foot of knotted fringe at the hem, and she wore a needlepointed blue-and-coral headband horizontally across her forehead. Her long braided hair had been dyed into unattractive streaks. At the moment, Agatha's pretty face had the hidden, sour look of someone who had been passed over for a prize. Perhaps she didn't enjoy being one of Lucille's henchwomen. The volunteers whisked platters around us out the kitchen door and gave our little confrontation sidelong glances. Stuttering, I backed up into the refrigerator.

"Checking on the cake," I said lamely, then whirled to open the refrigerator door before Agatha could question me further. And there it was—the shimmering four-layer creation of ultra-cool, ultra-talented Julian Teller. Julian, in addition to boarding with us and helping with

Arch, was an apprentice caterer and ace pastry chef, despite the fact that he was still a senior in high school. When I had told him the traditional wedding cake was white on white, but confessed I was partial to chocolate with mint, he'd run his hands through his bleached, rooster-style haircut and said, "Hey man, it's your wedding," then proceeded to concoct a dark fudge cake with white peppermint frosting. When I'd vetoed the traditional topping of bride and groom plastic statuettes—my first wedding cake had had them, and what good had they done me?—Julian had smilingly flourished his frosting gun and created row upon row of abstract curlicues, swaying rosettes, stiff leaves, and curling swags. The flower-mobbed cake resembled a frenzied rock concert.

"Excuse me, Goldy," said Agatha, less timid this time.

I turned. Agatha's dress barely concealed a scarecrow figure. She dispelled her unhappy look with a faint smile, and I remembered the last time we'd talked, at a barbecue I'd catered for her husband's hunting buddies. She'd been wearing a beaded sundress of the same fish-flesh hue, and given me the identical wan smile. Now she made an uncertain shake of the streaked braids.

"Goldy, if you don't go back to the sacristy, Lucille is going to be *extremely* upset."

"Yes, but the cake should be out by now—"

"Please. Hymnal House is almost set up. It's all going to be fine. You don't *know* Lucille when she gets upset."

Lucky me. I started back down the hall. Unfortunately, that narrow space was filling up with people depositing their it's-April-in-Colorado-and-might-snow coats in the Sunday School rooms. When they spotted me, Old Home Week officially began. The first to leap in my direction was Father Doug Ramsey, Olson's tall, gangly new assistant, who was also a member of the diocesan Board of Theological Examiners.

"The star of the show!" he cried, causing heads to turn. Doug Ramsey had a delicate, triangular face and long, loopy ringlets of black hair that made him look closer to eighteen than twenty-eight. His compensation for looking too young was talking too much. "The whole committee's here," he gushed, "which is *quite* a compliment to you. Of course, I don't suppose the candidates are here, but then again, *they're* probably studying for the tests we *mean old examiners* are dreaming up for them next week. . . . You know, I'll don a stern expression and ask about the Archbishops of Canterbury, and then Canon Montgomery will ask about the history of the Eucharist." He stopped talking briefly to flutter his knobby fingers dramatically on his chest. "And no matter *what* the question is, that *awful* Mitchell Hartley will probably flunk again—"

I said desperately, "Doug, please. Have you seen Father Olson? He seems to have forgotten today's the day. In a pinch, could you do a wedding?"

Father Doug Ramsey's face turned floury-white above his spotless clerical collar. A long, greased comma of black hair quivered over his forehead. Arrested in midspeech, his mouth remained open.

I felt a pang of regret. "I'm kidding, Doug. I just don't want to be delayed."

"Oh, no," he said tersely, then added with characteristic self-absorption, "then you'd *never* be back in time to do the candidates' examinations. But . . . a *wedding* . . . I don't know what I'd preach on. Love, I suppose, or maybe the trinity . . ."

This uneasy speculation was interrupted by a series of unearthly groans. I peered through the crowd in the hall and saw Lucille Boatwright sagging against one of the priests. She was moaning loudly. Remembering Agatha's warning, I guessed I was seeing Lucille Boatwright *very* upset.

"I'm coming!" I cried. "Just wait a sec!"

I shouldered my way through the folks in the hall, all of whom wanted to touch me or ask questions. *Where's Schulz?* asked one of the policemen, whose face I vaguely recognized. *Where's Arch?* asked a Sunday School teacher. *I was in traction and haven't seen him since I was healed* . . . A long-ago church friend's voice: *Goldy, what a stunning suit! So much better than that froufrou gown you wore last time, dear.* As politely as possible, I brushed the well-intentioned questions and fingers aside. Now my hair, my suit, *everything* was going to be a mess, I thought uncharitably. Why weren't these people out in the pews listening to the organist make approved music? Reaching the end of the hall, I saw a priest and a female parishioner ministering to Lucille Boatwright, who had slumped to the floor. Clearly she took the customary procedures more seriously than I ever imagined.

I said, "I was only in the kitchen—"

"We're going to have to call an ambulance," said the woman. "I think she's having a heart attack."

"But I just stepped down the hall for a *moment*—"

The cleric looked up at me. His face was very flushed. "I think your fiancé is on the phone," he said. "There's some kind of problem—"

I rushed past them into the choir room. The white telephone wire lay coiled on the floor. Bewildered and slightly panicked, I snatched up the receiver.

"Yes?"

"Oh, God, I'm sorry," said Tom Schulz. His voice sounded flat, infinitely dejected. In the background I could hear a faint tinkling, like windchimes.

"Sorry about what? Where are you?"

"Just a sec." The phone clacked down on something hard. He came back to the line after a moment. "Miss G." He sighed deeply. "Tell everybody to go home."

"What?" This wasn't happening. "Why? Tom, what's wrong?"

"I'm out at Olson's house. He called with car trouble, asked me to come get him. And I found him."

"You—?"

My fiancé's voice cracked. "Goldy, he's dead."

2

"Tom. I don't understand. Please. Tell me this isn't real."

"He just died a few minutes ago. When I got here, he'd been shot. Shot in the chest," Tom Schulz added in the distant, flat tone he used when discussing his work. "I've called in a team. Look, I have to go. You know the drill. I need to go stay by the body."

"But, how . . . ? Are we going to get married? I mean, today?"

"Oh, Goldy." Despair thickened his voice. "Probably not. The team will be here for hours." He paused. "Want to try to do a civil ceremony tonight?"

"Do I—" I did not. Not a hurry-up ritual. Like it or not, I was an Episcopalian, what they call a *cradle* Episcopalian, the Anglican equivalent of the American Kennel Club. If I was going to get married again, then it was going to be in front of God, the church, and everybody, and the wedding was going to be performed by an Episcopal priest.

Oh, Lord. My hands were suddenly clammy. *Father Olson.*

I ripped the hat off my head. A knot formed in my chest. This was a mistake. This phone call was some awful nightmare. Any moment I was going to wake up.

I stammered, "Tom, what happened to Father Olson?"

"I don't know. That's what we have to find out. Do you want to go back to your place and wait for me?"

"Just come to the church. Please. I'll wait." I cursed the tremble in my voice. "Take care."

I hung up. The air in the choir room suddenly felt thin. Father Olson's absence loomed. I tried to erase images of a gun being raised menacingly in his direction. Of shots. Beside me, the silver bar holding the burgundy choir robes glimmered too brightly from the neon light overhead. In the hallway, shouts, squawks, and cries of disbelief rose to a din that rivaled the hammering in my ears. I closed my eyes and tried to breathe.

"Goldy, what the—"

Slowly, I turned. Marla Korman's large presence filled the door to the choir room. The noise from the hallway roared louder.

"Goldy, you look like hell! Hey! Why'd you toss your hat? I went to four stores to find that thing." Marla closed the door behind her. "What's all the commotion out there about? And look at your suit. Have you been sitting on the floor? For crying out loud!"

She click-clacked over in her Italian leather heels and put her small hands with their polished red nails on my shoulders. An incongruously conservative navy suit hugged her wide body, which was usually far more outrageously clad. The tight French twist taming her thick, normally frizzed brown hair seemed somehow absurd. She had worn the suit and pinned up her hair for my wedding. My wedding that now, suddenly, was not to be. I wondered how long it would take for the noisy news-sharing of the hallway to reach the people out in the pews.

"Hoohoo, Goldy!" she said brightly. "I know you're in there. You want to tell me what's going on?"

I tried to reply twice before I could say, "Olson's dead. Tom . . ."

She grasped my shoulders more tightly. "Dead? *Dead?*" Her voice shrilled in my ear.

"Yes." I made a feeble gesture toward the hall. "That's probably the cause of all the racket. I don't know. Has anyone out there said anything about the wedding?"

"They can't—" Marla released me and pivoted on her heels. Her pumps gritted against the vinyl floor as she tiptoed back to peek down the hall. Again the noise roared in. After a few moments of observation, she quietly closed the door and turned back to me. "Looks like Lucille Boatwright passed out, but she's conscious now. What happened to Father

Olson? What do you mean, *he's dead*? Did he have a heart attack, or what?"

Tom's advice: *Give away nothing.* Abruptly I remembered his green eyes and handsome face turning grimly serious one night as he wiped his floral-patterned Limoges dessert plates and spoke to me about his work. *If I confide in you, Goldy, tell no details to anyone, not even to those you trust, because you don't know where those details are going to end up.* One did not divulge facts such as *shot in the chest* to Marla. I knew too well her large body and large spirit did not prevent her from being an even larger gossip, best friend or no.

Marla's small hands moved frantically along the pearl choker at her neck, another one from the upcoming raffle. "I mean," she was saying, "did he have some kind of medical problem we didn't know about? Aneurysm? Stroke? I mean, him of all people. With all that talk about healing, you know. Oh, listen to me. I even went out with him . . ."

I told her the minimal story as I knew it would soon become available: that Tom Schulz had gone to Father Olson's place to pick him up. That an intruder, or someone, had mortally wounded Olson before Tom arrived.

"Oh, my God, he was *killed*?" Marla's plump cheeks went slack with disbelief. There was a knock at the choir room door. Marla opened it, dispensed with the intruder, then turned back to me. Her voice turned fierce. "Oh, why did Olson insist on living way out Upper Cottonwood Creek?" She tensed up her plump hands, crablike, and gestured widely. "He thought all he'd need was a fancy four-wheel-drive vehicle. Didn't he realize not having neighbors close by could hurt him? I just can't believe it. He was only, what, thirty-five?"

My mind reeled again, trying to compute. "I guess. But I do know that the . . . ceremony is off." The deep breath I attempted to take didn't alleviate a cold wave of shivers. "All the food . . ."

Marla tilted her head to consider. "Want me to get one of the folks tending Lucille in here for you? I heard someone say they were calling Mountain Rescue."

"No, no. Thanks."

"I still don't understand how Olson was killed."

"Well, I guess that's what the police team will find out." I was suddenly deeply embarrassed by the thought that my parents, son, friends, and acquaintances were all sitting in the church pews, waiting for my wedding procession to begin. "Does everyone out there know what happened?"

"I haven't the foggiest." She hesitated, then minced tentatively back out the door. The din in the hall had shifted to a more pronounced tumult of raised voices and stamping feet out in the congregation. The pain in my chest made an unexpected twist. I was still having trouble breathing. Within minutes Marla returned to report. "Apparently, when Tom called, he wanted to talk to you but Lucille wouldn't let him. They argued. You can imagine Lucille insisting the bride couldn't be disturbed. Even if it was the groom calling. And the groom was a cop. So Schulz finally told her about Olson. He said to send someone for you *immediately.*"

Marla began to pull the pins out of the French twist. No ceremony, no fancy hair.

"So then Lucille collapsed," she went on grimly. "There was a priest nearby who tried to tend to her, and she told him that your fiancé wanted you on the phone. Eventually she gasped out the news that Olson was dead. Father Doug Ramsey just made an announcement that your wedding would be postponed. And why. Good old Doug is trying to start a silent prayer service. Of course, silence is the last thing the poor guy's going to get. It's pretty crazy out there. Looks as if the cops who were here, Schulz's friends, are scrambling outside for their car radios." She shook out her mass of crimped hair, stowed the hairpins in her suit pocket, and with sudden resolve took my arm. "We have to get you out of here. People are going to be coming in to use the phone. And you're the bride, you don't need to have everyone asking you questions. Let them read it in the paper. Where were you before Lucille put you in the sacristy to wait?"

"Olson's office."

"Anybody else there?"

I shook my head.

"Let's go."

She steered me out of the choir room. Lucille Boatwright was now sitting, slumped, in a kid-size chair hastily provided from one of the Sunday School rooms. She was moaning again, so I assumed she was not in imminent danger. Marla and I made a quick left out the side door beside the sacristy, the same door I had come through with so much hope only fifteen minutes before. All the attention focused on Lucille meant the exit of the would-be bride and her matron of honor went unnoticed. *Thank God for small favors,* my father would say.

The chilly air outdoors was a pleasant shock after the too-warm, too-close air in the church. When my beige shoes slipped on the ice, I begged

Marla to sit with me on the bench by the side door for a moment. I needed to clear my head of the image of a bloodstained Father Olson. She reluctantly took a place beside me and muttered that someone could find us here. But she took my right hand anyway, and firmly held it in hers.

At length she said, "Look, Goldy. Don't think about Olson."

"I can't help it."

"Then let's go into the office."

"I can't."

I shivered and glanced at the columbarium that Lucille and the parish Art and Architecture committee were having built in honor of old Father Pinckney. Lucille hadn't obtained Father Olson's permission, much less a building permit, but excavation was moving ahead anyway, despite the fact that St. Luke's, and the columbarium, were in the county floodplain. The idea of Father Olson's ashes being the first interred there made me avert my eyes and look up the steep hill across the street, where the old Aspen Meadow Episcopal Conference Center's Hymnal House and Brio Barn overlooked our church and Cottonwood Creek. I could see Lucille's henchwomen still moving through the doors of Hymnal House with platters of food. So much for our wedding reception in the historic district.

"Let's go," I said. "This is depressing me."

Once we'd entered the church office building, Marla sat me down and asked if I needed anything.

"Just Arch. And nobody else, please. Maybe Julian," I added. "I don't want to go home, and Tom promised he'd be along as soon as he could get away."

"Gotcha." Marla shut the heavy wooden door behind her.

The air in the office building seemed stuffier than the church. Some of the remnants of the ongoing renovation were piled by the desk in the secretary's outer office: torn-out drywall, pipes, an old faucet. My street clothes and garment bag hung forlornly on a door hook beside a faded reproduction of Leonardo Da Vinci's *Last Supper.* I gazed at the painting, in which a sunlit Jesus and eleven followers talk and gesticulate while Judas reaches for food, his face in shadow. My eyes were drawn to the photographs above the desk: Father Olson, somber with Sportsmen Against Hunger and the carcass of an elk, smiling with the Aspen Meadow Habitat for Humanity Committee, standing proudly with the committee I was on with him, the diocesan Board of Theological Examiners. Had been on with him. Someone would have to call the diocesan office. A photograph over the desk made my ears ring: dark-bearded

Olson, holding a tiny white-robed infant and bending over the baptismal font. Someone would have to arrange the funeral. The first rites to the last.

I tried to open one of the old windows, but it was painted shut. I turned away and willed myself not to think of Ted Olson dying. Dead. What ran through my head were images of him alive. Olson laughing and arguing at our Theological Examiners' meeting; Olson rolling his eyes as I shook out an enormous molded grapefruit salad for the Women's Prayer Group; Olson preaching on his favorite topic—renewal.

And then in my recollection his face was suddenly, vividly, up close, in one of our early premarital counseling sessions. I had never really known Ted Olson until we began that very personal journey into discussing Tom's and my relationship. I recalled the skin at the sides of his eyes crinkling deeply when he laughed, his slender fingers absently stroking his dark beard when he listened. For the sessions, he had worn jeans topped with dark turtlenecks instead of his customary black clerical shirt and white collar. Sitting in his tweed-covered swivel chair, he had lifted one dark eyebrow and eyed me skeptically.

"And why exactly do you want to get married again?"

"Second time's the charm."

A mischievous smile curled his mouth. "Do you always hide behind the flip answer?"

"It helps."

Sometimes it helped. And now Olson was gone. I tried again to breathe deeply and told myself to stop thinking about him. But I couldn't.

"Mom?"

Arch stood uneasily between the secretary's desk and a stack of contorted water pipes. He bit the inside of his cheek and tugged on the hem of the tux.

"Do you want me to leave? Marla said I should come over."

"No, no, I'm glad you came." I asked him to sit down so I could explain that Father Olson, who had been due to present Arch for confirmation this month, wasn't going to show up. And why.

"Yeah, I heard," he said haltingly when I'd told him the news. He raised his chin and pushed his glasses up his freckled nose. In Aspen Meadow, a mountain town that was more like a village than a suburb, Arch had had much experience of death. Here, the two of us knew a larger group of people than I ever had in the towns I'd lived in before moving to Colorado. For Arch, to experience townspeople killed in skiing and car accidents, in avalanches, by cancer or of heart attacks, was unfortunately commonplace.

He asked in a low voice, "Do they know how it happened yet?"

"Tom will."

Beneath his freckles, Arch's face had turned translucently white. The skin under his eyes was dark as pitch. "Where is Tom? Will he be here soon?"

When I nodded, he said, "Julian wants to know what you want to do with the food."

"Oh, Lord. I don't know."

Arch waited for me to elaborate. Then he went on. "Something else. Mrs. Boatwright, you know?" When I nodded, he said, "Well, they're waiting to take her when the Mountain Rescue Team gets here. But . . ." He stopped.

"What is it, Arch? Things couldn't get much worse."

"She was sitting out there in the hall, you know, after she passed out. Then she saw me and like, signaled me over. She told me in this loud whisper to ask you to donate the food to Aspen Meadow Outreach. 'Obviously your mother won't be able to use it today,' " Arch whispered in an uncannily throaty imitation, " 'and I've seen this kind of thing before.' "

"Seen a priest die before a wedding?"

"No." Arch drew his lips into a thoughtful pucker, then continued. "Mrs. Boatwright said she'd seen a groom change his mind." He singsonged, " 'Sometimes they just *can't* go through with it.' " He'd always had a talent for imitation, but I'd never been devastated by the results before.

"What did you tell her?"

"I said I'd have to ask you. About the food. I didn't say anything about Tom. I mean, is that rude or what?"

"Very. The nerve. Listen, Arch," I said defiantly, "Tom called here and asked for me, for heaven's sake. He didn't change his mind. Father Olson is *dead.* And Tom asked if I wanted to get married tonight, just not in the church."

"Yeah, well, you're not, are you?" my son asked. When I groaned, he added, "So what should we do with the food platters?"

I rubbed my temples. I was developing a blinding headache. "I'll figure something out when I get home. I can't fret about it now. Would you please ask Julian to pack everything into the van?"

"Okay, but there's one more thing . . ."

"Arch!"

"Mom! Sorry! Julian wants to know what he should do with your parents."

"Give them to Aspen Meadow Outreach."

"Mom! And I hate to tell you, but Grandma and Grandpa asked me if the groom had changed his mind, too."

"Great." I reflected for a moment. I couldn't just abandon my parents at the church. They'd been reluctant to venture from the Jersey shore to the high altitude of the Rockies in the first place. They felt uncomfortable in my modest house, with my modest life. I mean, I'd married a doctor, which they'd deemed good, gotten a divorce, which they saw as unfortunate, and gone into food service, which they found lamentable. Now I was marrying a cop. My parents did not view this as a move in the right direction, and unspoken behind their cautionary words about hasty marriages was the sense that they hadn't done very well on their investment in their only daughter. "Invite them back to the house," I told Arch. "Their plane goes out late this afternoon anyway, wedding or no wedding. Tell them I'll be along as soon as Tom gets here. Then we can make a few plans. And Arch—thanks. I'm really sorry about all this."

He hesitated. "So there isn't going to be a wedding, then."

I gave him a brief hug. "No, hon. Not today."

"I'm really sorry, Mom." He pulled away and concentrated his gaze on the bookshelves. "*You* don't think Tom Schulz would just not show up, do you?"

My ears started to ring. "With the priest dead? No. It's just, you know, with this—" I did not finish the thought. "Don't worry," I said finally. "Tom and I are going to get married. Here at the church, too. Just not this very minute."

When he raised his head, Arch's young face was taut with disappointment. Wordlessly, he clomped out of the office door.

An oppressive silence again descended on the old building. I sat pleating the beige silk between my fingers. Within moments there was the sudden overhead scraping from the family of raccoons. When they were undisturbed by the presence of people, they noisily reclaimed their territory. Their scratching made my flesh crawl.

"Enough!" I shouted as I heaved a hymnal at the ceiling. It slammed against the rafters with a satisfying *thwack*.

That shut them up. I picked the hymnal off the floor and threw it against the wall. The shock reverberated through a bookshelf. A pile of theology books thudded to the floor; notes popped off a bulletin board;

my streetclothes fell from the hook. I walked across the office, lowered myself into the tweed swivel chair, then quickly jumped out. The chair was Ted Olson's.

Disconsolately, I threaded my way through the debris of torn pipes and broken drywall to the secretary's office. Through the thick windows I saw the Mountain Rescue ambulance arrive and then swiftly depart, presumably with Lucille Boatwright. Guests streamed out of the church, heads bowed, as if it were the end of the Good Friday liturgy instead of an aborted wedding ceremony. So much for the silent prayer service.

Gripping bowls and then the cake, Julian Teller did his loyal-assistant routine and made several laborious trips out to my van. I yearned to help him. But I couldn't bear the thought of clearing the parish kitchen of food that was supposed to be served after my own wedding. Finally Julian escorted my bewildered parents, with Arch, to the parking lot. The van revved and took off.

What seemed like an eternity later, a cream-and-black Sheriff's Department vehicle pulled up in the lot. First one, then a second and third official car skidded on patches of ice. Their tires spun and spewed small waves of gravel before coming to a rest on the other side of the columbarium construction. Uniformed officers emerged. My breath fogged the window as I waited anxiously for Tom Schulz to appear. I folded my chilled hands and debated about rushing out. I should have told Tom I would be in the office.

I tapped on the glass when two grim-faced policemen I knew, partners named Boyd and Armstrong, climbed out of their cars and strode to the church entrance. After a few moments, both officers emerged from the church's side door. They walked up the muddy flagstones to the office building. I knew they were on duty that day as they had been unable to come to our wedding. Pacing behind them somewhat stiffly was a woman with long brown hair. She carried a bulging Hefty bag. She was familiar looking. A policewoman, perhaps.

Boyd and Armstrong pushed into the office first. Like most policemen, they had a brusque, businesslike air about them. Boyd, short and barrel-shaped, stopped abruptly at the sight of me. He stood, feet apart, and rubbed one hand over black hair that had been shorn close in a Marine-style crewcut. Underneath his unzipped Sheriff's Department leather jacket, his shirt was too snug around his bulky midsection, a pot belly that had increased in size since he'd stopped smoking several months ago. He was gnawing one of the wooden matches he had taken to chewing to keep from overeating. Behind him, tall, acne-scarred Armstrong, whose few wisps of light-brown hair had strayed off the bald spot they were supposed to conceal, surveyed the room bitterly. The woman, whom I judged to be about fifty, unbuttoned her oversized black coat. That task concluded, she held back, clutching her bag to her chest, mutely watching me.

"Where's Tom?" I demanded.

Boyd and Armstrong exchanged a glance. Boyd bit down hard on the match. The woman gave an almost imperceptible shake of her head, sending her lanky hair swinging.

Boyd said, "Sit down, Miss Bear."

"Why?" I remained standing. "Don't patronize me, please. And you know my name is Goldy, *Officer* Boyd. Where's Tom? He called me about Father Olson. Does Tom know I'm still here?"

Boyd stopped chewing the match. His eyes flicked away from me before he said, "Bad news, I'm afraid."

"What?" Panic creaked in my voice. What else could go wrong on this day that was supposed to be so wondrous? "Is Tom all right? Where is he?"

Armstrong held up one hand. He looked seriously down his pock-marked nose at me before replying. "Somebody must have been out there. Still there," he announced with agonizing logic. "We think. Out at the priest's place. Schulz called us, then you. Looks like he went back out to be by the body. Maybe he wanted to look around."

"Where is Tom?" I repeated. "Why are you all here?" I demanded, too loudly.

Boyd stopped rubbing his head and looked me squarely in the eyes. He gestured at the woman. "Helen Keene here is our victim advocate."

I said, "Victim advocate? But Olson wasn't married, he lived alone. Who's the vic—"

"I'm sorry, Goldy." Boyd shifted the match from one side of his mouth to the other, inhaled raggedly, and looked at a small notebook he'd pulled out of his pocket. "We got to Olson's at 11:46. Didn't see Schulz, but his vehicle was there. Signs of a struggle near Olson's body, which was near the bank of Cottonwood Creek." He studied a grimy page of his notebook, then added, "Looks like Schulz might have fallen or been pushed down the bank. He dropped some articles, then dragged himself up the creek bank."

"Where is he?"

Boyd took another deep breath. "It appears somebody got the drop on Schulz." He glanced at Armstrong, avoiding my eyes. "Looks like the perp was still there. Something happened, there was a struggle—"

"Tell me."

"Schulz is missing," Boyd said tonelessly.

3

"No." My legs felt as if they were disintegrating. "No, no." The walls seemed to sway. Get a grip, I ordered myself. Boyd's face was a study in misery I could not bear to contemplate. Armstrong shrugged and looked away. Helen Keene eased between the two men. She grasped my elbow firmly, then guided me toward the small striped couch in the secretary's office.

I could not assimilate Boyd's words. *Got the drop on him. Fell . . . pushed down the creek bank. Schulz missing.*

It was simply not believable.

"I don't understand. Where did this happen?" My voice came out like a croak.

Wordlessly, Helen Keene, victim advocate, advocate for *me,* I realized dully, drew a quilt out of the Hefty bag she was carrying. Gently she pulled it around my shoulders. I was shivering uncontrollably. There was a painful buzzing in my ears. Hold it together, girl, I commanded my inner self. Hold it together *now.* For Tom.

Boyd and Armstrong exchanged a look. Boyd's carrotlike fingers caressed his worn notebook. "Sorry. You weren't even a cop's wife yet. They get used to this kind of crisis. Or at least used to the idea of this kind of crisis. Well. We're not sure about the actual events. We believe that's what happened." His face was fierce; he held his rotund body in a tight, aggressive stance. "It looks as if Schulz was hurt. But we're going to find him. We'll work around the clock." This was not the matter-of-fact Officer Boyd I had met the previous spring, the Boyd who had proudly announced in January that he'd given up smoking. This wasn't business-as-usual. This suddenly ferocious Boyd took Tom Schulz's disappearance as a personal affront.

"What do you mean about his being hurt?" I demanded. Helen Keene put a hand on the quilt that covered my shoulders. She sighed softly, regretfully. I refused to look at her.

"Just from falling down into the creek, we think." Armstrong *tsk*ed.

"Okay, look," said Boyd, scratching his close-cropped head furiously and chewing the match, "we'll tell you what we know. Schulz told Dispatch he was going to call you, because of the wedding. Did he?" I nodded. My heart was racing. "We need to talk to you about your conversation with him. But first we need you to go out there, to Olson's place, to have you look at some stuff."

"What stuff? Stuff at Father Olson's house?" Sick with confusion, I looked around the church office. Wouldn't there be something here that would help? I tried and failed to summon Tom's logical voice, his explanations of the inevitable steps in an investigation.

Boyd interjected, "Don't worry, we're going to come back here. Eventually."

I said, "I just don't understand."

Armstrong's tall shape loomed too close to me. "It goes like this: A cop gets surprised. He's going to try to distract the perp, especially if the perp has a weapon. So say the guy wants to kidnap the policeman. Our guy's going to drop stuff at the scene, make clues, anything for us to follow—"

I pressed my lips together and Armstrong abruptly fell silent. His words fogged my brain. Too much information, too disorganized, was coming too fast. Helen Keene patted my back. I longed to leave this room. Tom Schulz had disappeared. I wondered where Arch was, then remembered he had gone with Julian and my parents.

"Miss Bear," said Boyd. "Goldy. We really need your attention. Time's important here."

"I'm sorry. I'm coming with you. I want to go right now." I did not add *this instant,* although that was what went through my mind.

Helen Keene helped me to my feet. Armstrong yanked on the office door. As we walked, my eyes caught the high mounds of dirt where

Lucille and her committee intended for ashes to be interred. The columbarium was just an ice-filled ditch at this point, like a fresh wound in the earth. The fuss over the memorial project seemed so stupid now.

Boyd flipped a page in his notebook as we crossed the snow-pocked parking lot. "Schulz was supposed to get married at noon. Call comes in, 11:14. Dispatch takes it, Schulz says he's got a body, gives us the location of," he squinted at the page, "the Reverend Theodore Olson. Out upper Cottonwood Creek, fire number 29648. Dispatch tells him it's going to take us thirty minutes to get a team up there. He, Schulz, says Olson was the priest. Olson's been shot and he just bought it—er, died. Looks like two gunshot wounds in the chest. Schulz tells Dispatch he has to call you. No wedding." Boyd tapped the notebook. "He didn't think there was anybody around, obviously. He didn't mention another vehicle. Olson was dead. We're analyzing the Dispatch tape now, trying to pick up background noise—"

I stopped walking. "Do you think Tom chased the killer? Isn't there a trail or something? Please. Tell me. I have to know."

Helen Keene picked up the quilt which had fallen from my shoulders. Shifting from one foot to the other, Armstrong hovered over us. My questions made him uncomfortable. Finally he said, "The trail ends at a vehicle. Two sets of footprints: Schulz and somebody. We just don't know what happened. But finding an officer is our top priority. Always."

I whirled to face Armstrong. My voice was shrill. "If you'd killed a priest, wouldn't you just leave? Why would someone hurt Tom?"

Armstrong made another helpless gesture. "Maybe the perp heard Schulz. Or Schulz spotted him. Recognized him. So the perp panics, hides, and then just loses it. Figures he'll be caught if he doesn't take Schulz with him. Or maybe Olson wasn't dead when Schulz got there, told him something and the shooter went nuts . . . or maybe Schulz followed him and . . ." He didn't finish that thought.

"For what it's worth," Boyd interjected, "we figure this is some kind of amateur. Not that you're likely to get a professional hit on a priest," he added uncomfortably.

"You said there was some stuff Tom dropped. May I see it? Now?"

"We couldn't bring it to you." These were the first words Helen Keene had spoken since her arrival. Her voice was surprisingly young and musical. "We have to leave it at the scene for photo and video. But we need you to come out and take a look. You may be able to help us identify it."

Armstrong's and Boyd's faces said, *Let's go.* Silently, Helen Keene put her arm around me again. We walked quickly, heads down, to the waiting squad car.

Father Theodore Olson's house was located northwest of Aspen Meadow proper, in the area the locals call Upper Cottonwood Creek. Driving out of town under a darkening sky, we followed the meandering path of the creek, past ancient shuttered summer dwellings, past the entryway to Arch and Julian's school, Elk Park Prep. After the school, there was a spate of immense custom homes built in the latest real estate boom—this one fueled by people fleeing the high cost of living in California. Farther up, the landscape turned pastoral. We passed the few ranches that remained from Aspen Meadow's proud cowboy past. The ranches boasted wide, lush meadows that sprawled along the creek bed. Then Aspen Meadow Wildlife Preserve loomed suddenly into view, its peaks still covered with winter snow.

While the police car sped along the winding road, Boyd and Armstrong asked me to repeat my brief conversation with Tom. I reconstructed every line of dialogue as best I could. Were there other voices, background noise, cars starting, any sounds like that? I said no. When I faltered, exhausted, Helen Keene began to talk. Her voice was warm and soothing. Quietly, she asked if there was anything I wanted or needed—coffee or water from their Thermoses? Were there family members who needed to be notified of my whereabouts? I glanced at the dashboard clock and remembered my parents' flight from Stapleton Airport in Denver. Helen used the cellular phone to call our house. She asked Julian to drive them to their flight for me. I'd be home as soon as I could, she promised him.

Outside, frozen pellets of snow began to drop, making a staccato noise on the windshield. So we would have had a snowy wedding. I could imagine the snow falling in soft waves past the diamond-shaped window above the St. Luke's altar, my parents with tears in their eyes, Marla weeping unabashedly, Julian giving Tom and me the V-sign.

Arch beaming.

Stop.

Helen Keene's voice murmured into the receiver about my delay and helping the authorities. Helen did not mention that Tom Schulz was missing. I was grateful for her help; my voice would give me away, I knew.

After Helen carefully clicked the cellular phone back in its holder, she turned back to me. She had wide-set brown eyes, thick dark eyebrows, and her long brown hair contained much gray. From the thin folds of dry skin on her square face, I judged her to be older than fifty, possibly even in her early sixties. I wondered if she had ever been an advocate for a bride before.

She said, "My background is in crisis counseling. My training is in psychology. Schulz told me that was your training, too."

"College major. I cook for a living."

She smiled, showing large teeth streaked with yellow. "And you're a mother. So am I, although my children are grown now."

I pulled the quilt over my shaking knees. I'd never talked with one of the Sheriff's Department victim advocates, although their existence was well-publicized in the county. The advocates, both men and women, brought teddy bears and homemade quilts to the victims of accidents and crimes. Tom had told me that after a recent landslide, the advocates had spent the day in a hospital emergency room, giving out over forty quilts. They did a lot of good work, he'd said, with people who were hurt, with people who had lost loved ones. . . .

Helen's smile held through my silence. Tom would have said, *Tell me how you see her.* What he meant was, *describe her.* Suddenly I could imagine Helen Keene bringing an oversize container of Kool-Aid into her children's elementary school classes on Field Day. When the Shriners' circus came to town, I saw her shuffling onto a schoolbus to help chaperone the boisterous class on its bumpy trip. Now her gentle smile faded to seriousness. "Goldy, we need to talk. You're going to have to decide what people you're going to tell about this. Among your friends, I mean. If you're going to keep it together and help us, you need to take care of yourself."

"Decide who I'm going to tell about the canceled wedding, Tom disappearing, what? I want to help find him," I said, without adding a doubtful comment on how effective I was afraid the Sheriff's Department could be without Tom Schulz.

Again Helen put her hand on my arm. Her short nails were spotted with chipped orange nail polish. Outside, the snow shower thickened; Boyd turned on the windshield wipers. "It's like any kind of assault," Helen told me. "It's a personal violation. Your fiancé has disappeared. So maybe you feel stranded. High feelings, emotional vulnerability." In the front seat, I heard Boyd snap his match between his teeth. I flinched. Helen went on, "But people won't think of you as being in need of care. They're going to think of you as a switchboard operator, full of information. They'll feel they have to call you to find out the latest developments. Or maybe they'll just be nosy to see how you're holding up." She continued firmly, "You need to decide. Who're you going to tell how things are going? Who are you going to talk to about how you feel?"

"All right," I murmured. I did not know what I would say and to whom. I just wanted Tom back.

"Something else." Her voice was still matter-of-fact. "People are going to talk. They're going to joke. They're going to say Schulz staged this disappearance to escape getting married to you." She chewed her bottom lip and looked at me expectantly.

My face became hot. A spasm of pain swept over me. I said, "They already have. Or at least one woman at the church has. And of course my parents think he's skipped," I said with an absurd squeak of laughter.

Helen shook her long hair. The police car turned right by a row of mailboxes where a Sheriff's Department car was stationed. Its lights flashed blue and yellow in the snowy gloom. We started up a rutted, muddy road. "Look, Goldy, part of my job as victim advocate is working on how people are going to respond to unexpected cruelties. One of the hardest things I have to deal with is when a child is kidnapped, and the neighbors insist he ran away." She said firmly, "I know Schulz loved you very much."

"Helen—please. *Loves.*"

"Sorry."

Our car skidded through an ice-covered puddle before stopping by the broken-down split-rail fence that led to Father Olson's house. With my nerves put on edge by Tom Schulz's disappearance, I needed to find significance or clues in every detail. Had the fence been broken when I catered a vestry dinner here last month? I could not remember. A lanky policeman standing by another Sheriff's Department vehicle motioned Boyd through.

Boyd gunned the engine up the precipitously steep driveway. My mind snagged on a memory. The inclined driveway had been one of the reasons Father Olson had insisted to the vestry, that group of twelve lay people elected to run the temporal affairs of the church, that he needed a four-wheel-drive vehicle. And not just any four-wheel-drive, vestry member Marla had laughingly told me, but a Mercedes 300E 4Matic. The vestry, charged with raising and managing the church finances, had balked. But eventually, according to Marla, the group had acquiesced. This year, they'd even agreed there was sufficient money to hire a curate. Olson had hired the fidgety, over-talkative Father Doug Ramsey. What the vestry had grudgingly admitted was that unlike Father Pinckney, who only visited his favorite parishioners, Father Olson *was* diligent when it came to visiting shut-ins, even when they lived in the most remote locations. And when those shut-ins died, the treasurer meekly noted, they often left money to the church in direct proportion to how much the priest had come to call. The parishioners whom Father Pinckney had visited had, apparently, not been so generous. In the three years since Olson had arrived, only five shut-ins had died. Nevertheless, parish giving was way up.

Not only that, Marla told me darkly, but Father Olson had hinted during the heated negotiations for his Mercedes that there was interest in him from another parish seeking a new rector. Forty thousand for a Benz was a lot cheaper than the hundred thou it would cost the parish to search for a new priest, especially since they had just gone through all that when they were looking for a replacement for Pinckney. *A hundred thousand dollars?* I had asked Marla incredulously. Absolutely, she'd replied, what with putting together a parish questionnaire, crunching and publishing the resulting data, making long-distance calls and flying candidates and committee members hither and yon for interviews, looking for a new rector was *absolutely* a far more expensive undertaking than buying a German luxury car. And besides, Marla said with a laugh, with the latest bequest, the parish could afford any vehicle or assistant Olson wanted.

As we passed the first of what I judged to be a dozen police cars, I hit the button to bring down the window, then greedily inhaled icy air. What had happened to the parish with the interest in Olson? With Olson dead, our own church would eventually have to begin a rector search; unlike the Vice President, Doug Ramsey didn't automatically step into the leader's shoes. But we were a long way from all that, and the hiring of a new priest was the least of my worries.

The Sheriff's Department *had* to find Tom. I squeezed my eyelids shut as we passed the coroner's van. Either that, or *I* would try to find him, I thought absurdly. I would not consider any other outcome. I summoned up Tom's wide, handsome face, his laconic manner and affectionate smile. I clung to these images. What were Helen's words? *You need to take care of yourself.*

Our vehicle drew up to Ted Olson's garage. The dusty silver Mercedes sat, hood lifted, amid an array of boxes and lawn clutter that included a badminton net and croquet mallets and wickets. Welcome to the Rockies, I thought, and recalled Tom's dry comment on easterners who attempted to play croquet on their sloped properties: The guy uphill has the advantage.

Parked behind the Mercedes was Tom's dark blue Chrysler. Granite formed in my heart.

We piled out of the squad car and threaded through lodgepole pines to the front of Olson's place, a rambling single-story structure with dark horizontal wood paneling and a slightly buckled green shingle roof. Typical Aspen Meadow architecture from the late sixties, it was not too different from the rectory, a parish-owned house, that Father Pinckney had inhabited in Aspen Meadow before he retired. The rectory had been sold when Ted Olson arrived. He'd insisted he wanted to buy his own place outside of town.

The snow ceased as suddenly as it had begun. A yellow police tape was strung across the walkway to the front door. I glanced up at the covered entranceway and saw a cloisonné pair of intertwined serpents. One of Father Olson's memorabilia from a pilgrimage to England, no doubt. A mosaic of the serpents was on the floor of some English cathedral. Which one? I couldn't remember. If the snakes were supposed to bring good luck, I thought uncharitably, they hadn't worked.

Another policeman directed us around the side of the house. Here the property sloped down to Cottonwood Creek. I pulled the donated quilt around my shoulders, and with Helen Keene, Boyd, and Armstrong, skirted the perimeter of taut yellow tape. The four of us made our way down the hill littered with fallen logs and underbrush that sloped to the creek. My wedding shoes skidded over slippery pine needles. I knew there was a short path down to the water out the back of Olson's home. Because the weather had been unusually warm the night of the dinner meeting last month, the vestry had made the descent to and from the creek while I steamed pork dumplings in the kitchen before the stir-fry. From the noise to our left, it was clear that path was still being scoured for some indication of what had happened.

As I plodded and slipped on the way down, my heart seemed to be taking a thrashing. It was like being caught in the undertow on the Jersey shore where I'd spent childhood summers. Within moments we slid into a narrow strip of meadow. Snow clung thick as dandruff to tufts of withered grass. Bare-branched cottonwoods edged the creek's path. When I tried to walk toward the water, dark mud sucked on the soles of my shoes. Law-enforcement types trudged along the creek bank: One group was doing a video of the crime scene, another took photographs, a third painstakingly measured distances. A cluster of people stood or crouched around a covered bundle on the snow. A white-haired policewoman from one group noted our presence. She motioned us toward them.

"We're reconstructing how Schulz was taken," she said to me without preamble. "Come on over and take a look." T. Calloway, her nametag said. On the way to the creek bank, she thanked me for coming out and brusquely explained that they would not be ready to move any of the evidence until I identified it. This, she explained, was standard police procedure. "Which was why we needed you right away."

"So how could Tom Schulz have been kidnapped?"

Investigator Calloway shook her head, then stopped abruptly at the six-foot drop-off to the water. She pointed to the other side. "The vehicle was over there. A four-wheel-drive of some kind. Somebody appeared to be prodding Schulz to move forward."

But my eyes were drawn to the creek bed itself, where the mud, sand, and rocks had been churned with activity. I saw footprints and ridges. I saw . . . ah, Lord.

"I'm sorry," said Investigator Calloway. "Tell me what you see. I need to know."

I pointed toward the water. At first my voice refused to engage, but I forced it out. "That's Tom's wallet. . . . That's his key ring."

"Look out of the water itself. By that large rock."

Shallow water rushed around a boulder in the middle of the stream. I squinted. A sandy spit of land almost touched the boulder. On the sand was a small box, which I knew from its size and shape was covered with dark green velvet. The name embossed in gold on the top would be *Aspen Meadow Jewelers.*

My headache cut like razor blades. Investigator Calloway's distant voice said, "The box has a—"

"Yes," I interrupted. "He would have had that box with him." I did not need to be reminded of the box's contents, the thin gold band Tom and I had picked out. His ring was still in Father Olson's office at the church. I said, "He was so big, strong . . . I still don't understand how someone could have, that is, could there have been more than one person—"

Calloway held up one finger. She shook her head. "Besides Schulz's, there's only one set of footprints."

There was a fresh rustle of activity from the group by the creek bank. Investigator Calloway motioned us back toward the voices.

"Yeah, it's his."

"I think so."

"It doesn't make sense to me . . ."

Calloway lifted one bushy white eyebrow. "Looks like we might have one more thing for you, Miss Bear."

Together we walked to a group of police officers by the thick stand of cottonwoods. My eyes were drawn to the corpse-sized lump covered with dark material. It was hard to believe I would never see Father Olson again. The crowd fell silent, then parted abruptly in front of us.

"Schulz might have tossed it over here. Have her take a look at it." The speaker was an angular man with shaggy red hair and a gravelly voice. He pointed to a small soggy spiral notebook under the cottonwoods. Someone threw a poncho on the wet grass and mud in front of the notebook. Awkwardly, I knelt as directed, feeling all eyes on me. Investigator Calloway crouched beside me and spoke gently.

"Don't touch it. Again, you're more familiar with him, you can tell us if it's Schulz's."

The top page of the notebook was wet. The writing on it was slightly smeared. I barely noticed Boyd as he squatted beside Calloway and me. Slashing strokes written with a blue ballpoint indicated the notes had been hurriedly taken, undoubtedly scribbled in an awkward position. Timidly, I read aloud:

w Nissan van
1049 v alv gswx2chst
d d
B. - Read - Judas?
vm p.r.a.y.
1133 vdd

My head throbbed. I reread the scribbles.

"Well?" demanded Inspector Calloway.

I said nothing.

Boyd grunted.

Frustrated, Investigator Calloway asked, "Is there *anything* you can tell us?"

I pulled back and looked into Calloway's shrewd hazel eyes. Her look and her questions were urgent. I knew she needed my help to find Tom and solve this horrific murder. Pain squeezed my voice. I told her, "The handwriting is Tom Schulz's. I don't know what he was trying to say."

4

Boyd pressed his thin lips together, scowling down at the sodden spiral notebook. "Schulz and his notes. Memory enhancer, he called it." He flung his match into the snow and craned his stubby neck to reread the scribbles. "*GSW times two.* Two gunshot wounds, we knew that. *DD.* Looks like he might have gotten a dying declaration."

Investigator Calloway sighed. "Now if we could just figure out what the victim said. And we'll need to read up about Judas." She concentrated her gaze on me. "Know anybody with a white van? People with names, initials *VM* or *B*?"

I felt dizzy. His handwriting. I could hear my teeth chattering. A vision of a shotgun welled up. Where was the gun now? How much ammunition did it have?

"Please, Miss Bear. A van. A white Nissan van. Sound familiar?"

"Ah, I have a white van. It says . . ." I groped for words. "*Goldilocks' Catering, Where Everything Is Just Right!* on the side. But it's a Volkswagen, not a Nissan."

"Is your van missing? Where was it this morning?"

With difficulty, I thought back. My van had spent the morning being filled with platters of food for our wedding reception. I told her so. Investigator Calloway nodded. She assured me her investigative team would check with Olson's neighbors as well as with people who lived along Upper Cottonwood Creek Road, to see if anybody else saw a van.

I stared at the wilted notebook that Tom had, presumably, somehow managed to toss into the bushes. The paper in front of me must hold some clue to what had happened out here. Impenetrable hieroglyphics stared back.

"Don't you cops use some kind of standard shorthand? That's what it looks like to me."

Boyd pulled out his pad and began writing on it. "Nothing standard," he said gruffly. "*GSW* and *DD* I already told you. Gunshot wounds. Dying Declaration. The victim was alive. The victim was dead. Somebody drove a van. A reference to praying and the Bible. We'll get you a copy of this. If you can puzzle over it some more, that would sure help."

"Wait, though," said Calloway. "Wait. Look at it again, Miss Bear. *VM P.R.A.Y.?* Could all those periods in there have some significance for Schulz? Or something from your church, maybe? Is P.R.A.Y. an acronym for some church organization? Schulz used V for victim on the first line, so could VM refer to that? We'll check through his files, see what we can come up with. Maybe you have something else he's written, some notes to you, something with abbreviations?"

I said no and did not mention that Tom Schulz had written me few notes in the time we'd known each other. Our courtship had emerged from crisis. When the attempted poisoning of my ex-father-in-law had led to the temporary closing of my catering business, I had responded reluctantly to Tom's interest in me. As our relationship developed over the last eighteen months, we'd had phone conversations, barbecues, outings in the mountains or in Denver. These outings invariably concluded with meals I fixed in my professional cooking area or dinners Tom prepared in the fabulously equipped kitchen of his cabin. And only very recently, when we were alone, those meals were followed by lovemaking.

We had not written.

Calloway persisted. "But you must have *something* of his, a notebook, journal, calendar, anything that might contain some of these abbreviations. If you did, or if such written material existed, would it be at your house? Or his?"

I knew she was doing her job. Trying to find their premier homicide investigator, the police would ruthlessly unearth every scrap of information. But I wasn't up to discussing our complex domestic arrangements, especially when it involved so much stuff in boxes that had just been moved to my house from Tom's cabin. In fact, I wasn't up to discussing much of anything. I said, "I'm not sure. But I'll look. I promise."

"Who has keys to his place?" she wanted to know. "And his car? I mean, besides that set in the creek."

My eyes were burning, my hands were numb with cold. I muttered that I had a set of keys to his home but not with me. Anyway, I added, his place was empty. At that moment, another officer summoned Calloway. She promised that Boyd or Armstrong would stay in touch, and directed that I keep the phone line to my house open. I asked Boyd when I could have the articles Tom Schulz dropped at the crime scene. He clomped off, then reported back that when the lab was done with them, someone would come by my place with Tom's things.

"Was there any blood?" I asked Boyd. I cleared my throat. "Tom's blood? You said he was hurt."

Boyd winced sympathetically. One of his rough hands reached out impulsively for mine. Quietly, he answered, "Looks like he got scratched on the rocks. Maybe he turned his ankle or broke a leg bone coming down the bank. I'm not going to lie to you: He could be hurt bad." I couldn't listen, couldn't look at Boyd, couldn't bear to have him touching me. I turned my gaze to the snowy ground and pulled my hands away. Boyd went on. "That's the only way the perp could have overpowered him, we think. If that's what happened. You know, Schulz is muscular, he's a tough guy. Street smart and regular smart. We're going to bring you a copy of the note," he added, changing the subject, "for you to study."

A cold, wet breeze swept the frigid meadow. The end of the snow and advent of watery afternoon sunshine had not materialized into anything warm and springlike. I clasped my upper arms but couldn't stop trembling. Helen Keene shambled over to me and again threw the victim-advocate quilt around my shoulders. Slowly we walked down the muddy driveway to Boyd's squad car. She asked me for directions and then drove us home. We passed the ranches, the custom homes, the preparatory school entrance. The time spent in Olson's meadow had been hard on my wedding suit; cold, wet silk clung to my legs. In my mind's eye, I kept seeing Boyd, Armstrong, and Helen Keene walking across the flagstones to the St. Luke's office with their terrible news. I couldn't control a gutteral groan. I needed to get home, to be with Arch and Julian.

"Please keep your phone line open," Helen said after I'd turned down her offer to come into my house and stay for a while. She handed me her card. "And keep the quilt," she added softly. "A group of women from your church donates them to the Sheriff's Department and to Aspen

Meadow Outreach just for situations like yours." The questions bubbled up in my brain: Situations like mine? What exactly was my situation? But Helen held me in her steady gaze. "Goldy—please call me if you need me."

I thanked her and extricated myself from the police car. On the sidewalk across from my house, a trio of neighbors watched, apparently oblivious to the cold. How bad news traveled so quickly in this town I did not know. Stumbling dizzily toward my front door, it was all I could do to keep the quilt awkwardly clutched around my muddied wedding suit.

Once I had come through our security system, I called for Arch, then Julian. The silent house felt deserted without the customary rich smell of cooking. My suitcase, packed for our honeymoon, sat forlornly in the front hall. I turned away from it.

"Oh, Mom, you're here!" cried Arch as he galloped down the stairs. He had changed from the tux to a gray sweatsuit. "Julian took Grandma and Grandpa to the airport. He's taking our tuxes back, too. I was just about to start putting the food in the walk-in, the way Julian told me. Where's Tom? How come your clothes are so messy? Where'd you get that blanket thing?"

"Oh, hon. It's a long story." I begged off immediate explanations by announcing I would take a shower while he put the platters away. Wearily, I climbed the stairs. Every muscle in my body ached. In the bedroom that Tom had begun only recently to share with me, I stood in front of the mirror and gazed at the ruined beige silk outfit. *A middle-aged Miss Haversham,* my reflection mocked back. A flood of anger sent my fingers ripping at the tiny pearl buttons. Two flew off and *pinged* on the wooden floor. A half-formed sob squawked out of my throat. I carefully removed the churchwomen's necklace. *I don't deserve this,* I reflected bitterly. Selfish to worry about what I didn't deserve, but I didn't care. Tears leaked out of my eyes as I groped around on my knees until I found the buttons. *I have suffered enough already. Hey, God? Did you hear me? If you're really there.* After placing the buttons on my bureau, I reached for Tom's pillow on the bed, then buried my face in it. I sobbed and gasped, then inhaled deeply. Even though he'd spent the last few nights at his cabin, the pillowcase had the wonderful smell of him.

In the shower the spray went to scalding as I rocked back and forth, back and forth. Eventually I wrapped myself in a thick terrycloth towel and sat on the bed, dizzy and exhausted. I rose and pulled on a sweatsuit. Again I caught a glimpse of my wan reflection. What to say to Arch? To Julian? I didn't even know what I was going to say to myself.

In the kitchen the counters were empty except for a tray of marzipan-covered petit fours and chocolate truffles that had been meant to be take-home presents for our wedding guests. I asked Arch if anybody had called. He said no and went back to methodically pulling off the wrapping and then eating truffles, one small bite at a time. I hugged myself and began to rock again. Arch stopped in midbite, his eyes narrowed behind his glasses.

"What's going on, Mom?"

"Oh, Arch . . . I'm afraid I have some bad news."

"Father Olson. I heard."

"No. This is about Tom." Arch was one of the people who had to know. I braced myself, then flatly recounted the bare outlines of the story: Tom finding the mortally injured priest and then apparently being hurt and forcefully taken.

As I spoke, my son's freckled face went numb with shock. When I'd finished, he sat motionless for a long time, then, carefully, he put the half-eaten truffle back on the paper napkin embossed with *Tom and Goldy, April 11.* He pushed his glasses up his nose and clasped his hands under his armpits.

"Tom Schulz was kidnapped?"

"They think so."

"They're going to find him, aren't they?"

There was no point in equivocating. *I hope so,* or *The police are working on it* would only lead to a tangle of unanswerable questions and a flood of worries. There was no reason to voice the unwanted fears that chilled my spirit the way winter winds howl down the mountains. I saw myself picking out a plain coffin for Tom Schulz. In a few short years, Arch would go off to college. I would live out my days alone.

"Yes," I told my son firmly, with more conviction than I felt. "They will find him."

Arch started to sweep the kitchen floor, an order-restoring chore he often undertook when his outer life was in chaos. My stomach said I should eat, but one glance inside the walk-in refrigerator at the platters of beautifully decorated reception food made me turn away. Would whoever abducted Tom feed him? I paced around the kitchen, felt the gnawing in my stomach develop into spasms, willed the pains away. Arch finished the floor, took out his drawing materials, and sat at the kitchen table. He knew I would want him within sight.

My business line rang. The sudden noise made me cry out as if I'd been struck. I dived for it.

"What?" I shouted. If it was a client, I thought belatedly, I could kiss this booking good-bye.

"Goldy?" came the tentative, frightened voice of Zelda Preston. "Are you all right? I mean, I know you aren't all right . . . you can't be after what's happened . . ."

Zelda Preston, mother-in-law to scarecrow Agatha in the church kitchen, was a current Altar Guild member and, until very recently, the organist at St. Luke's. Zelda and Lucille Boatwright had both been widowed about a decade ago. The two women were almost constantly in each other's company now, except when Zelda met with the master swimmers and did her weekly three miles' worth of laps. With her attenuated face that always reminded me of a camel's, her wiry muscles, and her long braid of gray hair wound on top of her head, Zelda Preston seemed the tall, rod-thin counterpart to Lucille's stodgy, solid self.

I said, "Are you calling about Lucille?"

"Oh, my dear Goldy. No. I'm calling about you. I want to do something for you, poor dear. . . ." Her voice faltered.

Zelda carried a painful past, but we'd never had any sisterly soul-baring talks. An older female Episcopalian would rather die impoverished than discuss psychic wounds, a conversation she would put in the same category as comparing bra sizes. Nevertheless, Zelda's attempt to offer sympathy touched me, and awakened guilt. I hadn't called *her* this past month, when the many disagreements she and Father Olson had had about ecclesiastical music had ended up with his firing her. Still, what would I have said? *You want to have lunch and talk about how getting fired is like getting divorced?* I didn't think so.

"Zelda. You are thoughtful to call. I don't need anything, thanks." I cleared my throat, keenly aware that I needed to keep both phone lines clear in case the police needed to reach me. I didn't know which number they had. Since I had no call-waiting, I couldn't risk giving the police a busy signal. But explaining all this, plus Tom's disappearance, were more than I could handle at the moment. "I need to go."

"Oh, all right. But Goldy," she went on meekly, "I am so terribly sorry to bother you about this, but I'm just trying to see what you want done with your wedding flowers. Lucille isn't available, as you probably know, so I need to step in for her to help plan the Holy Week services and the funeral for Father Olson." She paused. "Have you heard anything? I mean, about what happened to him?"

"Not yet."

"Well . . . If you wish, we could try to use these flowers for Father Olson . . . I know it sounds petty, but someone must start to make the decisions, and Doug Ramsey is *impossible.* . . . If you donated the flowers, it would certainly save the parish money, goodness knows. However, I do not know what our *new* priest will want. Not our new priest," she corrected herself, "whoever those people down at the *diocese* send to us." Zelda's voice dropped on the word *diocese* in a way that left no doubt as to her opinion of that ecclesiastical body.

"Tell you what," I said placatingly, desperate to clear the phone line. "Why don't you donate them to the Catholic church? Their parish is bigger; they're sure to have a wedding coming up soon."

"The Catholics! Having a wedding during Holy Week? For heaven's sake, the least you could do is donate them to someone from our parish who is ill. Honestly, Goldy. The *Catholics.*"

"Fine, Zelda. Really. Who's in the hospital at the moment? Whatever will make you happy." This whole conversation was absurd. But however much we might disagree or be upset, Episcopalians did not hang up on each other.

She trilled, "Roger Bampton is home from the hospital, although . . ." She broke off and announced, "Victor Mancuso has shingles, but I don't know which hospital he's in, and of course it would be difficult to track down the church secretary, since she took her Easter vacation early." She paused again. "And it's *you* I want to have happy, my dear."

"Victor Mancuso?" I said, incredulous. *VM.* I demanded, "Who's Victor Mancuso?"

"No one really, he's the secretary's uncle. She just put him on the prayer list before she left. Nobody else knows anything about him, I already asked."

On the prayer list, on the prayer list. *P.R.A.Y.* I struggled to think: The prayer list contained names of all those for whom the parish offered intercessory requests. Or, as Arch maintained, it was the list of people and things we wanted God to fix. The charismatic segment of the congregation, those parishioners who put ultra-enthusiastic emphasis on spiritual gifts and a personal relationship with Jesus, offered intercessions on a much more regular and serious basis than most of the rest of us. There was also a small noncharismatic women's prayer group that met weekly.

Zelda, I remembered, was a member of this group. Maybe she could help decipher the acronymns in Tom's note.

I asked sharply, "Is there an ecumenical or parish organization with the initials P.R.A.Y.? Maybe something like, Protestant-Roman Catholic Association of Youth?"

Zelda drew in her breath, confused. "Goldy? What in the *world* are you talking about? Are they the ones you want to donate the flowers to? Because I can't be calling all around—"

"Zelda, is there such an organization? P.R.A.Y.? I'm sure I've heard of it somewhere."

"Well, I'm sure I haven't, and I've been in this parish for twenty years, ever since Father Pinckney—"

"Okay, thanks, Zelda. Please. Use the flowers in any way you wish. I'm sorry, I *have* to go." We both stuttered good-byes and gently hung up.

Arch glanced at me, frowned, and left the room to look for some colored pencils. I stared at my catering calendar. The days were blank. Of course, I had cleared it in anticipation of our three-day honeymoon. Now there was not even work I could do to take my mind off this spiral of events.

Worry for Tom exploded in my chest. Should I have asked Helen Keene to stay with me? When would Julian be back from the airport? What could Tom's cryptic notes mean? I lay down on my kitchen floor, pulled my knees to my chest, and felt tears slide down my cheeks unchecked. *I'm losing it.*

The doorbell rang; again, my heart jumped. Leaping to my feet, I raced down the hall, then stared disbelievingly through the peekhole. Marla. She made a face at me and held up plastic bags of food. Just what we needed: more to eat. Arch, who had trotted down the hall behind me at the sound of the bell, moaned in disappointment and muttered that he was going to watch television.

"What are you doing here alone?" Marla demanded as soon as she had heaved herself and her bags into the kitchen. "I swear." Still wearing her dark matron of honor suit, she took in my sweatsuit and my face, then shook her head. "Somehow I knew you wouldn't want me to take you out to dinner tonight."

"I'm not alone; Arch is here." To my horror, it all spilled out. "Marla—Father Olson's killer took Tom. I had to go out to Olson's place, and it was awful . . ."

She pulled me in for a long hug. "I know," she murmured in my ear.

"I was down at the church looking for you. Father Doug told me. Do you need to cry?"

I thought about the weeping I'd already done, solitary and helpless on the floor. "Thanks, but no. Not at the moment, anyway."

"Need to talk?"

I pulled away from her, picked up a bag, and set it on the counter. "How did Doug Ramsey know Tom was missing?"

"From the cops." Marla heaved the other bag onto one of the kitchen counters. "Some of them are still at the church. They wanted to see if Schulz's phone call to the church office might have been taped."

"Oh, Lord." I stumbled morosely into a kitchen chair.

Marla eased down beside me. She put a hand over mine. I stared unhappily at the black front of Tom's range, unable to rid myself of the vision of him flipping pieces of chicken on the grill. He'd had friends from the Sheriff's Department haul the Jenn-Air grill-with-convection-oven over from his cabin and install the ventilation pipe a week ago. He had said he couldn't live without his oven. With a wink, he'd added, "Sort of like you, Goldy."

After a few moments, Marla rose and began to unload her stash. Individually wrapped Beef Wellington. Frozen Scampi. We'd often joked that our ex-husband had found two women who loved food more than they loved him. My passion was working in the kitchen, and Marla was the queen of packaged gourmet.

She looked at me. "Where's your choker?"

"Upstairs. Why? It's a miracle I didn't lose it out at Olson's place, tramping around in the mud."

"Goldy, don't say *it's a miracle* to me." She flopped back down next to me. "We've got a problem. Actually, more than one."

"What? With the pearls?"

"Before your wedding was supposed to begin, I was out in the narthex with the jewelry raffle committee. I told them both of us were wearing the chokers that were going to be sold, and they ooh'ed and aah'ed."

Oh boy, I thought, here we go. Some left-wing group had threatened a pearl boycott.

"I'll get to the pearl problem in a minute." She sighed. "Apparently," Marla continued glumly, "some of the goings-on in our parish have started rumors floating around in the diocese."

I sniffed. "Goings-on in our parish? Rumors? Wait until they hear our priest has been murdered." I shook my head, seeing the flash of Father

Theodore Olson's warm smile behind his dark beard when he appointed me to the Board of Theological Examiners.

Marla nodded. "Right. 'Show me a parish in the diocese without some wild stories,' I say. And so they say, 'Hoho, word's out Roger Bampton claims his healing was *miraculous.*' As in feeding-of-the-five-thousand miraculous."

"Oh, please," I said, in no mood to discuss disease. "Roger's sick. I heard he was a little better. Miraculous? That's what our ex-husband is going to say when he hears Tom Schulz didn't show up for the wedding." I felt a sudden chill, thought about making tea, then dismissed it. Too much effort. "Anyway," I added, "Roger has leukemia."

"He's out of the hospital." Marla grimaced. "Get this. He's not just a little better, he had a *normal* blood test. To me, it was a miracle old Scotch-swilling Rog didn't die of liver disease before they diagnosed him with leukemia. And they're saying there've been other miracles, too."

"Come on, Marla. I've heard some of those stories, the bad knee healed and all that. Who listens? They're like the stock market. You have a wave of good luck and then a wave of bad. How is this a problem?"

"Goldy, we've been busy with other stuff, we haven't been tuned into all the *latest.* I mean, you've been getting ready for the wedding, and I've been planning a jewelry raffle and sale with dozens of orders for tickets and chokers. But Agatha Preston enlightened me: Three weeks ago, sick-to-death Roger was suddenly pronounced well. Last week, a Sunday School teacher swore she'd been cured of chronic back pain. An infant born blind got his sight somehow. So I told these folks that I need to lose twenty pounds, where do I sign up?"

I said, "I need Tom Schulz back."

"Just thought you'd like to know."

"Father Olson wouldn't have approved."

"Listen," she protested, "Agatha and these women swear Olson was the one whose actions got the rumors started in the first place. It's Father Pinckney who wouldn't have approved." Getting up abruptly, Marla hauled out three bags of Chinese-style vegetables and two frozen Sara Lee cakes. I wondered briefly what had happened to the wedding cake. Marla emerged from my walk-in refrigerator and put her hands on her ample hips. "But remember I said I had more than one problem? Here's the other: Father Olson kept the rest of the pearls. Out at his place. Twenty chokers, two thousand dollars each. The cops didn't find them at his house."

"They've already searched the whole place?" I could not remember ever being so confused. Another wave of weariness swept over me. I ran a hand over the black enamel of Tom's stove. "That's hard to believe. Why did you . . . why did Olson have the pearls in the first place?"

"He always kept the stuff for the jewelry raffle and sale." Marla sounded disgusted. "He kept the gold chains last year and the jade the year before that. He said a jewelry thief would never scope out Upper Cottonwood Creek. I told the police to keep looking for them, but they said his house wasn't burgled, so it's not as if they searched every nook and cranny. It's just that the motive doesn't look like robbery at this point. Of course Olson didn't have a safe. And they won't let me or anyone else go into his house to poke around. That Olson. He was such a squirrelly packrat, he probably hid them somewhere we'll never find." She groaned.

"Squirrelly packrat?"

"Sorry, I'm mixing my rodent metaphors. You going to eat these truffles?"

"Go ahead. Marla— Is there a church organization with the acronym P.R.A.Y.?"

She took a bite of chocolate and munched thoughtfully. "Pray? Not that I know of, and you know if anyone would know about church organizations, it's me."

"Well, when was the last time you read the story about Judas?"

Marla finished her first truffle, looked over the tray, and chose a second, this one a plump dark mound dusted with cocoa. She popped it into her mouth, put a hand on her large chest, and frowned. "I certainly don't know. Why?"

"Tom wrote something down before Olson died," I murmured. "He mentioned this P.R.A.Y. and Judas, but nobody knows what he was talking about."

"Judas? He wrote something about Judas? Why?" I shrugged. Marla licked her fingertips. "Let's see, what's today? Still Lent. I always wait for somebody to read the story to me. You know, in church. The Last Supper, Maundy Thursday, then the betrayal by Judas. No, no, it's the other way around. Wait a minute. You're the Sunday School teacher, you tell me. Is that all he wrote? What was it, some kind of ransom note?"

"No." I'd probably already said too much. I gritted my teeth in preparation for further interrogation, but Marla pushed away the truffle tray and gazed in my direction, concerned. Clearly, she was more worried about me as a friend than she was about the details of the homicide/kidnapping investigation.

"Goldy, want to come and stay at my place? I can take care of you. Honestly, it's the least I can do. Matron of honor and all that."

"No, thanks. I have to stay by the phone. Until they find him," I said uncertainly.

"They'll find him," Marla said firmly. She inched her chair over and put her hand on my arm. "Goldy, you cannot stay here alone."

"You're great, but honest. I'm not alone—Arch and Julian are with me. Talk to me about the church. Tell me how this could happen."

"I swear, I don't know. Olson was just—" She gestured extravagantly, like an Italian looking for a word. "—a cute charismatic who had a good grounding in theology? I don't know. Does that sound prejudiced? I mean, when I told him we cleared twenty thousand on the gold chains last year, he didn't say 'Praise the Lord.' "

"That doesn't help." Twenty thousand dollars on gold chains? I felt hysteria rising in my throat and pushed it down. "With these jewelry raffles—you sell some and raffle some, right?" She nodded. "Who ordered the pearls for the fund-raiser? Do you know how many people knew they were out at Olson's house? And what do the churchwomen use all that money for, anyway?"

"Hey whoa, Goldy, slow down." She pressed her lips together. "Bob Preston ordered the pearls this year. You remember, the oil guy, husband of Agatha, son of Zelda. I guess I should say, former oil guy. He got some kind of deal from a friend of his in the Far East. As to what the churchwomen use the money for, there's usually a *big* argument. Lucille and the Art and Architecture Committee want to build the columbarium before they redo the kitchen. I'm running the raffle, and I want to give the money to Aspen Meadow Outreach. So Lucille Boatwright and I are at odds, which, believe me, is nothing new. Speaking of the crotchety angel, are you up to hearing about what happened after she collapsed at the church? Or do you want me to fix you some tea first?"

I really couldn't focus on Lucille Boatwright and her autocratic ways. But decision making was beyond me. When I said nothing, Marla rummaged through cupboards, extracted a teapot and cups, opened a box of Scottish shortbread she had brought, and put a pan of water on to boil. The gestures reminded me of Tom. He loved tea. Loves. *Stop it.*

"Anyway, Lucille Boatwright," Marla persisted. "The Old Guard is still guarding. Old Lucy's fine; she informed the doctors not to let Mitchell Hartley and the rest of the charismatics touch her precious columbarium construction in her absence. She had some arrhythmia, and Zelda Preston is down at the hospital with her."

"Well, Zelda's back, because she just called me from the church. Trying to plan Holy Week and Ted Olson's funeral and wondering what to do with Tom's and my wedding flowers." Marla sipped her tea and rolled her eyes. "I told her to give the altar arrangements to the Roman Catholics."

Marla choked. "Treading a bit close to the edge, aren't we? I'm surprised Zelda's involved. You know, she was just so irate about the music, spent all last month screaming about going to see the bishop. Oh, wait. Speaking of the bishop. Guess who he's appointed to pastor the church through this crisis?"

"Marla. I really don't care. All I can think about is Tom. A priest appointed to get us through this crisis? Could the bishop really move that fast?"

"He has to. I mean, a murdered priest, a halted wedding, not to mention a funeral? Our flock needs emergency pastoring."

"Doug Ramsey, I guess."

"Wrong. He's too junior." She dunked a shortbread cookie into her tea and carefully bit into it. "The bishop is sending in the poet."

"The . . . oh, no. Not George Montgomery. He's the canon theologian. He's on the Board of Theological Examiners with me and always asks about the history of the eucharist."

"Montgomery may *examine* about the sacrament of holy communion," Marla said, "but he's going to *versify* about everything else." She finished her shortbread cookie and reached for another. "Be prepared for sermons that ask, 'Where were you, God/when I laid sod/and found it crass/to ask for grass?' " She chuckled sourly.

I stared at Tom's oven. The phone rang. I jumped for it.

"Yes!"

"Hello, is this Goldy?" A female voice, hesitant, raw from crying.

"Who is this?"

"Agatha," gulped the voice, "Agatha . . ."

I put my hand over the receiver and mouthed to Marla, "Agatha Preston."

Marla stage-whispered, "I saw her in the church kitchen. She looked like a WASP auditioning for *Song of Hiawatha.*"

"Agatha," I said into the receiver, "what is it? Do you have some news? What's wrong?"

Marla's eyes bulged. I shook my head firmly when she mouthed, "What? What?"

"I can't, I can't take it . . ." Agatha gagged, coughed, and let out a single sob. With great effort, she said, "Did you . . . I need to know if you . . . saw him." She burst into a fit of crying.

"Saw him?" I was bewildered.

"What happened?" she sobbed. "Oh, God, I'm not going to make it. Oh, where is he?" She cried harder, and then her voice became distant when the phone thudded against a hard surface.

"Hello, who's this?" A male voice.

"This is Goldy the caterer. I was trying to talk to somebody."

"This is Bob Preston. My wife coordinates the prayer list. As you can see, she is extremely upset. She'll have to call you later."

"But, Agatha asked me if I saw somebody. Who was she talking about?"

Bob Preston said: "I certainly don't know. My wife's beside herself. It would be in the best interest of the church if you could just let her call you back."

My frayed nerves snapped. I yelled, "Look, dammit—"

But unlike most Episcopalians, Bob Preston had hung up.

5

"What a creep!" I screeched. "Get out the phone book," I raged at Marla. "I need to call back the Prestons. Agatha said she wasn't going to make it, and had I *seen* him, and then Bob just more or less told me to forget it, she'd have to call me back! Where is my stupid phone book?"

Marla's eyebrows climbed toward the stratosphere. Telling Marla to forget something was her idea of denial of civil liberties. I scrounged wildly for, and then through, the thin Aspen Meadow phone book. No Preston. What about the church directory? I looked for it, but then remembered I had cleared that shelf to make way for Tom's cookbooks, which now lay in a disorganized pile above the counter. I had no clue to the directory's whereabouts.

Marla clattered our teacups into the sink and turned on the faucet. I gave up looking for the Prestons' number and announced I was out of physical and emotional fuel. I had Tom Schulz to worry about. Had he ever mentioned Agatha Preston to me?

"What is Bob doing now?" I demanded of Marla. I summoned up a mental image of Bob Preston, oilman extraordinaire: With his puffed-out chest and thinning red hair, Preston always reminded me of an aging rooster, although he probably wasn't much past thirty. Over six feet, maybe six-feet-four, he had prominent cheekbones, a receding chin, and narrow lips. I said, "What happened to his oil business?"

She began rinsing Tom's cups with their tiny stylized roses. "Bob was riding high until the price of oil crashed in the mid-eighties. The price of natural gas hasn't gone anywhere either, so it was too expensive to explore. His company went belly-up year before last. They haven't called for you to cater lately, have they?"

I put my hand on Tom's stove. "Caterers are always vulnerable to the vagaries of wider economic movements." My voice sounded so morose it was clear that financial vulnerability was not the problem.

"Come on, I'm going to cheer you up," said Marla decisively. "You have to get your mind off these things. I'll tell you all the gossip about Bob and the Bob-projects. Not only do they include Habitat for Humanity right here in your neighborhood, he's also heading this Sportsmen Against Hunger group. They go out into the woods with six-packs and rifles with scopes and shoot elk, then donate the—shall I call them 'proceeds'?—to Aspen Meadow Outreach. Now if you were a poor, hungry person, how would you feel about eating an elkburger? Do you have a recipe for such a thing? How about venison chili?"

I shuddered. "I know about that group and the Habitat project. Just tell me who Agatha wanted to see."

She gave me a look of determination. "Agatha is involved in everything down at the church. I don't know who she was referring to." She turned the last teacup over to drain on a towel and ran her fingers through her frizzled hair. "But you can bet I'm going to find out."

Outside, the gears of the van ground as the tires crunched up the driveway. Julian had returned.

"Marla, I can't stand being out of it. I can't stand to just sit here by the telephone waiting for the police to call. I've got to do something."

She sat down and squeezed my fingers, which were finally beginning to get warm. "Goldy, what you need to do is rest. Let Arch and Julian pamper you, if you're not going to come to my place."

Julian, dressed in a secondhand wool overcoat that was much too big for his compact, muscled body, clomped inside and threw himself into a kitchen chair. Marla, who is happiest when people are eating, asked him if he wanted some tea and shortbread.

"No, thanks." The corners of his mouth quivered downward. His bleached mohawk haircut was wildly askew, and the five o'clock shadow on his jaw made him look older than nineteen. He'd exchanged the rented tux for patched jeans and an oversized T-shirt distributed by a local roofing company that had gone out of business. The logo shrieked: *The roof is the hairdo on a house! Think about it.*

Julian snorted. "I went by the church to see if there was anything else I needed to pick up." He gestured with his thumb. "The wedding cake's in the van. I gotta freeze it. The people at the church told me what happened to Schulz. I can't *believe* it, man. Schulz is so fast, so smart, I'm like, you're *kidding.* Have you heard anything?"

I said no and tried to appear pulled-together. Julian had suffered his own share of upheavals, starting when the boarding department at Elk Park Preparatory School, where he was a scholarship student, closed. We had both been live-in employees for a few ill-fated months at a wealthy couple's mansion, and when things fell apart there, Julian came to live with Arch and me. Less than two months away from graduating from Elk Park Prep, he was an excellent student, star swimmer, and ferociously good cook. He was desperate to get into Cornell so he could study food science. Eventually, he wanted to become the first vegetarian caterer from Bluff, Utah, to be written up in *Gourmet.* I thought he had a good chance to get into Cornell, although I had my doubts about his aspirations for *Gourmet.* That, however, could wait, as it was the coming week that would bring the college acceptance and rejection news. Adding this to the wedding preparations had put Julian's anxiety into high gear. Still, Arch and I loved having him around, high anxiety or no. But now, with Tom gone, the teenager would be impossible. I knew from sad experience that the emotionally volatile Julian became volcanic in the face of danger to those he loved.

"So what are the police doing about Schulz?" he demanded when I didn't answer immediately. He glowered at me as if this were somehow my fault. "I mean, do they, like, know who snatched him, or *what*?"

I patiently explained that a concentration of law-enforcement types were prowling about at Olson's house the way they were searching the church, that they had found some things of Tom's and a note containing abbreviations nobody could decipher. Julian chewed on his knuckles when I said Tom's note seemed to be his catalogue of events up to the moment he was abducted by somebody whose identity we did not yet know.

My personal phone line rang; I snatched it. "What?"

"Uh, Goldy? This is Father Doug Ramsey, and I need to talk to you about . . . some church matters. First, of course, I am concerned about you. How are you doing?"

"Terribly, Doug. Sorry, I can't talk now. I'm trying to keep my phone lines open for the police."

"Well. This will just take a minute. It's about the meeting next week, and the food—"

I put my hand over the mouthpiece and hissed at Marla, "Get rid of Father Doug for me, will you? Quickly?"

Marla puckered her lips, then took the receiver. "This is Goldilocks' Catering and we can't talk now." But instead of hanging up—she was, after all, a cradle Episcopalian—she listened to Doug Ramsey launch into one of his long strings of words: explanations, queries, thoughts. I whispered a prayer that the police would do an operator interrupt if there was news.

"What do you mean, abbreviations? What kind of notes are you talking about?" Julian asked me in a conspiratorial tone.

"Just his notes on what was happening when he arrived out at Olson's place. They think it was to help him remember." I looked questioningly at Marla, who still held the phone to her ear.

Marla shook her head and told Doug Ramsey to hold on. To me she said, "He's saying Bob Preston called him after Agatha phoned here. He wants to know if you want Schulz put on the prayer list."

"Of course," I said. "*Please* tell him I have to leave this line open for the cops, so don't let him go on and on with exaggerated descriptions and hyperbolic worries." Which was precisely Father Doug Ramsey's style, unfortunately.

Marla returned to the phone. After a minute, she said, "No, no, no, I'm sure she won't. . . . She's under too much stress, that's why." Again she put her hand over the mouthpiece. "Did this guy flunk pastoral theology or what?" she whispered. Doug's voice still droned through the receiver; Marla smiled widely. "Doug," she told him loudly, "you can find *another* caterer." More muffled protests were followed by, "All right, I'll ask." She turned to me. "Father Insensitive wants to know if you're still going to cater the Board of Theological Examiners' meetings starting Tuesday night. And attend, too, since you're a member, that's what he says he's upset about, can't get another qualified laywoman on such short notice, and especially with Olson gone, they just won't have enough people to do the examining. Or so he claims. He says it'll help you get your mind off your other crises. Although I think he's more worried about food, if you want to know the truth."

"Goldy, you can't," Julian began fervently, "not when you're going through this other mess. Tell them I'll do it."

"I agree," said Marla, her hand still clasped over the mouthpiece. "The police will want to talk to you—"

"Tell him I don't know yet," I interrupted firmly. "The meeting's in three days—he can wait until tomorrow for a decision." Besides, I added mentally, Father Olson had been head of the Board of Theological Examiners. I owed doing this catering to him, and perhaps cooking for the board would keep me from obsessing about Schulz.

Resigned, Marla spoke quietly into the phone, then hung up. When Julian asked if I wanted him to fix dinner, Marla replied with a snicker that Father Doug had said the Altar Guild was sending in meals. Starting tonight.

"Oh, wow," Julian muttered as he raked his mown blond hair with his short fingers. "Tuna fish and cream of mushroom soup."

"Don't be ungrateful," Marla chided. "I've brought you frozen zucchini quiche, your own mini-wheel of Camembert, and spinach tortellini. And there's Beef Wellington for the carnivores. Not to mention that you still have plenty of wedding goodies tucked away in your refrigerator. You can munch on those for as long as—"

Wedding goodies. I put my head into my hands. *I know he loved you. <u>Loves.</u>* Julian and Marla simultaneously lunged forward to hug me, which only made matters worse.

"I didn't mean to, I really didn't." Marla's voice choked with guilt near my ear. "At least let me take you out tonight, Goldy. There's no point staying around here."

"I need to be near the phones," I said for what felt like the hundredth time. "But thanks, Marla. Please. Julian, if it'll make you feel better to cook, go ahead."

With a wild and angry energy, Julian began to bang around the kitchen. Arch appeared from the TV room and asked for an update. When we told him there was none, he assessed the two glum adults and one manic teenager, then announced he was going back to finish watching his show. After a while, Marla said she would go home and make some calls for me, to let people know what was going on so that they wouldn't tie up my lines with their dumb questions. But she would stay if we needed her, she offered hopefully. I assured her we would be fine. When she left, I went to find Arch.

In the spare bedroom that we used as a recreation space, Arch had the television on but was lying face-up on the tartan plaid couch. When he turned to me, I knew he was assessing my mood, the way he had as a child. He seemed to be wondering: How should I react to this crisis? If Mom is upset, I should be upset.

"I'm going to be all right," I said to his unspoken question. "Are you?"

He groaned. His gray sweatsuit was pleated in a rumpled mass that he didn't bother to straighten. He avoided my eyes. "Mom, how soon do you think the police will call?"

I turned the television off and sat in the matching plaid chair. "Very soon. They're going to bring me a copy of the note, and some things of Tom's."

Arch paused, mulling something over. Finally he heaved himself up.

"What is it, Arch?"

His thin chest and shoulders collapsed with a loud, disgusted sigh. Lying on the couch had flattened his hair straight up at the cowlick. "You really don't think he could have decided to, like, run away, do you? Maybe he just didn't want to . . . you know, I'm not saying it's you, Mom . . . maybe he just was afraid of all of us being together. In a family. Maybe he just didn't want to get married," he concluded fiercely.

I waited until Arch looked at me, then I took one of his cool hands. "This is what I believe: that they'll find him. That he wants to be a family with us more than anything."

Arch's eyes had gone from narrow to vacant; clearly, he was doubtful.

"Please, hon, won't you come eat? You haven't had a regular meal all day."

Arch shook his head and pulled his hand away. "I don't think I should eat until they find Tom Schulz."

"Please. Don't do this. Julian's working like crazy out there to make a nice meal for you. And you know Tom would want you to take care of yourself." He didn't move. "Please, Arch."

He got up. With bleary eyes, he pushed past me down the hall to the kitchen.

Our dinner consisted of Julian's idea of comfort food: a spicy frittata served with his own heated sourdough rolls, a fruit cup, and a complex salad of tomatoes, scallions, lettuce, crushed corn chips, and grated cheddar and jack cheeses, all coated with a thick, smooth avocado dressing. I recognized this guacamole concoction as a specialty of Tom's. Julian had retrieved the recipe from the overstuffed square plastic file that I'd forgotten was on a shelf where Tom's cookbooks were piled on top of mine. I wondered if the card file had any abbreviations in it. VM? B.—Read—Judas? P.R.A.Y.? Not likely.

The boys exchanged a worried look when I stopped moving food around on my plate and brought Tom's recipe box up to my nose, inhaled deeply, then dumped the whole mass of handprinted recipes out onto the table. The spattered, yellowed cards smelled faintly of Tom's kitchen. It was an inviting, high-ceilinged room in the log home he had been about to vacate, after much discussion, to live in town with us. I reached for a card: *Monster Cinnamon Rolls.* His handwriting. And then a note in another, more recent pen: *Try for G.* I couldn't bear it; I turned it over and left the cards in an untidy pile.

The frittata and salad, unfortunately, merely assuaged hunger, which was by this time severe. Worse, I was unable to offer comfort in the area Arch and Julian most needed it: answers to their questions. First they wanted to be told—again—every detail of Tom's disappearance. I hesitated discussing my time in the meadow by Olson's house, with its memories of the shrouded corpse and the police tramping dutifully about, looking for clues. But Arch, who had eaten only a forkful of frittata, and Julian, who was digging into his third helping, would tolerate no avoidance on my part. They wanted to hear it all, as if such knowledge could give order to the sudden loss of the big-bodied, big-hearted police officer whom they had both come to love. I did not mention that it looked as if Tom had been injured on the stony bank of the creek. Julian pushed his plate away and looked at me quizzically.

"What about *before* the church?" he persisted. "Didn't Schulz, you know, call you this morning? And what about Father Olson? Is stuff missing from his house? I mean, if there is, why would some guy rob him, then shoot him down by the creek instead of just knocking him out and taking off?"

"Tom Schulz did not call before we left for the church this morning," I said, remembering the hassle of getting my garment bag, the ring, and all the food platters into the van. "And as to the why with Father Olson, I don't know. That's what the investigative team is supposed to be working on." Some kind of resolve was forming. *And what I'm going to find out,* I added mentally.

Arch put down his fork. I was not up to telling him to finish what was on his plate. He said, "I want to see the note from him. I have some books of codes. Maybe I could look the abbreviations up."

Exasperated, Julian got up and began to clear the table. "Arch," he said as he clanked dishes into the sink, "if he'd known somebody was watching him, he would have pulled out his gun, not written a message to us in stupid code." He threw open the door to the commercial dishwasher that had just cost me over a thousand dollars. The heavy door made a cracking sound as it bounced in place.

"Oh, yeah?" hollered Arch. His face flushed with anger. "Where d'you suppose he packed his piece? Inside his tuxedo with the ring he was going to give to Mom?" Arch glowered at Julian, who rudely ignored him as he dumped plates and cutlery into the dishwasher. "If I want to look up codes, I will! I'm allowed!"

"Guys," I begged, "please. Not now." I made a sudden decision. Pushing my chair out from the table, I snatched the van keys. "I'm going back to the church." To the two pairs of suddenly fearful eyes, I said, "Don't sweat it. I'm just going to pick up his wedding ring."

It was bitterly cold outside. The wind had picked up and was whirling snow off the ground like fanned smoke. The van growled in protest when I gunned it toward Main Street. The church parking lot was empty, which is what you'd expect at 6:30 on a Saturday evening. I hopped out of the van, walked carefully across the slippery frozen gravel, and pulled on one of the two main doors to St. Luke's. It was unlocked—so much for ecclesiastical security. On the shadowed altar, the pallid petals of my bridal flowers glimmered like leftover funeral arrangements. Gritting my teeth, I allowed the door to swing shut and trotted around the long way, up past the columbarium construction. I was panting by the time I arrived at the church office building.

That office door wasn't just unlocked: it was partially open. *Tom, be with me,* I prayed silently as I tried to catch my breath. I whacked the door open with my foot.

"Hello?" I called as I stepped boldly over the threshold. "What the hell—?"

At first, I was so shocked I could not register what I saw. Within seconds, however, dismay replaced surprise. The office had been vandalized.

The sawhorses leading to the renovation area lay in pieces on the desk. On the floor, papers from the secretary's files had been dumped every which way. Her phone had been pulled from the wall and smashed. Hymnals and prayer books were spewed on top of the disorder of pipes, and the couch on which I had sat with Helen Keene that afternoon had been slashed. Gouts of foam rubber lay everywhere.

"I can't believe this," I muttered. The old floor creaked as I tiptoed through the devastation to Ted Olson's office. If whoever had done this had stolen Tom's wedding ring . . . My skin prickled with rage. I knew I was a little crazed. But no one was going to take *that* away from me, too.

Olson's office was—if possible—even more of a mess. Not only had the phone been broken to smithereens, but the contents of upended file drawers had been spilled over the floor. So much for the police searching through them for the meaning of *VM, B.,* and *P.R.A.Y.* The bookshelves were empty—all the volumes were on the floor. The vandal had spared the Leonardo reproduction, although it now hung at a grotesque tilt. The bulletin board had crashed to the floor. *The ring,* I thought. *What did you do with the ring, you bastard?*

There was a sudden shuffling. I screamed and grabbed a heavy book. Something—a trash can lid?—banged. Out the office window, I could dimly see a raccoon shambling away from the building. I collapsed onto a chair, certain I was about to have a heart attack.

"Dammit! Where is the ring?" I said aloud.

And then I remembered that I had brought it in the pocket of my streetclothes. They had fallen from their hook when I'd heaved a hymnal at the wall. I stepped over the debris until I came to the plain brown cotton dress that still lay in a rumpled heap. Kneeling, I fumbled in the pocket and experienced a cold wave of relief when my fingers closed around the velvet-covered box from Aspen Meadow Jewelers.

I pulled it out and opened it. The thick gold band that was to have been Tom's glistened in the fading light. I popped the box shut, stood, and stepped quickly over the chaos. Clutching the precious ring box, I ran back to my van.

6

The van wheezed against the cold as I raced home. Back in my kitchen, I ignored Julian's vociferous inquiries and called the Sheriff's Department. Yes, I insisted to Dispatch's toneless question, it was an emergency. Dispatch put me through to Calloway; I told her about the ransacked church office. She thanked me, said Boyd was on his way up to my house anyway, and that she'd send a team over to the church. I hung up.

"Man, Goldy, I can't *believe* you went inside when you saw the place was trashed." Julian slapped one of his schoolbooks open on the table and glared at me. "Don't you think that was, you know, *dangerous*? I mean, you really ought to think about taking care of yourself, don't you think? And no offense, but you look terrible." Upstairs, water gushed into Arch's bathtub. I looked around the spotlessly clean kitchen. In his usual methodical way, Julian had finished the dishes, set Arch on his evening routine, and now sat leaning back in one of the kitchen chairs. Even though it was Saturday night, he'd brought out some work to do. Julian despised inactivity—for himself, anyway. "I think you should stay home," he advised. "You know, just wait for the cops to call." He shifted the chair to balance at a precarious angle and crossed his arms impatiently. "So. Did you get the ring or what?"

"Yes, I got the ring. And I don't normally think of the church office building in the early evening being a dangerous spot," I replied stiffly. But in light of the day's events, Julian was right. I was about to show him the ring box when something under the shelf of Tom's cookbooks caught my eye. In the spot where Julian usually upended drying pots and pans, he had cleared the counter and spread one of his bandanas. On top of the bandana was Tom's recipe box; on top of the box was a small pile of what looked like potting soil.

"Julian? Is that dirt on my counter?"

His face turned sheepish. "Well, yeah. Kinda."

"Are we into voodoo here or what?"

"I figure you need to cover all the bases."

"Julian? What base is this? The one under home plate?"

He slammed the chair down onto the floor, sprang over to where I stood, and pointed at the mound. "This is dirt from Chimayó," he announced, as if that would explain everything.

"I know Chimayó is in New Mexico," I said. My patience was wearing thin. "And I know it's famous for its chili powder. But you're going to have to enlighten me on the dirt."

Julian rubbed two fingers across his sparse hedgerow of bleached hair. "It's, you know . . . like magic. People make pilgrimages to the sanctuary at Chimayó because the dirt has this . . . special healing power. The Indians thought so, and they were in that spot first, you know. Then the Spanish Christians said it was miraculous too, so they built this sanctuary place. So when the swim team went to Santa Fe for a meet, I went over with some of the guys. You just scoop the dirt out of this big hole. I figured if the Indians and the Christians thought it was powerful stuff, then I should get some too, in case I ever needed it. So now I want to use it." Avoiding my eyes, he reached out to press his fingers lightly into the earth. "For Tom."

I was touched. Before I could think of something appropriately grateful to say, Arch joined us. He was wearing an enormous white terrycloth bathrobe Tom had given him. His wet brown hair stuck out like pine needles. He said, "Was the ring at the church?"

"Yes, hon. But somebody had broken into the church office. It was a mess."

"Oh, gosh." Arch stood beside me, bleakly silent. "Mom?" he said finally, his voice serious. "I've been thinking. The next time you go out investigating, I'm coming with you." I exhaled thoughtfully; it was nice to know I had both a twelve-year-old and a nineteen-year-old intent on mothering me. "What in the world is *that*?" He was looking at the pile of dirt.

"Something of Julian's. He can tell you all about it."

Julian began, "It's from Chimayó—"

"Oh, yes," said Arch knowledgeably, "I know all about Chimayó from *Stories of the Weird.* But Mom? If the Health Inspector pays a surprise visit and sees that? You are going to get into so much trouble."

Before I could protest, the front doorbell rang. We all bolted for it. It was Boyd. Behind him stood Helen Keene, carrying another overstuffed Hefty bag. Their bleak faces said they had not found Tom. I ushered them into my living room, where Boyd handed me a photocopy of Tom's note and a plastic bag containing his wallet and the other wedding ring box, sodden from being in the creek. With soft-spoken composure, Helen asked if she could meet with Arch and Julian one-on-one, to see if they needed someone to talk to. She'd brought them quilts, too. Julian replied by asking her if she was hungry. Without waiting for a reply, he led her out to the kitchen. Arch muttered that he didn't want a quilt if it looked as if it belonged to a girl, and traipsed along behind.

Boyd declined food, although he looked longingly in the direction of the kitchen. I told him about the mess at the church office and that I'd called the Sheriff's Department.

"Damn it to hell," he said angrily as he sat on the living room couch. He had changed into a bright green down parka that did not go with his uniform pants. From his uniform shirt pocket that had at least four ballpoints hooked on it, he drew out a pen and his battered spiral notebook. It was similar to the one Tom Schulz had tossed into the bushes. With his free hand, Boyd surreptitiously slid a wooden match into the side of his mouth. "You want to tell me what was in the church office? I mean, do you know anything someone would want to rip off? Or conceal, maybe?"

I told him that the tickets and chokers were supposed to be at Olson's house, not in the church office. Boyd had already heard plenty, he said, about the necklaces from both Marla ("that big, funny woman") and Lucille Boatwright ("hysterical battle-ax"). I showed him the wedding ring I had retrieved. The church office contained an appointment book, notes, and files, too, I added, but Olson was such a packrat, only someone who knew exactly where to look for something would be able to find it. And that was before someone broke in and trashed the place.

Boyd stopped scribbling in his notebook and picked up the ring box.

"I wanted to come to your wedding," he said with a remote sadness. He handed me back the box. "But I pulled weekend duty."

With the other crises hanging over us, neither Boyd nor I wanted to talk about the possibility of rescheduling. Instead, assuming a crisp tone, he ran through the names of Olson's neighbors. None had seen anything this morning but nondescript cars coming down Upper Cottonwood Creek Road. Hard to believe that this was all the same day, that it was only this morning that Olson had been killed. Yes, Boyd was saying, the neighbors had heard two shots, but in rural Colorado, you heard shots all the time.

Boyd's tired brown eyes gave me a level, detached gaze beneath black eyebrows that stood up like magnetic filings. "I'm telling you this, Goldy, because it's our policy to keep the next-of-kin informed of every detail when there's a kidnapping. And something I tell you might jog your memory or make you remember some detail that could help. Try to concentrate, and then let me know."

I rubbed my temples and wondered how many times in his career Boyd had asked distracted and grieving folks to concentrate. *The neighbors had heard shots.* The common experience of hearing gunfire was true even in my own neighborhood off Aspen Meadow's Main Street. Coloradans waste no time blowing away anything bothersome, from garden snakes to woodpeckers to bears; ecologists be damned.

Helen reappeared with her customary silence and sat down next to the cold fireplace. Boyd snapped his ballpoint open and closed several times, then asked if he could run a few things by me. I murmured that I wanted to be helpful.

He flipped through several crumpled pages of his notebook. "There doesn't seem to be anything missing from Olson's place. At least, nothing that we can tell, like a stereo ripped out of the wall, or pearls gone from a jewelry box. But you're right, the guy was a packrat. Looks as if he kept every piece of mail since the time he moved there. But the audio equipment, computer, church supplies—plates and goblets and stuff made out of gold, silver, brass—all look untouched. We're not sure what the guy had in the first place. But I'll tell you this," he said as he chewed furiously on the match, "I don't want a bunch of churchwomen traipsing around in there looking for jewelry while we're conducting an investigation."

I thought of Olson's living room with its shelves of thick books, its ornate sacramental vessels—called patens and chalices, not plates and goblets—and his mantelpiece with its beautifully carved crèche from Santa Fe. I wondered if Olson ever made a pilgrimage to Chimayó. Boyd shifted his bulk, tapped his notebook, and said thoughtfully, "Anyway, especially after this church break-in, we can't completely rule out burglary as a motive. Or somebody trying to destroy something. Here's one thing that's puzzling us: Olson's Mercedes started right up. He didn't have car trouble. So why d'you think he'd call Schulz to pick him up?"

Involuntarily, I thought back to the silly disagreement Tom and I had in last night's counseling session with Olson. Did any other couples argue about whether marriage lasted into the afterlife? Did they argue about it the night before their wedding? Probably not.

"Maybe," I said, then hesitated, imagining Olson's desire to deal with conflict. He tried to bring about reconciliation no matter what. That was his way. Had been. "Maybe Olson wanted to talk to Tom before the wedding," I ventured, "to reassure him that everything was going to be all right." I sighed. "I blew a gasket in front of both of them after our supper last night. Maybe Olson felt the only way Tom would accept some pastoring before the wedding was by pretending to have car trouble." I knew better than Boyd how reluctant Tom Schulz had been to see Father Ted Olson for counseling. *Shrinks,* he'd muttered, *they can drive you crazy in court.* I'd told him Father Olson wasn't a shrink, he was a priest. A *religious shrink,* Tom had grumbled. But in the course of our sessions together, Father Olson had insinuated himself into Tom's affections. Olson had genuinely admired Tom's powers of observation; he even professed envy of Tom's ability to bring about justice. All he ever got to do, Olson complained, was forgive people.

Boyd interrupted my thoughts. "Blew a gasket about what?"

"Oh . . . just some dumb thing about the marriage vows lasting forever. I was stressed out."

Boyd puckered his lips and shrugged. "Olson could have just talked to him at the wedding."

"No, there wouldn't have been time. Do you think Tom's disappearance has anything to do with needing to be in court next week? Someone involved in the case who needed him to conveniently disappear?"

Boyd shook his head. "Nah, it's a forger. The guy's still in jail, I checked. And no known accomplices. About your theory of the reverend wanting to talk to Schulz before the wedding. Maybe Olson was afraid of something. Didn't want to tell Schulz his fear over the phone. So he got Schulz out there with a fairy tale about car trouble. Maybe he wanted Schulz for protection from somebody. Was Father Olson having problems?"

"What kind of problems?"

"Woman problems. Money problems. Church problems. You tell me."

My fingers brushed over the moist crushed velvet of the box that held my wedding band. I felt my heart compress, the way that air becomes more dense when the temperature suddenly drops.

Boyd scowled. "Goldy. He was your priest, he'd been at your parish for three years. You must have known how he was doing."

I held the velvet ring box tightly. "There are a number of different groups within our church. One is the Old Guard. That would include priests like our former rector, Father Pinckney, and people like Lucille Boatwright, head of the Altar Guild and Art and Architecture Committee, and Zelda Preston, who was our organist. Emphasis on the *was.* Olson had just fired Zelda, and knowing how much he hated conflict, that must have been painful."

"Oh yeah? Zelda Preston?" Boyd wrote in his notebook. "What'd he ax her for?"

"They fought continually over the music. He would pick the hymns and she would change them without telling him." I stopped, uncertain of how to elaborate. "Father Olson was a charismatic, which means he wanted people to have a *personal* relationship with the Lord. The kind of music he favored was sort of, 'Jesus Loves Me' set to folk music. The Old Guard, on the other hand, prefers, say, 'A Mighty Fortress Is Our God.' "

Boyd stopped writing and raised his eyebrows. The match drooped from the side of his mouth. "That's it? Changed hymns? The Old Guard guards the hymns?"

"Well . . . not exactly. When it comes to Zelda, I mean."

There was a silence in which Boyd drummed his knee with his free hand.

"Okay, look," I went on. "I know what I know about Zelda because we were in a Lenten discussion group together when we were both going through some difficult times." Privacy was a precious thing, and little of it survived exposure, especially at church meetings. In a small town, gossip was the weapon of choice in destroying your enemies. And Zelda had been my friend.

Boyd grunted. "I'm trying to find Schulz, not write an article for the local paper."

"Don't even mention the local paper to me."

"Goldy!" interjected Helen Keene. They were her first words since she'd rejoined us from the kitchen. "For heaven's sake!"

"All right, all right." I paused. "It was five years ago. We were discussing something very innocuous, a book called *In the Wilderness,* and Father Pinckney was the leader. I went because I was depressed about the awful state of my marriage, and had to get out of the house. I figured a daytime church discussion group would be kind of nice." I held out my hands in a helpless gesture. "One day Zelda very unexpectedly broke down. You see, she had two sons. One is Bob Preston, who is a parishioner at the church. His wife's name is Agatha."

"Yeah, I want to talk to you about her," Boyd said. "But go ahead."

"Zelda's other son, Mark, had leukemia. Mark was the swimming coach at Elk Park Prep, and he was married to Sarah Preston, who lives in Elk Park with their son Ian, who was twelve at the time." I looked out my front window. But instead of seeing the cold night, I pictured Zelda's gray braid wobbling on top of her head as her body shook with sobs. "On Ash Wednesday of that year, Mark, who was in his mid-twenties and had had the leukemia for about six months, went into a coma in a hospital in Denver. What kept him alive while he was comatose were the daily blood transfusions Sarah had to okay. After a couple of weeks of this, I guess Sarah just decided she'd had enough. So she refused the daily transfusion."

I fell silent. Boyd and Helen were staring at me.

"Mark Preston died within hours." I brushed unseen lint off my sweatsuit, feeling my eyes fill with tears. "Zelda wasn't at the hospital. No one consulted her about stopping the transfusions. She didn't get to say good-bye to Mark."

"My Lord," murmured Helen.

"That wasn't the end of it," I said softly. "At our book discussion group, Zelda blurted out that Sarah had killed her son. She would never forgive her for that. She said she wanted Sarah out of her life forever."

Boyd and Helen Keene were silent. "And the grandson?" Helen finally asked. "Ian?"

"Zelda wrote off the grandson, too. She was just so angry . . ." I sighed. "Anyway, Sarah eventually remarried. I heard her new husband is a Catholic, and the three of them go to the Catholic church. From all the accounts around town, Zelda hasn't seen or spoken to Sarah or Ian in, well, five years."

Boyd tapped his notebook. "So how does this relate to Olson?"

"I'm getting to that. At the discussion group," I said reluctantly, "no one knew how to react to Zelda's outburst. Father Pinckney just shriveled up. I mean, the old fellow looked as if he could have crawled under a rock. And of course, the rest of the women were aghast. You have to understand, members of the Old Episcopal Guard never, ever, *ever* spill their guts in front of a group."

"But you were there," Helen prompted.

"Yes. I was there." Indeed. "I almost didn't go to the meeting that day. My head was throbbing from the whack John Richard—my ex-husband—had given me after he broke my thumb in three places the previous week. My hand was in a cast. When Zelda told her story and began to weep, I felt so bad, I cried with her. Despite the stupid cast, I put my arms around her and held her." I took a deep breath and thought back. "I guess everyone else was embarrassed. They left. No one even said a word. Hours later, it was just Zelda and me, sitting next to each other in our folding chairs, sniffling. When it was almost time for Arch to come home on the schoolbus, I insisted she drink a cup of instant coffee that I fixed in the church kitchen. After Zelda took a few sips, Lucille Boatwright suddenly appeared to drive her back home."

Boyd asked, "So did you and Zelda become friends?"

"Zelda spent the next two weeks sending me casseroles and discount swim coupons for Arch. But she and I never talked about what had happened again."

"Not meaning to be rude, Goldy," Boyd continued patiently, "but I'm still wondering what this has to do with *Olson,* since this happened during the time of the *other priest.*"

"Zelda was the organist. After Mark died, playing the music, and doting on her other son, Bob, and his wife, Agatha, became Zelda's whole life, even though Bob and Agatha are charismatics and supported having Olson as the new rector after Pinckney retired. Anyway, in Father Pinckney's time, Zelda picked the hymns. She also ran the choir and every aspect of the church's music. Then Olson came. He appealed to a whole different group in the church. He wanted the music changed, and technically, according to church law, he was the one in charge of the services. So he and Zelda fought. And fought and fought and fought." I shook my head, remembering some of the acrimonious exchanges.

"Did they talk about this . . . problem with the son who died?" Boyd asked.

"Oh, yes," I replied. "Remember, Olson hated conflict. He said he wanted everybody to have a personal relationship with Jesus and be reconciled to each other. According to Marla, who hears everything, Zelda and Olson weren't having any reconciliation in their weekly shouting matches. Supposedly it was over the hymns. But the rumor was that their conflict went much deeper, that he wanted to force her to make up with her widowed daughter-in-law. Zelda told him to mind his own beeswax. She had the Old Guard on her side though," I added, "when it came to the music."

"Why's that?"

"Look. The Old Guard just doesn't want anything changed from the way the Episcopal church was when *they* were little. As long as there are fund-raising luncheons, golf courses, and the 1928 prayer book, they're happy."

Boyd chewed on his match and wrote some notes. The inviting smell of popcorn wafted out of the kitchen. "Besides Zelda Preston, did these Old Guard people dislike Olson?"

"They did. Lucille is building a columbarium she intends to dedicate to Father Pinckney. I think she believes when it's done, he'll come out of retirement and be our rector again."

Boyd muttered sarcastically, "I don't know if I'd want to return to a church with an ash cemetery dedicated to me. What a place. I thought this was where everybody loved each other. You know, sing songs and give money to the poor?"

I said quietly, "You haven't been to church for a while."

"Yeah, maybe I'll go, and you can take me. All right, just a couple more questions. Did Olson get along with his assistant, this Doug Ramsey?"

Julian appeared with huge bowls heaped with hot buttered popcorn. The fragrance filled the living room, and I gestured to Helen and Boyd to help themselves.

"I guess they got along," I said after I thanked Julian and he disappeared. "Doug's on the Board of Theological Examiners." I cast around to remember in what other contexts I had seen Doug Ramsey work. He was involved in diocesan work and was Olson's liaison with the Aspen Meadow Habitat for Humanity. I told this to Boyd.

"Yeah, we know that. We also heard Ramsey was the bishop's spy."

"What?" I was nonplussed. Father Insensitive, with his overtalkative, exaggerating way and his lists of things to do, a spy? Spying on what? Or whom?

Somehow, Boyd had rid himself of the match. He took a handful of popcorn, ate quickly, and said, "We heard that the bishop thought Olson was out in left field and moving toward the wall. As in going, going, gone, bye-bye Episcopal Church, hello new denomination." He scooped up more popcorn, ate it, and reflected. "So tell me. Is moving out of your sedate church's ballpark the kind of thing people would kill for? I know, you say, you have to look at the different groups." There was still an edge of sarcasm in his voice.

"Look," I said with more ferocity than I intended, "let me give you an example of the kind of thing that can happen in our oh-so-sedate church. On the national level, we had a prolonged and very public fight over the ordination of women to the priesthood. After that was approved, there was an incident at an Episcopal church. A man came up to the altar and tried to strangle a female priest administering communion. He didn't protest, he didn't go to another church, *he tried to strangle a woman he did not know.* He screamed, 'You bitch, I hate you, what do you think you're trying to do?' "

Unmoved, Boyd said, "But Olson wasn't a woman. This is different. Or is it? Which group did the strangler belong to?"

My face was hot after my outburst. I grasped the ring box and tried to summon up Tom Schulz's calm. "I don't know whether it's different, that's the whole problem. I'd say the would-be strangler was part of the Old Guard. Did Doug Ramsey tell you he was a spy?"

Boyd grinned. "Of course not. You know anything about the financial status of your parish?"

I said that as far as I knew, the parish had typical financial problems. Typical in what way, Boyd wanted to know. Different church groups wanted money for their projects; there was never enough to go around. There was some squabbling over funds. But Marla had said giving was up.

Boyd's eyes narrowed. "Year before last, your parish had a gross income of a hundred thousand. Last year it was a hundred-twenty thou, pretty good growth rate in a recession, but a couple of invalids left money to the parish when they died. Year to date—we're talking a little over four months—the church's income was *three hundred thousand dollars.* This isn't Olson's dough, mind you, it belongs to the parish. Could that be something the bishop would be interested in?"

A dry laugh crackled in my throat. "If the parish was doing that well, and the diocesan office knew about it, I'm surprised they didn't send up a dozen priests to spy."

Boyd said, "One of the women told me that all the money was coming in because there was some magical healing stuff going on here. That Olson was the founder or perpetrator, and people were paying to get a piece of that magic."

"Miraculous claims aren't typical of our church." Unlike Chimayó, I wanted to add, but didn't. "Then again, neither are today's events."

"So you don't know anything about the money coming from some miracle agenda?" When I shrugged, Boyd continued. "Okay, two more questions. I need to know what you know about this"—he flipped a page in his notebook and scanned it—"candidate for holy orders." He said the unfamiliar words slowly. "Named Mitchell Hartley. Guy wants to be a priest," he summarized. "Flunked the oral exam for the priesthood last year. We hear Olson was behind the flunking."

I told them what I knew of Hartley, whose chief distinction as one of the charismatic parishioners was his vehement opposition to Lucille's columbarium project. *Idolatry,* Hartley had fumed at the parish meeting, his face flushed, his mass of red hair quivering. *Do you think the Lord would have wanted a columbarium?* I knew Father Olson had urged the Board of Theological Examiners to flunk Hartley last year. I did not know why. "Mitchell Hartley goes to the second service at our church," I said. "I don't really know him very well."

Boyd pulled in his stomach with a noisy breath. "Well, we're looking into that. Lots of money, miraculous healings, a candidate who was flunked. Now about this Agatha Preston—"

But before he could elaborate, his beeper went off, and he asked to use the kitchen phone. When he trundled back into the living room two minutes later, he had put his notebook and pen away. "We'll have to talk more about this tomorrow, Goldy. The team is done over at the church, and they want to go out to Schulz's place tonight, to see if he left any notes by his phone, or anything else that could help us out. We still have his keys from the creek."

Trancelike, I mumbled an okay. Boyd and Helen Keene moved awkwardly toward my front door. Helen dropped down on one knee and retrieved the victim-assistance quilt I'd once again inadvertently dropped on the floor. It was splotched with mud. Helen asked if I wanted her to wash it. I thanked her and said please give it to someone else; I had plenty of blankets. She folded the quilt, draped it over her arm, and gave me an affectionate, unexpectedly lovely smile. They would both be in touch, she assured me, and I should call if I needed anything. The front door closed quietly behind them.

I sat there in my silent living room and thought back to the cold March afternoon I'd spent with Zelda Preston and her pain. Lucille Boatwright had led Zelda slowly through the church doors, her arm around her slumped shoulders. I'd taken Zelda's untouched cup of coffee back to the parish kitchen. The powdered creamer was still lumpy and floated on top. Because of my cast, I hadn't been able to stir it in.

7

Still gripping the jewelry box, I moved over to a chair next to unopened boxes transported from Tom's place along with his oven. I put my hand on the cardboard and stared at the cold ashes in the fireplace. *Remember, o man, that dust thou art, and to dust shalt thou return,* Olson had solemnly proclaimed over each of us at the Ash Wednesday service, just as he dipped his finger into ashes and made the sign of the cross on our foreheads. He'd been more than Marla's assessment: *a cute charismatic.* He had been knowledgeable and kind; his faith was heartfelt. Olson had even charmed his way into Tom Schulz's heart. And now Father Ted Olson was dead. My chest ached.

I forced myself to get up and stow the two ring boxes and Tom's wallet in my china buffet. I allowed myself only a moment of what-could-have-been: In my mind's eye, I saw Olson smiling over us as Tom slid the ring on my finger. This was supposed to have been our wedding night. A terrible emptiness descended on me.

Julian and Arch, their torsos wrapped in blue diamond-patterned victim-assistance quilts, were finishing up a bowl of popcorn in the kitchen. Giving me a guilty look, Julian untangled himself and used the business line to make his overdue call to Beaver Creek, canceling Tom's and my hotel reservations. Arch asked politely to see the page of Tom's notes. I quickly penned a copy for myself, then gave the photocopied sheet to him.

The moon had risen, the boys had gone to bed, and it was past midnight by the time I had worked my way through all of Tom Schulz's boxes looking for letters, files or journals—anything with abbreviations. Feeling a pang of guilt for invading his privacy, I checked Tom's wallet, which had my business card and Julian's and Arch's school photos in it. In the boxes, I was rewarded only with bank statements, tax returns, and old bills. Maybe the police would find something out at Tom's cabin or in the trashed church office that offered a clue, for I surely hadn't.

Outside, the air was still fiercely cold and windy. Wearily, I backtracked to the kitchen, where Scout the cat meowed insistently to be fed. In all the confusion, I had forgotten the poor feline, whom I now moved carefully from the food prep area. While Scout tilted his head appraisingly, I ripped open a packet of cat food and dumped it into his dish. But it was not enough. After a few dainty mouthfuls, Scout sought affection by throwing himself on his furry spine on the kitchen floor. I rubbed his stomach and told him that we both should get some sleep. My eyes burned and my head throbbed. Waiting had never been my long suit.

I longed to get out my electric blanket, turn it to high, and sleep. But sleeping in a warm bed? I couldn't do it; it would be betraying Tom, who probably was neither warm nor comfortable. I thought of his handsome face with its penetrating green eyes, of his body with its warm folds of flesh that I had come to love. When I tried to rest on the living room couch, the wind whistled down the chimney flue and through the moulding around the picture window. Propelling myself off the cushions at three o'clock, I returned to the kitchen to do the one thing that had ever helped me cope with anxiety: cook.

I was glad I'd dumped out all of Tom's recipes before Julian made a dirt-covered shrine out of the box that had held them. The directions for Monster Cinnamon Rolls beckoned. *Try for G,* Tom had written. Scout, happy to see me again, and ever hopeful for a snack, twined between my legs as I melted butter in milk, proofed yeast, and beat eggs. The recipe made a large batch, which would do for the first church service that was now only a few hours away. Would the person who kidnapped Tom come to church? Could it really be someone from the church? I hoped not. So much for *Thou Shalt Not Kill.*

I kneaded the sweet dough vigorously. Because of Boyd's questions about St. Luke's, I found my mind wandering back to the Episcopal parishes of my childhood. My father's business ventures brought us to town after town with the same sign, *The Episcopal Church Welcomes You.* No matter where our family lived, there was the same church built of stone, with the same stony people inside. The priest had always been a faraway man with his back to a congregation that recited the same prayers and sang the same hymns no matter where you went. Those priests were a far cry from the smiling, disheveled, folk music–loving and sympathetic-to-everybody Father Theodore Olson. In the old days, Sunday School walls boasted pictures of a Jesus who looked more like a blond fellow in a nightgown than a rabble-rousing first-century Palestinian. In those days, the women's church groups held fund-raising events; the men's groups went on retreats; the youth groups caroled upperclass neighborhoods at Christmas.

You never had a murder.

I pounded out the air bubbles from the risen dough, rolled it into a long, thin rectangle, then slathered on softened butter mixed with brown sugar and cinnamon. The wind whistled around the back doorjamb; I recalled a particular windy moving day from my childhood, when I'd tearfully said good-bye to neighborhood and Sunday School friends before our family settled in New Jersey. I often suspected the reason I'd fallen in love at twenty with John Richard Korman was that he had the baby-faced features, blond-brown hair, and affecting smile of a Sunday School friend whose name I had forgotten.

I quickly rolled the dough into a fat log and measured where to slice. After my life fell apart and I'd pretty much managed to put it back together, Tom Schulz had appeared, with his large, handsome, self-confident body and spirit. Tom Schulz, who loved Arch and Julian and me with a frightening intensity, who had awakened vulnerability and affection that I had presumed dead, who was willing to do anything to keep us happy. Who had said to Father Olson last night that he and I would *not* be parted by death, no matter what the wedding vows claimed. And now he was held captive by God-knew-whom for God-knew-what reason. If he was still alive.

I cut the dough carefully at the evenly spaced intervals and placed the thick sugary spirals in a buttered pan. I needed to sleep; I needed to pull myself together and find out as much as I could about Father Olson, for surely the murderer's path led through our parish, or through a committee, or through the diocese. . . .

My eye fell on the pile of exams from the candidates I was to help examine in three days.

Olson had told me that in the third and final year of their seminary

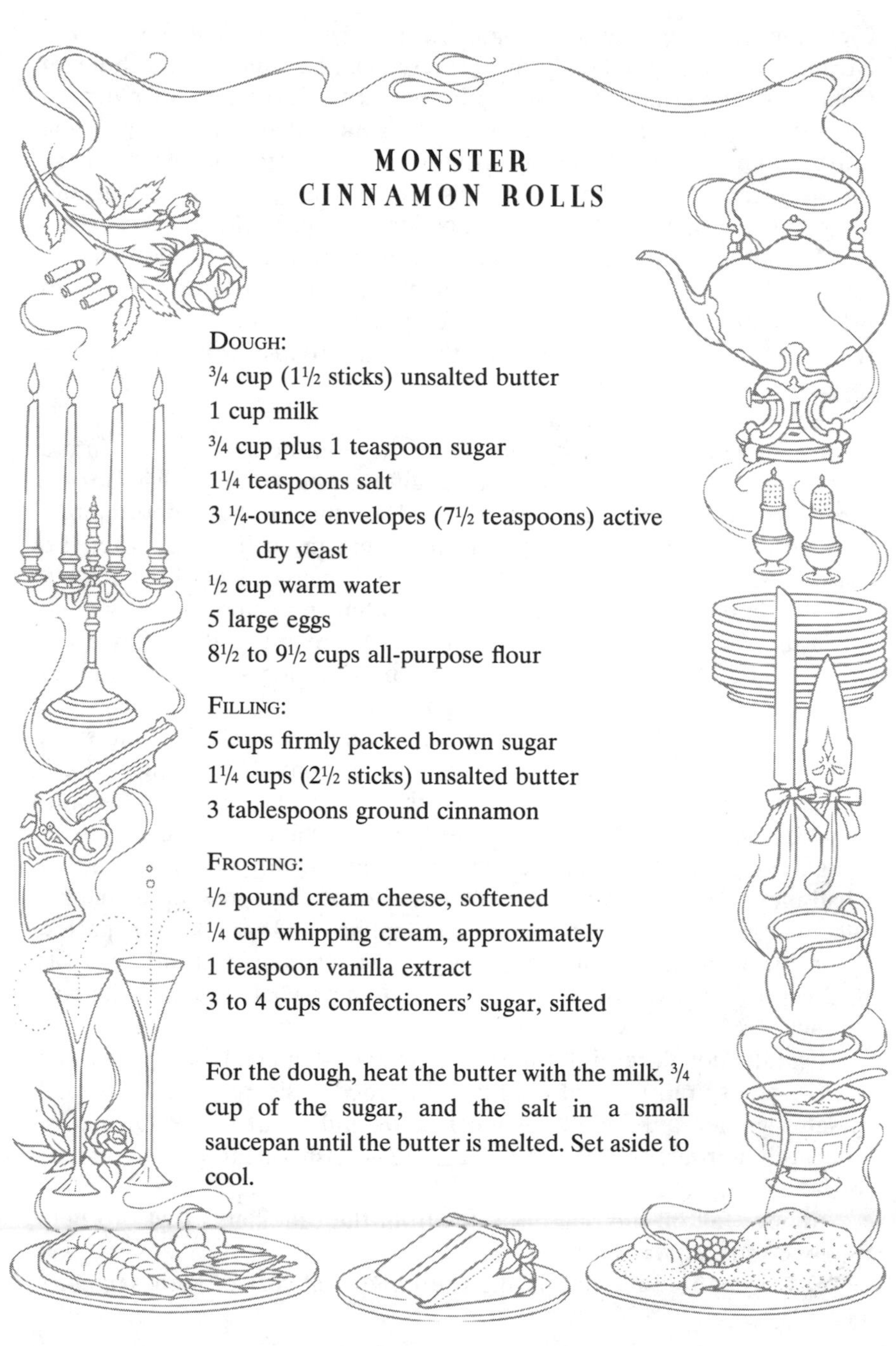

MONSTER CINNAMON ROLLS

DOUGH:

$^3/_4$ cup ($1^1/_2$ sticks) unsalted butter

1 cup milk

$^3/_4$ cup plus 1 teaspoon sugar

$1^1/_4$ teaspoons salt

3 $^1/_4$-ounce envelopes ($7^1/_2$ teaspoons) active dry yeast

$^1/_2$ cup warm water

5 large eggs

$8^1/_2$ to $9^1/_2$ cups all-purpose flour

FILLING:

5 cups firmly packed brown sugar

$1^1/_4$ cups ($2^1/_2$ sticks) unsalted butter

3 tablespoons ground cinnamon

FROSTING:

$^1/_2$ pound cream cheese, softened

$^1/_4$ cup whipping cream, approximately

1 teaspoon vanilla extract

3 to 4 cups confectioners' sugar, sifted

For the dough, heat the butter with the milk, $^3/_4$ cup of the sugar, and the salt in a small saucepan until the butter is melted. Set aside to cool.

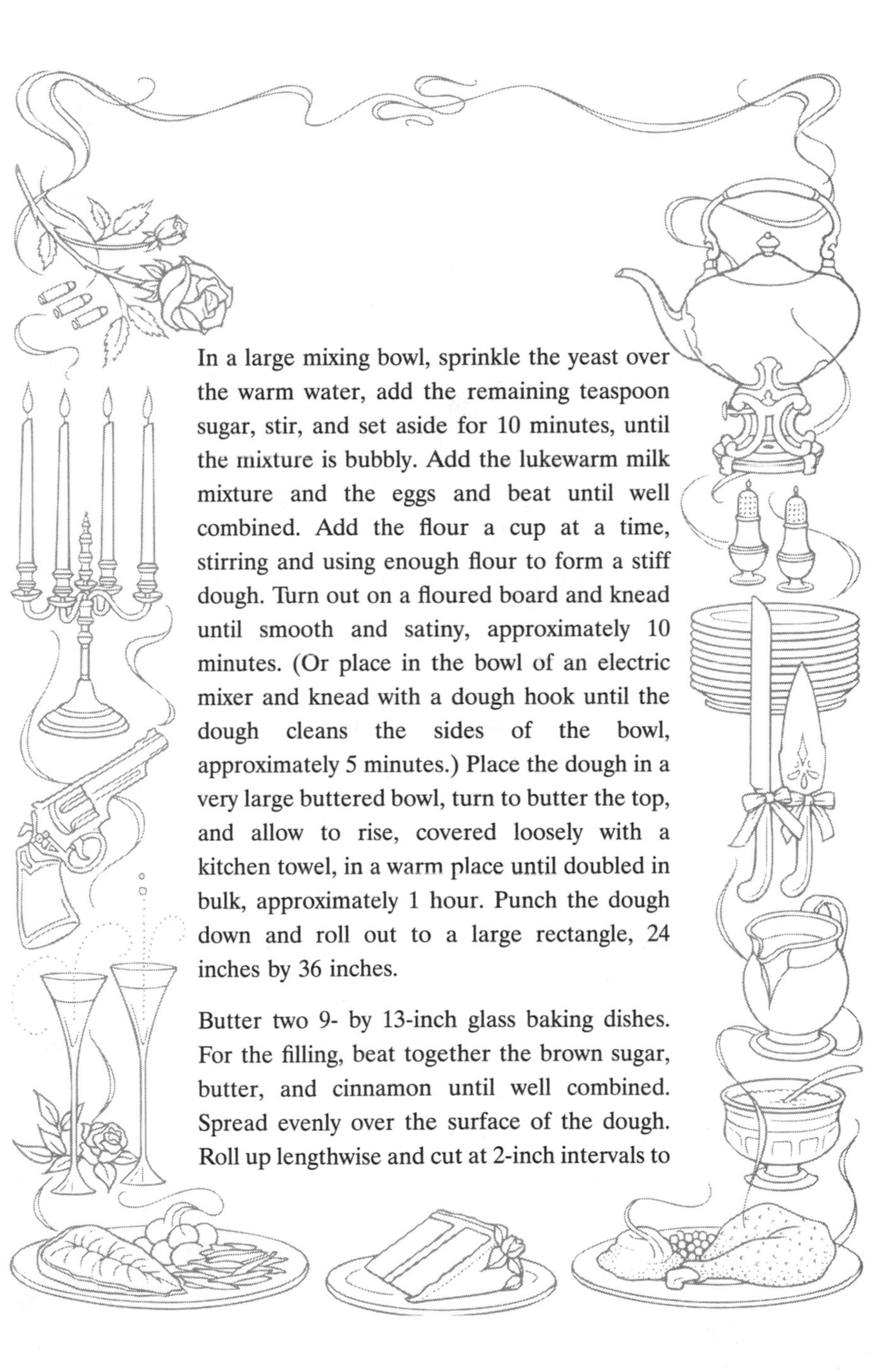

In a large mixing bowl, sprinkle the yeast over the warm water, add the remaining teaspoon sugar, stir, and set aside for 10 minutes, until the mixture is bubbly. Add the lukewarm milk mixture and the eggs and beat until well combined. Add the flour a cup at a time, stirring and using enough flour to form a stiff dough. Turn out on a floured board and knead until smooth and satiny, approximately 10 minutes. (Or place in the bowl of an electric mixer and knead with a dough hook until the dough cleans the sides of the bowl, approximately 5 minutes.) Place the dough in a very large buttered bowl, turn to butter the top, and allow to rise, covered loosely with a kitchen towel, in a warm place until doubled in bulk, approximately 1 hour. Punch the dough down and roll out to a large rectangle, 24 inches by 36 inches.

Butter two 9- by 13-inch glass baking dishes. For the filling, beat together the brown sugar, butter, and cinnamon until well combined. Spread evenly over the surface of the dough. Roll up lengthwise and cut at 2-inch intervals to

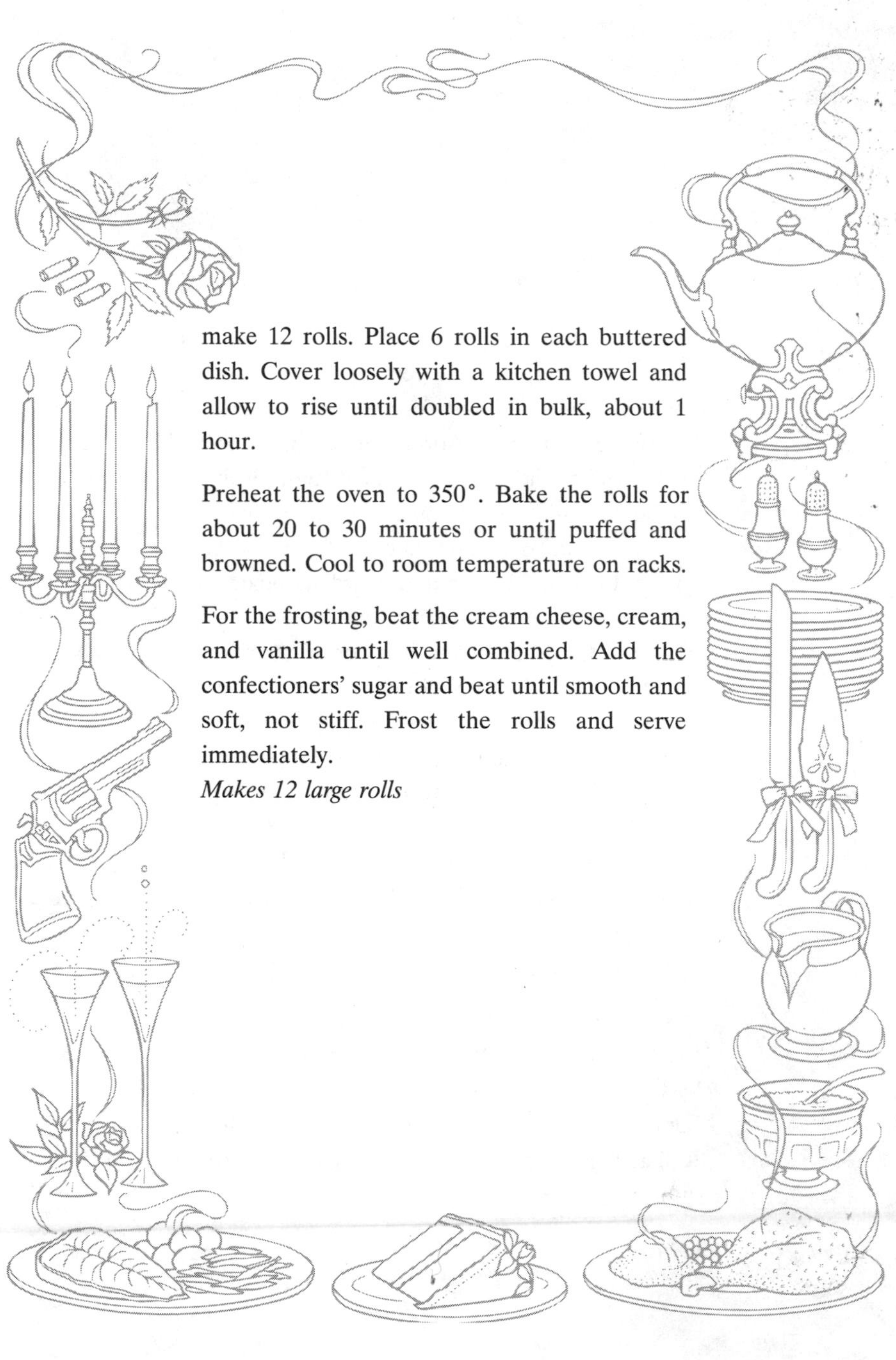

make 12 rolls. Place 6 rolls in each buttered dish. Cover loosely with a kitchen towel and allow to rise until doubled in bulk, about 1 hour.

Preheat the oven to 350°. Bake the rolls for about 20 to 30 minutes or until puffed and browned. Cool to room temperature on racks.

For the frosting, beat the cream cheese, cream, and vanilla until well combined. Add the confectioners' sugar and beat until smooth and soft, not stiff. Frost the rolls and serve immediately.

Makes 12 large rolls

training, candidates for the priesthood took the General Ordination Exams that now graced my counter. The battery of tests covered the seven canonical areas: Church History, Liturgics, Pastoral Theology, Ethics, Theology, Issues of Contemporary Society, and Scripture. The tests were graded by the General Board of Examining Chaplains on the national level, which then sent the exams on to the dioceses. In the diocese of Colorado, the Board of Theological Examiners read them, determined areas of weakness, and then gave oral exams to the candidates. A candidate had to show oral proficiency in all seven areas before he or she could be ordained. That sounded like a lot, I'd said to Father Olson. Maybe I wasn't really up to it. *Just read the exams and ask yourself whether you'd want to have this person as your priest,* he'd solemnly replied.

Mitchell Hartley's exam was in my pile, although I didn't know which was his. Numbers at the top of each candidate's test sheets kept the examiners from knowing who was who, to eliminate prejudice. I had my list identifying candidates by number somewhere. Unfortunately, there had been a mix-up at the diocesan office, and I had not received my photocopied set of papers to read until yesterday, when I was deep into pâte doughs, bridal bouquets, and Portobello mushrooms. I hadn't read any of the exams, and the last thing I wanted to do was get academic on what was supposed to have been my wedding night.

Still. When I looked at the sheaf of papers, I could see the indulgent grin on Father Olson's face when he'd appointed me to the twelve-person committee, saying that not only did he treasure my culinary abilities, he also valued what I had to offer the Board *intellectually.* Sure, the way people read *Playboy* for the interviews. But the diocese had paid the discounted rate I'd given them to bring Gorgonzola quiche, asparagus rolls, cauliflower salad, and chocolate cake to my first Board meeting, when the discussion centered on the ethics of breaking the seal of confession if a person's life was in danger. After years of casseroles and Jell-O, and without waiting to hear my opinions on confession, the Board immediately proclaimed their faith in me.

Before the meeting, Father Olson had said there were "a few rumblings" over the appointment of a laywoman who was a caterer to this powerful board that had the final say on whether persons were ordained. "Better tell them about your theological training," Olson had warned me, "so they, too, will value your mind as well as your mousse." So at my introduction, I'd dutifully told of the sixteen-week course for Sunday School teachers I'd taken two years before from Canon Montgomery, a member of their board, at the Aspen Meadow Episcopal Conference

Center. Canon Montgomery, now soon to be our emergency pastor at St. Luke's, looked like a ruddy toad. He'd beamed and lapped up my flattery along with his piece of cake. I didn't mention his aggravating tendency to pat his white hair along its middle part as he put spiritual experience into rhymed couplets.

Now the clock said almost four A.M. Soon it would be dawn. No time to start reading theology, that was for sure. I lifted the towel to check on the rolls, and fatigue struck with such ferocity that my knees buckled. I grabbed the side of Tom's convection oven for balance. I turned away from the unread papers, left the rolls to rise at room temperature, and flopped back on the living room couch.

The wind had died down, as it often did near sunrise. Still, the house felt cold. I burrowed into the hard cushions and regretted giving back my victim-assistance quilt.

Tom. Be all right.

Holding that thought, I tried to relax. Frightful nightmares of falling into mud accompanied fitful sleep. I awoke abruptly, feeling stiff and chilled, and realizing unhappily that the canceled wedding, the murder of Father Olson, and the unexplained disappearance of Tom Schulz had not been bad dreams, but odiously real.

I opened one eye to see what time it was. Something was wrong. Above Tom's boxes, my mantelpiece clock was just visible: half past six. Had a noise startled me out of sleep? Now, as I listened for Arch and Julian, the house was silent. What was wrong? What had awakened me with that sensation of something odd, out of place? I inhaled deeply and blearily scanned the room.

It was the light. The living room was suffused with a tangerine-colored glow. A red sky in the morning promised snow. Big deal. My neck screamed with pain; I stretched carefully. My body insisted I would regret attempting the usual yoga routine. I felt confused. Even with a red sunrise, the light in the living room was too orange. It was not the sunlight that was colored; something was coloring the sunlight.

With effort, I extracted myself from the cushions. I tiptoed to the window and looked through the knots of the lace curtains. I stared at, but could not comprehend, what I saw. Hanging from the roof of my front porch was a handmade knitted blanket. It was bright orange, and had a red heart at the center.

8

When you've slept in your clothes, forty degrees feels frigid. Ignoring the cold, I hopped gracelessly onto the porch swing and wobbled perilously there for a moment. Sunlight was brightening thin smears of cloud that shone like mother-of-pearl. Very gently, I pulled the orange blanket into the light and tried not to slip on the frosted swing seat while examining the tiny stitches. The coverlet was not knitted, as I had thought, but double-crocheted with a small hook and thin, expensive wool yarn. A chill wind blew through my sweatsuit and threatened my precarious balance. I snatched down the afghan, then looked around to see if any of my neighbors were about. But the cold weather, especially on a Sunday morning, meant people were still snuggling deep under their coverlets and blankets. Not to mention afghans that didn't come from a source unknown.

I scanned the crocheted rectangle for a note of some kind and saw none. From victim assistance? A thoughtful neighbor? The previous night's fierce wind might have blown off any attached notes. I bunched the afghan over my shoulder and jumped down from the porch swing. While my joints reminded me I was no longer a limber teenager, I noticed a foil-covered oblong dish sitting primly to the left of the front door. Casserole, courtesy of the Altar Guild. And this time there was a note in a firmly lettered hand on top of that: *Please take care of yourself. Our women's group is praying for you. Zelda.* With my free hand, I picked up the icy glass dish and scuttled into the house.

Her note hadn't mentioned the afghan. Imagining wiry Zelda Preston, or even stolid victim advocate Helen Keene, scaling the wall of my porch to make a dramatic visual statement by hanging a Valentine-type afghan made me smile. I made espresso and watched it spurt merrily into a cobalt-trimmed cup. It was Hutschenreuther, a gift from Tom Schulz. Pain seared through me. The phone rang and I grabbed it.

It was my mother calling from New Jersey, so concerned that she and my father hadn't been able to say good-bye, and was I all right? Remembering Helen's advice, I did not mention Tom Schulz's disappearance. They would only worry and call me incessantly. Yes, I assured my mother, we were fine. The two of them had just come back from the early church service, she said, and when was the wedding going to be? I stalled. Ah, well, we were working on rescheduling. Did they find out what happened to your priest? No. But will you get married when things are back in order at the parish? Of course, I promised. When we have a new priest.

And a groom, I thought grimly after replacing the receiver. Dread, worry, and stinging guilt made a simultaneous assault. If only I hadn't insisted Tom and I get married in the church. Tom Schulz never would have known Ted Olson. He never would have gone out there yesterday morning. He would be sitting here right now having coffee with me, instead of being in peril. Or worse. Or worse . . .

Stop this.

My espresso had turned cold. I slugged it down anyway, stared at Julian's pile of Chimayó dirt, and waited for my brain to click into gear. Not much happened; there's only so much caffeine can do on two hours of sleep. I slammed the risen cinnamon rolls into Tom's oven. With great reluctance, I showered and dressed in a dark blue suit, then put in a call to the Sheriff's Department. Without Tom there to tell me what was going on, the center for county law enforcement felt like a foreign outpost. Boyd was not at his desk. I left a message asking for an update, and gave the number to my personal line.

In a great rush, I repunched buttons on my business phone and got Tom's own voice mail. The sound of his rich, deep, vocal recording was nectar. I listened to it while Scout rubbed against my leg to remind me it was feeding time. I listened to it while writing a note to Julian and Arch and inhaling the deep, rich, mouth-watering smell of the just-baked cinnamon rolls. I listened to it again while assembling ingredients for the poppy seed muffins that I would make between the services in the church kitchen, since the cinnamon rolls would just be enough for the first service. At last, the clock said 7:30. As I was slathering cream cheese frosting on the warm cinnamon rolls, my business line rang. I snagged it.

"Goldy, this is Frances Markasian of the *Mountain Journal—*"

"Don't." I could just imagine stringy-haired Frances Markasian perched aggressively at her desk, smoking a cigarette with a great length of ash and swigging Diet Pepsi spiked with Vivarin. The woman never slept.

"Goldy, please, I'm sorry about this—"

"The heck you are." I cursed myself for not taking Helen Keene's advice. I should have disconnected as soon as I heard Frances's voice.

"We know about Olson and we know about Schulz," Frances continued as if I had not spoken. "We know Mitchell Hartley's a suspect. But I saw some big heart thing hanging on your porch when I drove by this morning, and I took a picture—"

In spite of my upbringing, I hung up. The doorbell rang; it was Boyd. His black crewcut glistened in the morning sun; a battered leather flight jacket did not quite cover his pear-shaped belly. He was chewing vigorously on his match, and he didn't look happy.

"We don't have him," he said abruptly when I opened the door, without waiting for me to ask. The uniform shirt he wore underneath the flight jacket was so wrinkled I was certain he'd been up all night. "But you and I need to talk."

"I was just about to go to church—"

"I'm coming with you. Think I look okay?"

"You look fine. But go to church with me? You've got to be joking. Why?" I looked at him sympathetically. "You look exhausted."

"I'm okay. And I don't joke."

Boyd wanted to take my van so we could talk on the way. I asked him to hold the rolls in his lap. He obliged and we took off.

"Go the long way," he ordered, "whatever that is. I need to know a few things before we get there. What do you know about Olson being the protégé of a priest named Canon George Montgomery?"

I obligingly swung the van right instead of left on Main Street. Our trip to church would take ten minutes instead of five. "Montgomery is the canon theologian and one of the staunchest conservatives in the diocese. He's not the kind of fellow who would fall on his sword over the old hymns. I mean, this fellow's dream is to go to sleep wrapped in the

Shroud of Turin. He used to be the rector of a big church in Pine Creek, but now he's semiretired. Montgomery's on the Board—"

"Yeah," said Boyd, "Theological Examiners, we know. Served with Olson at the cathedral some years back, when Montgomery was dean. They were real thick until they had a big spiritual disagreement, sort of like the ones you're telling me about in your parish. They get along on the committee?"

I remembered Montgomery complaining bitterly in one of our meetings about a candidate's explanation of prayer. "Well, the only disagreement I can recall was when Montgomery insisted that prayer was about *relationship* and not about *making coconuts grow.* He really worked himself up into a dither. The next meeting, Olson brought in a giant coconut. Montgomery didn't think it was funny. That's the only conflict I can remember they had."

"Late last night," Boyd drawled, "Mitchell Hartley told us Canon Montgomery and Father Olson had another argument. This one was last week in some other meeting. About whether miracles were happening at your church. Sounds as if there was a lot of yelling. Hartley said they could hear it through the doors of the meeting room at the diocesan center."

"I don't know anything about that," I said. I didn't add, *But nothing would surprise me, arguments are the church's way of life.* I'd made that pretty clear to Boyd yesterday. "Are you thinking their animosity was really bad? Bad enough to kill for? Because if you are, Father Doug Ramsey mentioned Montgomery was at St. Luke's yesterday waiting for our wedding to start."

"Ramsey. The guy with the windy explanation for everything. He said Montgomery was at the church?"

I nodded and swerved around a corner. Maybe I was driving too fast. I eased my foot off the pedal. "I invited all the parishioners, as well as the board. Twenty minutes before our wedding was supposed to begin, Ramsey said, 'The whole committee's here.' Nobody in the church could have gotten out to Olson's and back in that amount of time."

"Well, that's really not what we're thinking about. This guy Hartley says—"

"Hartley was at the diocesan center when he heard this argument between Father Olson and Montgomery? Doing what?"

"He says he works in the office of Congregational Services there, and he hears things. Was there resentment or anger over this miracles thing?

From anybody in the church? Maybe somebody wanted to get healed and didn't?"

I shook my head. "Sorry, I haven't heard anything about that. But my friend Marla might. She's a lot more involved with the various groups than I am. And by the way, a reporter called me this morning and said Hartley was a suspect. Is that true?"

"Everybody's a suspect at this point, Goldy. That's just our policy until we know differently."

Boyd shifted the rolls around in his lap and seemed to be formulating a new question. Poor Boyd, I thought. This wasn't the greatest way to introduce somebody to church life. I slowed down behind an exhaust-spewing truck.

"All right. You've told me about some of the people. What you didn't tell me was *why* the Old Guard hated Olson. I mean, besides the fact that they had different tastes in music."

I pulled the van onto a muddy shoulder one block away from the church. I cut the engine and looked over at Boyd. "It's what he represents. Represented. A lot of things have changed in our church over the last two decades. The Old Guard hates the liturgical innovations of the last twenty years, especially the passing of the peace, a point in the service when people embrace each other."

Boyd chuckled. "People in their sixties and seventies not liking body contact with strangers? Not surprising. Now give me the two-minute drill on what they hate about the music."

"Zelda and the traditionalists dislike the new hymnal. Intensely." I explained to Boyd that when the Episcopal hymnal had been revised in 1982, we'd lost "The Son of God Goes Forth to War" because it was deemed too militaristic, "Once to Every Man and Nation" because it supposedly undermined traditional theology, and "We Thank You, Lord of Heaven" because one of the things the hymn was thankful for was "dogs with smiling faces." This last never did bother me. Why not also be thankful for "cats with inscrutable faces"?

Boyd glanced at his watch. "Get to the point, Goldy. The service starts in fifteen minutes."

"Well, what the older crowd is most allergic to is the folk music booklets that Father Olson had tucked in every pew. The Old Guard wanted no part of the new songs. The way they settled the issue at St. Luke's was to have the earlier service traditional, the later service the one for the charismatics. To the traditionalists, the guitar-and-tambourine tunes are a flood of disrespectful noise that sounds an awful lot like 'Jesus, the Magic Dragon.' "

"Huh," muttered Boyd. "I can see we're getting into some important issues here." He fingered something in his breast pocket that looked suspiciously like a pack of cigarettes. Then he cast a longing look at the plump cinnamon rolls in his lap. Wordlessly, I reached into my supply bag for a knife, paper plate, and napkin.

"Please have one," I urged as I sliced through the thickened brown sugar syrup that clung to the rolls' sides. I lifted out a dark, dripping spiral, maneuvered it onto the plate, and handed it to him. He groaned with delight.

"Go on about the music."

"Okay. Even though the first service the Old Guard attends has traditional music, and the second service has the renewal music, they didn't want it at St. Luke's at all," I explained as I pulled the van back on the road. "To them it was like creeping communism, remember that? Anyway. The Old Guard had finally gotten a petition going. They called it *Halt the Hootenanny* and they had a bunch of signatures. Lucille Boatwright had just begun her rotation onto the chairmanship of the Altar Guild, and she was going to present the petition to Olson. They thought that might force him to drop the new music. That was the last I heard." I pulled into the church parking lot.

Boyd chewed thoughtfully. Finally he said, "I still need to talk to you about the Prestons."

"If you want to be at the service from the beginning, we need to go in now. Or if you want to talk—?" Boyd shook his head, folded the empty paper plate, and started to open his door. I took his plate to put in my van trash bag and said, "Wait. Don't come in with me. Don't sit with me or act like you know me. Please."

"You care to tell me why not?"

I took the rolls from him and carefully rearranged the plastic over them. "Two reasons. If people see you and your Sheriff's Department uniform, they won't tell me a thing. On the other hand, they might tell *you* something they wouldn't share with me."

"Yeah? What's reason number two?"

"People will talk," I said simply. I gave him a steady look. "They'll say Tom Schulz left me because I was having an affair with you. And I don't even know your first name."

"It's Horace. And now you know why I prefer Boyd. And there's not even a shred of truth—"

"So what? Horace. Boyd. *Please.* I'll go in first, you lock my van and follow."

He grunted. "I thought this was gonna be a place where people would be happy to see me."

"Welcome to the church, Horace."

When I came through the heavy wooden door into the narthex, I immediately realized it was Palm Sunday, a liturgical fact that had slipped my mind with all the disasters of the past twenty-four hours. My wedding flowers had disappeared. They had been replaced with the elaborate fans and sprays of the palms that symbolized Jesus' entry into Jerusalem, and in the church, the beginning of Holy Week. We were only seven days away from Easter, the most sacred festival of the church year, despite all the hype about bunnies and baskets. Whether Boyd knew all this or even cared I did not know.

In any event, Palm Sunday always brought out more folks than was customary during Lent. The activity in the church kitchen was at a fever pitch. I intended merely to leave my pans of cinnamon rolls for someone to dole out after the service along with the other baked goods. However, when I appeared by the oven, all activity ceased. Six women, including a remarkably stalwart Lucille Boatwright, eyed me with a combination of surprise, pity, and unnervingly intense silence.

"For after the service," I said lamely. I put down the pans.

A chorus of "We're so sorry" and "Isn't this just *so* awful" and "My poor dear, you *shouldn't* have gone to the trouble" sent me reeling back into the narthex. There I was greeted by a frantic Father Ramsey.

"Doug," I interrupted matter-of-factly before he could rattle on, "we need to talk. It's about Father Olson. And the bishop." Out of the corner of my eye I could see Boyd, looking extremely uncomfortable, leafing through the pamphlets at the back of the narthex.

Doug Ramsey raised startled dark eyes. "Oh, Goldy, how *are* you? I've been so worried, but with everything going on, a funeral to plan, the meetings . . . honestly! Are you managing all right? Did the food arrive?" His black clerical suit was wrinkled and covered with dandruff, as if he too had slept in his clothes. I wondered why he wasn't wearing his vestments. His eyes darted past me to see who was coming through the parish door. "Sorry, I can't talk now," he said. "We've had the most *extraordinary* mix-up. Have you decided to do the food for the board meeting?" When I did not immediately respond, he again assumed a sympathetic expression and made his voice low and serious. "Have you heard anything about the . . . your . . . ?" I shook my head. Doug

Ramsey strained his neck inside his white clerical collar and shook his head of floppy dark curls. "Well, ah, I *must* go tend to some last-minute problems. The money the churchwomen are raising selling raffle tickets for pearl chokers? I thought they had their spending plans all set. *Now* it turns out that a third of them want to give it to African famine relief, a third want to use it for the columbarium stones, and another third want to invest in more pearls for next year. They want *me* to arbitrate, which means two-thirds of them are going to hate me . . . Then Zelda came back in this morning wanting her old job back, and Canon Montgomery was trying to be pastoral, so he said yes—"

"Montgomery? Here already? I thought you were going to fill in for a while, at least."

"Yes, well, *so* did I." Ramsey cleared his throat noisily and ran the fingers of one hand through his hair, disarranging his curls. "Anyway, ah, then *Zelda* said she *always* picked the Palm Sunday hymns, and Montgomery had already chosen the music, and then the *new* organist showed up! And all this plus what happened to Olson . . . Oh, dear. So the new organist *stomped* out of the sacristy, and one of the churchwomen thought he was the fellow coming to give an estimate on the columbarium stones, and that he'd been *driven away* by the invest-in-pearls faction. Then, if you can imagine—"

I couldn't. And I thought catering was bad.

"*—just as* I am straightening out the organist fiasco, Mitchell Hartley shows up and starts asking about the oral exams for the candidates for ordination! The exams don't even begin until *Tuesday*! Now Canon Montgomery needs me to find a King James version of the Bible while he deals with the, er, music. Not to mention that of course, some time in the next five minutes, I have to vest."

"Doug, please. I need to talk to you about my fiancé. It would help me if I could ask you a few questions."

"Well, can't it wait until the *coffee* hour? *Please?*" He torqued around and went flying after the new organist, who had banged open the rear door of the church to make a dramatic exit. I turned in desperation to look for Boyd and saw the short, fully robed body and ruddy face of George Montgomery as he entered the narthex. Lucille Boatwright marched up behind him and snagged him by the robe. Canon Montgomery tripped and barely prevented himself from falling over.

"Father Montgomery, I must talk to you about the drainage from our columbarium project after the service!" Lucille rasped. Montgomery, recovering, did not immediately reply. He got Lucille's acid test: "Canon

Montgomery, did you know Father Tyler Pinckney?" When Montgomery was mumbling that he had not known Father Pinckney very well, I sidled up and gave him a welcoming smile. Lucille briskly turned on her spectator pump heels and stalked away.

"Thank you, oh, thank you from the bottom of my heart," said Montgomery. His voice caught, as if he had been crying. His mottled face had aged much in the two years since my Sunday School course. His hair seemed whiter and thinner than I remembered, and his eyes were bloodshot.

"Are you all right?" I asked impulsively.

He tilted his head and raised his bushy white eyebrows. "I've had a hard time. Olson was my right-hand man at the cathedral. He was very dear to me. I talk to grieving people all the time, but here I am—" His voice faltered.

"Yes. I . . . I'm sorry." I did not know what to say. You did not hug the canon theologian, even if you were on the same committee. Montgomery's duty was to articulate the theology of, for, and by the diocese, which in our case was all the Episcopal churches in Colorado. It was not his duty to be affectionate. Embarrassed to be staring at his sagging face, I looked at his robes. Montgomery was wearing an elaborately needlepointed red stole.

"That's Father Olson's . . . you're wearing his . . ."

"I know." Montgomery's haggard features crumpled. He lifted the thick, perfectly stitched edges of the stole. "I was called in somewhat late, and all my stoles are packed away. Actually, I'm still in shock—" He gave me the benefit of his close-set, kindly brown eyes, his warm, tentative smile that slanted sideways. He patted his white hair, parted exactly in the middle. "Father Ramsey told me you, too, have been suffering."

The formal address of Ramsey did not surprise me. "Yes, well, as Doug . . . Father Ramsey knows, the police are scouring the county. They're keeping me informed."

Montgomery nodded and reached out to brush my arm with his fingers, then drew back hastily as Doug Ramsey himself approached with a freckle-faced, red-haired young man taking long, aggressive steps beside him.

"Do you know Mitchell Hartley?" Montgomery said to me under his breath.

"Not very well," I replied, equally conspiratorial.

"The reality is much worse than anything you could have heard,"

Montgomery told me in a pleasant tone. He turned to Hartley and added stiffly, "I didn't know you were a parishioner."

"I'm not surprised you forgot," growled Mitchell Hartley, who was probably in his late twenties and had a head of thick orange-red hair that he combed up in an exaggerated pompadour. *Holy Elvis.* He had eyes the vivid color of blueberries and a wide jaw that jutted out defiantly. Doug Ramsey mumbled something about vesting and scuttled away. Hartley and his red tidal wave of hair leaned in toward me. He assumed a condescending, pastoral tone. "I am sorry to hear your sad news, Goldy. I am praying for you."

"Ah," I said, embarrassed. "Thank you."

Canon Montgomery pulled in his chin and leaned away from Mitchell Hartley, as if he had suddenly come upon some especially noxious form of poison plant. Mitchell Hartley quirked one orange-red eyebrow at me.

"I know you know," I said uncomfortably. "But I don't believe we've met. You see, I usually go to this service rather than . . ."

"Yes," he said impatiently. "I know that."

"Well," I faltered, "how nice. I guess I'll be off then—"

"You're the woman, the *caterer,*" Mitchell Hartley said with a bitter smile, "that Theodore Olson appointed to the board. And you've just had this tragic loss. . . ."

"Ah, well, yes."

Canon Montgomery cleared his throat and puffed out his chest. "Miss Bear is a very highly respected member of this parish. She represents, shall we say, the Woman in the Pew. I trained her in one of my Sunday School seminars. But she probably won't be attending our meetings next week, as she's in the middle of another crisis."

Mitchell Hartley snorted, lifted his wide jaw, and narrowed his bright blue eyes at me. "That's too bad. We don't usually get such a good-looking examiner."

Since we were in church, I avoided making a scurrilous remark. I began to see why Father Olson would have flunked Mitchell Hartley last year. A dawning realization told me being an examiner might not be that much fun.

While we were talking, parishioners had been streaming through the doors and looking around expectantly. When their glances caught on a robed priest engaged in conversation, they seemed to be reassured and wended into the pews. Doug Ramsey made a flustered, but vested, appearance while the teenaged crucifer twirled around the poled Victorian cross. As if on cue, the first few notes of organ music pealed out—the familiar strains of "Once to Every Man and Nation."

"What happened to the prelude?" squeaked Doug Ramsey.

"What happened to 'All Glory, Laud, and Honor'?" asked Canon Montgomery. His white eyebrows furrowed in sudden anger. "What seems to be the problem with St. Luke's?"

"Guess you two don't have much control of this parish," muttered Mitchell Hartley. His eyes glittered.

I slithered away.

Once in a pew, I looked around for Boyd. He was sitting in the back, eyes fixed on the altar. Canon Montgomery assumed the celebrant's role in a dignified manner, although his distress over his lack of control appeared to quiver below his passive exterior. Whenever he wanted music, he nodded sternly in the direction of Zelda at the organ. Clearly, he didn't want to risk announcing what could be a disputed hymn. The newly hired organist never made a reappearance.

As the service continued, I fought rising worries about Tom. I imagined him in pain; I saw him in his coffin. I shook my head, cleared my throat, and tried to sing. That proved impossible. I flipped aimlessly through the hymnal. People turned to frown at the slapping noise of the pages. I reached forward quickly to put the hymnal back in its rack. It fell on the stone floor with a decisive bang, which brought me more disapproving glances, including a glowering look from Montgomery.

Montgomery retrieved my attention with a short, theatrical silence before the sermon. "I know some of you have come to enjoy the . . . lines that I occasionally compose, so I will take the liberty to share some with you now." He cleared his throat, patted on his middle-parted hair, and puffed up his chest again. I pressed my lips together.

"Ah, Lord!" Montgomery intoned. "How we wax lyrical/when speaking of your work in miracle!" He paused, then raised his voice to a shout. "But truly! What is most divine/is seeing you in bread and wine!/And what we seek from you the most/is Father, Son, and Holy Ghost!"

It must have been the stress. An irrepressible gurgle of laughter came out of me. Montgomery charged down the nave, his shoulders stiff with rage.

"Are you *always* so disrespectful?" he roared. His mottled face was now an unhealthy crimson as it shuddered close to mine. His breath smelled like a very old person's.

I said in a low voice, "No. Sorry."

Montgomery's face withdrew slowly from mine. I was irresistibly reminded of a large, angry turtle who had abruptly decided to go back to the dignified encasement of its shell. The shell at that moment was the canon's—actually Father Olson's—imposingly voluminous red robe. Montgomery pivoted, and seemed to will control of himself. In the long, ensuing silence, he walked majestically, crimson robe flowing and shoulders stiff, back to the pulpit. *Hey!* I wanted to yell after him. *I thought you liked me!*

I wondered what Boyd was thinking about his introduction to the Episcopal Church. The graying heads in the congregation turned to each other, confused by the lack of direction. A few shot me sidelong glances. I ignored them. Canon Montgomery stood stolidly facing the altar, his back to us. Doug Ramsey cleared his throat desperately, looked to Montgomery for direction, got none, and reluctantly started on the prayers of intercession. My mind was elsewhere. I had never been yelled at by a priest, only by my abusive ex-husband.

And we most humbly beseech thee, of thy goodness, O Lord, to comfort and succor all those who, in this transitory life, are in trouble, sorrow, need, sickness, or any other adversity.

Tom Schulz had made me a lovely chocolate-raspberry cake the first night we had made love.

"Tom!" I said with a low groan, then blushed as more disapproving eyes studied me. Again I regretted coming to this service.

For servants departed this life in thy faith and fear, especially our beloved priest, Theodore Olson. Parishioners sniffed and coughed. George Montgomery slowly crossed himself. Lucille Boatwright knelt, stiff and stony-faced.

Then the intercessions were complete and the acolytes bustled with the offertory plates. Zelda Preston peeked out from behind the wall next to the organ and announced the anthem. Finally jolted back to reality, Montgomery declared the offertory sentences at the same time that Zelda took off on her organ solo and Marla slid in next to me in the next-to-last pew. A waft of rose-scented perfume enveloped her.

"Good God! Did the canon go off or what?" she hissed under her breath. "Anyway, *I* think what Episcopalians seek the most/is tea and marmalade and toast. Agree?"

"Please don't." I felt dizzy. "I thought you came to the later service."

"Ordinarily I do, not because I'm a charismatic and believe in the gifts of the spirit and all that. Actually, what I believe in is the gift of sleep. But I woke up early and called your house to see if there were any developments. Arch said you were here at church, and I was worried about you so I came. And I should have been worried about you. I came in when the Canon From Hell was shooting his mouth off in your face. I was dying for that cop back there to pull his gun, or something, but I just heard his beeper go off, and now he's left—"

Before she could finish, I was squeezing past her out of the pew and running down the nave. I sprinted past the Sunday School rooms to the choir room. The door was just closing; I lunged to hold it open.

Boyd was already talking into the receiver. He held up one finger when I opened my mouth to ask him what was going on. Then he shook his head.

"Okay," he said. "Bob Preston, got it. How quick can you get a car to me at this church? Great."

Boyd replaced the receiver. My heart was pounding.

"Now don't get your hopes up," he told me, seeing my face. My heart sank to new depths. "We think Schulz is still alive. We found the car he was transported in, abandoned in a ditch near Deer Creek Canyon."

"Oh, God—"

Boyd sighed heavily and scratched the top of his dark crewcut. "It's a Nissan four-wheel drive, not a van. The *van* in the note must have been for vanity plates. They said *EPSCMP,* for Episcopal camps. The vehicle belongs to the Episcopal diocese of Colorado."

9

I grabbed the bar holding the hangers for the choir robes. "They don't know where he is?"

"Not yet. No discernible footprints away from the car. The kidnapper must have had another vehicle already parked there."

Pain stabbed my head and a rock-size lump formed in my throat. I couldn't accept the facts Boyd was relating with the flat tonality I should have become used to already. I said, "The vehicle belonged to *the diocese of Colorado*? Do they know who was driving it? Was the vehicle stolen? How do you know Tom was—"

Boyd slid a matchstick into his mouth and leaned against the wall. He ticked points off on his fingers. "First, we think Schulz was in the vehicle because, again, we found some of his stuff."

"More? Like what this time?"

Boyd shifted his weight and looked doubtful.

"Please," I begged, "tell me."

"Well, we think we found his socks shoved under the front seat."

"What?" Boyd did not, after all, joke.

"Look, Goldy, it's just the way it was by the creek bank. Schulz fell, was pushed, got hurt, covered with mud. But at the same time, he was trying to drop stuff, give us clues, build a trail, that's what we're supposed to do in that kind of situation. So you figure, now he's in the Nissan. He's in the back seat, he's restrained." At the thought of Tom bound and perhaps gagged, I felt a groan rising but suppressed it. "He can move his feet so he takes off his shoes, eases off his socks and wedges them under the front seat, then slips his shoes back on so's the person who took him won't notice."

"How do you know they were his socks?"

Boyd chewed on the matchstick and crossed his arms. "Because he also wedged his college ring down between the seats in the back. University of Colorado, with his initials and the date. Look, I gotta go."

"But . . . he hardly ever wears that ring. And I thought you said he was hurt, limping, or something, how could he . . . ?"

"Looks like there was blood on one of the socks. And I guess he was gonna wear the ring to the wedding." He shrugged.

Too much. I stared out the choir-room window at the cold morning sky. The early-morning scattered clouds had ballooned and moved in. The sun had disappeared.

He said, "I need to get outside and watch for the department car. They left me at your place and now they're saying they need to come get me."

"Let's go, then," I said, and directed him out the same door Marla had taken me through the day before, when we were trying to escape the chaos of my nonwedding.

When we were outside, he said, "Remember when I wanted to ask you about Agatha Preston?"

"Yes, sorry, she called me yesterday, all hysterical. Wanted to know if I had seen him."

Boyd ferreted his faithful notebook out of his pants pocket. "Keep talking," he ordered as we walked toward the snow-covered parking lot. "Seen him-who?"

"Watch out," I said as we approached the columbarium construction. "We're going to have to go around these ditches."

We ducked under the low eave of the church roof, then squeezed single file through the narrow passage between the sawhorses and the corner of the St. Luke's building. The ditches that would eventually hold ash receptacles had filled with ice-edged puddles; it looked as if the unauthorized construction had unexpectedly encountered the water table.

Boyd asked tersely, "Agatha wanted to know if you'd seen . . ."

"But that's what I don't know," I protested. "I didn't have a clue if she was referring to Tom or Father Olson, and then her husband took the phone away from her and hung up on me."

"Her husband hung up on you? Bob Preston?" When I nodded, Boyd said, "He's the head of the diocesan Camps and Conferences Committee. He's the one who's supposed to be in charge of the keys to that Nissan. It was stored across the street—"

"Wait." Of course I knew the car; I'd seen it many times parked in the garage next to Hymnal House, when I'd catered for the musicians' conference during the summer. "Yesterday morning. The keys to the conference center were missing when we tried to set up for the wedding reception. It's a huge bunch. Maybe the car keys were on it."

Boyd's voice became exasperated. "I thought the Altar Guild had *those* keys, and Preston the *car* keys."

"Well, you'll have your chance to ask Bob Preston. Here he comes." I gestured at a shiny gold Audi now pulling up next to the creek. At that moment the doors to the church banged open. Lucille Boatwright came out, intent on her prey. Unfortunately, her prey this time was Officer Boyd. The heavy wooden door flapped shut as Lucille sailed over to him and used her hand like a caliper to grasp the sleeve of his leather jacket.

"Why did you leave the service early?" she demanded shrilly. Behind her, Mitchell Hartley pushed through the church door and walked swiftly over to Boyd and Lucille. Boyd released himself from Lucille's hold and stowed his notebook in his pocket. Lucille's voice rose. "What have you found out?"

Boyd began, "The police are in charge—"

"Oh, don't mind Lucille," Mitchell interjected, half-joking, half-snide. "She doesn't care who's *supposed* to be in charge of something, because eventually she's going to be running the show. Isn't that right?"

Slowly, Lucille Boatwright turned toward Mitchell Hartley. I could feel the lava rising. Since the service was over, other parishioners were coming outside. Some held lopsided paper plates, each one heavy with a cinnamon roll I had brought. The crowd eyed Boyd, Lucille, Mitchell, and me while pretending to pick at the rolls with tiny plastic forks. Canon Montgomery, last out the church doors, strode importantly toward us.

"You may wonder, Mitchell Hartley," Lucille began in a tone so icy I felt sweat prickle my arms, "*why* you have failed to become a priest, but your failure is *precisely* because of the way you are acting at this moment. Who would want you for their priest? Certainly not *me.*"

Mitchell Hartley leaned over Lucille. His face was bone-white and his vivid eyes shone ominously. Loudly, he said, "You wouldn't want *Jesus* for your priest."

Lucille Boatwright's mouth fell open. In a commanding tone, Canon Montgomery inquired: "Mitchell, don't you have some studying to do?"

It was then that I noticed Officer Boyd ripping cellophane off a new pack of cigarettes. While Lucille Boatwright, Canon Montgomery, and Mitchell Hartley glared fiercely at one another, Boyd lit a cigarette and inhaled deeply. Beside him, a newly arrived Bob Preston coughed lightly. In typical Aspen Meadow fashion, tall, roosterlike Bob wore a fringed leather jacket, plaid flannel shirt with Navajo bolo tie, jeans, and hand-stitched custom-made cowboy boots. Wearing a long black coat, Agatha stood mutely beside him.

Mitchell Hartley spat his words at Lucille. "Jesus is in charge of this parish, Lucille, not *you.*" To Canon Montgomery, Mitchell snarled, "The Lord is going to get me through these exams, George."

"Father Montgomery to you, young man, if you don't mind." Montgomery's skin had an unhealthy flush.

"Oops," said Marla from my side, where she had suddenly appeared. "Are we having a bit of a confrontation in the Episcopal church parking lot? The Frozen Chosen at war, for all the world to see?"

"Why don't you go break it up?" I said desperately to her. The hostility level among Lucille, Montgomery, and Hartley had risen to nuclear fission level. "I need to talk to Boyd."

"Are you kidding?" she cried in mock horror. "Lucille's already asked me to make five hundred cookies for Olson's funeral tomorrow. I said no, so now I'm on her shit list."

"Marla!"

"I forgot. We're at church."

A Furman County Sheriff's Department car pulled up to the entrance of the parking lot behind the rows of other cars and sat idling. Boyd took a last drag of his cigarette and dropped it at his feet.

"I'm going to need to talk to you," he said to Bob Preston, "as soon as I finish some other work. Don't leave the church."

Bob Preston, uncomprehending, opened his eyes wide as Boyd walked quickly toward the car. I scrambled after him.

"Please," I begged when I caught up to him, "tell me more about where they found Tom. Did it look as if he'd been hurt badly? What are they thinking could have happened?"

Boyd kept his eyes on the squad car as he hurried along. "They told me there was a small amount of blood in the car, some dents and tearing of the vinyl seats, maybe signs of a struggle. I'm going to look at it now. From the looks of things, we figure Schulz is still alive. We just don't know why."

"Tell me what you mean," I pleaded.

Boyd threaded through the first row of cars; I followed. He said, "Here's someone who's killed a priest. Before the priest died, he gave a dying declaration to a police officer. If the victim identifies his killer in a such a declaration, it'll hold up in court. Then Schulz is kidnapped by the killer. Why? Why wouldn't the killer just kill Schulz, too? He's the only living person who can identify him."

"I don't have any idea," I said helplessly.

"My guess is Schulz knows something," Boyd said as he held in his stomach to squeeze past a parked Volvo. "Or has access to something. Something the killer wants. It could be just that notebook of his. It could be the whereabouts of those missing pearls. The ditch where we found the car is near a hidden turnout in Deer Creek Canyon. It looks as if whoever shot Olson planned it well. Except for Schulz showing up, of course. Maybe the killer used the church car because he was afraid his own car would be recognized. Because the car belongs to the diocese, we have to assume the person we're looking for is someone associated with the church. Okay. Given Schulz's unexpected appearance at Olson's yesterday, and given that the perp didn't want to kill him at the priest's place, why not kill Schulz and just dump him in the canyon? Why keep him alive?"

"Why?" I echoed as I brushed past a Mercedes and smeared mud on my suit.

"Well, whatever it is, you better pray Schulz knows how to keep the killer at bay. As soon as he gets what he wants, you, me, the department, Schulz—we're all gonna run out of time."

We arrived at the police car. The engine was racing.

"I gotta go," Boyd said as he opened the door. He stopped and saluted me. "Be in touch."

This half-promise, half-command hung in the chilly air after the squad car pulled away. Boyd was my one link to Tom Schulz, and I hated to see him go. I wanted the intense, pear-shaped investigator to be completely absorbed searching for Tom rather than being driven to smoke by neurotic parishioners and their idiotic squabbles.

I faced the rows of cars. The last thing I wanted was to go back to the church entrance and face all those people with their probing eyes and nosy questions. I whirled and headed around the back of the church, toward the St. Luke's office. Within moments I was staring at the yellow ribbon the police had strung in front of the vandalized space. I ached to go into Olson's office and look around, but I knew Boyd would have a fit. Plus, it was illegal.

Oh, well, let him have a fit. I sprinted up the steps, ducked under the yellow ribbon, and pushed hard on the rotting door to get in. I passed quickly into Olson's office. On the desk blotter was a skewed pile of correspondence and notes. I suppressed qualms of guilt and leafed through the bits of paper. Some bills and advertisements, some printed church circulars, a list of phone numbers, a couple of letters to Olson from friends. Would there be an appointment book here, something to tell who the priest was supposed to meet with on Saturday before the wedding? Then I remembered what Tom Schulz had told me when he was working a homicide investigation, that the investigators would come to a victim's office to look around and gather evidence, primarily for the victim's appointment book. So if the book had been here, it wasn't here anymore. The police surely would have removed it.

Wait. Had I heard something? I stood still and held my breath. The raccoons? No. Was someone coming? The moments clicked by as my anxiety went into overdrive. I peered out one of the windows. I saw no one.

With clammy hands, I began to riffle through the pile of files that had been dumped on the floor by the vandal. There was no tab marked *P.R.A.Y.* I lifted out the folder marked *Diocese.*

The priest who saved everything hadn't felt the need to toss anything from his bulky, overstuffed files, this one included. It was chockful of newsletters from the bishop dating back three years. There were notices of upcoming conferences and meetings, announcements of priests who had renounced their orders, and other ecclesiastical communications that were meaningless to me at a cursory glance. I couldn't tell if something had been removed, such as anything pertaining to the *Halt the Hootenanny* petition. And the cursory overview was all I could manage at the moment, since it wouldn't be too cool to be caught sifting through the vandalized files of our murdered rector. Again I listened—for doors opening, someone approaching—but this time was greeted only with oppressive silence.

I put the notes from the top of the desk into the file and laid the copious diocesan folder aside. I flipped through pile after pile and finally found *Board of Theological Examiners,* which I lifted out. Father Packrat Olson had been head of the committee, and the folder was predictably heavy. There were old exams, announcements of meetings with agendas, lists of examinees from previous years, Olson's letter to the bishop telling about my appointment to the committee, and the last item, a brief notice from the diocese about the glitch in photocopying the exams last week. Olson would hear from the diocesan office, the note promised, as soon as the exams were ready.

I slapped the file closed. Out the dusty window, I could see parishioners dispersing, reverently clutching pale green sheafs of palm. They'd finished with their coffee-hour treats and were heading toward their cars. The 8:00 service was over and I hadn't discovered a thing.

Someone associated with the church.

I slipped the *Diocese* and *Board of Theological Examiners* files into two of Olson's books: a thick Bible and an oversized tome on the church's feast days. Hoisting the heavy volumes, I noiselessly closed the door to the little building and went back the way I'd come, around the rear of the church, toward the parking lot. With any luck I'd be able to stow the books in my van, unnoticed. My fingers ran over the worn leather covers. I wondered if I looked suspicious. After all, you didn't usually see caterers walking around hefting overstuffed volumes on religion.

Outside, the cool breeze and liquid rush of snow-swollen Cottonwood Creek blended with the hum of departing cars. Before I could reach my van, someone yelled from behind me, "Hoohoo! Gold-*y*? The woman in the *pew*?" At that moment, a huge roar erupted from the road. I flailed wildly and dropped the book on holy feasts. Papers scattered. In a fast, clumsy pirouette, I managed to hold on to the Bible, superstitious that it was like the flag and shouldn't touch the ground. Mitchell Hartley leaped from where he'd been waiting and almost blocked my view of the approaching cavalcade of roaring motorcycles. I looked furiously at Hartley, whose pale face seemed to contrast starkly with his red pompadour. Then I glared at the papers and files lying everywhere in the mud at my feet. Damn Hartley. Furious, I knelt and awkwardly tried to pick them up.

"Don't help me," I said angrily, although he'd made no effort to do so. "This is all confidential stuff."

I glanced up to make sure he wasn't memorizing the papers I'd stolen from Father Olson's office. But Mitchell Hartley was gazing at the loud parade on the road by the creek. The bikers were on their way to the Grizzly Saloon on Main Street. It was part of a spring ritual that shouldn't have taken me offguard. *It's the migration of the Harley-Davidsons,* Tom Schulz had noted enthusiastically. *The weather grows warm, and Aspen Meadow becomes the gathering place for flocks of hefty folk in black leather, mirrored sunglasses, bandanas, ponytails, and single earrings. Makes so much noise you could shoot off firecrackers and nobody'd notice.* The sole requirement for the motorcycles, unfortunately, seemed to be that all their mufflers were removed prior to setting out for Aspen Meadow.

"Wow! I'm always amazed when we get that kind of racket in a mountain town! It's like a jet runway!" shouted Mitchell Hartley from above me. I opened the feasts book and swiftly packed the last of the damp, dirty papers between loose dry ones, stuffed them in the book, and rose unsteadily. The sun emerged from behind the clouds. Mitchell Hartley's startling orange hair shone in the sudden bright light; his dark blue eyes scanned first the books in my hands and then my face. "Any news?" he asked, too cheerily for my taste.

I raised my voice over the roar of the motorcycles. "Excuse me. Mitchell, why did you call to me to stop?"

When he smiled, his crooked, wide-gapped teeth reminded me of something Tom had told me while explaining how he sized up suspects. *People who grow up poor have bad teeth, teeth that are either crooked from lack of orthodonture or worse, missing altogether from lack of proper care.*

"I came over to the conference center early to study," Hartley replied, with more false cheer. "I live next to a kennel, and it is noisy like you would not believe. I'm staying in Hymnal House." He waved vaguely upward in the direction of the Aspen Meadow Conference Center. "It's quiet now, before everyone gets there."

His awkwardness in my presence translated alternately into arrogance or too-familiarity. The effort to be polite made him nervous. It was as if he were waiting for me to say that I liked him, that this time he was going to pass his exams because God was in charge, that everything was going to be okay. But his resentment of my purported power over his career seeped through every pore. I almost blurted out that I'd been appointed to the committee because of my culinary, as opposed to theological, expertise. But there was something else.

The bikers continued to roar past us. "Mitchell, how could you possibly have gotten into Hymnal House? The place was locked yesterday morning when we were trying to get in for the reception and—" The motorcycles drowned me out. I fell silent.

"The place was open," he cried back defensively. "What reception was that?"

The last of the motorcycles growled past. I had invited Hartley to our wedding, as I had all the parishioners. But since he had responded that he wouldn't be able to come, I gave a brief overview of the previous day's postponement of the ceremony after Olson's murder. And about Tom missing. Ah, but he knew all about that. Hartley informed me that someone had put the news about Schulz on both the parish and the diocesan prayer chain.

He furrowed his brow; the red pompadour shook ominously. In a quickly assumed pastoral tone, he said, "Goldy, have you turned the search for your fiancé over to the Lord?"

I replied evenly, "I've turned the search over to the Furman County Sheriff's Department." His flinch almost made me laugh. "Mitchell. Who made the arrangements for you to get into Hymnal House? Was it before or after you heard about Father Olson? It just seems so weird," I added pensively, with an equally furrowed, equally pastoral brow.

Mitchell Hartley backtracked to give his story of how he'd come to know about Olson's murder. Last night, his calls to Olson to ask when the exams would start had gone unanswered. Frustrated, Hartley had then phoned Montgomery, the next most senior person on the Board of Theological Examiners. Montgomery had tearfully told him the news he'd heard from the bishop, that Olson had been shot by an intruder. Of course, Hartley informed me, he was dreadfully concerned about Father Olson's tragic demise, although he was joyful that Olson was now with the Lord. But, Mitchell went on in a worried tone, as a candidate for Holy Orders, he was also frantic about whether the exams would still be held. So, as he'd planned—I could check with the diocesan office, if I wanted—Hartley had come to Hymnal House last night. Like my own experience with catering up there, he'd never given a thought to the building not being open, which it had been because someone had broken a window.

"I put a piece of cardboard over the broken pane and locked the place up when I went to bed," he said in his own defense. "But I left it unlocked today, since I didn't have any keys." He shrugged.

"The police are on the way up," I said. I didn't mention the abandoned diocesan vehicle they had found. "Be sure to tell them about your arrangements." I had every intention of filling Boyd in myself about Mitchell Hartley's unorthodox residency across the street from the church. I'd also ask that the police check with the diocesan office on his reservation. When Hartley made no move to leave, I added, "Mitchell, I'm feeling really stressed out from all that's happened, and I need to go home and check on my son and finish some cooking—"

"I've been in this diocese for ten years." He leaned toward me. His voice was suddenly raw with anger.

"Well, I guess the ordination process takes a long time. . . ."

"A long time? A long time?" The blue eyes blazed. "*Some* people get through in three years. That's what it is in other dioceses. But not Colorado. They seem to take a kind of . . . pleasure in making people wait. Making *some* people wait, anyway."

I wanted desperately to put the books with the stolen files in my van, wanted even more desperately to be out of this conversation. I tried to look dour, the grieving bride.

I said, "Guess I need to shove off." He didn't get the hint. I added, "I don't believe in making people wait."

He lifted his chin and shot me a suspicious look. "You don't?"

I edged backward toward my van. Mitchell Hartley, unrelenting, followed. I wanted to ask, *Have you turned your waiting over to the Lord?* But I didn't want to hear the answer. Instead I sped up my retreat. Ever eager to impress, Hartley kept remorseless pace right beside me. "I know waiting is supposed to make you grow stronger," I said noncommittally, "but that depends on who or what you're waiting for, doesn't it? How does that psalm go? 'I waited patiently upon the Lord, he stooped to me and heard my cry.' Like that."

Effortlessly keeping up with me, Hartley glanced down at the books in my hands. He shook his head almost imperceptibly: This woman doesn't interpret the psalms correctly, and she hasn't turned the search for her fiancé over to the Lord. In a sadly condescending tone, he said, "Of course, I know the psalm." We'd reached my van. He leaned against the door so that I couldn't open it.

I took a deep breath. "I heard last year didn't go so well for you. At the exams, I mean."

"Some of the questions were really off base," he replied impassively. "In fact, I was wondering what kind of questions I could expect from you. If you're coming, that is."

Hmm. "How about," I said thoughtfully, "eschatology?" Maybe Hartley had a unique take on *'til death do us part.*

"What about it?"

"Anything about it."

"Well, that's not very helpful." His eyes had turned icy.

"Mitchell, please. I really must go—"

"Look, Goldy, I'm really sorry about your policeman. I just—I want to tell you something. But don't say you heard it from me, okay?"

Of course, I was immediately interested. "Don't say what?"

"Ted Olson had, like, a double life. He . . . well, I saw him in a restaurant on Colfax, down in Denver near the Diocesan Center. He was with a woman. I knew it was him because of that fancy Mercedes he always drove around. Then I heard he was having an affair, that the bishop was about to discipline him. They'd found some letters or something."

This was Mitchell Hartley who had avidly told Boyd about a heated argument between Father Olson and Canon Montgomery? What was he trying to do here? I asked, "Who was Olson having an affair with? Did your source know that? What did the woman look like? Not that it's against the law to have lunch with someone. Even if she is a woman."

He ignored my flippancy. "She had on a scarf and sunglasses. That's all I remember. I tried to talk to Ted about it once."

"And what did he say?"

"He acted like I'd hit him."

"You weren't trying to talk about what he was going to ask on the exams, were you? I mean, since he'd flunked you once already."

Mitchell Hartley's blue eyes darkened; he scraped one large, scuffed shoe across the gravel and pivoted to walk away. Over his shoulder he said harshly: "I thought Ted Olson was someone I could rely on. But it was revealed to me that he was not."

10

I heaved the stolen books and files into my van. Boyd thought Schulz knew the whereabouts of something, something perhaps belonging to Father Olson, a *something* the killer needed. And now that model candidate for the priesthood, Mitchell Hartley, was making more accusations, this time about illicit affairs, some letters, and what God had spoken in his ear. I sat for a moment in my van and tried to think. What would Tom be asking? What would happen if you had a letter or some letters, say, or needed to know where something was? What good would having that something do? I had a sudden image of Tom being interrogated, and Boyd's suspicions about something else going on. *That's why the killer is keeping him alive.*

When I went back into the church, Zelda Preston and Lucille Boatwright were engaged in a spirited conversation that ended abruptly with my appearance. Before I could figure out a reason to ask them about the Hymnal House keys, Marla sashayed up to my side. In the parking lot, I hadn't noticed that her hair had returned to its normal willful tumult, despite the fact that it was held here and there by barrettes covered with tiny flowers fashioned of green and pink silk. Outside of the pew, I now also had a chance to admire her fashionable floral-print chiffon dress, which clung in thin folds around her ample body. Tiny rows of appliquéd pink flowers adorned the neckline and hem. Marla always dressed according to the season. This was obviously the couture statement for spring.

"Well?" she demanded *sotto voce.* She pressed her fingers into my forearm. Her rings sparkled with pink diamonds and pale emeralds. "What did Boyd say? Have they found him? Did they figure out what that note meant?"

"No news. They did find the car that he was transported in." I didn't tell her the car belonged to the diocese. "Listen, Marla," I said earnestly, "you didn't tell anybody about that note Schulz left, did you? I don't think Boyd would approve of anyone else knowing about it."

She opened her mouth to protest, but before she could speak, Bob Preston strutted over and assessed us. With difficulty, he wriggled his hands into his double-stitched denim pockets and rocked back on his cowboy-boot heels. It was clear that the church was one of Bob's domains.

"I feel so bad about hanging up on you yesterday, Goldy! So to make it up to you, Agatha and I would like to take the town's prettiest caterer out to brunch. After the ten o'clock service."

"Gosh, Bob," said Marla, "don't mind me."

He didn't. I consulted my watch. Nine fifteen. I was becoming oddly popular. Bob Preston either didn't know or wasn't worried about the police coming back to Aspen Meadow to question him. Before I could respond, and just as Marla was saying a warning "Uh-oh," under her breath, Zelda Preston and Lucille Boatwright approached us.

"How are you, Goldy?" asked Zelda. Her voice was filled with concern. "Poor dear. Did you get the casserole?" Unlike Lucille, Zelda did not dress in understated, expensive outfits. Her faded turquoise knit dress, with its sloping shoulders and hemline from a decade past, screamed *thrift shop.* A single strand of not-exactly-antique glass beads decorated her throat. Her face was a wrinkled mass of worry. "You haven't mentioned it since you came to church."

"I'm . . . hanging in," I told her, "thanks. And thanks for that lovely orange afghan, too. So thoughtful of you, when the weather's still so cold—"

Her concern turned to puzzlement. "Afghan? I use electric blankets. Goodness! But at least my lasagne arrived safely." Her gaze drilled into the guitarists arriving for the second service. "I suppose I should be leaving."

"Oh," I begged hastily, "please stay. I really want to talk to you about . . ." How to say, about whether you had the car and Hymnal House keys? About the guitar music petition you were battling over with our murdered priest? "About . . . lasagne. And the *Halt the Hootenanny* petition."

Marla groaned.

Lucille Boatwright narrowed one flinty blue eye at me. Because I was divorced, because I was commonly engaged in food service, and probably just because I existed, Lucille did not like me. She would be suspicious of me if Mother Teresa were giving me a kiss. Now she bristled inside her dark gray double-breasted wool suit with its armory of tiny, ornate gold buttons. I thought she was probably still assessing where Schulz had run off to, abandoning me at the altar. Tahiti. Borneo. But instead she announced, "We had fifty signatures, but Father Olson wasn't interested. So we took it to the bishop."

Marla giggled. Incredulous, I choked. "You did what?" These two dutiful women in their sixties had bypassed their rector and taken their petition directly to the bishop? That kind of authority-flaunting behavior would have been unthinkable during old Father Pinckney's time. "What happened?" I demanded.

"That's what we don't know," Lucille replied defiantly, as if I were painfully dumb. "The bishop's office says they formally replied to our request to halt guitar music. But of course we never heard from Olson on the matter. You know that man would have misplaced his tax return. He probably never even filed, and now that he's dead, the IRS will come looking and the church will to have to pay—"

"Ah, Lucille," interjected Zelda sweetly, "you musn't get yourself upset talking about the music again—"

Behind us, Bob Preston snorted.

"Well," I said desperately, "why don't you stay and we can talk more about it after the next service?" Then I remembered that I had agreed to join Bob and Agatha for brunch, because I wanted to milk *them* for information. "Zelda, I'd really love to hear you play the organ again—"

"Ha!" cried Zelda. Her nostrils flared. She looked like a poodle refusing to eat what had been set before her. She gestured significantly at the musicians testing their tambourines. "There's no way I'm playing that blather they call music at the next service. I am a professional."

Trying with a remarkable lack of success to suppress more laughter, Marla overdiligently smoothed down the pleats of the green-and-pink dress and announced, "*I'll* talk to you about lasagne, Goldy. When it comes to pasta, *I* am a professional. I just don't do cookies."

I shot her an exasperated look and lightly touched Zelda's arm. "Please . . . wait. Was it someone from the Altar Guild who left the afghan for me?"

Zelda stared at me, her miserly mouth drawn into pinched folds. "Oh, poor Goldy, how should I know?" She patted my hand and turned to Lucille. "People think I know *everything* about this parish, and I'm always the last to know *anything.* Come along now, Lucille, we must get you back home to rest."

Lucille pointed her dimpled chin in my direction. "Do they know what happened to your fiancé?" she demanded brusquely. Recalling her suspicious interrogation of first Arch and then Boyd, I pressed my lips together and shook my head.

I said, "We're all hoping for good news."

"I see." Lucille raised one pencil-thin white eyebrow. "Did they figure out that message he left? We've put it on the prayer chain, you know, that the police will be able to decipher it. We're going to discuss it at prayer group tomorrow."

I turned venomously toward Marla, who shrank back in mock horror. Her plump, bejeweled fingers sheltered her face. Bob Preston guffawed. "You might as well have put it in the *Post.*"

Trying to keep anger out of my voice, I asked Lucille what time the prayer group meeting was scheduled. This was one meeting I needed to attend, if for no other reason than to shut everyone up. But I hoped that I wouldn't need to, that they would find Tom before then.

"Now, Goldy," warned Lucille, "you know we take our praying seriously."

"So do I. And, I was wondering, are we praying for anyone with the initials V.M.? Or does that stand for Virgin Mary or something? I mean, since you know what was in Tom's note, have you studied it?"

"Virgin Mary? What in the world—"

"Initials, then. Praying for anyone named V.M.?"

Lucille huffed, "Except for Victor Mancuso, I don't know. Perhaps it would be good if you did come, dear, you could remind us to ask." She touched a row of silver curls, then seemed to have an inspiration. "Would you like to bring some lunch? Just for about eight people. You're so good at that! And it'll help you get your mind off your other troubles. Fish for Lent, of course. Do you have any?"

"Fish?"

"No? Well," Lucille confided, "how about shrimp?"

I said, "Oh, sure," in a sarcastic tone that was clearly lost on her before she breezed off with Zelda. Well, I'd certainly been busy. After the service I was going out for brunch with the Prestons; tomorrow, I was making lunch for the entire prayer group. Nothing like food to quell anxiety.

"Now don't be mad at me," Marla began defensively. She kept her voice low. Bob Preston had moved off but was nearby, buttonholing a fellow Kiwanian. "You never said that note was a secret."

"All right, all right," I conceded. "Listen, I know how you can make it up to me."

"But I didn't *do* anything."

"You'll like this, I promise. It's your kind of thing. I need to know more about whether Father Olson was having an affair. Please, it's important."

When Marla had finished registering astonishment and was muttering that she'd be delighted, I spotted Father Doug Ramsey out of the corner of my eye. Leaving Marla, I moved unobtrusively in the direction of our late rector's assistant, the purported ecclesiastical intelligence agent.

"Need to chat, Father D."

Unfortunately, I startled him; his first tentative sip of hot coffee splashed down the front of his white alb and stole.

"Oh, dear, I'm sorry," I said.

His delicate, triangular face was more rueful than his voice. "Don't worry about it," he said uncertainly. "I can sponge it out."

I said I was mixing together some muffins between the services, and could we sponge out the stains in the kitchen and chat? There were some things I was wondering about, things the police had said to me about him and the bishop.

Doug Ramsey did not immediately reply. His doleful brown eyes fearfully roamed the room. I followed his glance and saw Mitchell Hartley chatting reconcilably with Canon Montgomery while Bob Preston regaled some newcomers. Agatha gave her mother-in-law Zelda a tentative hug as she departed, then stood uncomfortably next to her husband. She had taken off the dour black coat and wore a light orange outfit the color of a Creamsicle. I knew the Prestons' orientation was of the charismatic sort, and that coming early for the second service meant Bob would have more of a chance to draft folks into Bob-projects. The narthex was nearly empty, and the service was not due to begin for thirty minutes. Still, Father Insensitive Ramsey seemed oddly nervous. Interesting.

"Where do you want to talk?" he said under his breath.

"In the kitchen," I whispered back. "No one will suspect. If we go outside, people will wonder what it is we're being secretive about."

"Oh, Lord, that's not what I want," he said with a gulp. He ran his fingers through his black ringlets.

I smiled at him. "If we go in the kitchen, people will think we're doing dishes. They'll avoid us like one of the plagues that struck Egypt."

Without further ado, I strode purposefully into the church kitchen, which was empty. Doug Ramsey reluctantly followed. I silently offered a clean, wet sponge to him, and he dabbed at his alb.

Then I got out the eggs, evaporated milk, oil, and premeasured flour I'd brought and said, "First of all, I'm wondering who has access to the set of keys to Hymnal House and the Episcopal camps vehicle."

He scowled. "That's what the police want to know about the bishop? For heaven's sake! They keep that set of keys down at the diocesan office in the winter. For special events, someone from the parish goes to get them. Why on earth do you need—?" He cast another anxious glance around. "Don't you think I should be doing something out here? So it won't look suspicious."

"How are you at lining muffin tins?" I thrust a box of paper cupcake liners at him and gestured at the muffin pans.

"Uh—"

"Okay," I continued briskly, "why do the police think you're the bishop's spy?"

"Ack!" His face turned bright pink. For once he wasn't able to think of some long set of words to justify and amplify his response. "Well, I—" he began finally as he opened the box and shook out a tower of pastel liners. He stopped and looked at them as if they were cockroaches. "You know I was hired by Father Olson—"

"Cut the crap, Doug. Why did the bishop recommend you for this post?"

He held a pale blue liner between the very ends of his index finger and thumb. After a moment's hesitation, he dropped it in a cup, inspected it, did the same with a green one, then a pink. At this rate, the tins would be ready by sundown. He said, "How did you know the bishop recommended me?"

Did this pompous dork think people in this parish didn't talk? Rather than explain, I merely revved the electric mixer through the eggs, oil, milk, and sugar, and waited for an answer.

"You know, Goldy,"—*drop, drop*—"er, some strange things have, or had, been going on in this congregation, and Father Olson,"—*drop,*

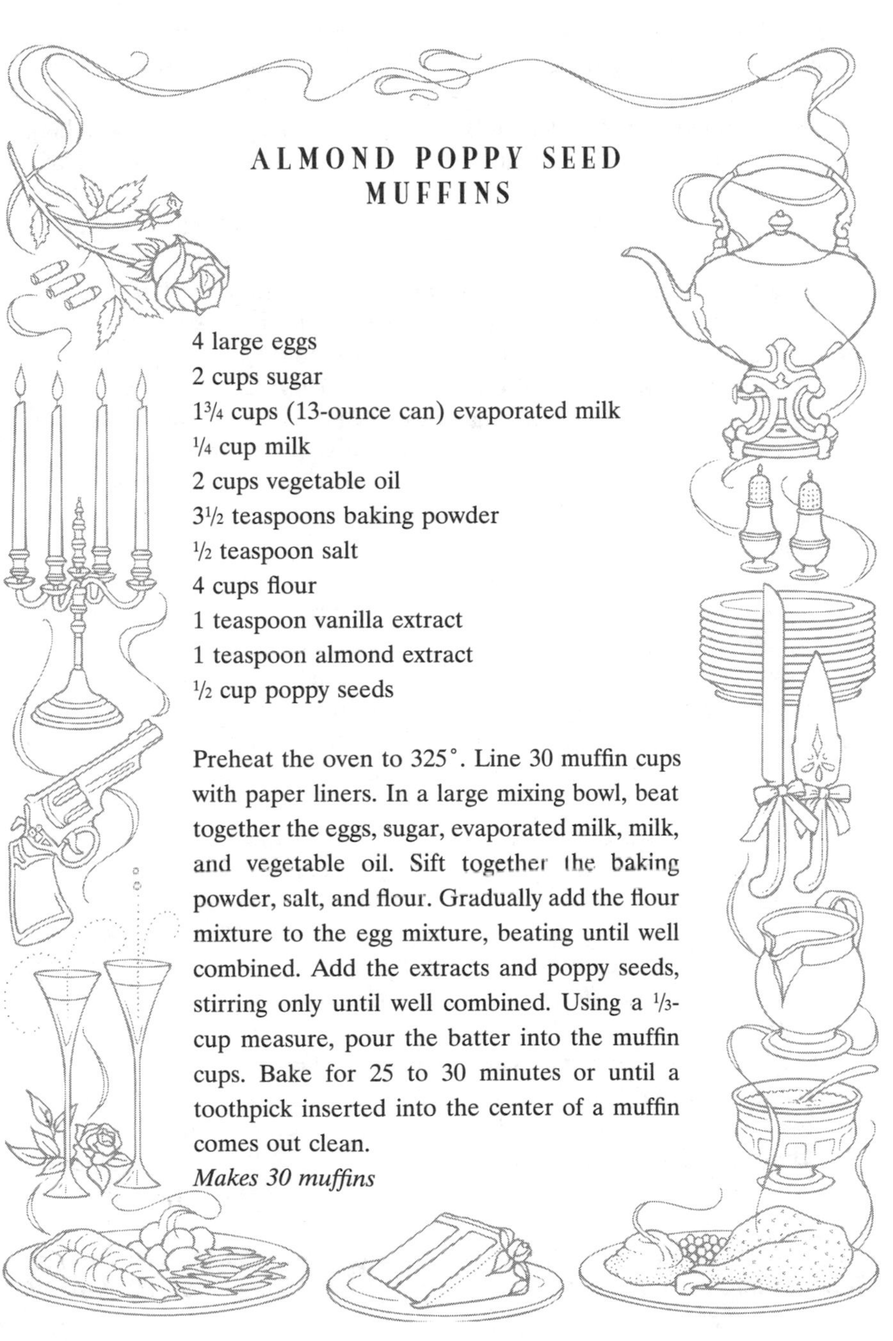

ALMOND POPPY SEED MUFFINS

4 large eggs
2 cups sugar
1¾ cups (13-ounce can) evaporated milk
¼ cup milk
2 cups vegetable oil
3½ teaspoons baking powder
½ teaspoon salt
4 cups flour
1 teaspoon vanilla extract
1 teaspoon almond extract
½ cup poppy seeds

Preheat the oven to 325°. Line 30 muffin cups with paper liners. In a large mixing bowl, beat together the eggs, sugar, evaporated milk, milk, and vegetable oil. Sift together the baking powder, salt, and flour. Gradually add the flour mixture to the egg mixture, beating until well combined. Add the extracts and poppy seeds, stirring only until well combined. Using a ⅓-cup measure, pour the batter into the muffin cups. Bake for 25 to 30 minutes or until a toothpick inserted into the center of a muffin comes out clean.
Makes 30 muffins

drop—"Ted, was never one to be terribly *communicative* with the bishop's office. I mean, he didn't even go to *deanery* meetings, and then when diocesan *convention* rolled around—"

He stopped abruptly when Bob Preston vaulted into the kitchen. Preston, seeing we were engaged in domestic activities, beat a hasty retreat.

"Doug, why don't you go a little faster?" I suggested lightly. "Why did the bishop need you to spy?" I said brusquely when Preston was safely out of earshot. "The service is going to start in twenty minutes! Do you want to tell me, or do you want to tell the police and four newspapers? 'Priest held for questioning over secret role in parish' ought to look real good in *The Denver Post,* not to mention *The Rocky Mountain Episcopalian.*" I angrily dumped the flour, baking powder and salt into the batter and began to beat furiously. "Time is a problem here for the man I'm supposed to marry. But, since I don't have too much to do now that he's been kidnapped, I'll certainly have time to phone each of the newspapers personally."

Doug Ramsey gave me a helpless expression, then began to drop paper cups in the pan again. "Goldy, don't threaten me. You know I'm under the bishop's discipline—"

I swirled in the vanilla and almond extracts, which turned the thick batter golden and fragrant, and then the poppy seeds, which gave it an inviting, speckled appearance. "Why does the bishop need a cleric to report back to him from St. Luke's in Aspen Meadow? What was he afraid of?"

"That people were worshiping Olson, that's what!"

"What?" I stopped the beater and gaped at him.

"You heard me." He shook with frustration. The muffin tins dropped out of his hands onto the counter just as the sun came out from behind a cloud and shone through the windows. Doug's alb turned brilliant white. His anger shimmered out in all directions.

"Worshiping him how?" I demanded.

Doug glared at me. He said tersely, "Father Theodore Olson belonged to the Society of Chad, as do I, as do Wickham and Montgomery and twenty other clergy in this diocese." He inhaled mightily. "You probably think the Society of Chad has something to do with African famine relief."

Lucky for me I'd taken that course from Canon Montgomery. I picked up the bowl and began to ladle batter into the few muffin cups Ramsey had set out. "Seventh-century English bishop, traveled around his diocese on foot. Died of the plague. What about him? And would you preheat that oven to three-twenty-five for me?"

"We are dedicated to preserving the apostolic tradition, just as Chad was," Father Doug replied huffily, twirling the oven dial. "And this year as our chosen study we have been looking at miraculous healings. As they validate the sacraments, of course."

"You're losing me, Doug." I took up his abandoned task and started to put the paper liners into the rest of the muffin cups.

"Well, it's one thing to talk about Lourdes and Medugorge," he said fiercely. "On the other hand, quite a bit closer to home, a Sunday School teacher suddenly says she doesn't have any more back pain! Well, that could be because we replaced most of those antiquated chairs in the Sunday School rooms. That infant a month ago that was supposedly born blind? There are conflicting reports on whether his reflexes had even been tested when this healing allegation came up!"

"Lourdes and Medugorge," I prompted him.

"Yes! Well. It's quite another thing to get some wild report that Olson lays hands on a terminally ill St. Luke's parishioner at Lutheran Hospital, and one hundred percent deadly mylocytic leukemia just disappears! I mean, *please.*"

"But nobody really knows what happened to Roger Bampton, isn't that true? This doesn't really sound like the Episcopal church, Doug." I scraped the last of the batter into a paper liner and set the pans into the oven. I looked at my watch: 9:45. I'd have to sneak back during the service to take the muffins out when they were done.

"Oh, tell *me* it doesn't sound like the Episcopal church. As you may or may not know, Goldy, there is no ecclesiastical . . . *mechanism* within our communion to verify miracles. And no one actually *saw* the parishioner's blood tests. Oh, those much-touted blood tests! As if I hadn't heard enough about *them.* . . . But soon after the Bampton incident, *another* Sunday School teacher claimed she was cured of lupus after Father Olson laid hands on her. Someone else said somebody's shingles disappeared. The stories spread and our prayer list is suddenly the length of the phone book. The money isn't just pouring in, it's flooding in." Not to mention, I added mentally, the number of terminally ill folks who will want to be Sunday School teachers. "And who's containing this?" Doug fumed. "Who's testing it against church doctrine and experience? It's as if the *Martians* have landed! Come to Aspen Meadow and throw away your crutches for the entire Anglican communion to see! Talk about headlines!

We've been expecting the *National Enquirer* here any minute! Now if Olson just would have come to *one* deanery meeting—"

"Who's we? Who would have been threatened by this, besides the bishop? Someone like Mitchell Hartley?"

Doug Ramsey made a raisin face of disgust. "Mitchell Hartley is one of the ringleaders of this sort of thinking! There's no foundation to it, I'm telling you! It's all Jesus-is-my-buddy and the Holy-Spirit-is-my-voodoo. These people are *ruining* the church. Of course, we all thought Olson was grounded in the orthodox faith—"

"You keep saying 'we.' "

"Why, everyone in the hierarchy, of course. We're talking about the apostolic tradition here, Goldy—"

"Doug! What about sexual misconduct?"

He shrank away from me and colored deeply. "*Excuse* me?"

Several early arrivals for the second service, enticed by the delicious vanilla-mixed-with-almond aroma wafting out of the oven, poked their heads in to see what was cooking. Father Doug Ramsey and I bustled to start washing bowl and beaters. Disappointed, the curious churchgoers withdrew.

Over the sound of hot water filling the sink, I murmured, "I heard a rumor that Olson was romantically involved with someone. Having an affair. How's the Episcopal church's mechanism for dealing with that?"

Doug squirted about five times as much liquid detergent into the sink as we would need. "Goldy, he could have been involved with *ten* women, I mean, the man could have had a *harem* the way they fell all over him. They used to wait outside the door of our Society of Chad meeting! We began calling Olson the magician. Women and miracles, what more could you ask for? Montgomery asked for his resignation from the society, but of course he didn't get it. Then the bishop called me in and said, 'Find out what Olson's doing. He's pulling in so much money, there must be something to it.' Lord!" He flourished the dish detergent. "So here *I* am having to act the sycophant in Aspen Meadow, and *praying* that some of this chicanery will be exposed!"

"Doug, that's enough soap." He pulled back the container and looked dejected. I turned off the water. "I'm sorry, I know you're terribly upset. Just tell me, what women were waiting outside the door of the committee meeting?"

He slapped the detergent down and pulled his alb around him as if it were a blanket. His eyes blazed. "I don't remember. And you needn't waste your pity on *me.* I will continue to carry on, as I always have. I will go in as an examiner day after tomorrow, with a level head, good organization, and the belief—no, the *knowledge* that the orthodox faith prevails—"

"Doug, I meant it. I can tell how upset you are. Please, help me. I'm just trying to find Investigator Tom Schulz. What I don't know is who resented Olson. Do you know who his worst enemies were?"

Doug Ramsey released his alb and leaned in toward me. He hissed: "Olson's worst enemy was himself."

11

At the ten o'clock eucharist, the one favored by the charismatics and people who brought children (heartily loathed by the Old Guard, regardless of what Jesus had to say on the subject), Montgomery's sermon was the same. This time, however, he ignored me as carefully as I did him. First he'd been friendly, then he'd yelled at me, and now he was indifferent. Grief could make people strange.

The second service was completely different from the first. If the 8:00 service was the liturgical equivalent of a golf game, the 10:00 was a soccer match. Perhaps it was the three women and one man enthusiastically strumming guitars, playing the drums, and banging tambourines near the altar. Or maybe it was the people themselves crowded into the pews, their hands raised in the air as they energetically sang the hymns. In addition to advocating a personal relationship with the Lord, the charismatics put great emphasis on praise through song. *Hearty* song. And of course, the wildness could have been at least partly attributed to the great multitude of children, all either chattering, sobbing, dropping books, or scrambling over the wooden pews. By the time we got to the intercessory prayers, I was ready for someone to blow a whistle. Instead, Bob Preston got up with a prayer book and a pad of yellow legal paper. His few strands of hair glimmered in the light from the electric candelabra. The deep hollows of his cheeks made him look uncannily like Zelda. It was the first time I had noticed a resemblance between mother and son.

"I'm sure everyone knows by now that Father Olson was tragically killed yesterday." Bob Preston paused to be certain everyone had heard him. His eyes swept the room. In the sudden hush, the only noise was the clicking silver ends of his bolo tie. "We put the news out on all the phone trees . . ." He tilted his head to one side and raised his voice. "The funeral will be Tuesday morning at ten." At the first service, this announcement had been accompanied by tiny, discreet sniffs. Now sniffles developed into a wave of lamentation that quickly rose to a crescendo. People clutched each other as they wept; they patted each others' backs and offered tissues. Father Olson had been, after all, one of them.

"We believe he did not die in vain." Bob Preston's voice soared over the sobs. "We believe that he did not die in vain!"

"Amen! Yes, Lord!" accompanied this announcement.

Father Doug Ramsey opened his eyes wide and tilted his head to catch Canon Montgomery's attention for an I-told-you-so glance. I wondered if Canon Montgomery thought all this was better or worse than people snickering at his poetry. I perused the congregation for Mitchell Hartley. He sat in the pew across the nave from me, his red pompadour bobbing as he appeared to agree with Bob Preston.

"Now you know," Preston bellowed, "Father Olson would have wanted us to continue with the prayer list. We need to pray for Victor Mancuso. Father Olson laid hands on him in the hospital, and we're waiting for the tests to come back. We need to keep praying for Roger Bampton, who continues to show no sign of illness!"

In the midst of the tears, the congregation burst out clapping. Montgomery closed his mouth and twitched. Doug Ramsey put his face in his hands. I didn't dare look at Mitchell Hartley again. Bob Preston went through the rest of the names on the list, pausing to make comments on the progress, or lack of progress, of each person. I began to squirm when we got to the part of the list entitled "for those in troubled relationships." My fears were confirmed when we heard of Hal and Marie, that Marie was still drinking and we needed to pray for strength for Hal. But the worst was yet to come.

Bob Preston held up his right index finger. It boasted a silver ring with a hunk of turquoise the size of a small boulder. At first I thought he was going to make an announcement about the jewelry raffle, but when he stabbed the air in my direction, my heart sank. "We need to pray for somebody who doesn't usually come to this service. We need to pray for Goldy back there," he bellowed ruefully.

All eyes turned to me. I thought I was going to throw up.

". . . As you've probably heard, Father Olson died before Goldy's wedding. Goldy's fiancé," Bob consulted the yellow pad importantly, "Homicide Investigator Tom Schulz, found poor Ted Olson in his final moments on earth. But then something happened to Investigator Schulz; no one knows what. The police think maybe he was abducted. But he left a note before he was taken." He stopped to take a deep breath. "So Jesus," he intoned, clamping his eyes tight, as if he were about to blow out candles on a birthday cake, "we just want to ask for strength for poor Goldy and that the Sheriff's Department will be able to find the notorious criminal who did this!"

"AMEN!"

My throat closed. My skin had turned clammy. *I have to get out of here.* When Montgomery finally began the opening lines of the General Confession, I nipped into the kitchen, removed the muffins from the oven, and placed them on the counter to cool, then trotted out to my car. I remembered from Montgomery's course that the confession was generally omitted at the Palm Sunday liturgy, at the discretion of the celebrant —in this case, Montgomery himself. But the canon clearly felt that the folks at the later service needed a dose of communal penitence. I, on the other hand, didn't want to confess anything. I didn't look back.

Ten minutes later I sat facing an enormous insulated pot of bad coffee at Carl's Stagecoach Stop, a restaurant on Aspen Meadow's Main Street. The Stagecoach Stop had been pure cowboy until Carl, a restaurateur from Zurich, had bought the place a year ago and attempted to make it Swiss.

"Business is gonna fall off," Tom had announced when we'd celebrated our engagement by coming here for breakfast. "Carl needs to put back what everybody likes. *Müsli with Fruit* won't hack it without *Stagecoach Steak and Eggs.*"

Of course, he had been right. When Tom and I had visited again two months ago, the menu had been revamped, and the waitresses' uniforms had been transformed into something along the lines of Dale Evans-meets-Heidi. "Listen to that," Tom said, pointing to one of the speakers. It was not the usual piped-in German folk music. But Carl hadn't reverted to pure country music, either. Tom had raised his bushy eyebrows and commented, "Waylon Jennings plays the polka."

"Be all right," I urged the image of Tom Schulz in my mind. It would be at least half an hour before either of the Prestons showed up for our brunch. To protect myself from people who might want to disrupt my solitude, I piled Father Olson's Bible as well as the tome on feasts in front of me. With a not-quite-steady hand I poured myself some of the coffee—better than Carl's cappuccino, which tasted like milky motor oil—and opened the Bible to look for Judas.

I perused through similar stories of the betrayal in Matthew, Mark, Luke, and John. The common thread was that Judas offered to betray Jesus to the high priests for a sum, that at the Last Supper Jesus knew what was coming and confronted Judas, who left. Later, in the Garden of Gethsemane, Judas arrived with an armed crowd. By kissing Jesus, Judas betrayed him to the soldiers. Things didn't turn out too well for Judas when he was paid his thirty pieces of silver. According to the story, after the Crucifixion he hanged himself.

I reread the stories. What could Olson possibly have meant when he gasped *B.—Read—Judas* as he was dying? Had Tom been able to figure out what Olson meant by that command? Who was *B.*? Read *what* about Judas?

I put the Bible aside and picked up the book on feasts to look up Chad. Not the country in Africa, not half of the singing group Chad and Jeremy. There was a muddied photograph of Litchfield, England, where Chad had been buried in A.D. 672. Trained in the Celtic Christian tradition, Bishop Chad had been humble and devout. I noted the trademark of the Society of Chad, two entwined snakes that certainly looked Celtic, like something you might find in the Lindisfarne Gospels. I did not see how a society named after Chad could have as its nemesis *these people who are ruining the church.* But the thought of conversing with Doug Ramsey again about *these people* did not fill me with enthusiasm.

"Excuse me? Goldy?"

I looked up to see a gaunt-faced Agatha Preston hovering above me. Her apricot-colored sweater, skirt, and headband made her skin look jaundiced. Over a wide lace collar that was absurdly girlish, her only adornment was a long, expensive-looking double strand of jade beads. Her streaked hair was woven into two tight braids.

"Yes, Agatha. Hello."

"Hello. Well. First of all, I want to apologize for that phone call yesterday." She looked around at the assortment of bikers, churchgoers, and yuppies-in-corduroys and added, "I was quite upset, and I just sort of fell apart." Her delicate fingers fumbled with her jade beads. "Bob couldn't come, or rather, he might arrive in a little bit, he had to stay at church to talk to the police . . . about Hymnal House." She glanced down at the book in my hands. "I'm sorry. Were you studying?" Without waiting for my reply, she looked around for a waitress. "I'm hungry. Aren't you?"

She was making me nervous. "Sit down, Agatha."

"Oh sure." She pulled out her Swiss-style wooden chair with its heart-shaped back. A waitress wearing a ruffled blouse, skirt edged in fake leather fringe, and cowgirl boots thumped up.

"I'm ready," I said crisply. Ever partial to European fare, I ordered Müsli with yogurt and blueberries while Agatha stammered, changed her mind twice, and finally settled uneasily for a cheese omelet. The waitress slapped her order book closed and hightailed away.

"Start with the phone call yesterday," I commanded with a smile and swig of coffee.

Her blue eyes turned huge. "Well, it all really starts before that." She hesitated. "You see, you work, or I guess I should say, you work outside the home, so your relationship with the church is different." Color flooded her sallow face.

"My relationship *with whom* in the church is different? Different from *whose* relationship?"

"Your relationship with the other women. *From* the other women. They just . . . don't expect the same things of you. You get respect. I mean, I always wanted to do volunteer work, especially since I thought it would help Zelda . . . you know . . . have support. She's gone through so much."

"And did it?"

Her laugh was dry and brittle, a you've-got-to-be-kidding laugh. "I'm like their little pet. Hers and Lucille's." She raised her voice. "C'mere, Agatha! Answer the phone sixteen times a day! Go fetch! Stuff these envelopes! Mail out these raffle invitations! And whatever you do, don't have any fun! You're doing this for the church!" She regarded me intensely. "People talk about heaven all the time, but you know what's weird? I think a lot about *hell.* And who I'd like to have there." She smiled conspiratorially. "Do you ever think about that?"

"Let's see." I sipped coffee and tried to think. "I saw the IMAX film on Antarctica. I thought *that* would be a great place for my ex-husband to spend eternity."

"Oh." She giggled and twirled a streaked braid with her index finger.

"How about your husband? Does Bob have fun in the church? Or is he one of the hell-folks?"

Agatha thrust her head back and giggled even louder, as if now I was being really naughty. "Oh, Bob, well, you know. He loves to run things, and he has the time to do it now. In the spring and summer he does construction projects like Habitat for Humanity, in the fall he goes out with Sportsmen Against Hunger, and they just have a blast shooting off their Remingtons at all those poor, innocent elk—"

"Did Father Olson get respect?"

Color again climbed her neck above the childish lace collar. I felt as if I'd said "Underpants!" to a conservative seventh grader. "Ah," she said, "I wouldn't know. I guess I'd have to say no."

"So . . . how did you know about this lack of respect for him? Through your volunteer work?"

"Well, yes. Zelda and Lucille informed me it was my turn to be head of the Episcopal Church Women." She was frowning at something over my shoulder. "Father Olson was also . . . counseling me. You know," she added, suddenly earnest, "he could have gone to any parish. Everyone loved him. Well, almost everyone . . ."

"Did you love him?" I asked impulsively.

She blushed again and twirled the braid so tightly I thought she was going to pull it out. "I didn't think that I did, I mean, I just admired him, but then I heard this thing on *Stories of the Weird* about how people can be soul mates, you know? That's why I wondered if you'd seen him, you know, his body? Was there much . . . blood? Did he suffer?" Her eyes probed my face.

Oh, Lord. I said, "When you called, I didn't know if you meant Olson." I immediately felt somewhat light-headed, probably a side effect of dealing with an underappreciated woman who claimed to be worried about me, yet who put great stock in *Stories of the Weird.* "I don't think he suffered too much," I improvised. "Who didn't love Father Olson?"

Agatha wrinkled her nose and absentmindedly fingered the milky green beads. "Oh, you know, some people thought he was just showing off with a fancy car, trying to act rich, but he wasn't, he just needed to get around! Ted didn't believe in having a lot of money. Ted just believed in *love,* you know, don't you?"

Instead of answering, I poured us both more coffee. She frowned at it.

"Gosh, I guess I should have ordered tea. I always drink tea, but it just hasn't seemed cold enough lately, but it's not quite warm enough for iced tea—"

"Agatha!"

The vacant eyes were suddenly startled. "What?" She pulled her row of tiny bottom teeth in front of her top teeth and wrinkled her forehead.

"Where was your husband yesterday?"

"Yesterday? You mean Saturday?"

"Yes. Where was Bob all day?"

"Gosh. Um. You mean, like in the transcendental sense?"

"I mean, like was he at the hardware store, was he at the barber, what?"

Agatha's youthful face remained puzzled. But as the overhead speakers began another set of cheerful Alpine square dancing music, her features brightened. "With Aspen Meadow Kiwanis. Yes, you know. They're building a house, for Habitat for Humanity, off Main Street on that empty lot where the house burned down last year, remember? And the guy who owned it was in Saudi Arabia or something, so he sold it to the Kiwanis for next to nothing. The lot, I mean, anyway—"

"And Bob was there all day."

"Well, most of the day, I guess. He came home terribly exhausted and I was just so upset about Father Olson, and on the phone with you. . . . Why?"

"Agatha, was Bob," I leaned toward her, "*jealous* of your relationship with Father Olson?"

"Only when I didn't clean the house on the days we did our counseling work—" She stopped abruptly, looking stricken.

"Did you ever work with P.R.A.Y.?"

"Pray? About what?"

The waitress arrived with our food. The Müsli with yogurt and blueberries spilled out over a wide porcelain bowl. I took a mouthful. Creamy yogurt coated the sweet, juicy blueberries and luscious crunch of Zurich-style granola. I was suddenly ravenous. It felt as if years had gone by since I had eaten anything. Melted cheese cascaded down the side of Agatha's steaming omelet. She made mm-mm noises as she dug in.

"Agatha," I ventured after a moment, "do you have any idea who might have wanted to hurt Father Olson? Someone who could have killed him? Anybody who might have been a traitor?"

"Who, me? Have an idea? No." She chewed an enormous mouthful of omelet thoughtfully. "No, really. But listen, I've been so worried about *you* with what happened to your fiancé and all—"

"What do you know about Victor Mancuso?"

"Vic—? Oh. Nothing." Her face brightened again. "Didn't they make an announcement about him? I do know about Roger Bampton. He had leukemia, and then he got better after Ted . . . Father Olson laid hands on him. Do you really think miracles happen? Or do you believe that it's just all in our minds? On *Stories of the Weird*—"

"I'd guess I'd have to talk to Roger. Talk to his doctor or something."

"Well, I saw Roger. When he was sick." She put down her fork and made a face. "He looked awful. His skin was the color of deer feces, you know, when it's been there for a while—"

"Agatha, I'm trying to eat Müsli here."

"Oh, sorry. Well anyway, I'm not one of those people demanding to see the blood tests, before and after."

"Who's demanding that?"

"Oh, Goldy, I don't know."

I wondered if anyone had ever tried to give this woman a lie-detector test. Would she pass or fail? Or would she just not understand the questions? I said, "Was Ted Olson his own worst enemy?"

She put down her fork and sighed. "People wanted stuff from Ted all the time, that's what I'm trying to tell you, nobody respected him. I mean as a *person.* Everyone wanted a little bit of him, as if he were some kind of stuffed animal or something. No one would notice a little bit of stuffing missing, do you know what I mean?"

"I guess I don't."

She doused her coffee with creamer and wiggled her mouth disapprovingly. "They wanted him to *take care of them.* They wanted him to *pray for them.* They wanted to talk to him about issues in the parish, and mostly what they wanted was for him to *get so-and-so to stop doing something.* Or get someone to *start* doing something."

"Was there anybody who wanted him to do something, and he didn't do it?"

"Come on." She took a small sip of coffee, approved of it, and sipped more. "He couldn't do everything. He was supposed to have Mondays off, you know."

"And did he?"

"Oh, no. People would call, call, call all day. One day he just didn't answer the phone. You know, when there was that big problem over the music. Zelda wanted to find out if he'd heard from the bishop, and when he didn't answer the phone, she drove all the way out there and stalked right up to the door and banged on it."

"And did he answer?"

"Of course he didn't! But then she came around back!" Agatha was indignant. "Peering through his windows and trying to see what was going on! So she opened the back door and she shrieked, 'I knew you were home! Your car is right there in the driveway!' like she'd just won a game or something. That woman is impossible. I don't care if she is my mother-in-law."

I spooned up some more Müsli and tried to think of how to phrase the next question.

"Did Ted tell you all this, Agatha?"

"Well," she said with another sip of coffee, "I was in counseling with him at the time."

"He was your counselor, so he told you *his* problems? Or he was your counselor that day at his house?"

She looked up. A shadow crossed her face. "Oh, Bob honey, we didn't see you come in."

12

Bob Preston peered down at our plates, then glanced around the restaurant. He sat tentatively, frowning at the Western-style light fixture hanging down over our table.

"This is awfully bright," he announced. "Makes it hard to see." He proceeded to start unscrewing the bulb. Unfortunately, it was too hot. Bob yelped, dipped his fingers into his wife's ice water, carefully wiped them on the clean napkin of the place setting in front of him, and unscrewed the bulb a few more revolutions before dipping, drying, and unscrewing again. Finally he had the bulb out. He reached across and with extreme delicacy placed it on the empty seat at our table for four.

Agatha tilted her head to focus on this little drama. "Poor Bob," she murmured sympathetically once the lightbulb was dispensed with. "Can't stand bright light."

"Ahhh," said Bob when Heidi/Dale rushed up. But before she started to take his order, she sent a confused look at our light fixture. "Don't worry about it," Bob assured her with a wave of pinkened fingers. "All we need you to do now is turn off that damn noise."

"What?"

"Turn off the polka!" he bellowed. Several bikers turned unshaven faces in Bob's direction, but he glared back. "Look, I need hash browns on one plate, two poached eggs on another, and sliced fruit—no honeydew melon on that, okay?—on a third. Got it, honey?" The waitress finished scribbling, nodded once, and took off.

"Bob," I began conversationally, "we were just beginning to miss you. Everything okay at church?"

He grunted. "I guess. If you don't mind listening to Montgomery. I swear, that man is *boring.* And after what our congregation has been through, you'd think the diocese could send us someone who could preach. What do we get? A froggy-looking guy who shouts bad poems at parishioners. And then that obnoxious seminarian, what is his name, Hartley? Kid drives me nuts. He sees me getting into my car, an Audi that I earned the bucks to buy, thank you very much, and he starts preaching at me about the evils of money."

Agatha had undergone an astonishing personality change since her husband's arrival. Instead of being spaced-out, she was now demure. She smiled vapidly.

I asked, "What do you think's going to happen to the parish?"

Bob Preston puffed up. "If the Lord wants us to—"

I said, "Stop right there, Bob." Agatha regarded me in horrified silence; her husband merely shrugged. I went on gently, "For the sake of argument, let's assume the presence of the Lord, okay? What do you think the people are going to do?"

He shook his head and pulled in his chin, assuming the dismayed expression of an oilman who'd drilled a dry hole. "I don't know if you can assume God's presence, Goldy. That's what they did during Pinckney's time, and the place was as dead as smashed and bloodied roadkill, I'm telling you."

I pushed the plate of unfinished Müsli away. "And you thought the place came to life under Father Theodore Olson?"

The waitress arrived with Bob's order. She looked at me quizzically, then hesitated, I thought, because of the lack of light and the unwillingness to risk Bob's rude tongue again. Then she said, "You're the caterer. Goldy. I heard what happened. Sorry."

I murmured a thanks. Bob Preston took a bite from one plate and brayed: "These potatoes are cold." The waitress rolled her eyes at me—*demanding clients!*—and whisked away the offending hash browns.

"Yes," said Bob, picking up where we left off, "the place came to life under Olson. Didn't you find him more centered on the Lord than Pinckney and that old-church crowd?"

"I thought Father Olson was very nice." I kept my gaze on Agatha.

"He was very . . . attractive to parishioners." She looked away. I went on, "I didn't have the same approach to the faith as Olson, but he was a great counselor for Schulz and me. Arch had him for confirmation class and thought he was marvelous. I just wish the police could figure out why—"

"Well, that's their job, isn't it?" Bob interjected brusquely. He craned his neck around, probably seeking the unfortunate waitress. "What did Schulz say in that note?"

My skin prickled. I exhaled and shrugged noncommittally. "Haven't the foggiest. It was policeman shorthand. Olson was alive, Olson was dead. What did the police have to say to you?"

With his right hand, Bob made a lasso-type movement in the air. He grimaced. "They said they found a diocesan vehicle. They wanted to know who had access to the keys, who had access to the car, who had access to Hymnal House—"

Our waitress returned with Bob Preston's new hash browns. I pressed my lips together. *Who had access to Hymnal House and Brio Barn?* I thought of the old conference center, where I had taken my Sunday School teachers' course and where I had catered many times. The conference center boasted many rooms, now closed off. It also contained numerous sequestered storage areas. Hmm.

"Bob and Agatha," I announced as I got to my feet, "thank you for a lovely brunch. I need to be getting home to stay by the phones and take care of Arch. Let's get together again soon," I added insincerely.

Bob Preston reared back slightly. His brow furrowed. Then, not one to let piping hot hash browns go to waste, he dismissed me with a small wave.

"I'll take Goldy to the door," Agatha said hastily. With his mouth full, Bob shrugged. Agatha rose suddenly and sent her Swiss-style chair reeling. This brought more interested looks from the bikers. They loved brawls, even at brunch. To discourage such an eruption, Agatha and I walked decorously to the entrance of the restaurant.

"Please tell me," she began in a low, imploring tone. "I have been so worried about you, and about Schulz, but did Ted—Father Olson—say anything to Schulz about . . . anything from me?"

"Anything from you? Like letters? Talk fast, he's looking at you."

She glanced nervously in her husband's direction and waved her fingers halfheartedly. "I was in counseling with Ted because I thought Bob was getting ready to leave me," she blurted out in the same confessional whisper. "Money disappeared out of our checking account and I didn't know where it went. I thought Bob was hiding it somewhere, getting ready to file for divorce. After the first few months, I just couldn't bear to see Ted only once a week. I had so much on my mind. So I wrote to him . . . about all that I was going through and feeling . . . every day. And I cashed in a whole-life policy that my father had given me, and stashed the money. Father . . . Ted was the only one who knew about my financial arrangements. I was so happy to have somebody to write to about how I was going to use my money. Now I'm just so afraid that Ted could have left those letters somewhere that Bob could get hold of them . . . and use them against me." Her eyes brimmed with tears.

"Were you in love with Ted?"

"What difference does it make?" she hissed. She dashed at her eyes, shook her braids, and sniffed. "Did he say something about the letters or not?" We both looked at Bob, who was pointing to his poached-egg plate and once again giving the waitress elaborate instructions.

"Agatha, just tell me," I urged, "about Ted. And if your husband knew."

She stepped to one side of a cuckoo clock and Swiss flag display. Her face was ashen. "Why? Why do you want to know? Ted is gone."

"Because it'll help me," I said desperately, "in case the man I'm supposed to marry is still alive. Can't you just tell me what was going on, and if your husband was jealous?"

"Ted *loved* me," she protested. "I'm sure of it. I know he would have waited for me."

"Waited for you for what?"

"Waited until I could get some more money together and dump Bob."

"Agatha, did you tell the police this?"

Her face crumpled. "Of course not! I'm the married head of the Episcopal Church Women. Our rector was single. What am I supposed to say: 'I was in love with our priest, and I've been squirreling away cash for the last five years? Please don't tell my husband?' "

"Where is the money?"

"I'm not going to tell you. It's no one's business but mine." Fury bubbled through her voice.

"You were at Olson's house when your mother-in-law, Zelda, came out that day about the music, weren't you?"

She choked and smoothed the skirt of her apricot suit. "Help me," she pleaded. "Help me find my letters, and I'll tell you."

Her plight touched me. "I'll do what I can."

She whispered, "When Zelda came out, I was hiding in the bathroom." Abruptly, she turned and scampered back to the table where her husband sat abusing the waitress.

I zipped the van two blocks down Main Street, turned left at my street, and gunned the engine up the hill. I whizzed past the lot where the skeleton of the Habitat for Humanity house stood abandoned for the weekend. I was sorely tempted to drive the extra five minutes it would take to go directly to the Aspen Meadow Conference Center, but I decided I needed some tools, just in case. As soon as I was in the house I called for Arch, who came bounding down the staircase.

"Gosh, Mom, what took you so long?" He was still wearing the sweatsuit he'd put on yesterday after my wedding-that-wasn't. He pushed his glasses up his nose and looked behind me in the direction of the front door. No Tom Schulz. "What's going on? Was that Investigator Boyd at the door this morning? I saw the police car out my window, but figured you would have told me if they'd found him." His young face was tight with anxiety. "I thought for sure they'd have figured out some clues by now."

I gave him a hug. "They did find something, Arch. What they found was the car they think took Tom away from Father Olson's house."

"But they didn't—"

"No. Not yet. Where's Julian? Did you eat breakfast?"

"He's at the grocery store. He says someone actually did send over tuna noodle casserole, so he's out buying ingredients for a Mexican pizza he's going to make tonight. And yes, I had one of the cinnamon rolls you left."

"Great. Listen hon, I'm going over to the conference center—"

"But . . . what if Investigator Boyd calls?" His sherry-colored eyes were large with worry behind his glasses. "Why are you going over there? Are you just going to leave me here to take messages? *Why* are you going to the conference center?"

Kids. From as early as I could remember, Arch had been inquisitive. Not just on philosophical questions such as, *What happens after you die?* Arch wanted answers to everything. *What do they do with your tonsils after they take them out? Why do you have to sell the cookies you make? At Todd's house they get to keep the oatmeal cookies his mother makes.* And, most troublesome of all, *Why does God let people suffer?* Of course I had figured being a good mom meant you had to explain everything, or try to. *They throw the tonsils away. We have to sell cookies to live. God is with us in our pain.*

"I'm going to check on the broken window," I lied.

"You hate broken glass. You won't let me touch it."

"I'm just going because I'm going, that's why!"

He squinched his face into an accusatory expression and pointed a finger at me. "It has something to do with the church, doesn't it? And Father Olson. You're going to that old conference place because . . ." He stopped talking to appraise me. "Because you think somebody's hiding Schulz over there. That's it, isn't it? You're going to try to find him all by yourself. I'm going with you."

"The heck you are, buster."

"If you don't take me with you, I'll ride over there on my bike. Then maybe the killer can get you and me together."

"Oh, for heaven's sake, then, let me call the police."

I put in a call to Boyd and identified myself to the person who answered. I asked that the Sheriff's Department send a car over to the Aspen Meadow Conference Center, that I had a good idea Tom Schulz might be there.

"They were already there," the policeman said. "But if you have another idea about Schulz, they'll go back. Twenty-five minutes, tops," he said and then hung up.

"Okay, Arch, the police are on their way."

He gave me a baleful look. "I miss Tom, too, you know."

"All right, all right, we'll go over and meet the police there. But I have to go find some tools and my Mace, just in case . . ." I didn't finish the thought. "Get your coat, hon. It's cold."

He raced up the stairs and announced sonorously over his shoulder, "Mom—we're going to need at *least* two flashlights."

13

Within minutes my van was whining up Meadow Drive toward Hymnal House. The air was unusually chilly for an early Colorado afternoon in April, and a bleak sky threatened snow. No law-enforcement types had arrived by the time the van crunched over the gravel of the long conference driveway. Silently I castigated myself for agreeing to bring Arch into a potentially dangerous situation. I wavered about going back. I saw a jogger in my rearview mirror, backed up, and rolled down my window. Yes, the police had been here, he informed me, panting. It was a while ago, maybe half an hour.

I would not go into any of the buildings until they got back, I vowed. I would not put Arch in danger.

I pulled the van up to the split-rail fence by Brio Barn. We jumped out onto ice-slickened grass at the edge of the cliff overlooking Main Street, Cottonwood Creek, and St. Luke's. Across the creek, the church lot held two cars. But it was empty of people. No signs of activity animated the conference center, either. The two ninety-year-old conference buildings were distinguished by dark cedar shake shingle siding, stone entryways, red roofs, and an air of benign neglect. Red paint curled off the window frames and dead pine needles lay in a haphazard pattern across the windowsills. The place looked like a Victorian summer camp shuttered for the off-season.

Up the hill from us, next to Hymnal House, stood the old garage. It was a one-story edifice originally built to accommodate three horse-drawn carriages. Now its door yawned widely. Arch and I walked up slowly. The notion of Tom being hidden somewhere in the center was an idea I found alternately brilliant and inane. I glanced around the empty conference garage with its ancient hedge clippers and rusted engines, its workbench cluttered with tools and leaning towers of snow tires. Had Tom been in here? The dusty surfaces revealed no signs of human presence.

"When do you think the Sheriff's Department will get here?" Arch asked impatiently when we returned to the van and I slid open its side door.

"Any minute," I assured him with more confidence than I felt.

"Forgot to tell you," Arch said as he snapped the buttons on the flashlights to test the batteries. "A guy named Canon Montgomery called. Wanted to apologize for his little outburst, he said. Wants to get together with you before the exams. What outburst? What exams?"

So Canon Montgomery had called. If he truly was feeling contrite, maybe I could play off his guilt to get him to discuss the woman waiting for Ted Olson outside the Society of Chad meeting. "You know," I replied, "the exams for the candidates for the priesthood. They start Tuesday night . . ."

But Arch wasn't listening. "What's all this?" he asked. He shone his flashlights in the corner of the van that held the two thick files and books I had pilfered from Olson's office.

"Oh, that's just—" Startled by the approaching whine of a car engine, I stopped talking. For a moment, we were transfixed by the sight of the small foreign automobile barreling down the conference drive.

"Mom," said Arch, "that looks an awful lot like—"

"Don't tell me. Quickly, hustle up to Hymnal House. We need to hide."

I slammed the van's sliding door. And then we ran. But the steps were snowy, and Arch was unsure of which way to go. We were not fast enough to elude Frances Markasian. The *Mountain Journal*'s investigative reporter lunged out of her Fiat, hoisted up her voluminous bag, and bounded up the stone steps to Hymnal House in hot pursuit. Gasping for breath, she caught up with us on the old stone patio by the double-door entrance. We stood panting just feet from the window that hung, snaggletoothed and cardboard-covered on the inside, after Julian's breakage and Mitchell's repair.

Holding my side, I noted that the shoes enabling Frances to sprint up the steps were sneakers held together with duct tape. Above these hung her oversized black trenchcoat that was either a journalistic affectation or the only piece of outerwear available at the same garage sale where she'd unearthed the sneakers. The recession had obviously left its mark on Aspen Meadow. She dropped the big handbag on the flagstones and sent her dark stringy hair shaking wildly as she pounded her chest and coughed hard.

"Gee, Goldy, where're you going so fast? You're going to give me a heart attack." As if to remedy this situation, Frances leaned against a pile of metal deck chairs on the stone patio, leaned down to retrieve the bag, and groped inside. After a moment's search, she pulled out a pack of cigarettes and book of matches. She shook out a smoke and looked us over. "Whatcha doin' with the flashlights? Looking for something?"

"We're going in to find some pans of mine," I said laconically. "I know by order of the Aspen Meadow Fire Department that there's no smoking within ten feet of any of the conference buildings."

"That's too bad," said Frances. She lit the cigarette and inhaled greedily. With the hand holding the cigarette, she pulled a curtain of her hair off her face so she could see what she was doing. With the other hand, she brushed snow off one of the deck chairs, a rusted green contraption that looked as if it had been salvaged from the *Titanic.* Blowing smoke out in a thin stream, she dragged the chair over to the short stone wall that edged the deck. Fifty feet below, cars passed along Main Street. Without giving the view even a cursory glance, she plopped on the wet chair and put her feet up on the wall. "If I don't sit close to the building for a smoke, then I won't be able to tell you what I've learned about your parish."

Arch raised one thin straw-brown eyebrow above the frame of his glasses. I cursed inwardly. But the flesh is weak. I brushed snow and ice off two more chairs.

"Is this something Arch can hear?" I demanded as I scraped our chairs across the flagstones to the wall.

"You don't need to protect me, Mom," my son said grittily. "I am a week away from being thirteen, in case you forgot."

Frances waved this off and carefully balanced her cigarette on the edge of the stone wall before again reaching down into her bag. She brought out a Jolt cola, shook it lightly, then popped the top and sucked fizz.

Arch watched in open-mouthed awe. He said, "That is so cool!"

Frances retrieved the smoke and smiled beatifically. "What, the drink or the cigarette?"

"The pop! I'm not allowed to have that stuff. *Triple* the caffeine of regular cola? Are you kidding? Man! You must be cruisin'!"

"Uh, excuse me?" I interjected mildly. "What happened to your Diet Pepsi and Vivarin?"

"That's only for morning." She set the can on the stone wall and sucked on the cigarette as if it were an oxygen machine. "This is for afternoon. Listen. Bob Preston is b-r-o-k-e."

"No kidding?" I looked off the deck at the tops of pine trees that grew along the steep slope. An evenly spaced line of antique cars passed sedately on the road below. The Model-T Club of Denver often brought their point-to-point rallies through our little burg. It was better than the motorcycles. Beyond the chugging cars, the A-shaped roof of St. Luke's resembled an enormous tent top.

"Flat broke," added Frances. "Busted. And in hock up to his sanctimonious ears."

"I thought he had oil well royalties or something."

She chugged more Jolt and made a satisfied lip-smacking noise. "That's why I'm the reporter and you're the caterer."

"Cut the chorizo, Frances. What are you saying? And who'd you get this financial information from?"

I tried to stare her down. Unfortunately, her eyes were mostly concealed by that dark stringy hair that looked as if it'd just been released from dreadlocks. "Bob's well," Frances intoned with a swipe at the hair, "is dry. Literally and figuratively. But then there are forty thousand dollars worth of pearls floating around somewhere." She rubbed the cigarette between her fingers and smirked. "Forty thousand clams—or is it oysters?—might not be enough to kill for, but it would give somebody a nice little stake. Now about Agatha and your priest, Olson—" Frances studied my face avidly. Since I didn't have any dreadlocks to hide behind, I kept my expression resolutely blank. She went on. "—I heard she wanted him a whole lot more than he wanted her."

"Really? Who told you that? Please, Frances, I need to get into the conference center to look for my stuff. The police were here, and they'll be back soon."

"What's the hurry?" She glanced over her shoulder at the broken window. "What'd you leave over here, pans? They're probably stolen by now, if anybody would think to look up here."

If anybody would think to look up here. This woman was driving me crazy. I shrugged. If I let her know I was waiting for the police so we could look for Tom Schulz, I'd never get rid of her.

Frances chugged more Jolt. "How are you feeling about the kidnapping of your fiancé?"

"One more personal question and I'm driving home."

"Okay, try this. Think your bishop would have put up with a priest having an affair?"

My parish, my priest, my bishop. Pretty soon she'd have me owning the Anglican church worldwide. "No, Frances, of course I don't." All across the country, female parishioners had been suing dioceses, claiming psychological damage when their priests were their lovers. All it took was a few million dollars lost when the women won their suits for the church to take notice.

I said, "You think we're looking at a lawsuit? Or that we were?"

She blew smoke rings to Arch's rapt admiration. "I think we might have been looking at *blackmail.*" Arch raised his eyebrows dramatically.

"Blackmail from whom?" I demanded. "From Agatha Preston? And where would Olson figure in that?"

"Say the priest is having a little illicit tickle between the sheets, or he's scared people will *think* he is." Arch's brow wrinkled, and I could imagine his mind working: *Who is getting tickled?* Frances continued, "Don't you think that Bob Preston could use this knowledge to blackmail Olson? Maybe to find out where those pearls were?"

"And then shoot him? Why not just sue and recover a couple mil?"

Frances inhaled noisily and warmed to her subject. "Say the priest refuses to give him information he wants, about his wife or the pearls or something. Or," she added pensively, "maybe the canon theologian, Montgomery, has a little heart-to-heart with his beloved former student, Olson. The heart-to-heart turns loud, and a bunch of folks at the diocesan center overhear them yelling." She paused. "Maybe the diocese is saying to Olson, give up fair Agatha or else."

"Or else *they'll* kill him?"

She held out her arms and shrugged dramatically. The big trench coat collapsed like a nosediving black kite. "Look, Goldy, I'm just trying to put this together. That's all I want to do," she whined with unconvincing naïveté. "There's one more thing. You know the Habitat house they're building over by you?" I nodded. "There's a flap among the neighbors, in case you weren't aware. They've just gotten the project red-flagged. They say it violates the neighborhood covenants 'cuz it's too small. The neighbors enlisted Olson to be their go-between with the Habitat board, where Bob Preston is a big old striped bass in a teensy-weensy pond. Know anything about that? There's going to be an article in the paper this week."

I said no and wondered if Arch was following all this. To my dismay, he was staring open-mouthed at Frances Markasian. I wasn't sure, but I thought I saw awe in his eyes.

She gave me a skeptical look before lighting another cigarette with the glowing end of the one she'd been working on. "So what do you think was going on between the head of the Episcopal Church Women and your priest?" The first cigarette landed at her feet.

"Gee, Frances, guess you'll have to ask the head of the Episcopal Church Women that one." I crushed the cigarette stub under my heel and stood up as an act of dismissal.

Frances took a deep drag, looked across the street at the roof of St. Luke's, and blew smoke. "What do you know about Roger Bampton?" she asked.

"Nothing that isn't common knowledge in town. How much of it is true is another question."

"Do you believe his healing was a miracle?"

"Do you?"

She shoved herself to her sneakered feet, sighed, and heaved the bag over her shoulder. "The only thing I believe in is the power of the press. That's where the truth is. For me, anyway." She gave me a good-natured handshake and half-smile around the drooping cigarette. "Well, Deep Throat, if you hear anything else, be sure to give the *Mountain Journal* a jingle."

"My pleasure," I lied.

"Stop by the office some time, Arch. I keep a fridge full of Jolt back by the press."

Arch's face turned momentarily jubilant until he caught my don't-even-think-about-it glare. When Frances had hopped back down Hymnal House's stone steps and roared away in the smoke-spewing Fiat, Arch and I picked up our flashlights to go back to the driveway and wait. When we got near the entrance to Brio Barn, we heard something. Something like a drawer or a door being closed hard. Or a metal chair sliding across a floor. Arch shot me a look.

"What was that?"

"Honey, I don't know."

"We have to go in, Mom."

"Forget it." Despite my words, I eyed the barn door.

"It could be him! He could be trying to get out! Mom! Are you listening to me? He might be trying to signal somebody! But maybe he's about to pass out or . . . And anyway, check it out!" He gestured widely to the houses near the conference center, the row of old cars puffing through Aspen Meadow. "This is like, a neighborhood. Nobody's going to bother us in the middle of the day in a *neighborhood.* But if you say we can't, then he'll probably be unconscious by the time the police get here, and we won't find him until—"

He stopped talking again as the scraping sound again reached our ears.

"Okay, look." My voice quavered. Arch already was walking down the old stone steps to the barn. "Don't call out to see if anybody's there until we get inside and have a look, say, on the stage, underneath the stage, in the storage areas, and so on. Do you want the Mace?"

Arch's voice said firmly, "Okay. I don't know where anything is in this place."

"I've catered here enough to know the ins and outs. Just follow me." I spoke with more confidence than I felt.

The padlock chaining the barn doors was unhinged. I didn't stop to wonder why as I threaded the rusty metal loops over and up to free the door handles. We swung the creaking doors open to the cavelike, shadowy space and were immediately greeted by a current of icy, dank air. What the hell am I doing here? my inner voice demanded. I groped for the switch to the overhead light that I knew existed. When I snapped it, nothing happened. Of course. Although winter was technically over, the electricity would be off until the summer conferences began. That meant that anywhere except Hymnal House, there would be no power, and anyone kept here would be cold. I thought of Tom shivering from exposure.

"Turn on your flashlight." My voice sounded like gravel. We swept fragile beams of light into the interior. The theater-shaped space was primarily used for rehearsals, choral concerts, and conference liturgies. In front of us across the wooden floor, the old pipe organ stood like a tall museum ghost. Sensitive to cold, it wasn't used here, merely stored. The stage was on our right; chairs were stacked haphazardly against the walls. The smell of old, musty wood was strong. I didn't want to shine my flashlight upward. The thought of creatures that could be skittering through the rafters was a distinctly unpleasant one. Gooseflesh prickled my arms. I was going into a cold, abandoned, semidark space on a cloudy Sunday afternoon to look for Tom Schulz. I didn't know which was worse, the ear-ringing fear or that recurring thought that I must be losing my mind. Actually, what was worse was the fear that Tom might indeed be . . . worse than unconscious.

"You do remember my birthday is this coming Sunday," Arch said in a low voice.

Leave it to a kid to bring up a birthday. Discussing something completely unrelated might relieve anxiety, after all. And where were the police?

"Yes," I said as I moved tentatively into the room. My voice came out too loud and echoed along with my footsteps. "It doesn't usually fall on Easter, but it does this year."

"I think when I grow up," said Arch courageously as he parted from me and walked in the direction of the stage, "I'm going to be the kind of guy who does people's taxes. Four days after tax day every year is my birthday. Then I'll always be able to have a big celebration, even though I'm grown up." He hesitated, then hissed, "Shouldn't we be calling his name, anyway? Since it doesn't look as if anybody's here? If he's in a storage area, maybe he could make noise . . ."

Good idea. "Tom!" I called weakly. My voice echoed from the cold, wooden walls. "Tom!"

Nothing.

I continued forward into the semidarkness, focusing my flashlight on the dusty wooden floor a yard in front of my shoes. Every few steps, I lifted the beam to the old organ. Its dull metal pipes rose toward the ceiling like prison bars. Once I shone my flashlight all the way up to the pitched ceiling. Hanging from the barn beams were not bats, but dusty embroidered banners from parishes whose organists had attended the music conference for many years. From the teas I'd catered in this space, I knew there was a closet behind the organ that served as storage for music and educational materials. This closet was opened for the July and August conferences of choir directors and Sunday School teachers. After I checked it we would go underneath the stage to check the dank stone basement that was used to store old church files. Neither sounded like much fun.

"Mom?" The beam of Arch's flashlight shone weakly in my direction.

"Over here. You were talking about what kind of party you were going to have when you grow up."

"Okay. I'm moving up onto the stage." The beam of his flashlight disappeared.

"Are you worried you won't have a party this year?" I asked, slightly louder.

"Sometimes I think I'm too old for that kind of stuff." His voice was muffled. From his shaded, moving light, I knew that he was checking behind one of the stage's heavy velvet curtains. "I would like a cake, though," he announced when he emerged. His small voice echoed. "Maybe a little family party. Are there dressing rooms or anything back here, any place where Tom could be? Maybe he's gagged."

I stopped walking. "Flash your light along the wall." He did, and revealed nothing but dusty paneling. With false cheer, I said, "What do you want for birthday presents?"

His voice was both earnest and fierce. "Tom Schulz back, Mom, what do you think? Did you look behind the organ?"

"I'm about to." I swallowed, ignored the pounding in my ears, and walked briskly to the organ. Going behind a large instrument, into a dark space where who-knew-what could be lurking, was intimidating. The keys and pipes were covered with cobwebs. I'd been bitten once by a poisonous spider. It wasn't fun. I shuddered and came around behind the pipes. A pile of chairs stood in front of the closet door. I put my shoulder to the middle of the stack and strained hard to push it out of the way. The chairs didn't budge. I took a deep breath and tried again. They made an unearthly scraping noise. They also moved an inch.

"Gosh, Mom," came Arch's horrified cry. "What are you *doing*?"

I put my shoulder against the chair-pile and shoved. If Tom Schulz was in this closet, whoever had put him in there was extremely strong. I pushed again, then stopped to rest. I pulled the bench around to use as a lever. I groaned and heaved my weight into it. After a moment, the bench and the pile of chairs scraped in an arc away from the door. The thought of Tom trapped in the closet gave me the strength to pick up the organ bench and smash the doorknob. Both disintegrated in the process. By the time Arch and I finished with this place, they'd need a federal grant for renovation.

I grabbed the flashlight with one hand, stuck the fingers of my other hand through the hole made by the missing doorknob, and yanked the door outward. I took a deep breath of dusty air and flashed the light into the windowless closet space.

Lining the walls were floor-to-ceiling shelves spilling over with yellowed papers and booklets. The smell of mold was dreadful. Except for dust devils and intricate spiderwebs lining the corners, the room was empty. Disappointment congealed heavily in my chest.

"I want to tell you what kind of cake I want," said Arch's distant voice. I came out of the closet in time to see his flashlight shining huge and scarlet in back of the stage right curtain.

"What?" I directed my beam up on the stage just as Arch's shape emerged from behind the curtain. His footsteps echoed across the wood.

"Pepper-*mint*!" His light wobbled against the ceiling. *"Agh!"* A loud cracking noise, like wood breaking, made me momentarily lose the grip on my beam. I refocused it shakily on the area where Arch was. Or had been. The stage floor was collapsing beneath him.

"Help!" my son shouted.

"Oh! Lord help us!" came the cry of a woman from the floor below.

14

My body felt impossibly cumbersome as it clattered over to the stage. I jumped up three steps, tripped, then crab-crawled to the place where the boards had given way. Arch had fallen through. I knew he was alive because I could hear his surprised voice half-talking, half-crying. I directed my light downward and peered through the hole of jagged boards to a whitewashed stone room lined with gray file cabinets. Arch was struggling, a knot of dark sweatsuit and long legs, on top of Lucille Boatwright, a wide and clumsy apparition in expensive-looking dark slacks and matching sweater. She was moaning, and her outfit was being ruined by the rolling action she was making on the dusty floor. I speculated wildly. Was Arch's back broken? Would the phone up at Hymnal House be connected? Would Mountain Rescue be willing to send an ambulance for Lucille Boatwright two days in a row?

"Arch! Are you okay? I'm up here! Are you hurt? Don't move if you feel anything's broken!"

"I hate this place, Mom!" he shrieked. Sweat prickled coldly over my body at the relief of hearing him respond. "This whole place is just so old!"

Poor kid. He was embarrassed and trying to cover it up with anger. Making a huge effort, he untangled himself from Lucille. Recriminating questions crowded my brain. Hadn't Lucille heard us in the barn? Why didn't she let us know she was down in the file room? Would the neighbors come running when they heard the commotion?

As I stared helplessly from above, my eyes gradually adjusted to the fact that there was more light in the basement than there was in the barn. A fuzzed stripe of dim grayness from the cloudy afternoon sky filtered in through the small basement room door that Lucille had left open. On the table was a tin-colored, battery-operated camping lamp that looked too new and expensive to belong to the conference center. It cast a metallic glow over the once-white masonry walls and the crowded row of file cabinets. With his knees drawn up, Arch leaned against one of the cabinets and vigorously rubbed his shins. One of the drawers in the adjoining cabinet was open. Next to it, a small stack of drab-colored files lay in a neat pile on a massive oak table. Groaning, Lucille rolled over on her side. She grasped the leg of the table and struggled to get to a sitting position. I knew the woman well enough to know that as soon as she was standing, she would set about scolding Arch. I needed to help him get out of there; I needed to protect him. I scrambled off the stage and out the barn doors. Slipping on wet pine needles, I skidded down the small slope to the basement and through the door of the storage room. The two were still seated on the filthy floor; both looked dazed.

I came in close to Arch's face, which was liberally smeared with dust. His glasses were askew. "Can you move? Are you okay? Oh, honey, talk to me."

"I'm *fine,* Mom. Just leave me alone, okay?"

"My goodness gracious, land sake's," Lucille huffed. Disconcerted, she tried to get control by brushing ineffectually on her filthy green outfit. Her silver hair was disheveled; dust covered her everywhere. The physical surprise of the fall made her seem more elderly, and there was a wild look in her eyes. The Mace. Oh, Lord. I offered her my hand. She took it without compunction and jerkily cranked herself to a standing position, breathing heavily.

Arch groped to straighten his glasses. His fingers slid back over the floor. He picked up the Mace canister and then something small and round, which he examined close to his lenses. "Are you all right, Mrs. Boatwright? Did I get you with the Mace?" He made a gargling noise, and I was afraid he was going to be sick. "Looks like you broke your necklace."

"Arch, please, hon, stand up." Clutching his finds in two tight fists, he again refused my hand and struggled to stand up next to me. His cheek was scraped, and his sweatsuit was covered with thick stripes of dust. But mercifully there was no blood.

"Did the Mace hurt you?" I asked Lucille. I didn't quite have the courage to ask, *What the hell are you doing here?*

"No, but that is dangerous stuff, heaven knows. Now, your son. How is he?"

We both looked at Arch, who avoided our gaze. He was mortified, but not in pain. He'd had a fright, and probably should take some aspirin and go to bed for the rest of the day. Of course, neither of these was likely. I looked up at the broken ceiling. It appeared that the wood had rotted through. This place needed renovation more than the church office, no question about it.

"Lucille? Are you hurt? I am so sorry this happened. I can't believe the conference center doesn't have somebody check these floors before they rot!"

"Well, my dear . . . Honestly! There I was, one minute," she gestured helplessly toward the file cabinet with a shaky finger, "and then he, why, I thought the whole place was caving in—" She swallowed. "I suppose we should notify someone of this. And then be leaving, of course. This is a dangerous place, no situation for a child—"

"Let me see if the police have arrived," I interjected. "If you're sure you're all—"

But she was not all right. She took one step and cried out in pain. Her aristocratic face crumpled. "The spray bottle didn't get me, but my ankle is twisted," she announced stoically.

"Stay with Mrs. Boatwright a few minutes," I quietly ordered Arch.

He nodded sullenly. I vaulted up to the barn. No Sheriff's Department, inside or out. When I arrived back at the storage room, Arch was handing a seated Lucille Boatwright the last of the beads from her broken necklace, which she held in a piece of crumpled paper in her palm. She awkwardly folded the paper and put it into her purse, next to the neat pile of folders in her lap. In my absence, she had managed to smooth her hair and her clothing. Because of her injured ankle, I felt obligated to suggest that I drive her home in the van before finishing what I'd come for. She insisted that we all go back to her house to get cleaned up. I told her I had to stay at the conference center to do some looking around.

"For what?" Lucille demanded in her customary regal manner. "There's nothing here." She gave me a look that said, I am always right and am seldom disobeyed. I glanced at the files in her lap. A faint pink wash of color climbed her cheeks.

"I'll tell you all about the church's filing problems when we get back to my house," she said in crisp defense. "But my ankle is turned. I can drive my car, I simply cannot walk to it. I need to be *brought* to it." She pressed her lips together and with rusty effort added, "Please."

At that moment, Investigator Boyd stuck his head through the door of the storage room. His eyes took in the broken ceiling, the mess on the floor, and our forlorn trio. He swore under his breath.

"What is going on here? You three all right?"

He seemed satisfied by the simultaneous cacophony of assurances he got from us.

"We're going through the conference center," said Boyd. He wagged a finger at me. "We got permission. That's *we,* not *you,* got it?"

"Aye, aye," I said agreeably. "Lucille, please give Arch and me a few moments to make space for you in the van."

Disheartened, Arch packed flashlights into the back of the van while I tried to start the engine.

"Arch, you realize the noises we heard probably came from Mrs. Boatwright opening the file cabinets, don't you?"

"Yeah, yeah." He paused. "You never did tell me what all this stuff was back here," he said with a sulk in his voice. There was the sound of rustling papers. "Gosh, Mom, don't these files belong to Father Olson or the church or something? Y'ever heard of 'Thou shalt not steal?' "

"Chill out, buster." The engine refused to turn over. I turned the key again and pumped the gas. "Officer Boyd told me to look through anything that would help figure out that note, and this is all I have. You want to find Tom, don't you?"

He *tsk*ed over the reluctant whine of the engine. After a moment, he said, "Father Olson always said, 'Y'have to wrap your faith around you, like a blanket.' I think he said somebody famous said that."

The engine almost caught and then died. I sat back, infinitely frustrated, and ran Arch's remark through my brain. I said, "Sounds like Linus. And I don't need a blanket, I need my van to start."

"Yeah, I didn't need a blanket either. So I asked him, if I had faith that the mean kids at school would stop picking on me, would that be like having a blanket? And he said the only behavior you could control is your own."

I twisted the key and the engine turned over. Maybe the only power you could control was your own; those built by the auto industry belonged to fate. Anyway, Olson certainly had been capable of giving the right answers about behavior. At least for others. "Sounds as if Father Olson made you think about faith, anyway."

Arch snorted. "Hate to tell you, Mom, but I think about Jolt cola, and that doesn't mean I have any."

"Arch!"

"Just kidding."

I gave up. The van skidded loudly over the wet gravel by the outside bench where Lucille Boatwright was sitting primly with her files and her purse. I put my head on the steering wheel and murmured to Arch, "Just cover up the stuff back there and help Mrs. Boatwright into the van, will you?"

Arch muttered, "Did you ever hear of Watergate?" But before I could reply he had rustled around and then gingerly jumped out. We drove Lucille to her silver car, which was the pristine, sleek Park Avenue in the church parking lot. She insisted she could drive, even with a sprained left ankle. Because I was anxious to know why she felt she had to ferret through church files on a Sunday afternoon, and why she had parked at the church lot instead of Brio Barn, I acquiesced to her insistence that we come over for a bit. My van chugged and popped behind the Buick to Lucille's Tudor-style home in the Aspen Meadow country club area. Refusing help, she limped ahead of us into the marble entryway, past polished cherry buffets, tables, and a magnificent étagère featuring animal figurines made of ivory. Arch made appropriate cooing noises until Lucille took him by the elbow and led him to the bathroom to get cleaned up. She disappeared herself for a few moments, then reappeared with the green outfit sponged clean of its dust.

"I settled Arch in front of the television with a soft drink," Lucille said with that characteristic lift of her dictatorial chin. "I didn't want him to hear how disorganized that church is." She led me into her kitchen, a vaulted-ceiling, ultraclean space with tall cabinets of glowing light-blue laminate and a brick-colored tile floor. I had a sudden, blinding realization: that Lucille wanted, as I had with Frances Markasian, to protect Arch from hearing what the church was really like.

I waited while Lucille ladled Droste cocoa and sugar into her gilt-edged Royal Crown Derby china teapot, then mixed the two together with cream. Whisking with her free hand, she expertly poured steaming milk into the pot and set it aside. I wondered what she'd done with the files. In her usual highly ordered fashion, she slowly brought to her cherry kitchen table two cups, saucers, and spoons, sugar cubes in a Waterford bowl, cream in a matching pitcher, and finally a small plate with butter shortbread. As she poured the hot chocolate, another, more painful thought assailed me: I realized how much Schulz would have enjoyed chatting with Lucille about English bone china, ivory figurines, Queen Anne cherrywood, and the merits of Scottish shortbread.

"If Arch doesn't like what's on TV, he'll come to see what we're doing," I warned. "I'm sorry you were hurt, Lucille, but isn't it dangerous for you to be down in that file room in Brio Barn? I mean, it's so decrepit!"

She shook her rows of silver curls and gestured for me to drink my hot chocolate. While it's hot, she seemed to be saying. "I was looking in the file storage area because that man Olson was such a *pig.* I mean, Father Pinckney would never—" I made a tiny, impatient throat-clearing noise. Lucille plunged ahead. "You just don't understand, Goldy. Olson was ruining our church. He was taking it in a direction, I mean, with those charismatics—"

"Whoa, Lucille!" I set down my cup. "We were talking about files, and then you made the leap to ruining the church. Please explain how you got from one to the other."

Lucille reached up to smooth the base of her neck, and with a sudden jerking motion of her wide, age-spotted hand, realized her necklace was not there. She sipped her hot chocolate and seemed to be struggling with where to begin her story.

"We used to be a family. Our congregation, you know. Maybe there were things that didn't work, like the annual giving, but we all got along. It was tragic that Father Pinckney had to retire. He loved everybody, you know that's true."

Actually, I knew it had not been true. Pinckney had pastored his little clique; the genuine pastor-to-all had been Ted Olson. But disagreeing on points of view wasn't going to get Lucille's motive for shuffling through file storage on a Sunday afternoon.

Her voice rose. "Now it's like we're two separate churches," she shrilled. "The charismatics pushing against the old traditions, destroying everything with their guitar music and their huggy-kissy, trying to take over everything, even the Altar Guild. You know what we called Olson?" When I shook my head, she said triumphantly, "Father Touchy-Feely. And of course he only cared about them, you know that."

Again, I did not. But lucky for me I'd majored in psychology and could pull out the Carl Rogers routine on command. I said, "You felt he didn't care about you."

She sipped the cocoa, shook her head, and looked at my cup. "Now, drink that while it's hot, Goldy. You know it's not going to stay warm forever."

Lucille was incapable of getting more than two sentences out without giving a command. But I obliged anyway. The chocolate was marvelously hot and creamy. And it smelled wonderful. I set my cup down delicately and commented, "You didn't feel appreciated."

"Why, of course not! With all I did for that church, do you think he appreciated even one thing? Oh! I could tell you about the weddings I've done, about the hours I've spent on the phone! About the money I've raised . . . and all that man Olson ever did was disagree with me. Disagree with me and make it difficult to deal with these frantic families who were trying to get their children married. Not to speak ill of the dead, but you know. We had a terrific argument about the office procedures, then more conflicts about the fund-raising—"

"So you got the files. Why?"

"Well now, just wait. Let me tell you. Where should I start?" She pressed her lips together. "All right, listen. Zelda Preston has been the organist at St. Luke's for many years. You know she trained at Northwestern, just has years and years of training. Not that Olson ever appreciated her. And she has been extremely loyal to St. Luke's. I know personally that she's given thousands of dollars over the years, thousands, much more than that riffraff that Father Olson has brought into our parish could ever appreciate."

I could see where the locus of disagreement over office procedures would have occurred between Olson and Lucille. All the pledges and treasury information were supposed to be completely confidential. But if the police had been able to find out about the money flowing in, then it was not too much of a stretch to think that Lucille Boatwright had known about it long before. I was willing to bet that thrift-shop Zelda didn't share *that* much of her money.

"So when Olson fired Zelda," Lucille fumed, "after all her loyal years of service, picking hymns and practicing with the choir and Lord only knows what all, why, I thought back to that petition. The bishop was supposed to write to us about the guitar music. They promised us from the diocesan office, I don't know how many times, that we would get a reply, that a reply was on the way. We wanted it banned, don't you see? And since Olson—so disorganized!—hadn't told us about the response, whatever he'd received, I thought I'd go look for it—" She stopped and took a sip of chocolate, gesturing with her free hand for me to draw the obvious conclusion. Which was not so obvious. I knew she was lying.

I said, "You were looking for the bishop's letter answering the petition because you thought it would help now? What difference would it make with Ted Olson dead? I should think that you'd be planning his funeral or something."

She fluttered her hand again as if to say, Immaterial, immaterial. "So we won't have to listen to that music anymore, what do you think? How can I plan a funeral if the charismatics are going to come waving their guitars at me? And if we have a letter from the bishop, we'll be able to get off on the right foot with whoever our new man is."

"I just think it's . . . awful early for that."

"Listen," she said suddenly. Her eyes brightened. "I want to talk to you about the luncheon tomorrow. I do want to pay you for all your supplies. I know how expensive food is, believe me, in this day and age! So send me a bill, won't you? Don't tell Zelda or the other women, we don't want them to worry about it."

A kind of muddle descended on my brain, which was probably her intent. I can talk about business or I can talk about nonbusiness. I am incompetent at mingling the two in one conversation. Arch had not rejoined us. I figured he'd found a cable channel. I didn't know what to say about the luncheon. As it stretched on, the silence between Lucille and me became increasingly uncomfortable.

"Tell me," I said with feigned puzzlement, "about the pearl choker raffle."

"Oh! Well, you know, none of the women want to work in the church anymore. They all have *jobs.*" Except poor Agatha, I thought. "We couldn't have our annual Home Tour because we simply could not get enough women to be guides in the homes! Would you loan your luxury home to the church for the day if there weren't enough guides? I mean!"

"But you thought if you got necklaces . . ."

She handed me the platter of shortbread. I declined. "For the past two years, it's been a painless way to make money. This year, of course, we wanted to finish the columbarium. Bob Preston—you know, Zelda's son-in-law—had a friend in the Far East from his oil-dealing days. He found a supplier in Hong Kong. Even with the duty fees, we would make five hundred dollars per necklace, and we would raffle several for those who couldn't buy. We figured, women in the church and in town, here in the club, would want to buy them, or at least buy a single raffle ticket. So we wouldn't have to try to get women to work who simply weren't willing to. You must have received your flyer about this in the mail, Goldy. What's the matter with you?"

"I was trying to plan a wedding," I said flatly.

Lucille Boatwright shivered slightly, as if to say that she would not have ignored a mailing from the church, even if she were planning a dozen nuptials. "This was supposed to take place the week after Easter. Didn't want to do it during Lent, of course, although some women said if they won the pearls, they would want to wear them to church on Easter. Frankly, I could see their point, but Lent is Lent."

"Ah. And why did Father Olson keep the pearls?"

Her facial expression evolved into a sad I-told-you-so. "He thought his house was safe. But *where* in his house? That's what no one seems to know, and of course the police won't allow us to look. Thank God I took out a rider on the church's insurance policy to cover them, or the church would have lost a bundle. We had to pay Bob Preston when those pearls were delivered. *Why* Olson insisted on keeping them, I don't know," she concluded, exasperated.

We looked into each other's eyes for a long moment. I said softly, "You felt he deserved to die."

"Of course not. Don't be ridiculous." But the aristocratic chin quivered.

I sipped my cooled cocoa and reflected. "Lucille, you've never told me a thing about how the church is run—"

"You never asked," she interjected.

"—but now you've asked me into your home and offered to pay for lunch tomorrow, for which I was already going to send a bill to the churchwomen, thank you very much. You've been extremely nice, really, and told me all kinds of things. What I'm trying to figure out is, why are you telling me all this?"

She looked down at her hand, which she was running slowly over the cherry tabletop.

"I think," I persisted, "that you're afraid of something." I thought back: the pearls, the petition, the file room. The files. "You weren't just straightening up at the conference center."

She looked away from me and out into her living room. At her Queen Anne wing chairs with their hieratic floral pattern on polished cotton. At her striped sofa in the same muted colors. At the well-polished Stieffel lamp next to the arrangement of dried eucalyptus in a ginger jar. At her money, her familiar order, her security.

With dawning clarity, I remembered Saturday morning, right before my wedding was supposed to begin, the new organist playing the triumphant opening bars of Jeremiah Clarke's *Trumpet Voluntary.* And then

Zelda's words: *I am a professional.* What would a professional most fear? Being maligned as a professional. Not being able to be a professional anymore.

I said gently, "You were looking for some letter from the bishop, because you think Zelda wants it. Isn't that right? You think she needs it, for some reason." Lucille rubbed her fingers delicately against the side of her china cup and remained stubbornly mute. "You think Zelda wanted the bishop's letter from Olson, so that she could save face. Find a job someplace else, maybe." A tear was rolling slowly down one of Lucille's elegant, powdered cheeks. "Lucille. You think Zelda killed him. Don't you?"

15

She sniffed and stood up. "Absolutely not. How can you say such a thing? I think it's time for you to go."

"You have to call the police. Right now, from here. If Zelda has Tom Schulz—" I couldn't finish. "Where was she yesterday morning?"

Lucille forced a smile. "I don't know! Why do you keep insisting?" She moved toward the kitchen door. "I am so glad your son is feeling better. I'll just go call him down from upstairs. The churchwomen have a funeral to plan, and I'm due at a meeting at five o'clock."

She minced neatly out of the room, all of her control reasserted by the threat of my urgent desire to extract information. I watched her wide retreating body, her neat silver curls shining like a metallic shield. Dammit to hell.

In the corner of her kitchen I spotted a light-blue wall telephone, almost invisible because of its exact color match to the cabinets. I grabbed it and dialed 911. Identifying myself, I said I needed to leave an emergency message for Boyd, that I had found out some things about the Olson murder and he should question Zelda Preston. I swallowed and added that Zelda was strong, a swimmer, that she might have Tom Schulz. When I hung up and turned around, Lucille Boatwright was standing at the door of the kitchen with her arm around Arch's shoulders.

"We're just getting to be the best of friends," she said to me, presumably of her relationship with my son.

Arch said, "Huh?"

I said, "I'm sorry. We need to go."

"Arch," said Lucille, "I just need to talk to your mother for another moment."

Arch gave me a questioning look. "You want me to go to the van, or back up to the TV room? Is this about the church again? I guess you want me to just go."

I said evenly, "Stay where you are."

Lucille's cheeks colored. She said fiercely, "The problem is that she won't tell me where she was yesterday morning. If she would just tell me. That's all I ask."

"Does Zelda live near here?"

Lucille opened her mouth to talk, but nothing came out—first time I'd ever seen that happen. Arch sighed deeply, the same sigh he always gave when faced with an interminable number of boring errands. "Mom," he begged, "can't we go home? Nobody knows where we are, and somebody might have called, and Julian will get worried—"

I said, "Yes, soon. Where does Zelda live?"

"I'm sorry." Lucille faltered. "I should have told you yesterday, or the police, or something." She caught hold of herself and wagged a finger. "You mustn't frighten her." When I made an impatient noise, she went on, "A one-story white brick on Golf Course Lane. Less than two blocks away, on the left side of the street. You know she might be swimming. Her back is acting up severely, and she thought it might help to do some extra laps."

I didn't answer. We were walking hurriedly through the marble entryway on the way to the van. Arch was trotting ahead of me. Since he was dedicatedly unathletic, this was a sure sign of his desperation to leave. I felt the need to keep a semblance of relationship with Lucille, in case Zelda knew nothing of Olson's death and Tom's disappearance. There wasn't a soul in the church who knew more about its inner workings and dark secrets than the elegant woman escorting me out of her house. And after all, she *had* apologized.

"Is it possible she might have been at the doctor yesterday? Seeing about the back pains?" I asked.

"We don't talk about it," Lucille said without looking at me. She put her hand to her throat again. No necklace. "When you get to be our age, it's too depressing to discuss your aches and pains and those of your peers. It would be all that we talked about. Not that you would be interested in something like that, of course. People don't want to hear about getting old."

We came out her gleaming front door and stood on the stone steps. The April afternoon air had gone from chilly to intensely cold. I said, "But I care—"

She waved this away. "And when you don't have someone to look out for you, you just have to do it yourself. Or do as Zelda and I do, take care of each other. Ted Olson," she added fiercely, "did not give a tinker's *damn* about us. In fact, I think he would have been glad to see us gone."

"Oh, Lucille, you can't be serious."

"My dear, I am entirely serious."

This outburst of personal bitterness meant either Lucille was letting her guard down or pretending to do so in a very convincing manner. In spite of my anger over her refusal to help and my desire to be out of there, I felt an intense pang of sympathy for her. I knew well what it meant to be unnoticed by a man whose appreciation and affection you craved. I had wasted seven years trying to get from The Jerk what he was incapable of giving to any human being. I reached out for the papery skin of Lucille's forearm. Maybe I could act convincing, too.

I said, "I know about taking care of myself; I've done it for almost a decade." Lucille shrugged my hand away; we kept walking. "If Zelda's in a lot of pain," I ventured, "why didn't she . . . talk to Olson, even if she didn't like him? I mean, after all I've been hearing lately, things like that Sunday School teacher, and then Roger Bampton—"

Lucille's sudden laughter was crude and shockingly hoarse. "What hogwash! What utter and complete nonsense! You don't honestly believe that, do you, Goldy? If you do, you're even less intelligent than I thought."

We had reached the door of my van. I let Lucille's opinion of my IQ pass. "So you don't believe Roger recovered from leukemia?" I asked with a brow I hoped was innocently furrowed. Arch, who was already sitting in the front seat, gestured impatiently for me to come on.

"The whole thing was a lie!" Lucille faced me, her ice-blue eyes blazing with indignation. Her wrinkled hands made a dismissive gesture. "A complete fabrication! Roger Bampton is a drunk. Going in to see a doctor because he felt bad? I ask you. He probably thought chemotherapy was like sticking a needle full of Jack Daniels into one of his arteries. Of course, Father *Pinckney* tried to get Roger into alcohol rehabilitation, but no one remembers that."

"You remember."

Her laugh this time was much lower, kind of self-mocking. "One of the few who does, my dear. Not that it matters." She hesitated, then returned the affection of my gesture, pressing her fingers into my arm. Soft green cashmere brushed my skin. "Zelda is my dear friend," she said earnestly. "You mustn't upset her. You mustn't let the police frighten her. She is easily hurt—you know what she went through when her son died. Surely you know that she hasn't dealt well with the way Olson treated her."

I wanted to hug her, but remembered in time her objection to displays of affection. Besides, what I wanted most was to be away from this perfect Tudor house with its perfect rooms and perfect landscaped garden. "Look, Lucille. Probably this will turn out to be nothing. When the bishop gets back, maybe his office will find a copy of the letter in his files, or maybe they'll find out he never wrote to Olson after all." Although I hoped not. Oh, God, I wanted Tom Schulz to be over at Zelda's house, I wanted Zelda to have killed Olson in a fit of passion, I wanted this all to be over.

"Will you call me?" Lucille pleaded earnestly when I had climbed into the van and rolled down the window.

"I thought you had a meeting." When she gave me a blank look, I added, "Do you have an answering machine?"

"Of course not. I hate those infernal things." Her authoritarian chin wobbled ominously. "Don't disrupt Zelda," she warned with the same commanding tone and finger she had used during the prewedding instructions. She took a quick step in front of my van. "And call me as soon as you know anything. Promise."

"Yes, Lucille!" I revved the engine and cursed her silently for making me feel like a dutiful twelve-year-old daughter. "Thanks for the cocoa." When she did not move, I threw the gearshift into reverse and backed out of her driveway, miraculously avoiding the laddered plantings of shrubbery and aspens.

"Doesn't have an answering machine!" Arch cried when I paused to read a street sign. "Man! She doesn't have cable! She doesn't have remote control! Not to mention that she doesn't have any video games! Where has that woman been for the last fifty years? Brother!"

I finally figured out how to get to Zelda Preston's one-story white brick house on Golf Course Lane. On the way, I reflected that ecclesiastically as well as technologically, Lucille and Zelda both would have preferred to turn back the clock.

"Man, Mom." Arch was still disgusted. "I don't know why you stay at the church. If I went to a church like that and everybody was mean, I'd leave."

I groaned. "It's my family, hon. And not everybody is mean."

Two police cars already had arrived in front of Zelda Preston's home. Not more than fifteen minutes had passed since I'd called from Lucille's. When they were looking for a fellow officer, they sure could move quickly. No red and blue lights flashed; I had heard no siren. I remembered Tom's words: *When you're trying to catch somebody, you don't announce your arrival.* I was stopped by a deputy who recognized me.

"They're securing the perimeter."

"Please let me go with them," I begged. "I have to see if Tom is in there."

His face turned from impassive to stony. "There isn't a chance in hell you're getting any closer to that house than you already are."

Cops.

At that moment a very confused-looking Zelda Preston, wearing what looked like a bathrobe, appeared at the door. She squinted at the officers on her steps, at the police cars, and at my van stopped on the grass by her driveway. Her front door immediately opened as she let the officers in. My heart sank. If she'd had Tom inside, she surely would have at least put up some kind of resistance.

Ten minutes later, Boyd and Armstrong came out together. Boyd hoisted his rotund self up the driveway while Armstrong, long and lanky, strode alongside. I glanced at the sky, now turned darkly ominous with a promise of evening snow. Whether my teeth were chattering from the cold or nervousness at the message I was about to receive, I did not know. As if to prepare me, Boyd shook his head. I crossed my arms and sagged against the van.

"This Preston woman is beside herself," he began. "She wants us to search through her house so that she'll be above suspicion. Her words. We did a quick look-see. No Schulz. Whatever made you think—"

"Now don't start," I warned, my voice shaking. "You told me to call you and I did. Where was she yesterday?"

Towering above us, Armstrong cleared his throat and answered for Boyd. "Interviewing for the organist's position at the Catholic church. Although she doesn't want the people at your place to know."

My eyelids felt like sandpaper. My brain had turned to the consistency of dryer lint.

"Look, Goldy," said Boyd. His tone was compassionate but undeniably impatient. "I told you we'd keep you informed. I've asked you questions about that church of yours, sure. But there's a difference between your answering questions and trying to do our job for us, okay? This is the second time today I've responded to a frantic call from you about where you think Schulz is."

"Haven't you found *anything*?" I despised the pleading in my voice, but wanted to hear any shred of news or hope.

Boyd bit on each word. "I can't *find* anything when I'm running around on your wild-goose chases!" He shook his head. "I'll call you."

As I gunned the van and rolled it past Zelda's house, Arch muttered, "Man! Was that guy grouchy or what?"

"They're just trying to find Tom, hon, you know that."

But lack of progress brought depression. Or perhaps it was the end of the day, the hardest time to be reminded of separation from someone you love. To the west, there was no fiery sunset, only a further darkening of the sky caused by the sun slipping past the clouds and behind the mountains. The temperature had dropped at least fifteen degrees. As we rounded Aspen Meadow Lake on our way home, large, wet snowflakes powdered my windshield. In front of the van, the wind whirled the flakes into thick tornadoes of white. Spring snow: good for the crops, or so they were always telling us on the radio. But bad for someone kidnapped, who might be in an unfamiliar and unheated place. When I finally pulled the van in front of the house, it felt as if all the energy had drained out of my body.

"Come on, Mom," said Arch. "Cheer up." He pointed at the Jaguar parked at a precarious angle by the sidewalk. "Look, Marla's here."

And indeed she was, fretting around in the kitchen, setting the table and standing back to admire the enormous basket arrangement of flowers she had brought with her. Oblivious of her, Julian pinched and pressed pizza dough into springform pans. When we came through the door, the two of them stared at our disconsolate faces.

"Goldy?" Julian's eyes were wide. "Any news?"

I shook my head grimly. I didn't trust my voice.

"Dinner is Mexican Pizza," he announced, turning away so I couldn't see the despair on his face. "Fifteen minutes."

I sat heavily in one of my kitchen chairs. "Tell me how you're doing," I said to Julian. "I'm getting tired of always focusing on my own crises."

He looked up from his work. "Me?" He had not shaved; the circles under his eyes made him look haggard. The college admissions. He was supposed to hear this week, and he hadn't ventilated any of his worry. He shrugged and wiped his hands on the white apron he was wearing over a much-washed black sweatshirt that had frayed at the sleeves. His baggy black cotton pants had lost their knee patch. It was one of Julian's scrounged outfits from the Aspen Meadow secondhand store. He carefully sloshed picante sauce over the dough in the pans. In his typical offhand manner, he said, "Don't worry about me."

"But I do," I said, and my voice choked. I felt a sob welling up, the first one in twenty-four hours. "I am worried about you," I cried. Involuntary tears came in earnest.

"Come on, Goldy," commanded Marla. "Out of the kitchen. Into the living room. Arch, do you know what sherry is?"

"It's from Spain, right? Comes in a bottle in a burlap bag? Mom uses it for cooking."

"Yeah well, right now Mom's going to use it for her psyche. Could you find it and bring it out to the living room with two small glasses? Please? And Julian," Marla added, "keep going with that pizza. I'll bet she hasn't had food in a while, either."

Julian nodded grimly as he sprinkled handfuls of cheddar cheese on his creation. Out in the living room, Marla sat me on the couch, eased down on the adjoining cushion, and pulled out a tissue from one of her pockets.

"Do you need a hug?" she asked when the outburst of crying was over and I was reduced to sniffles. She waved a hand at the bottle of Dry Sack that Arch had brought out. "Or do you just need sherry?"

"Both."

She obliged. The sherry warmed my throat. Arch, who had been watching me nervously from the hearth, set about constructing a complex fire of aspen, pine, and Russian olive logs.

I said to Marla, "Tell me why all this is happening."

She gazed at the first flames licking the fireplace wood. "How about, because the church is a strange place?"

"Our church in particular, or the church in general?"

She turned her mouth down at the corners. "Aw, go for the broad view. Big hospital for sinners. Only some people stay sick." She tipped up her glass to finish her sherry.

"But you knew Father Olson," I insisted. My voice had a watery, hiccuping tone from crying. "I mean, you went out with him a couple of times, didn't you? Was he really so bad? Why would someone hate him that much? I mean, so he had charismatic churchmanship. So what? Just

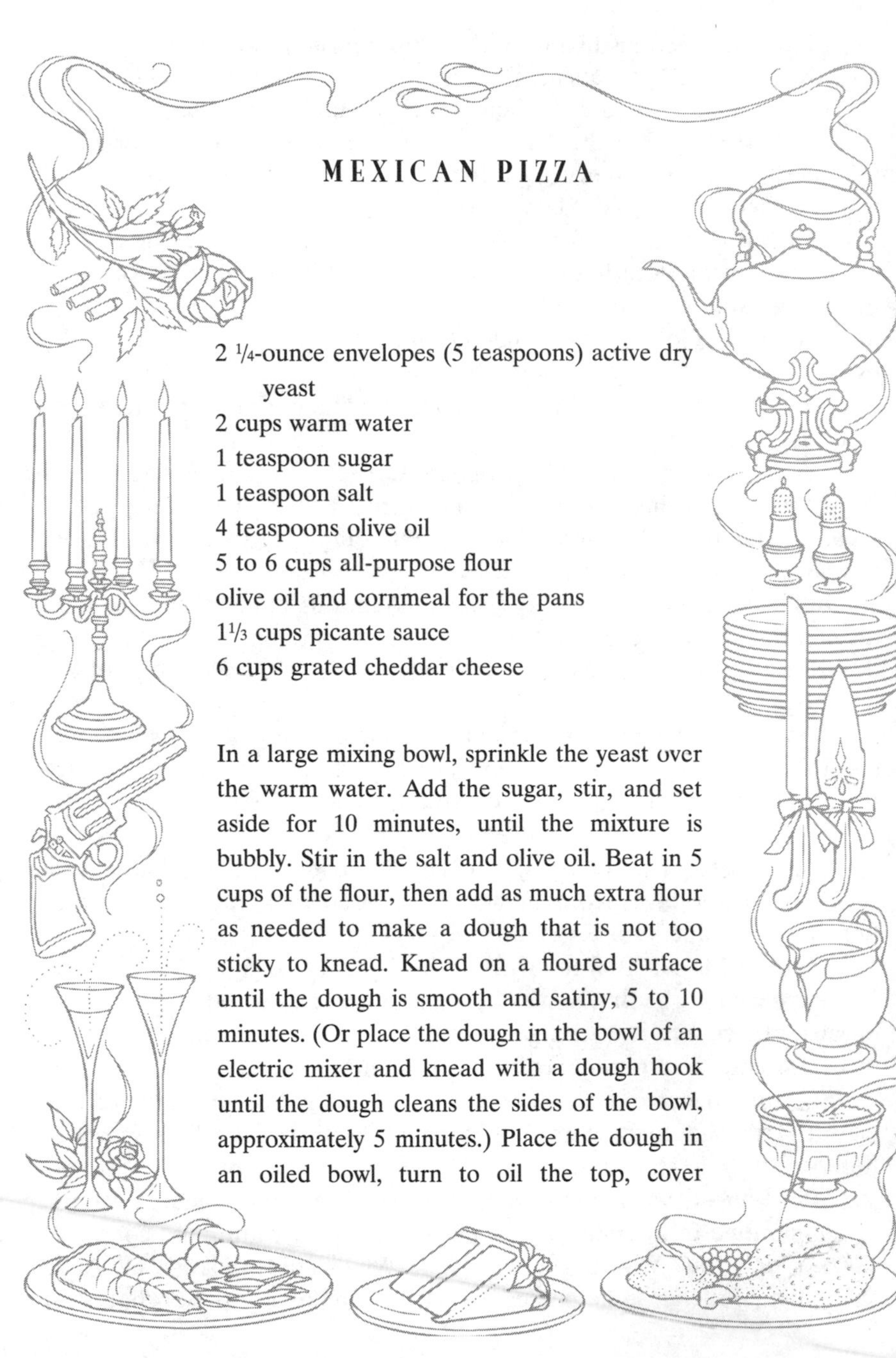

MEXICAN PIZZA

2 ¼-ounce envelopes (5 teaspoons) active dry yeast
2 cups warm water
1 teaspoon sugar
1 teaspoon salt
4 teaspoons olive oil
5 to 6 cups all-purpose flour
olive oil and cornmeal for the pans
1⅓ cups picante sauce
6 cups grated cheddar cheese

In a large mixing bowl, sprinkle the yeast over the warm water. Add the sugar, stir, and set aside for 10 minutes, until the mixture is bubbly. Stir in the salt and olive oil. Beat in 5 cups of the flour, then add as much extra flour as needed to make a dough that is not too sticky to knead. Knead on a floured surface until the dough is smooth and satiny, 5 to 10 minutes. (Or place the dough in the bowl of an electric mixer and knead with a dough hook until the dough cleans the sides of the bowl, approximately 5 minutes.) Place the dough in an oiled bowl, turn to oil the top, cover

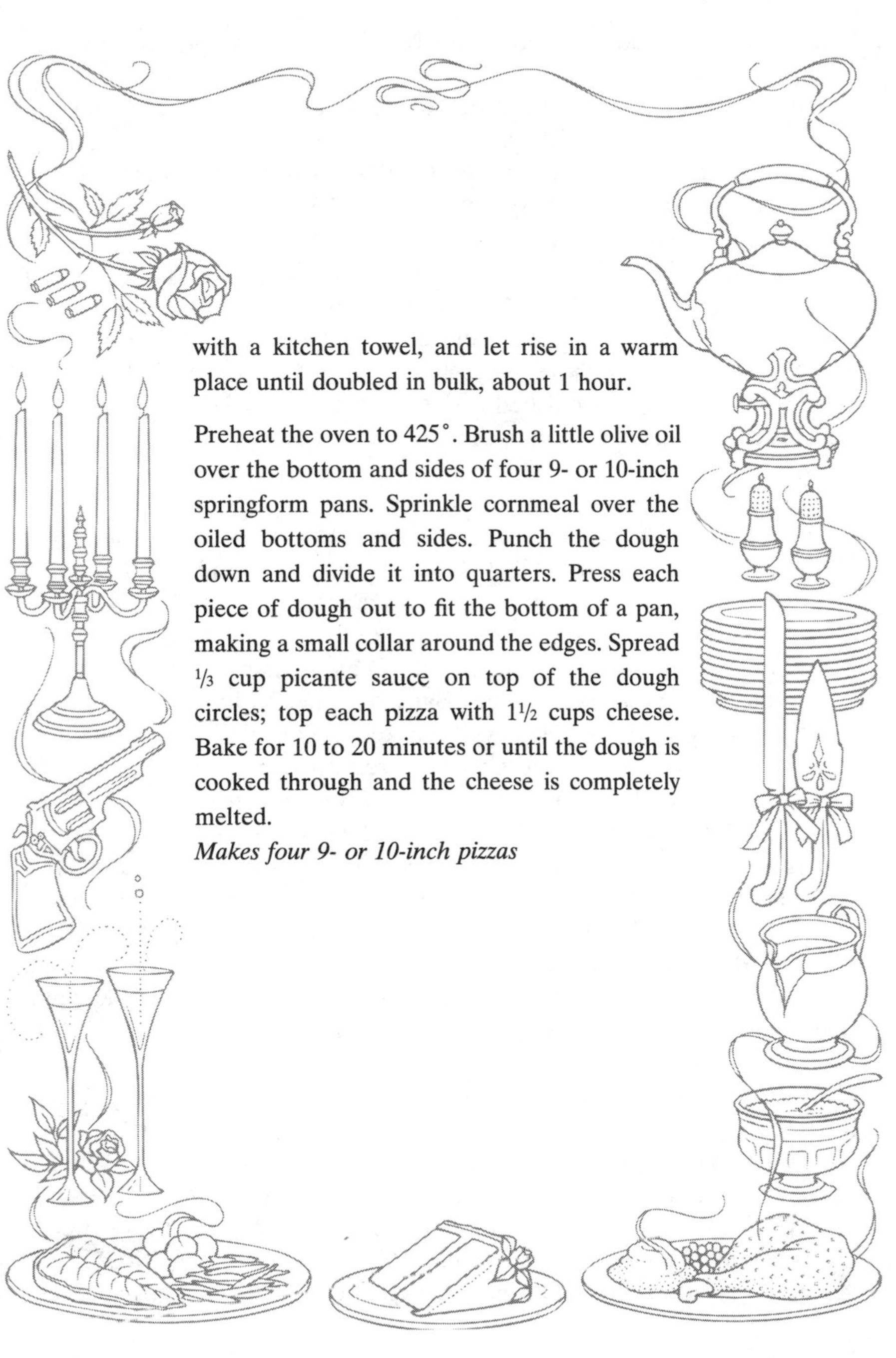

with a kitchen towel, and let rise in a warm place until doubled in bulk, about 1 hour.

Preheat the oven to 425°. Brush a little olive oil over the bottom and sides of four 9- or 10-inch springform pans. Sprinkle cornmeal over the oiled bottoms and sides. Punch the dough down and divide it into quarters. Press each piece of dough out to fit the bottom of a pan, making a small collar around the edges. Spread 1/3 cup picante sauce on top of the dough circles; top each pizza with 1 1/2 cups cheese. Bake for 10 to 20 minutes or until the dough is cooked through and the cheese is completely melted.

Makes four 9- or 10-inch pizzas

because someone doesn't agree with you doesn't mean you have to kill him."

Marla's expression was full of sadness and affection. "Depends on how much they disagree with you, I guess." She smiled and looked at her Rolex. "Fifteen minutes! Come on, Goldy, it'll make you feel better to eat." As if on cue, Julian swept into the living room carrying a tray with plates and steaming pizzas.

After she'd had a few mouthfuls and made the appropriate noises of praise, Marla said reflectively, "You know, I didn't really date Ted Olson. I was single, he was single, we went out for dinner a couple of times. I always thought he was more interested in my net worth than my body or soul." She giggled and finished a last bite of pizza. "Not necessarily in that order. Besides, I told you, the guy was squirrelly."

Arch tore a piece of crust from his mouth with sudden interest. "You don't mean, like a *rodent,* do you?"

"Of course not," said Marla as she smilingly accepted a second large piece of pizza from Julian. "This is my last piece, I promise." She took a dainty bite. "I mean, he'd say, 'Don't leave a message on the church voice mail or the women will say we're having an affair.' What was the matter with that, I wanted to know? Give the religious man an air of mystery. Which he got anyway, once Roger Bampton opened his big mouth."

"Squirrelly in what other ways?" I asked. I bit into the pizza and felt a shiver of delight: Hot melted cheese oozed around spicy picante sauce and a light, chewy homemade crust. Julian was an artist.

"Well," Marla went on, "when I ran the jewelry raffle last year, we had the worst ruckus over who was going to keep the gold chains. You know Lucille always insists on getting a separate insurance rider, and I have a safe in my house. Either of those would have been better than letting Ted Olson keep them out at his unsecured place in the boonies. But no. He insisted on being the caretaker for the chains, said he could outwit any thief, and he had to take responsibility for something of that value."

I stopped eating and leaned toward her. "Do you know where he kept them?"

"What are you looking at me like that for? I don't know. When I drove out there to get them, he just gave me that chipmunky look—sorry—and handed me a package. It was a gift-wrapped box, mind you, but the box was one that said, Church Frankincense. When I opened it, he said, 'Sorry, no myrrh today.' Then he laughed like he was some kind of biblical jokester and should go on *Jeopardy.* I mean, the guy had an attitude." With that, she smiled broadly at Julian and took another slice of pizza.

"He was a good confirmation teacher," said Arch.

"He was weird," said Julian.

After Marla left and Arch reluctantly had finished his homework, while Julian was still banging around cleaning up the kitchen—at his insistence—I took my second shower of the day and resolved to get some sleep. I had been so tired when we finished dinner that twice I had felt myself sway forward with my eyes closed. The Sheriff's Department would call if anything developed. As my head touched the pillow, I belatedly remembered my promise to call Lucille Boatwright. Undoubtedly Zelda had already done so, and with much embellishment told of the policemen's untimely arrival at her door. I wondered if she had also mentioned the interview at the Catholic church.

I closed my eyes and tried to sleep. I visualized the ocean on a calm day. I saw Arch as a baby, laughing. I imagined seeing Tom Schulz again, what I would say, how I would hold him and not let go. I sent him a silent message to hang on.

All for nothing: Wakefulness pierced every thought. The dishwasher finished its cycle. The distant whine from Julian's radio subsided. Snow whisked against the house. When I felt panic rise in my chest, I opened a window, inhaled the chilly, moist air, and exhaled steam. Since traffic through town was sparse, the rush of swollen Cottonwood Creek was unusually loud. I closed the window and sat down on the bed. Sleep would be impossible.

I stared at the wall. The one utterly predictable aspect of being a caterer is that you always have cooking to do. The work never ends unless you go out of town. With a noisy sigh, I trundled down to the kitchen to get a start on preparing for the women's luncheon.

I fixed myself an espresso and pulled out the pile of Tom's recipes. Immediately, I felt better, as if his presence emanated from the three-by-five cards. At church, Lucille had requested a seafood dish. Since it was Lent, she'd said. I had nodded to her arched eyebrow and question, I don't suppose you have any shrimp? I had told her, Oh sure. So much for fasting.

Tom's collection yielded a shrimp and pasta concoction that would ideally suit the churchwomen. With a cheese-based sauce, it would hold well in a chafing dish; the deep green of peas beside the pink of shrimp would make it look beautiful; and if I used wagon wheel-shaped pasta instead of spaghetti, nothing would dribble embarrassingly down anyone's chin. Since cooked shrimp demand last-minute preparation, I set the recipe on the counter and turned with zest to the dessert section.

I flipped through Tom's cards for apple cheese tart and Chocolate Truffle Cheesecake. Ladies' luncheons do better with cookies for dessert, I'd discovered long ago, for a couple of reasons. The dieters can take only a few and not feel cheated. Unlike cake, where the public taking of more than one piece is viewed as piggish, the nondieters can have numerous cookies in unobtrusive fashion. I would offer two types, I figured, one with chocolate and one without. For the chocolatey ones, I decided on Canterbury Jumbles, a chocolate-chip-and-nut affair that had such a wonderful Anglican name the women would feel duty-bound to eat them. I mixed up that batter, put it in the cooler, and then flipped through Tom's recipes until I came to Lemon Butter Wafers. On the side of the card, Tom had written, *B. - Dinner - Captain.*

There was that *B.* again. *B.* for what? *B. - Read - Judas.* In the dinner context, it looked less like someone's name. Before? British? Bring? Big? I had no idea.

In any event, the Lemon Butter Wafers called for ingredients I had on hand, so I softened unsalted butter and wielded my zester over plump lemons. A fine mist of fragrant oil from the golden citrus fruit sprayed my face. I closed the door to the kitchen so as not to wake Arch and Julian, then pulverized almonds in a small food processor and carefully mixed the ingredients together. I did a trial batch: The first hot cookie was buttery, crunchy, and as lemony as a meringue pie. It melted in my mouth. I set the rest of the batter in to chill and mentally thanked Tom for his culinary expertise. The churchwomen would think their dessert was sent from heaven.

It was two o'clock. I told myself I wasn't going to sleep; I was just going to rest on the living room couch. Within a moment of stretching out on the uncomfortable cushions, I fell into slumber like tumbling on ice: hard. When I awoke before dawn, my mind was clogged with an undispersed nightmare, this one of an onrushing pig. Or was it a boar?

Do not cast your pearls before swine . . .

Good Lord. I vaulted up painfully: five o'clock. At this time of year, that meant over an hour until daylight. I rubbed the crick in my neck and

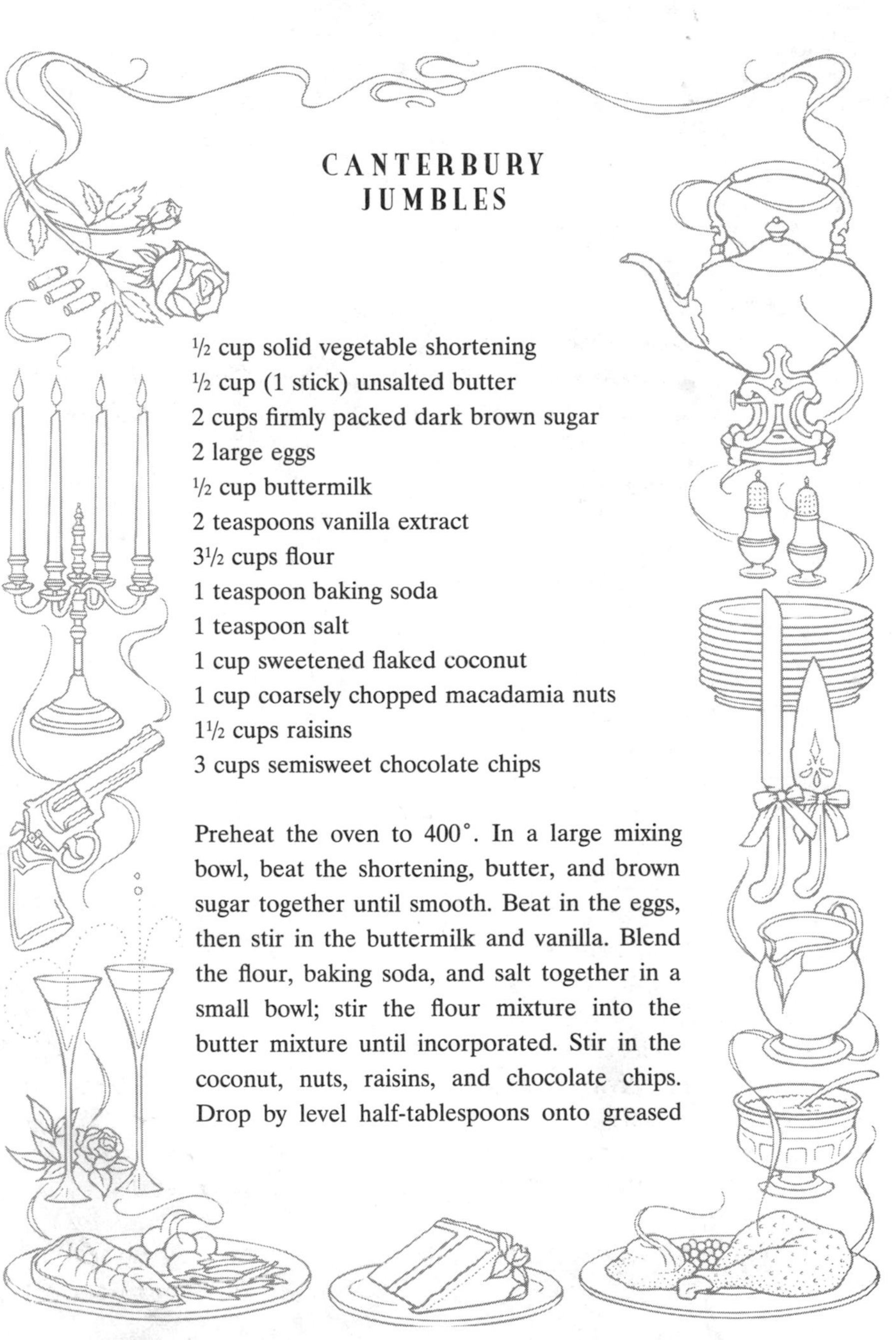

CANTERBURY JUMBLES

½ cup solid vegetable shortening
½ cup (1 stick) unsalted butter
2 cups firmly packed dark brown sugar
2 large eggs
½ cup buttermilk
2 teaspoons vanilla extract
3½ cups flour
1 teaspoon baking soda
1 teaspoon salt
1 cup sweetened flaked coconut
1 cup coarsely chopped macadamia nuts
1½ cups raisins
3 cups semisweet chocolate chips

Preheat the oven to 400°. In a large mixing bowl, beat the shortening, butter, and brown sugar together until smooth. Beat in the eggs, then stir in the buttermilk and vanilla. Blend the flour, baking soda, and salt together in a small bowl; stir the flour mixture into the butter mixture until incorporated. Stir in the coconut, nuts, raisins, and chocolate chips. Drop by level half-tablespoons onto greased

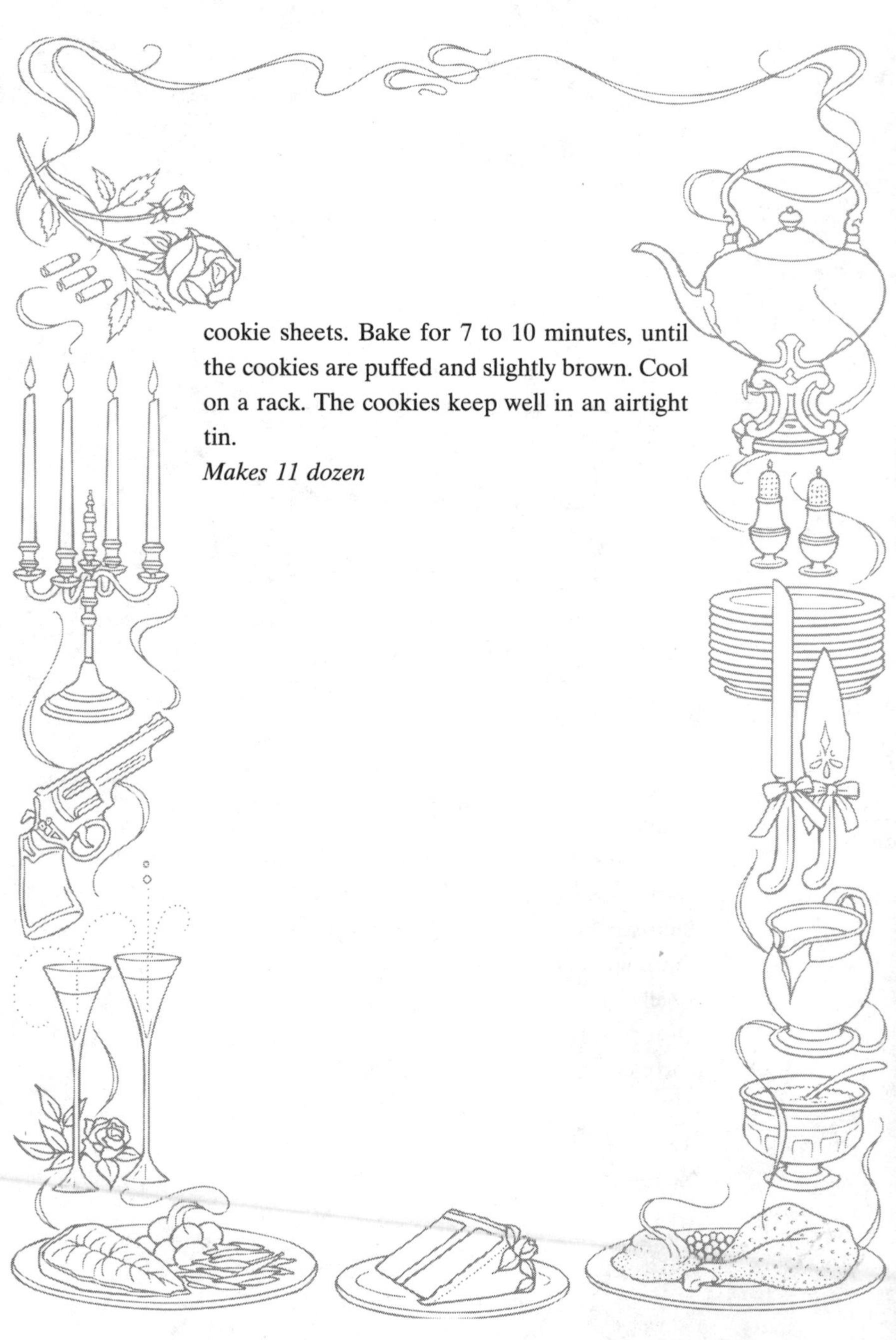

cookie sheets. Bake for 7 to 10 minutes, until the cookies are puffed and slightly brown. Cool on a rack. The cookies keep well in an airtight tin.

Makes 11 dozen

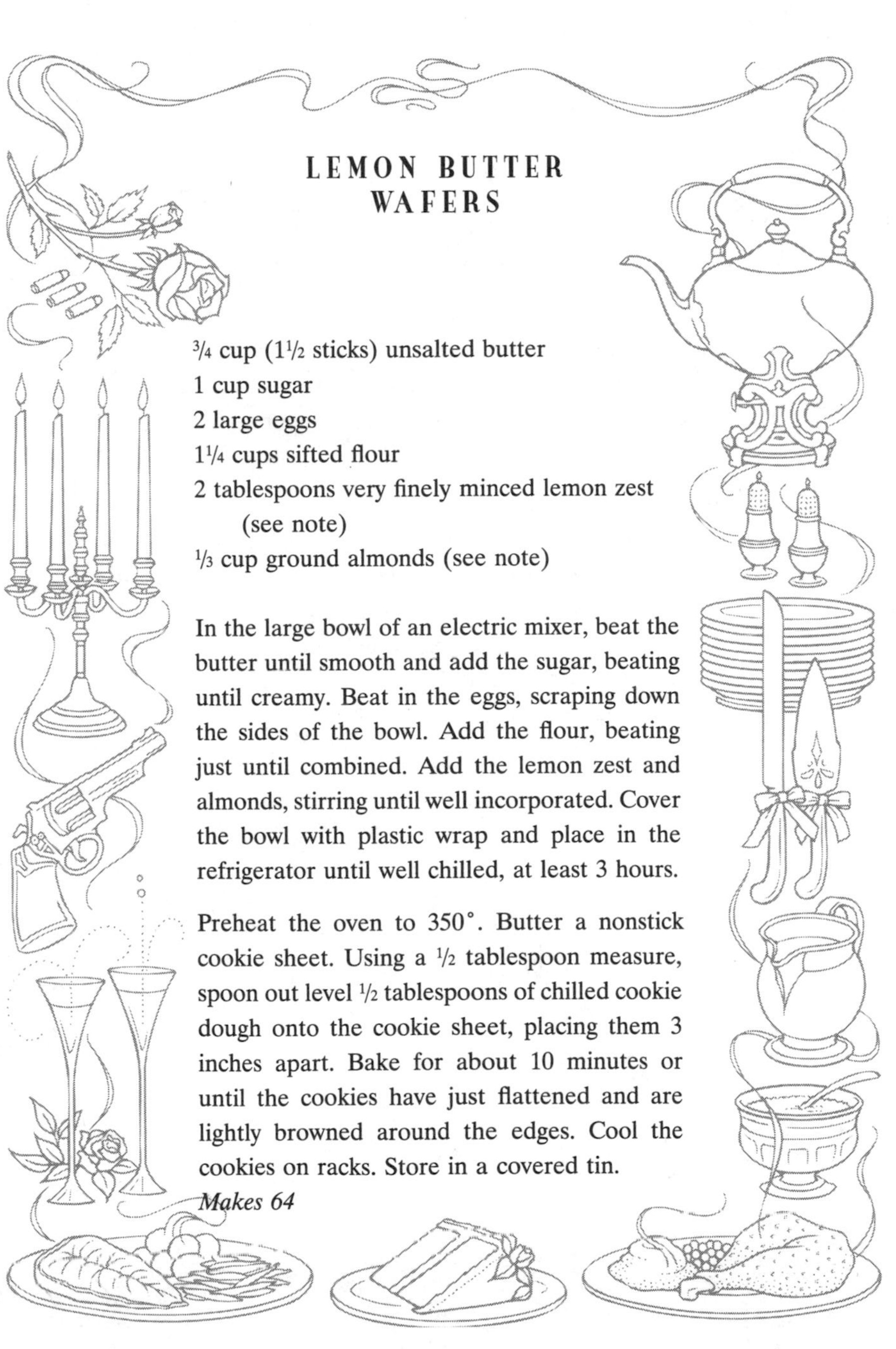

LEMON BUTTER WAFERS

¾ cup (1½ sticks) unsalted butter
1 cup sugar
2 large eggs
1¼ cups sifted flour
2 tablespoons very finely minced lemon zest (see note)
⅓ cup ground almonds (see note)

In the large bowl of an electric mixer, beat the butter until smooth and add the sugar, beating until creamy. Beat in the eggs, scraping down the sides of the bowl. Add the flour, beating just until combined. Add the lemon zest and almonds, stirring until well incorporated. Cover the bowl with plastic wrap and place in the refrigerator until well chilled, at least 3 hours.

Preheat the oven to 350°. Butter a nonstick cookie sheet. Using a ½ tablespoon measure, spoon out level ½ tablespoons of chilled cookie dough onto the cookie sheet, placing them 3 inches apart. Bake for about 10 minutes or until the cookies have just flattened and are lightly browned around the edges. Cool the cookies on racks. Store in a covered tin.

Makes 64

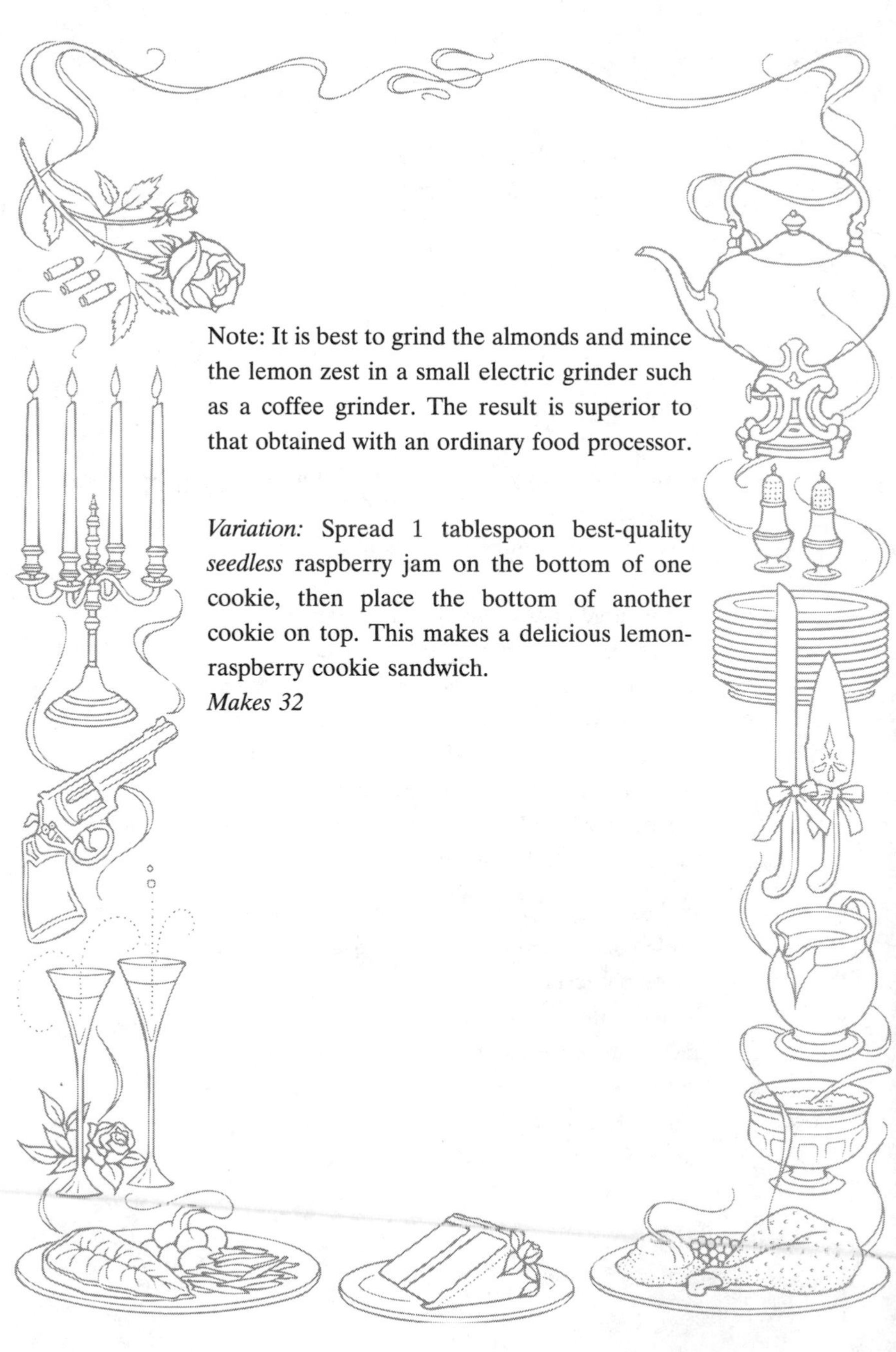

Note: It is best to grind the almonds and mince the lemon zest in a small electric grinder such as a coffee grinder. The result is superior to that obtained with an ordinary food processor.

Variation: Spread 1 tablespoon best-quality *seedless* raspberry jam on the bottom of one cookie, then place the bottom of another cookie on top. This makes a delicious lemon-raspberry cookie sandwich.

Makes 32

stared out the picture window. Beyond the porch, the snow had stopped and the moon shone brightly over a predawn landscape of fluorescent gray. I slipped to the hall closet and donned a ski jacket and snow boots.

I had to go back out to Olson's.

16

I fed Scout, who mewed happily when he saw he was having an early breakfast, and left a note for the boys: *Gone to Father Olson's house; back by eight.* No doubt when I got there the police ribbon would still be up. Whether this would be good or bad was an unknown. After all, I'd already crossed the one at the church office. I decided it would be good if no policeman was stationed at Olson's to make sure the line wasn't crossed; bad if someone was and I was rebuffed. I'd say to Boyd, I was just looking for pearls. He'd say, Oh, yeah? Try a jewelry store. I shooed away this thought and quickly filled my espresso machine with water and coffee. While it was heating I rummaged through the hall closet and found one of the flashlights Arch and I had taken to the conference center. When the dark liquid twined into my insulated mug, the clock said 5:15.

If I could just find the pearls, perhaps in some biblically related hiding place, then maybe with them, I'd find whatever it was the killer was looking for. I remembered what I'd said to Boyd: *Olson was such a packrat, you'd have to know exactly where to look to find something.* Now I had an idea of where to look. The church office had been trashed, perhaps when someone was searching for the pearls, or something unknown. *Figure the motive and you've got the perp,* Tom was fond of saying. I sipped the rich espresso and decided my best bet would be to drive around the way that the intruder had, via the dirt road that led to Upper Cottonwood Creek and the back entrance to Olson's house. Four-wheel-drive was a must, especially since I'd had such trouble starting my own van yesterday. I took the keys to Julian's vehicle, a Range Rover inherited from our wealthy former employers. *Sorry to take your car,* I hastily penned, *I promise I'll be back!* And with that I picked up my coffee and quietly slipped out.

Aspen Meadow in the so-called spring is about as inviting as a snow cave, especially when daily television images of azaleas and cherry blossoms remind us of April in the rest of the world. The Rover's steering wheel was frigid under my grasp; the engine barked its reluctance. I had always harbored a vague notion that T. S. Eliot lived in the high country when he wrote that April was the cruelest month. This dark morning certainly did not promise kind weather.

The Rover growled down my street in first gear, past the Habitat for Humanity construction site. Above the foundation, ice-covered two-by-fours loomed ominously in the bright moonlight. No red flag was visible; I wondered if construction had indeed been blocked. My attention was immediately drawn back by the Rover tires skidding through a stop sign; treacherous black ice glazed the pavement. Once I had edged out on Main Street, the Rover's headlights picked out stalactite icicles along the storefronts. The bank thermometer said 18°. Instead of allowing the morning's unbearable chill to penetrate my bones, I imagined the cocoon of warmth Tom's body had made nestling around mine. I wondered what the churchwomen would have said about the fact that Tom Schulz and I had been sleeping together in the five months since we'd become engaged. Lucky for me, I didn't give a hoot about ecclesiastical opinion.

A fox scurried under a split rail fence just before the turnoff for Olson's place. Half a mile later, I turned left on the dirt road that led across a bridge, then bumped over ruts in a wide arc to the other side of Cottonwood Creek. I parked between ponderosa pines as tall and ominous as frozen giants. When I jumped from the Rover, my breath made clouds of vapor in the moonlight. I fumbled with the flashlight and cursed the cold. When I finally could see where I was going, I headed for the creek bank. My boots crunched over the new snow. Every now and then, they cracked through mud puddles thinly covered with ice.

I was going into Olson's house when no one was there, I told myself firmly, because Boyd had ordered me to let the police do their job. In other words, I wasn't supposed to call them in every time I had a hunch. Besides, they had already gone through Olson's house. What I was looking for, and it really was a wild hunch, were the missing chokers, with *something,* in an unusual hiding place, a place where a squirrelly person who laughingly gave the head of the raffle committee gold chains gift-wrapped in a frankincense box would stow them. There were references to pearls in the Bible: Don't throw them before swine, a merchant who finds a pearl of great value and sells all he has to obtain it. There were probably others, I just couldn't think of what they were. I had already looked up Judas: He'd only dealt in silver coins.

I tried to focus on what Tom would think about this crazy excursion. Overhead, the wind swished through the snow-covered trees and showered my head with fine, cold flakes. *I always look for what's out of place, what's there that shouldn't be there, what's not there as well as what's there,* I could hear Tom say. I stepped over a snow-covered log and tried to visualize Olson's home as I'd seen it during the vestry dinner: the Stickley couch, wood floors, worn Kirman rugs, shelves of books, religious artifacts and knickknacks, the plants, the teapots, and trays. That was the problem with a packrat. In all the jumble, it was hard to remember exactly what stuff Olson had possessed.

Well, you're going to have to. Schulz's voice invaded my thoughts with his patented chuckle. I felt a great wave of affection for him then, and did not know if the sigh I heard was my own or the wind moving through the cottonwood trees at the edge of the creek. I stopped by the precipitous bank and saw a fragmented reflection of the moon in the rushing water seven feet below. This was where Tom had dragged himself, or been forced, across. I firmly placed my right boot at an angle and made a series of careful steps down the muddy, snow-covered bank.

My feet squished through the mud as I focused my concentration on seeing Olson's rooms: shelves of Bibles in several translations, biblical commentaries, leatherbound biographies of the saints, oversized art books featuring Chartres, Canterbury, and other cathedrals. In the realm of religious artifacts, I pictured the rubbings on Olson's living and dining room walls. Medieval, I thought, from my college course in art history. And then on a shelf were his own beaten silver paten and chalice, for serving the sacrament, and his portable ambry, a hammered bronze box rimmed in brass for storing the consecrated host. A portable wooden case in his home office held his sterling flatware service. When I'd stored the overflow of covered pans in Olson's office before the vestry arrived, I'd noticed a mind-boggling number of disheveled piles of papers on the desk and on the floor: the true mark of the Highly Disorganized. Without a secretary at home to keep his act together, Ted Olson had undoubtedly had a vague desire to sort through his correspondence one of these days. But when I'd asked him where to put the pan of pork dumplings, he'd swept the dish out of my hands and left it teetering on what looked like a stable pile. I'd realized Olson had no intention of ever sorting through the paper disaster, much less throwing anything away. After the dinner, he'd repacked the silver flatware himself and left it on an unused bed in the bedroom-turned-office.

I turned my attention back to the creek. The stones protruding from above the roiling surface of the freezing water looked wet and slippery. This was where Schulz had dropped the box containing my wedding ring. *Don't think about it.* I hopped lightly across the rocks. Breathing hard, I clutched the flashlight and scrambled up the other side of the creek. When I arrived at the snow-whitened meadow below Olson's house, it looked as if the sky was beginning to brighten. Or maybe it was just wishful thinking on my part after the deep shadows of the creek bed.

My eyes involuntarily traveled to the place where the police had found Father Olson's body. Instead of being smooth like the rest of the meadow, that area was indented. Odd. I breathed deeply and walked over to the spot.

My flashlight played over the shallow rectangle. Someone had carefully spaded up and removed the dirt from the area where Father Olson had lain. The artificially made ditch was covered with snow, and at one edge of the dug-up area, someone had put a crudely made cross of lashed-together twigs. This couldn't be part of police procedure, I reasoned. They might analyze the soil where someone fell, but they wouldn't leave a cross. *You're going to have to call Boyd and tell him about this.* I could hear Tom Schulz's voice in my brain as clearly as if he were standing next to me. Boyd wasn't going to be happy. The fresh snow on top of the rectangular hole left by the Mad Digger indicated that this activity had not taken place in the last few hours. That was good, anyway. The last thing I needed was to be hit over the head by a lunatic wielding a shovel.

I swept the flashlight beam in a circle around the spaded area and saw a clear path of small ruts: the outline of footprints leading up to and away from where I stood. Successive sweeps of the light revealed shallower footprint ruts surrounding the spaded area. I guessed them to be from all the police activity here on Saturday afternoon. And shallower still, of course, there would be the footprints of Tom Schulz and the suspect. Didn't want to think about that, though.

Time to go up to the house and look for pearls. Maybe Olson had a hollowed-out Bible. *Maybe he has a phone that you can use to call Boyd.* I ignored the sour taste in my mouth and, careful to avoid the footprint path, walked to the wooden steps leading up to Olson's house.

There was no yellow police ribbon around the back, at least that I could see. I climbed the stairs and tried the back-door handle. To my surprise the door was already partway open, and I ended up crashing into one of the kitchen counters. My chest shuddered painfully. I rubbed my hip, which had taken the brunt of the blow. My free hand moved along the wall and flipped on the kitchen light.

This was not just disorganization, I thought as I looked at open cupboards, pots pulled out on the floor, cornmeal and flour indiscriminately dumped. Fresh snow had blown into the kitchen through a smashed window. It lay on top of the dumped-out food like confectioners' sugar. The place had been vandalized, and not in the last few hours.

"Damn it to hell," I said aloud, and looked for the phone. A black wall model, it had been wrenched from the wall. So much for fingerprints, I thought as I picked it up and examined the cord. I plugged the cord back in, was astonished to get a dial tone, and dialed 911. Boyd was going to yell at me and I deserved it. I told the dispatcher where I was and that the house had been vandalized. No, I said, I did not think I was in any danger. She wanted me to stay on the phone, but I could not. There would be plenty of time for accusations and recriminations as soon as the Sheriff's Department showed up.

I stepped over an upturned kitchen chair and shined my flashlight on more chaos in the living room. I flipped on the overhead brass light fixture. The answering machine had been axed in two. The Stickley's dark plaid cushion had been slashed and emptied; down and feathers lay sprinkled over the detritus on the floor. I couldn't even see the Kirmans. Mountains of books lay by overturned brass lamps, dumped potted plants, and the remains of the framed rubbings. They had been torn from the wall and smashed. Shards of glass glittered in the wreckage.

I was so angry I thought I would shriek. First the church office and now here. Couldn't I ever get somewhere before it was destroyed? Had the intruder found the pearls? Or something, anything else? Boyd had said whoever was keeping Tom Schulz *might* want a particular thing whose location the expiring Olson *might* have told the trusted police officer who had found him. Too bad Tom's note hadn't mentioned it in any way the rest of us *might* have been able to figure out.

"I hope you didn't find it," I said loudly to the devastated room. My boots crunched across the broken glass and piles of feathers. But at that moment my eye caught the shelves where Olson had kept his church-related supplies. No chalice, no paten, no ambry. Perhaps the motive for his murder had been robbery, after all. The criminal just hadn't gotten everything the first time around.

I moved hesitantly down the hall toward the bedroom-turned-office. I stepped over coats, hats, gloves, and hangers dumped from the hall closet. Whoever did this is gone, I reminded myself as I entered the new space; snow was everywhere in the kitchen.

I switched on the overhead light in the office, one of those square, frosted-glass types that must have been an original fixture with the house. It cast a sallow light over the piles of papers. The contents of file drawers lay strewn on top of what had already been there. It looked as if all the papers had been gone through, but instead of being left in a mess as they had been in the living room, these had been neatly restacked in piles and pushed against the walls. Why would you trash the house, but organize the papers? *The silver,* Schulz's voice said sharply in my mind, *where is it?* Stacks of papers covered the office's incongruous bed. I stepped carefully around the side of the bed and saw the cherrywood case for the silver. It had been emptied. Glinting in the weak light, Grande Renaissance knives, forks, spoons, and serving utensils lay haphazardly everywhere, like a child's game of Pick-Up Sticks. Either robbery had not been the motive for this rampage, or this was one incredibly stupid thief.

I picked up the cherrywood case and pulled out the small drawer at the bottom. A slim packet of letters was wedged into the back. The sloped, feminine handwriting of the return address said they were from A. Preston.

Judas had received silver. Agatha had betrayed her husband. Olson had put the traitor's letters in the silver box. Whoever had trashed this place either hadn't found her letters or hadn't cared. I put the letters in my parka pocket. Maybe Tom's mystifying notation of *B. - Read - Judas* had something to do with Bob Preston and his wife. Damn. More ideas for Boyd.

Two more places to check: Olson's bedroom and the one bathroom. I knew there was a single bathroom and that the office had been the only other bedroom besides Olson's. Olson had bought the old place at a bargain because it had only one bath and two bedrooms, not much space for today's families. I wondered if the vestry would have been willing to move him into a mansion if he'd brought the church's receipts for this year up to half a mil.

Concentrate, Tom Schulz's voice in my mind reprimanded. I wondered if I was hallucinating. Is that what happened when you really missed somebody? Or was hearing voices a phenomenon of sleep deprivation?

I felt a pang of sadness, or perhaps it was the guilt of intrusiveness when I turned on the light in Olson's bedroom. The covers of the bed had been pulled off and lay in a heap on the floor. The mattress leaned against the box spring at a steep angle. Both had been slashed open. Olson's bureau drawers yawned, their contents of socks, underwear, and dark clothing in piles. On Olson's bureau, a painted Florentine tray lay heaped with an assortment of keys, receipts, and clerical collars.

Something hanging on his wall made me stop dead. Dark maroon, with a purple heart at the center. It was an afghan. Except for the colors, it was the exact design of the one that had been left on my porch.

Nausea swept over me. I tripped on my way out of his room and fell hard on the bed frame. I forced myself to get up and careened back down the hall to the living room, where there was at least a chair to sit.

Come on, Miss G., get a grip. I allowed Tom Schulz's affectionate imperative to flow from my brain down into my body, which was cold, very cold, from the lack of heat in the house. Still, I couldn't help but wonder if the afghan left at my house was meant to be some kind of sign. Something along the order of, *You're next.*

I had the ridiculous notion that if Boyd was going to bawl me out anyway, I might as well turn on the heat. I scanned the living room walls for an adjustable thermostat and saw that it was on the other side of the room, beside the empty shelves. Exhaustion paralyzed me. I wasn't going to turn on the heat, even though it was unbelievable how much the temperature had dropped in the last twenty-four hours. The splintered answering machine lay on the table. It was the kind with a receiver, too, and I wondered if it had been from here that Tom had made his call to me at the church.

I hugged myself and rocked back and forth to get warm. Where was the Sheriff's Department, anyway? It felt like forever since my call. There was no working clock remaining in Olson's destroyed house, of course. Outside his living room window overlooking a deck and the creek, the gradual brightening between the trees indicated the sun was finally making an appearance. Even though I hadn't found any pearls, it was time for me to go; Julian and Arch would need a hot breakfast on such a frigid morning.

I sat cemented to the chair. The last time we spoke, Tom had been here. He had called me at the church when I was so full of hopeful anticipation. I closed my eyes and for a moment felt sleep hover just behind consciousness. It had been warmer on Saturday morning when Tom had called from here. Why, I'd even heard windchimes through an open window in the background.

Windchimes?

Wakefulness came with a jolt. My flashlight hadn't picked out any windchimes. This doesn't matter, my tired brain insisted. Just go home. What had Tom said when he called the church office? He'd told me about Olson and that there would be no wedding. Then there was a distant tinkle, and he'd told me to wait. He hadn't found anything or he would have told me, wouldn't he? It was so insignificant that I'd even forgotten to tell Boyd and Armstrong about it.

I hauled myself out of the chair and headed toward the back door. There had been a jingling, glasslike noise in the background. Windchimes, I'd thought. But Coloradans usually stored their windchimes until June. The danger of harsh winds and unexpected ice could reduce the chimes to fractured bits. *But this guy kept his croquet set in the garage,* Tom's voice said to the far reaches of my brain. Maybe he didn't know you were supposed to store your windchimes.

I'm losing it, I reflected ruefully as I scrambled onto the deck off Olson's kitchen. Light crept up from the eastern horizon. My flashlight beam played over the deck. No chimes. I inched down the short outside wooden staircase, careful to avoid the center of each step, where a dark glaze of ice crystals no doubt lay under each fresh layer of snow. At the bottom of the stairs was a crawl space under the house that Father Packrat Olson had used for storage. My light scanned a paint-chipped lawn mower that would never cut another blade, at least a dozen straw baskets still wired with rotting floral clay, a higgledy-piggledy collection of boxes stamped with the name of the moving company that had brought Olson to this abode. One of the boxes was upturned, its contents spilled. They were tall iced-tea glasses made of a light green, translucent shell-type material.

The kind used to make windchimes.

The Sheriff's Department would not have noticed this. How could they? I had forgotten to tell them of the background noise when I was on the phone with Schulz. I knelt down, scooted forward, and flashed my light inside the box. Some glasses were broken, some unbroken. I took a deep breath and dumped the entire contents on the ground, and heard the same noise I'd heard in the background on the phone, only louder. It had not been windchimes that had caused the noise—it had been this box being upended, or a box like it. This was why Schulz had told me to wait.

He'd heard it and gone to see what was going on. The killer had been hiding under the house.

I flashed my light over the mess on the ground. It was hard to see in the darkness. But there were no chokers or jewelry of any kind in the pile of broken glass. When I set the box upright, a wet piece of paper clung to its side. I pulled my right glove off with my teeth and cautiously peeled the damp paper off the side of the box.

It was a standard piece of 8½ by 11 paper, typewritten and photocopied. There was no name on it, but at the upper left were four brief lines:

92-492
Set I
Part A
Page 25

It was the last page of one of the candidates' exam essays, already read by the General Board of Examining Chaplains, and soon to be read by our own diocesan Board of Theological Examiners. 92-492 was the encoded identification number of the writer. The typed words began, *"such actions can only be attributed to false prophets, whose actions undermine the true mission of the church."* And it went on, but I was not going to read it now; I wanted to get home.

I listened for the sound of a Sheriff's Department vehicle and heard none. *If a burglary isn't hot and no one's in danger, it's not one of the first things we respond to,* Schulz had told me. No telling when the police would arrive. I needed to rouse Julian and Arch. Besides, the frigid weather was permeating my skin. I carefully snatched up the paper, scooted out from the crawl space, and started walking fast through the trees to the creek. Once home, I could look up the identification number of the examinee on the master sheet I wasn't supposed to open until I'd finished reading the exams. This candidate shouldn't have left the last page of one of his exams underneath Olson's house.

In the broad meadow space, the brilliant moonlight melted into the faint sunbeams touching the frosted tops of trees on the surrounding hills. Pink light suffused the air and made the snow glow. On a neighboring slope, a dog began to bark. I couldn't wait to get home. Behind me, a morning breeze swept through the trees.

When I arrived at the creek bank, a faint cracking noise caused me to whirl around.

"Boyd?" When there was no reply, I lifted my voice. "Furman County Sheriff?"

The sudden stillness made me think I'd been deceived. *Tom?* I called internally. As if he were guiding my face with the tips of his fleshy fingers, I slowly turned toward the creek. This was the exact spot where he had been dragged or prodded across. Snow lay around not only my own footprints down the bank, but a second set. Transfixed, I stared at the prints. *Leave quickly,* I could hear Schulz's voice say.

At that moment, I heard a whooshing of air behind me. In a moment that went too fast, a hard blow hit the middle of my back. I heard myself expel breath, felt the pain explode across my vertebrae. I fell to my knees. Blackness engulfed me. I had an unexpected vision of Arch as a baby, then as a toddler. I'm dying, I thought. My life is flashing before me. My face fell into the snow, and I felt the rushing air of someone pulling the sheet of paper from my hand and then moving past me. *I'm trying to help you,* my mind cried out to Tom, who seemed suddenly far, far away. Very faintly, before I passed out, I could hear his response.

You are.

17

"Goldy! Gol-*dy*!"

Somewhere above me and far away, voices called. Louder and more insistent was the bone-splitting pain in the middle of my back. I gasped chilly, wet air. Was I drowning? Or had I undergone surgery for an unknown ailment and was I now struggling miserably to dispel the anesthetic? The voices grew close.

"Don't touch her," warned one, a woman. "See if she wants to move on her own."

I opened my eyes. With infinite slowness and a searing pang across my spine, I tried to maneuver onto my side. "Help." My voice was so faint I hardly heard it.

The floating faces of two people came into sight. I knew this man and woman. Their names were just out of reach.

"It's Helen," prompted the female face. "Remember me? I've called Mountain Rescue."

"No." I tried to raise my head and sagged backward helplessly. "Don't need it," I added unconvincingly. Imagining the scene at my house if I arrived in an ambulance brought a wave of dizziness. Julian and Arch would go nuts. "No stretcher. No EMTs. Please," I begged. Talking required an impossible effort. Every time I breathed, my body shrieked at the exertion.

"The heck you say," said a male voice.

I squinted. The sky had become bright without my witnessing it, and my clothes were chilled and soaked. "What day is it? What's the time?" I croaked.

The man and woman looked at each other, and I had a sudden memory of my parents above my crib. But these were no relatives of mine; these were Sheriff's Department Investigator Horace Boyd and Victim Advocate Helen Keene. And I had something to tell them, but the agonizing vice cramping my spine made it impossible to think. I struggled to move my legs, to see if my body worked. Summoning an enormous effort, I pulled my knees into my chest, then pushed up into a crouch. My spine shuddered in anguish.

"Don't move if it hurts," Boyd's voice ordered.

"I am getting up," I announced, and shakily came to my knees.

"Please wait," Helen said softly, too late.

In the distance I could hear the whine of a siren. The ambulance. A stretcher. Arch and Julian having a fit. I cried out as I stood up on the icy ground. My knees wobbled and the ground seemed to be coming back up to my nose.

"Oh, Jesus," muttered Boyd as he grabbed me on the shoulder and under the arm, then hauled me back to an upright, balanced position.

"I was attacked," I said weakly. "Someone hit me. The paper." I looked around on the ground. Snow and mud wavered in and out of focus. "Where is it?"

But it was gone. Boyd and Helen thought I was hallucinating and wanted *The Denver Post.* I asked them to help me walk. They said I should wait, see if anything was broken. I told them nothing was broken. I needed to move; lying motionless could worsen frostbite. With Boyd and Helen reluctantly walking beside me as I moved unsteadily across the field, we unraveled the story. My call had come in and been triaged. When someone in Dispatch had realized that the robbery location was the same as murder victim Olson's, Boyd had been informed. When Boyd wanted to know who had placed the call and Dispatch gave them my name, he had cursed and phoned Helen. I pointed to the dug-up area with the cross and told them about the missing sacramental vessels: chalice, paten, and ambry.

"Hombre?" said Boyd. "Like a Spanish buddy?"

"Like a small tabernacle to hold the consecrated bread. It's often kept in a built-in area behind a church altar."

"Glad we got that cleared up."

I told Boyd the local rumor that had Olson involved with Agatha Preston, then handed him Agatha's letters that I'd taken from Olson's silver box. Boyd shook his head, but took the packet. I also mentioned the afghan that resembled the one left for me. I ruefully added that whoever had struck me had stolen a sheet from one of the exam essays, an exam that was currently being read by the Board of Theological Examiners.

"Of course, I don't have the page," I said as we stopped to rest next to a leafless cottonwood. I took a shallow breath and shivered. When I tried to breathe deeply, a thick line of horizontal discomfort streaked across my back. "But I remember the number. 1492. Like Columbus. Only this was 92-492."

Emerging from the trees at the edge of the field were emergency medical folk with blankets and a stretcher. I willed them to go back, as if I were rewinding a movie. But they kept coming, spurred on by Boyd's impatient gestures. Helen was hovering solicitously. I felt utterly defeated. I had come so close, and now—

I turned back toward the creek. With acute disappointment I saw Julian's Range Rover parked past some trees on the other side of the creek. It might as well have been in Africa. Although the pain was excruciating, I wanted nothing more than to drive home. Besides, I remembered, I had a luncheon to cater today for the prayer group. Better not mention that to Boyd and Helen. I could hear Boyd now: *Forget the damn luncheon!* Sure, and never have the churchwomen ask me to do another affair for them. Or worse, have them spread it all around town what an unreliable caterer I was. Besides, I wanted to find out what or whom they were praying for.

"Have you found out anything about the missing pearls?" I asked. "In my mind's eye, I sort of saw them, imagined them being hidden—"

Boyd had started on a new match. At least he hadn't gone back to the cigarettes. His wide face turned grim. "Goldy, you're stressed. You're seeing things."

"I'll bet those pearls have something to do with Olson's murder." My voice quivered. "Something else. I could hear Tom's voice in my head."

"Hearing things, too," concluded Boyd. He motioned two EMTs over. I felt my control falter.

"Look," said Boyd. He leaned in close to me. To give him credit, he tried to make his voice sympathetic. "I don't want to take somebody off the search for Schulz. We can't spare an officer to keep an eye on you. Okay? So after these guys take you to get checked out, I want you to stay home with that friend of yours. That big, good-looking gal. Marla. In fact, I'm telling her to come stay over at your place, and I'm going to make the call from here."

I choked out Marla's number. Tears spilled uncontrollably from my eyes as the EMTs gently helped me onto the stretcher. Helen Keene held my hand the whole time, through the woods thickly aromatic with the smell of melting snow on fallen aspen leaves, around Olson's house, which bounced in and out of view, to the driveway where Tom Schulz's dark Chrysler was still sitting, glazed with ice.

My back felt broken, although I knew it was only badly bruised. It's impossible to get comfortable on a stretcher. When the two uniformed fellows worked to maneuver it up the ambulance ramp, Helen disappeared momentarily. She came back with another victim-assistance quilt draped over her arm. This was a pink and green strip quilt, like something you'd see in a preppy nursery. But I meekly allowed her to tuck it around me, then asked her to get hold of Julian and Arch, to tell them I would be home soon. A negative look passed between the two medical technicians. I ignored it.

Since there was no hospital in Aspen Meadow, the daytime emergency procedure when there was no blood, no fever, and full consciousness was to take the victim to a doctor in the mountain area who then made a medical assessment of the situation. The paramedics took me to the office of Dr. Hodges, or Stodgy Hodge, as we called him in town. In his late seventies, quick-moving, stoop-shouldered Hodges was the best diagnostician I had ever known. Unlike most of his generation, Hodges had made the transition to computers, on-line hookups, and other modern equipment with ease. But he also knew how to make his patients laugh, frequently the best medicine. When I had first visited him fourteen years ago, I had told him I was trying to get pregnant. Without missing a beat, he replied, "My dear, I am too old for you."

Now an unsmiling Stodgy Hodge was waiting at his office in response to Mountain Rescue's call; he dutifully opened the doors wide so the stretcher could be wheeled in. After gently poking around and trying to assess whether my kidneys had been damaged—they had not—Dr. Hodges concluded from the welt on my back that I'd been hit hard by a long weapon. Or, as he put it as he gave me the full benefit of his rheumy gaze above his smudged half-glasses, "Somebody tried to hit a home run using your body as the ball, but it was a bunt."

Could I walk, he wanted to know. I could, I said, with more confidence than my achy body warranted. He squinted dubiously, then ordered rest at home until I felt better. No exertion. I smiled without assent as he nipped away to call in a prescription for pain pills. Helen Keene used the other line to call my house, where she got Marla, who had just arrived and would be more than willing to come get me. I checked my watch: 7:30. Monday morning. Tom Schulz had been gone less than forty-eight hours. It seemed like decades since I'd left my house to snoop at Olson's. If I moved very slowly, and had Marla's help, I could do the prayer group luncheon. Correction: I *would* do the prayer group luncheon.

What I could not tell Stodgy Hodge or Boyd or even Helen Keene was that I also had no intention of taking it easy until the Sheriff's Department found Tom Schulz.

When I had somehow dressed myself and shuffled back out in the waiting room to sit by Helen Keene, it occurred to me that Roger Bampton might also be one of Hodges's patients. When the doctor returned bearing a sample of pain medication for me to take when I got home, I decided to find out.

"A neighbor of mine has mylocytic leukemia," I said. Talking was still a challenge. I tried to dispel shakiness from my voice. Helen Keene patted my arm. "What exactly does that mean?"

Stodgy Hodge paused and removed the half-glasses. He looked disapprovingly at the fingerprints on the lenses. "It means your neighbor is a goner."

"Yes, but . . ." I shifted in the hard chair, trying unsuccessfully to get comfortable, "If you had a case like that, how would it present? I mean, what would make you know that was the problem?"

The doctor scratched his impeccably shaven chin and replaced the glasses without polishing them. "Fellow came in here once, he was like death warmed over. Looked haggard, and his teeth hurt. He'd had a temperature for three days. I ordered a complete blood workup. It came back with a white cell count of eighty-seven thousand, and lots of abnormal mylocytes. Blood cells," he added helpfully.

"So you concluded he had this kind of leukemia."

"Yes, but wait." He held up a gnarled hand. "I put him in the hospital that day. Turned out he had a rectal abscess. That's what was causing the temperature. It's also a major complication of mylocytic leukemia."

I held my breath and let it out. "So what happened?"

The stooped shoulders shrugged. "He began chemotherapy in the hospital. But the disease is ninety-nine percent fatal." He sighed. "I hope your neighbor has a will."

"Did your other patient die?"

Dr. Hodges's grim expression altered. "Actually, that was the strangest case I've seen in four decades of practicing medicine. Ten days later, the fellow was feeling better. They ran more blood tests. His white count was normal. Under twelve thousand."

"Oh, wait," I said, aware that Helen's eyes were on me. Surely, she was wondering, at a time like this, with my fiancé missing and my body bruised from a callous attack, I shouldn't be worrying about my neighbor's health? "I did hear about this. Roger Bampton, from the church, right?"

"You heard about it? I shouldn't be surprised, the way news travels in this town."

"Yes. I guess I just didn't believe it." The office phone rang, and my next words came out in a rush. "Do you think it was a miracle?"

Stodgy Hodge's voice rustled in a dry laugh. He let the answering machine pick up the call. "I've seen good people die, and I've seen bad people live," he said when I looked at him expectantly. "Let's say it was . . . unexplained. We'll see how long he lives without a recurrence."

"But then, how would you know when something is a miracle?" I persisted. "Some of the folks down at the church say Roger got better because Father Olson laid hands on him."

He shrugged. "Maybe that's true."

"Doctor Hodges!" I cried. "Either it is or it isn't!"

Outside, a vehicle roared up to the curb and then stopped. A car door slammed.

"Please," I begged, knowing my time was short, "you saw Roger Bampton. What do you think?"

He chuckled. "I know he was having copies of his blood tests framed for Father Olson." When I glowered at him, he went on, "I also know our church isn't the most harmonious place in the universe. So why would God choose us to do something like this? The folks at St. Luke's can't even agree on the size of pipes to use in plumbing renovation. How would they explain a miraculous healing?"

My eyes still questioned him.

Stodgy Hodge, the best diagnostician I had ever known, shrugged. He said, "All right, I guess I believe the healing of Roger Bampton was a miracle."

"Goldy!" shrieked Marla as she banged through the office door. She was wearing an enormous white raincoat over a brilliant yellow sweatsuit. She looked like a large, angry egg. Her unbrushed brown hair flew out in unkempt tendrils. She stopped and glanced around at Dr. Hodges, Helen Keene, and then gave me and my wet clothes the once-over. "Went for an early morning swim, did we?"

"Don't start."

"No wait," she said, winking at Helen Keene and throwing her frizzy mass of hair back for effect, "the churchwomen wanted fish, so you thought you'd throw a line into Aspen Meadow Lake. The things caterers will do for food! But then you fell in—"

"Marla—"

"Don't bawl out the person who's come to nurse you." She put her chunky arm around me, helped me up, and started to guide me out the door. "I even have a covered cup of fresh cappuccino in the Jag for you."

Helen Keene bid me good-bye, and Stodgy Hodge placed the sample bottle of pain meds in my palm. Both knew I was in good hands.

"The police tell me you've been terribly, terribly naughty," Marla chided once she had me settled into the front seat of the Jaguar. I uncapped the hot, creamy coffee she had brought and tried to sip the froth as she rocketed the sedan over the icy streets. "What were you looking for at Olson's that was so important? Copies of *S and M Fantasies*?"

"I was looking for those doggone pearls that were going to be used for the women's jewelry bazaar. You said he hid things in strange places, so I just thought—"

"Oh, excuse me, *I* said he hid things in strange places? So this is *my* fault? You think the motive was robbery. That's the theory you risked getting *killed* for? If stealing was the motive and it failed, don't you think the police would have found the pearls when they first went out there, when Olson died?"

I didn't answer. We pulled up by the curb in front of my house.

"What's that supposed to be?" demanded Marla.

I followed her pointing finger. Yet another crocheted afghan swung gently from a rafter on my front porch. This one was green and had a white cross at the center.

"Oh, Lord, why—"

But my exclamation was interrupted. Julian and Arch vaulted out the front door. Their faces, full of curiosity and worry, pinched my heart. These last few days had been so hard on them.

"I still don't see why you went out to Olson's before the sun was even up," Marla said with an exasperated laugh. "I have plenty of pearls if you need to borrow some."

"I keep telling you not to start, but you just keep doing it."

Julian and Arch insisted on knowing everything that had happened. I gave a few brief details and concluded with the fact that I had not found Tom Schulz. Also, I'd been slightly hurt in the process. Marla settled me in a chair—I refused to go to bed—with an electric heating pad wedged against my back and a fresh mug of cappuccino. She took down the newly donated afghan while I dutifully took a pain pill with a glass of water. It was a mild muscle relaxant that I knew would still allow me to function, especially after the double dose of caffeine Marla had just given me.

She said, "I'm taking Julian back out to get the Rover so the guys can go to school. Can I trust you?" Her eyes challenged me to protest. I wasn't sure I had the strength.

"I'll stay with her," Arch piped up. "I learned CPR in Scouts." He gave me one of his goggle-eyed looks and a full, beneficent grin. Marla laughed while Julian, mute and anxious, stared at me as if I were an apparition. He could not seem to believe I was alive. I knew better than to try to explain my motivations to him in his present emotional condition.

"What's the deal with that knitted thing on the porch?" he demanded. "I think it's pretty weird that someone keeps leaving stuff for you, and you don't even know who it is."

"Someone at the church," I said casually. I brightened. "I probably won't get up when you get back. Hope your classes go well today." And then I remembered again the importance of this week to Julian. Would the college admissions or rejections come this day? I'd become so preoccupied with my own crises that I hadn't been very sympathetic. "Good luck," I added lamely.

"Don't worry about me," he ordered impatiently, then hustled off with Marla. "We'll be back for you in forty minutes," he warned over his shoulder to Arch.

Arch did not move from the kitchen table. "You just got one call this morning," he announced to me, as if anticipating my first question. "They want you to set up at the church around eleven-thirty. Should I phone and say you can't come?"

"No, I have to go. Maybe you could put some water on to boil the pasta. Then if you don't mind, you can scoop out the cookies. I made two kinds. They are recipes of Tom's."

He gave me a solicitous look, then retrieved my pasta pot. "So, out at

Father Olson's," he said conversationally, "was it really scary? I wish I knew who clobbered you. That is so gross."

"It went too fast for me to be scared. But I was wondering if you'd hand me that pile of exams over there, please." I readjusted the heating pad and felt the medication kick in. My head felt light, and the sharp pains in my back ebbed to a dull ache as I started flipping through the pages the diocesan office had sent me to read.

"Did the robber-guy take much?" Arch asked as water gushed into the pan. He heaved it over to the stove with a minimum of sloshing.

"Hold on." I ripped open the envelope containing the candidates' names coded to their exam numbers. As I suspected, candidate 92-492 was identified on the master sheet as Mitchell Hartley. I put in a call to Boyd's voice mail; after the fiascos at Brio Barn and Zelda's, the last thing I was going to do was have the cops go scoop Hartley up. Besides, the police already had checked the conference center, where Hartley was staying, for Tom. When I got off the phone, Arch was looking at me quizzically.

"What was your question, Arch? Oh. What did the robber steal. Some church vessels. But not a whole lot more that I could tell. For a reason I can't figure out, the robber or somebody dug up the area around where Olson's body had been, and put a cross there."

"Really? Wow. I've heard about that kind of thing on *Stories of the Weird.*"

"What kind of thing?" Normally, the fact that Arch had a fascination with the *Weird* meant that he knew statistics on UFOs, extraterrestrial explanations of Stonehenge, and metaphysical theories on Jimmy Hoffa's disappearance that were nothing the FBI would investigate. And of course, Chimayó. I said, "You heard about robbers digging up dirt?"

"Oh, no," he replied in his you-are-so-unsophisticated tone. "Okay, look. If the blood of a martyr falls to the ground in a certain place, people believe you have to dig up the bloody dirt . . . sorry, Mom," he added when he saw my expression. He gestured broadly. "Then they pour holy water, or just plain water maybe, over the dirt, and the dirty, bloody water that comes out has magical healing properties."

"Oh, please—"

"I'm just telling you."

"Thanks. The cookie batters are in two covered bowls in the walk-in. Next to the shrimp."

He frowned at my incredulity and emerged from the walk-in refrigerator balancing the butcher paper–wrapped shrimp on top of one of the bowls. I bargained with myself: I would stay seated and try to work. If the back pain became unbearable, I'd send the food over to the church and go to bed.

With infinite care, I leaned over to preheat Tom's oven. An arrow of pain shot up my spine: I decided I could live with it. Arch took out measuring spoons and the two of us scooped mounds of luscious-looking dough onto the buttered cookie sheets. Working with Arch in this way reminded me of the last time we'd cooked together, when Tom, Julian, Arch, and I had laughingly patted out silky discs of *focaccia* with garlic and pine nuts. Don't think about it, I ordered myself.

Arch placed the sheets in Tom's oven and drained the pasta wheels. Soon the kitchen was wrapped in a scent as rich and sweet as any country inn. I breathed the heavenly aroma in deeply: it was another gift from Tom, his memory, his recipe. Tom's cookies emerged as golden, moist rounds delicately fringed with brown; Arch and I each took one. As before, buttery lemon flavor melted over the crunch of almonds. They were out of this world.

"Those churchwomen are so lucky," Arch said with undisguised envy. Outside, the whine of Marla's and Julian's vehicles announced their return.

"Try a Canterbury Jumble."

He palmed one and patted me on the shoulder, then picked up his bookbag and trundled out. I glanced at the clock: 8:50. The boys wouldn't be too late for school. When I was going through the divorce from The Jerk, a therapist had told me that during a time of crisis, staying on schedule with a child's normal events was essential. Missing school, delaying mealtimes, getting to bed too late, would all say to Arch that his world was falling apart. The last thing I wanted was for my son to feel that chaos was taking over. Even if it seemed that way to me.

Marla traipsed in, took one look at my anguished expression, and popped a warm cookie in her mouth. I did the same, and tasted the warm chocolate oozing around the rich crunch of macadamia nuts and sweet, chewy raisins and coconut. Marla raised one eyebrow at the assembled ingredients on the counter. "Tell me how to fix this shrimp," she said dejectedly, trying without success to conceal her distaste for cooking. It wasn't the first time I had been reminded what a good friend she was, but tears smarted in my eyes as I set about instructing her in boiling the prawns.

An hour and a half later, and with periodic pauses in her clumsy culinary activity to massage my back, Marla had finished putting together

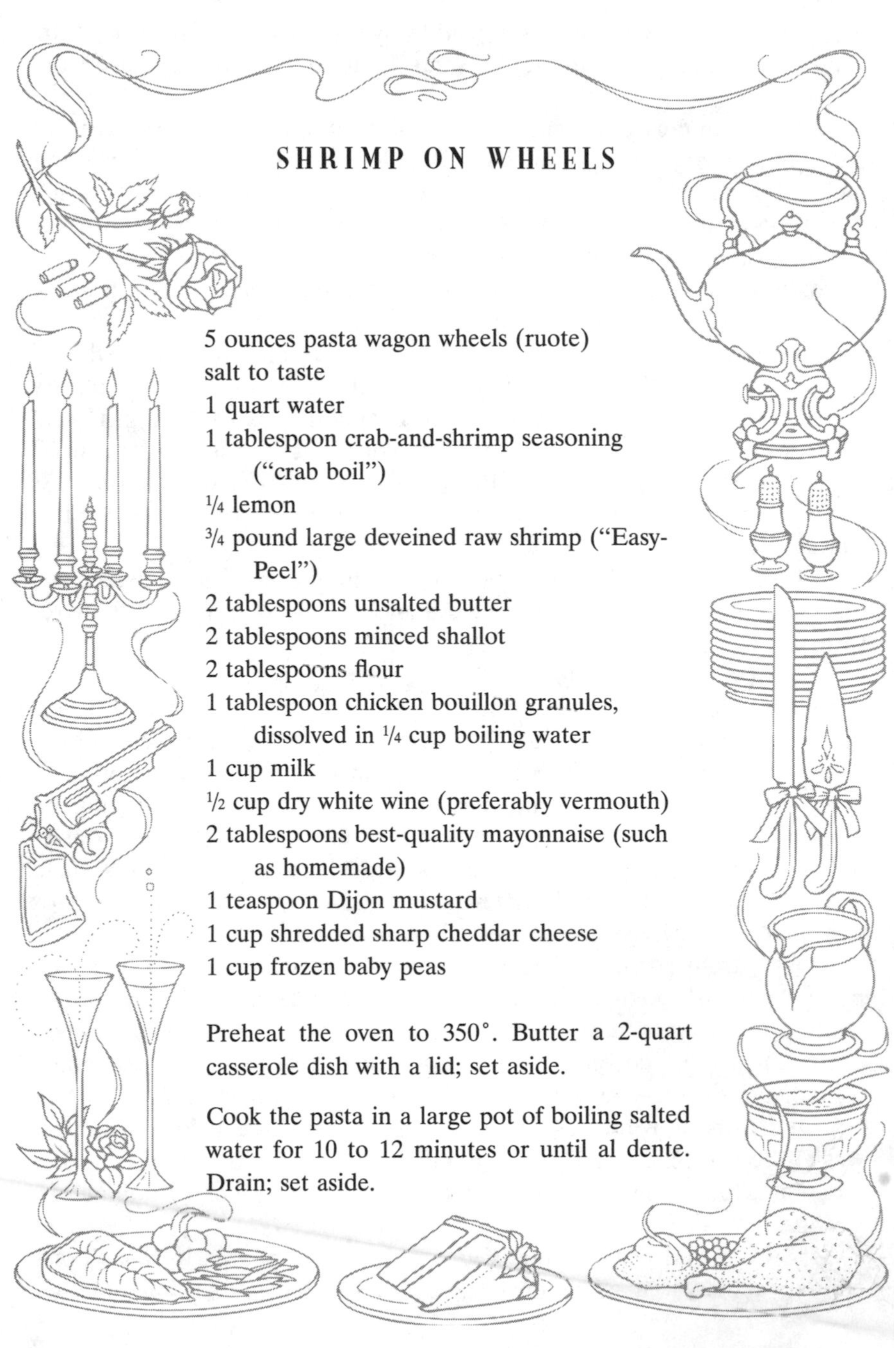

SHRIMP ON WHEELS

5 ounces pasta wagon wheels (ruote)
salt to taste
1 quart water
1 tablespoon crab-and-shrimp seasoning ("crab boil")
¼ lemon
¾ pound large deveined raw shrimp ("Easy-Peel")
2 tablespoons unsalted butter
2 tablespoons minced shallot
2 tablespoons flour
1 tablespoon chicken bouillon granules, dissolved in ¼ cup boiling water
1 cup milk
½ cup dry white wine (preferably vermouth)
2 tablespoons best-quality mayonnaise (such as homemade)
1 teaspoon Dijon mustard
1 cup shredded sharp cheddar cheese
1 cup frozen baby peas

Preheat the oven to 350°. Butter a 2-quart casserole dish with a lid; set aside.

Cook the pasta in a large pot of boiling salted water for 10 to 12 minutes or until al dente. Drain; set aside.

In a large frying pan, bring the quart of water to a boil and add the lemon and the crab-and-shrimp seasoning. Add the shrimp, cook until *just* pink (about one minute), and *immediately* transfer with a slotted spoon (leaving the seasonings behind) to a colander to drain. Do not overcook. Drain, peel, and set aside.

In another large frying pan, melt the butter over low heat and sauté the shallot in it for several minutes, until limp but not browned. Sprinkle the flour over the shallot and cook over low heat for 1 or 2 minutes, until the mixture bubbles. Stirring constantly, slowly add the chicken bouillon, milk, and wine, stirring until thickened.

Combine the mayonnaise and mustard in a small bowl. Add a small amount of the sauce to the mustard and mayonnaise and stir until smooth, then add that mixture to the sauce. Stir until heated through. Add the cheese, stirring until melted. Add the pasta, shrimp, and peas and stir until well combined. Transfer the mixture to the buttered dish and bake, covered, for about 15 to 25 minutes or until heated through.

Makes 4 servings

the women's luncheon food. The medley of succulent shrimp, sweet peas, and tender pasta lay under a blanket of wine-and-cheese sauce, awaiting only heating in one of my large chafing dishes, the kind used by caterers: a hotel pan. An inviting bowl of purple radicchio, dark green oak leaf lettuce, pale nests of chicory and baby romaine leaves glistened under plastic wrap next to a jar of freshly made balsamic vinaigrette. The cookies lay in alternating rows on a silver platter. To go with the main dish, Marla had thawed homemade Italian breadsticks taken from my freezer. When she had laboriously transported everything out to the van, she nipped over to her Jaguar and brought out a garment bag. Within ten minutes, she emerged from my bedroom, wearing a lovely wool dress the color my mother called dusty rose. With a monumental sigh, she collapsed on one of the kitchen chairs.

"Damn! Catering's hard work!"

I said, "Let's get going. I'm just fine." I leaned over and gave her an awkward hug. "This luncheon wouldn't be happening if it weren't for you."

"Don't get sentimental on me," she said as she unplugged the heating pad. I shambled into the bathroom and changed into the front-buttoning black dress Marla had picked out. The pain in my back was noticeable but not unbearable. Standing hurt more than walking. When I arrived back in the kitchen, Marla was already wearing a *Goldilocks' Catering* apron; she slipped one on me and tied it in the back.

"Seriously, Goldy, this work is too hard. I hope you're putting some money away in a retirement fund. If not, I need to get you together with my investment guy."

It hurt when I laughed. "To be perfectly honest, I haven't thought about retirement lately. If you're talking about a major life change, at this point, I'd rather get married."

She had finished tying my apron and I turned around. Dear cheerful Marla, my best friend, who sashayed through difficulty with flippancy and aplomb, had a look of such sadness and disappointment on her face that I knew it could mean only one thing, a thing she would never say. She thought Tom Schulz was dead.

18

We drove to the church in silence. The air was still cold, and gray lamb's tails of cloud wafted just above the rim of the mountains. Several older women had already arrived in the church parking lot. They watched Marla's and my arrival with hungry interest. When I tried to help Marla unload the boxes, a razorlike pain screamed across my back. Marla saw my wince: she promptly ordered me into the church.

"Besides," she announced, "here comes Bob Preston, and I just know he's desperate to help me unload."

Preston, who had clearly driven up in his just-waxed gold Audi only to leave Agatha off, submitted to Marla's orders after she rapped loudly on his car window with her ringed fingers and hollered at him through the glass. Sheepishly, he untangled himself from the gleaming car and picked up two boxes from the back of the van. I prayed that he would not have a hernia while carrying in a box and sue *Goldilocks' Catering.* But for Bob, a macho display was more desirable than being embarrassed in front of a gaggle of churchwomen.

Inside the church, Zelda Preston was already at work. Her wiry body and intent face were bent over a long table covered with a floral-print tablecloth. Her strong hands expertly set each place with the church's beautiful matched silverplate, Inlaid Rose. *When I arrest the wrong guy,*

Schulz had told me once cheerfully, *I do my best to be real nice to him the next time I see him.* I hobbled over to Zelda, knew better than to give her a hug, so merely picked up forks and started putting them around the table.

"Eight," was her laconic greeting. Well, at least she didn't ignore me. I guess I was forgiven. On the other hand, maybe she was embarrassed that I knew she'd interviewed for the organist's position with the Catholics, the same Catholics she'd deemed unworthy of receiving my unused wedding flowers.

Unused wedding flowers. I looked up at the altar and the diamond-shaped window. I had imagined the ceremony so many times that just being in the church again with food and women bustling around made the welt on my back throb. The pain pill was wearing off. When I finished setting the table with Zelda, I walked out to the kitchen and downed another one. Might as well pretend I was an angel and float through the prayer meeting.

By 11:35, eight women had assembled in the tiny church library that doubled as a meeting room for small groups. Marla announced it would make her nervous if I watched her fill the chafing dish with boiling water. That made two of us. I plugged in the electric heating pad I'd brought with me beside one of the library bookshelves, settled into a high-backed chair, and prepared to pray.

"Oh, my dear," said one of the women, all of whom were older than me by at least three decades, "what happened to you?"

"I hurt my back."

"We'll add it to the list," Lucille Boatwright declared solicitously as she settled onto the library couch like a hen adjusting to her nest. "Poor Goldy. Any word yet?" When I shook my head, she added, "Perhaps we should start with a prayer for Father Olson."

Beginning with Lucille, the women took turns delivering halting words of supplication. This was very different from the higher-decibel, gut-spilling type of prayer I'd heard at the late Sunday service. A silence followed. I closed my eyes and conjured up an image of Father Olson. On the screen of my brain, he appeared and said urgently, "Call me."

"What?" I said out loud.

"What?" chorused four women, their perplexed eyes suddenly open. Lucille Boatwright rolled her lips against her gums and gave me a stern look that demanded: *Are you on drugs?*

Prescribed pain pills, thank you very much. Still, I kept my mouth firmly shut as the women began a short prayer that God would lead the police to the murderer, and that Tom Schulz's note would be deciphered and Tom found. I had intended to ask these women questions about the parish during this meeting. But the pill I had taken was making logical thought impossible. During their prayerful silence, I allowed my eyes to slip shut. This time I'd conjure up Tom Schulz. Instead, Father Olson's face loomed again, his mouth open in supplication.

"Ca-a-a-ll me-e-e."

No doubt about it, I was losing it. I heard serving utensils clatter loudly to the floor out in the narthex. That was all I needed—I made a slow, clumsy retreat out to where the catering action was taking place. Unfortunately, the very person I was not in the mood to chat with was Canon Montgomery. His toadlike presence filled the narthex. Or maybe it was the poetry that invaded my mind when I saw him smile approvingly at the pan of pasta: *Only a wimp/eats shrimp.*

"Ah, Goldy," he said with a large, synthetic smile. He moved toward me. "Just the person I've been looking for."

Marla gave me a helpless look as the *Mountain Journal*—in the person of Frances Markasian—breezed through the church doors. When Frances spotted me talking with Montgomery, she grabbed the wooden door behind her and eased it closed so that it would make no noise. I felt an equal amount of discouragement and unease.

Ignorant of either woman's presence, Montgomery confided, "Goldy, I'm so very, very sorry that I was hard on you during the service yesterday." He made a gesture of apology with his meaty hands. "I feel terrible that my grief expressed itself in an ugly outburst against you. I called and left a message with your son. But I wanted to tell you so myself."

I muttered, "Okay." In her duct-taped sneakers, Frances Markasian tiptoed up behind Montgomery so she could eavesdrop on our conversation. The Stealth Reporter. I said nothing. In fact, I rather enjoyed the prospect of the canon theologian getting a painful dose of our local journalism.

"It's just," Montgomery went on, casting his eyes heavenward and warming to his topic, "that I'm still so terribly upset over losing Ted Olson. And this parish . . . I don't know." A cast of tragedy hung over every word. Frances Markasian was getting it all down. I couldn't help it, I laughed. Again. Perhaps it was the lack of sleep, the stress, the pill. Or maybe it was the way Montgomery took himself so seriously that brought out the hyena in me. "In any event," he rushed on with a self important sniff and pat of his middle-parted white hair, "we've decided to move up the exams by one day, since Olson's funeral is tomorrow and the whole committee's already here. Will this be a problem? To have dinner for fifteen at the conference center at six? Tonight? Do you have a staff that can help you? Penitential season, better have fish." Frances scribbled madly but noiselessly; I wondered wildly if I should set an extra place for her. My mouth hung open. Dinner for fifteen a problem? Montgomery had to be kidding. "Afterwards," he added in a rush, "we can go through the first three answers to the coffee-hour questions. If I could just figure out the fax machine in the choir room, I think I could notify the last of the candidates. I do remember we were planning on having you do the food . . ."

Tom Schulz's voice in my head said, *Who's we, white man?* At least it was Tom's voice this time. Anything was better than having the dead rector insist that I phone him up in the Hereafter. Maybe this was what schizophrenia felt like. I waited for Frances Markasian to introduce herself, but instead she just held her fingers up to her lips in a shushing motion. I wondered if this was legal. We were, after all, in church.

"Goldy?" Canon Montgomery raised his voice a shade. The last thing I needed was to have him holler at me again. Marla was shaking her head wildly and mouthing the words *No food.* But I knew I had to keep busy, even if the pain pills were playing tricks with my mind. The worst aspect of missing Schulz was the terrifying notion of having nothing to do, of being motionless at home waiting for the phone to ring. Not that I had done that much sitting around in the last forty-eight hours. But still . . .

"Yes, dinner will be fine. Will the place be open?"

He lifted his peaked eyebrows. "I've told Mitchell Hartley to leave the doors unlocked around the clock. That Bob Preston fellow protested—a little late for the person responsible for security to be upset, wouldn't you say? I'm having a broken window fixed right now. Can you imagine?"

"Actually, I can. That's our fault—"

He waved my protest away. "I'm assigning you and Doug Ramsey to examine Mitchell Hartley tonight, just for an hour. Go ahead and open your letter matching numbers with candidates, and concentrate on his written work. We hope Hartley'll do better this time . . ."

There was that *we* again. "How's Father Doug doing?"

"Oh, well," said Montgomery with a sniff. "You know he was upset with Olson over the miracle claims, and I do believe he was a trifle jealous, perhaps. Olson was so handsome and charismatic in *every* sense, a lady's man, you know." Frances Markasian wrote furiously.

"He was never a lady's man with me," I said, my voice as stiff as my aching back. I didn't wish to see any undocumented insinuations about Father Olson in the *Mountain Journal.*

"I'm just saying," Montgomery replied, testy and oblivious, "that I've been working with the clergy in this deanery to change suspicious, jealous attitudes. There have already been some meaningful changes. However, I do admit to frustration over priests' feelings that the pie is only so big—"

"Pie!" cried Marla. "I just knew there was something I needed to talk to Goldy about. Sorry that you're feeling frustrated, Canon Montgomery. Actually, I've been meaning to tell you about this other canon I knew. His name was Canon Glasscock. I said, 'Glasscock? Is that your real name? Do you have crystal balls, too?' " Montgomery gagged; I bit my lip; Frances Markasian wrote. But Marla was unyielding. "You know what the clergy should do?" she said, wagging a bejeweled finger at him. "Give *you* a jingle when they feel blue. Here, tell the *Mountain Journal* all about it. Frances here can write, 'When you want/to feel all summery/you can call/ Canon Montgomery!' " With that she grabbed my arm, whirled us both around, and marched in the direction of the kitchen.

Behind us, I heard Frances say with potently false humility: "Hi, I'm from the paper, and I'd like to talk to you about your relationship with the murder victim. Father Olson? Could you talk a little bit more about those jealous attitudes?"

"Brr-auugh!" howled Canon Montgomery.

I didn't dare look back to see how the canon theologian looked. I felt like a Filipino racing away from an erupting Mount Pinatubo. A Filipino with a bad back, no less.

Marla took the hotel pan from the church's oven. She set it in the chafer with a minimal amount of overflow splashing, from which she deftly leapt away. "Hey, Montgomery deserves it after the way he treated you on Sunday, so don't give me a lecture," she said defensively. She scooped up the salad bowl, swayed her body from side to side, and chanted, "I truly don't know/which is worse/Listening to his sermons/Or listening to his verse!" The woman was on a roll. I saw Montgomery storm out of the church with Frances Markasian in hot pursuit. My bet was on the journalist.

The bakery-fresh smell of breadsticks heating filled the kitchen. I watched Marla toss the salad with the balsamic vinaigrette and wrap the warmed breadsticks in a linen napkin inside a wicker basket. When the ladies emerged from the prayer meeting, they *ooh*ed and *ah*ed over the sumptuous array. In a fuzzy part of my brain, I registered that Agatha Preston hadn't shown up; maybe Frances Markasian had nabbed her, too. Between refilling the salad bowl and breadstick basket, Marla remarked that she hadn't seen Agatha either. But when I went outside to get a breath of fresh air and stretch my back, I saw Agatha on her knees, digging around in the columbarium construction area. With its deep mud and frozen puddles, steep-sided ditches and erratic surface, perhaps Agatha was working in the mud and thinking about her favorite topic: hell.

The women raved about the Canterbury Jumbles more than any other dish. This bore out the truth of the caterers' maxim that you must serve a rich and sweet dessert after a fish course. This was true even if the fish is shrimp in a wine-and-cheese sauce. After virtuous behavior, even if it is not truly virtuous, people feel they have earned their right to calories.

"Tata, dear!" one woman called gaily to me as she tied her Hermès scarf under her chin. "I hope they find your fiancé!" Her tone was along the lines of, "I hope you buy a new car!"

I glanced at my watch as Marla cleared the plates. 1:00. Tom Schulz had been gone for fifty hours.

"You can*not* cater tonight," Marla insisted once we were back at my house, sitting in the kitchen with our feet up. "I won't let you. *I'm* too tired. Besides, we don't have any food left."

I shook my head. The only message on my machine had been from Alicia, my supplier. That afternoon, she was bringing up the Chilean sea bass and vegetables I had been planning to prepare for the first meeting of the Board of Theological Examiners. This was fortunate, as I was indeed out of shrimp. I said, "This committee is counting on me. I can't just show up with no food."

"They were counting on you for *tomorrow*. Not tonight."

I got up slowly and took unsweetened chocolate, vanilla, and Amaretto from my pantry. "Look, Julian will be home soon, and he won't mind helping. Dinner will be very simple," I said as convincingly as possible.

Marla scowled. "What kind of medication did Stodgy Hodge put you on, anyway, hallucinogenic Darvon? Was lunch your idea of *simple*?"

Actually, the pain pills were helping. I melted butter and whirled chocolate cookies in the blender to make a crust. If we were going to have bass, especially steamed bass, then the caterers' postfish maxim made chocolate cheesecake a dessert necessity. Besides, I wanted to use another of Tom Schulz's recipes. It made me feel close to him.

"I don't believe I'm watching you do this," Marla muttered. "At least it's chocolate. Then we can both have some. Not to mention that your back will feel a lot better after a dose."

Nudging me aside gently, she beat cream cheese with eggs, sugar, and melted chocolate, then doused the smooth, dark mixture with cream, vanilla, and Amaretto while I patted the crumbly crust into a springform pan. When the cheesecake was safely in the oven, Marla poured herself a generous glassful of Amaretto. She announced she was going out to rest on the living room sofa.

"If you leave this house, I'll never speak to you again," she mumbled once she'd downed the liqueur and slipped off her shoes. "And another thing I'll never do again is think catering is this easy, fun, glamorous profession."

I shook out the heart-in-the-center and cross-in-the-center afghans and gently placed them over her. "It's nice to be appreciated," I told her. But immediately I felt a wave of sorrow: Here I was catering a fancy meal to a bunch of examiners and examinees, when I should have been on my honeymoon.

I dutifully hobbled back out to the kitchen and pulled out the pile of exams. I leafed through to Mitchell Hartley's first set of questions. This section of the exam was constituted to replicate that most pastorally challenging part of Sunday morning, the coffee hour. Many parishioners saw the priest's presence at coffee hour as an opportunity to get free advice. Think *Ann Landers meets Dial-a-theologian.* This year's written questions reflected the kind of bizarre interrogatories that were common. At our last meeting, Father Olson had told the board that a long paragraph was acceptable as an answer to a coffee-hour question. We examiners were always to remember that the candidate was supposed to be pastoral first and theologically correct second. The Episcopal church didn't want to make anyone feel unwelcome, no matter what. At least, that was their official line.

The first question went, "My neighbor asked me if I'd been born again. I said once was enough, thank you. She said I needed it, and I said I didn't. Who's right?"

Mitchell Hartley had written: "Your neighbor is right! You have to be born again, even Jesus says so. You need to get with the program."

"Uh-oh," I groaned. On the living room couch, Marla stirred in her sleep. *Not exactly pastoral,* I wrote in pencil, *and what happened to the long paragraph?*

The second question was, "Our teenager babysat for some neighbor

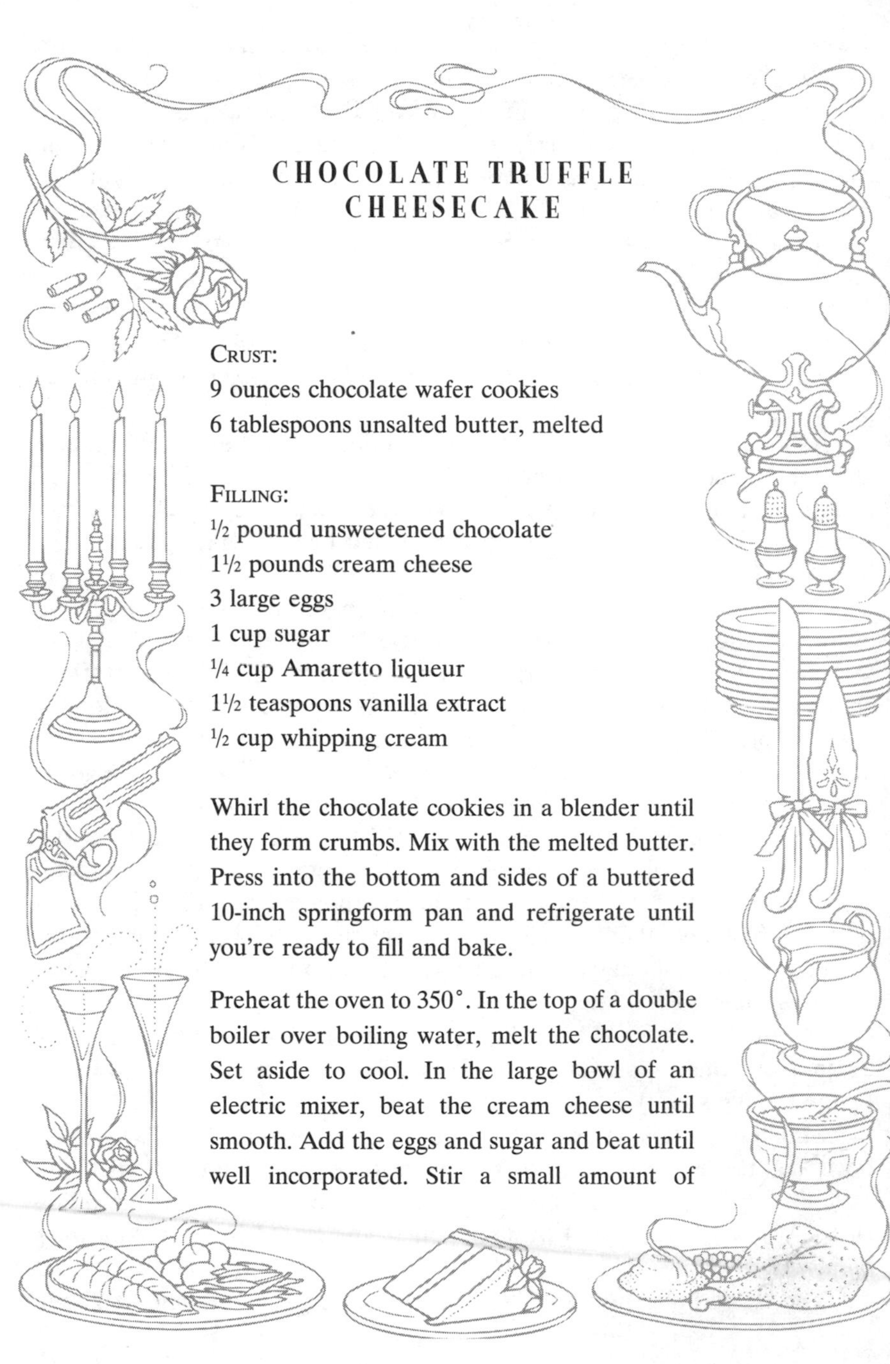

CHOCOLATE TRUFFLE CHEESECAKE

CRUST:

9 ounces chocolate wafer cookies
6 tablespoons unsalted butter, melted

FILLING:

½ pound unsweetened chocolate
1½ pounds cream cheese
3 large eggs
1 cup sugar
¼ cup Amaretto liqueur
1½ teaspoons vanilla extract
½ cup whipping cream

Whirl the chocolate cookies in a blender until they form crumbs. Mix with the melted butter. Press into the bottom and sides of a buttered 10-inch springform pan and refrigerate until you're ready to fill and bake.

Preheat the oven to 350°. In the top of a double boiler over boiling water, melt the chocolate. Set aside to cool. In the large bowl of an electric mixer, beat the cream cheese until smooth. Add the eggs and sugar and beat until well incorporated. Stir a small amount of

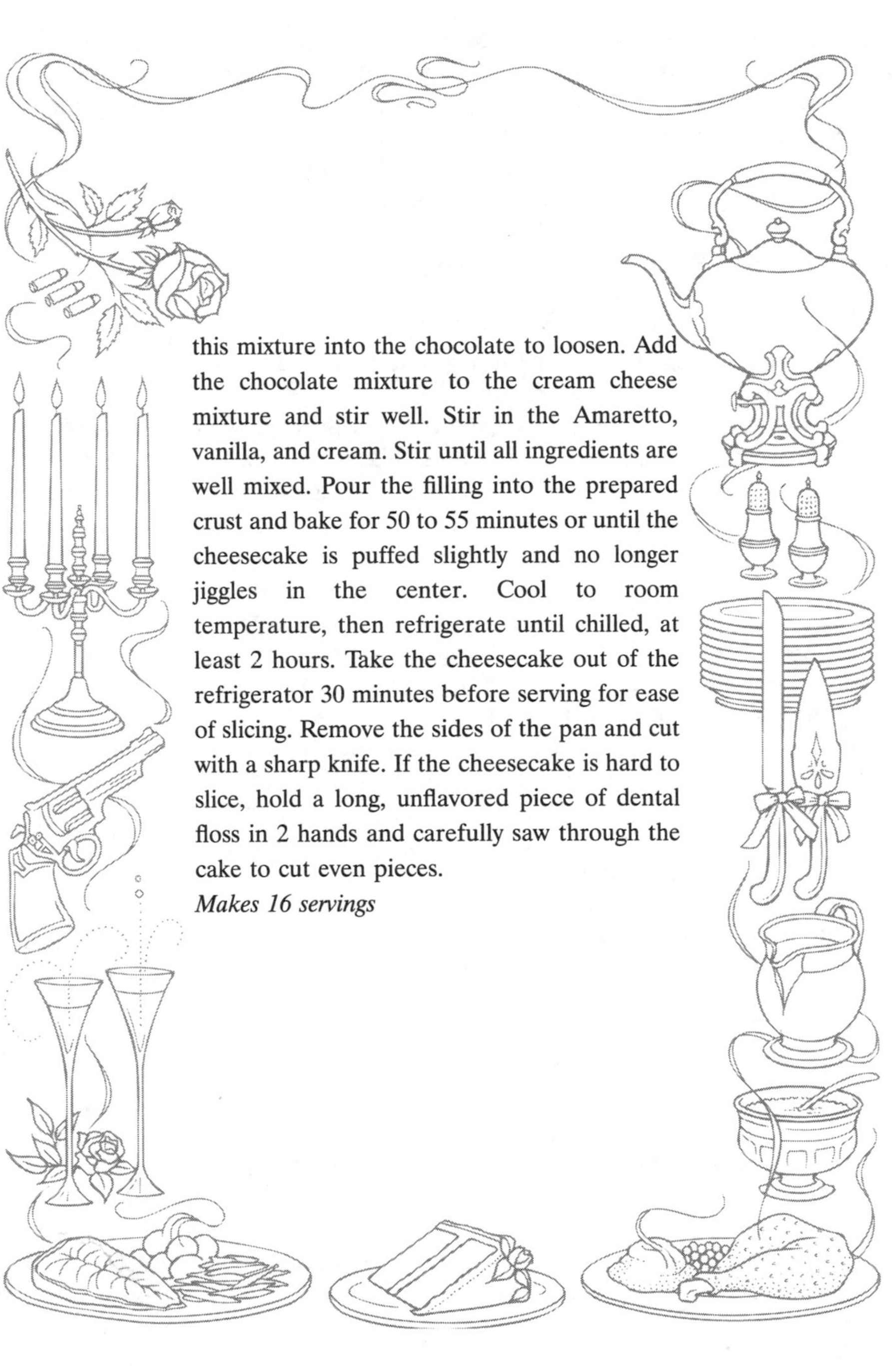

this mixture into the chocolate to loosen. Add the chocolate mixture to the cream cheese mixture and stir well. Stir in the Amaretto, vanilla, and cream. Stir until all ingredients are well mixed. Pour the filling into the prepared crust and bake for 50 to 55 minutes or until the cheesecake is puffed slightly and no longer jiggles in the center. Cool to room temperature, then refrigerate until chilled, at least 2 hours. Take the cheesecake out of the refrigerator 30 minutes before serving for ease of slicing. Remove the sides of the pan and cut with a sharp knife. If the cheesecake is hard to slice, hold a long, unflavored piece of dental floss in 2 hands and carefully saw through the cake to cut even pieces.

Makes 16 servings

kids whose bedtime prayer began, 'Our Mother and Father in Heaven . . .' I thought God was a man! What do you think, Father?"

Mitchell Hartley's tall, loopy handwriting replied: "God *is* a man! Don't let your teenager babysit there again."

Candidate Hartley was beginning to tick me off. Again.

The third question. "I don't understand, Father. Is AIDS God's judgment against homosexuals?"

Mitchell Hartley's reply was unequivocal. "Yes!" he'd written.

I wrote, *This guy flunks the coffee-hour section of the exam.*

So much for Mitchell Hartley. My only question was why the diocese had allowed him to stay in the ordination process for all these years. Maybe he was somebody's relative.

I carefully took the cheesecake out of the oven to cool, stowed the exams, and slapped open the files I had taken from Father Olson's office. Readjusting my heating pad, I scanned them again, page by page. I paid particular attention to the Board of Theological Examiners' file, which contained the correspondence between Father Olson and the bishop. The only paper of significant interest was the correspondence regarding Mitchell Hartley's flunking last year. This coming year, the one we were in now, would be Hartley's last chance at passing his written and oral ordination exams. In his part-time job with Congregational Resources, Hartley was at the diocesan center every day. And part of each weekday, the bishop testily reported to Ted Olson, Hartley was trying to find out from anyone in power if there was some way around taking these exams from—Hartley's words—*those liberals.* After this letter was one from Aspen Meadow Outreach thanking Father Olson, Bob Preston, and the rest of the Sportsmen Against Hunger for their donation of 600 elkburgers to Outreach's commercial freezer. Finally, there was a letter from the bishop's office approving the parish's support of Aspen Meadow Habitat for Humanity; the diocese said if St. Luke's wanted to give $10,000, and could afford it, that was fine.

The mention of the Sportsmen and Habitat made me think back to the Prestons. Too bad I hadn't had a chance to visit with Bob or Agatha before or after the prayer meeting. They probably would have the best idea of where those pearls actually were. If they were telling. The thought of going and searching for anything, when I'd already had unsuccessful forays into the church office, Brio Barn, and Olson's place, did not fill me with excitement.

Do they have other places to hide things? Schulz's voice insisted inside my brain.

I tried to think back. I was so tired. I put my head in my crossed arms on the kitchen table. Nowhere to hide. Hmm. I sat up with another jolt. *Habitat.*

"Where do you think you're going?" said Marla groggily when she opened one eye and saw me putting on my heavy jacket.

"The Habitat house. Right down the street. Want to come?"

She groaned as she creaked her way up off the sofa. "You know I have to come. The cops have told me I absolutely cannot leave you alone. Just tell me," she mumbled as she searched for her shoes, "why are you torturing me?"

"Because of Tom Schulz. I miss him and I need some help." I handed her one of the large garden shovels from the rear of the closet.

"Oh," said Marla, "what are we doing, digging up graves?"

"I don't really know what we're doing."

"This is getting better and better."

We zipped up our coats against the cold and walked the block and a half to the Habitat house. Marla insisted on carrying both shovels; this bit of consideration didn't keep her from grumbling every step of the way. At the deserted site, we stepped gingerly through frozen mud and over strewn boards, and looked around inside. The spaces for windows were large empty rectangles through which an icy breeze blew. Sheets of all-purpose white vinyl floor had been partially installed over the wooden subfloor. It was this white vinyl that got my attention. I looked down across what would eventually be the kitchen, and saw what appeared to be a large spider. When I came closer and bent over, I picked up the missing keys to Hymnal House and the diocesan vehicle, *EPSCMP.*

19

They were even labeled. *Hymnal House. Brio Barn. Nissan.* I didn't know what finding them here meant, but I knew it meant something. Marla and I scoured the rest of the construction site, but came up with nothing else: no sign of pearls, or letters, or sacramental vessels. No sign of Tom Schulz.

We walked back to my house as quickly as my throbbing back would allow. I held the keys tightly in the pocket of my jacket the whole way. Habitat. Bob Preston. The Bob-projects. I couldn't wait to tell Boyd, who still was due to report back to me about Mitchell Hartley. I called and left a breathless message with the Investigations secretary. Within minutes, Boyd called me back.

"We called Hartley and asked to meet him at his apartment. He wasn't too pleased to have to meet with us. Anyway, his place is so small, he'd have to be a magician to have somebody hidden there." Boyd's voice was barely audible above the static; I couldn't imagine where he was calling from. "The guy doesn't have much, that's for sure. And he sure doesn't have Schulz."

I told him about the missing keys Marla and I had found at the Habitat house.

"They were just lying there on the floor," said Boyd suspiciously.

"Not hidden in any way? You just found them. The way you found those letters. Which, by the way, don't tell us squat, except that Agatha Preston has a couple thousand stashed away in a checking account in Denver. So. The keys were on the floor?"

"Yes, they were on the floor. No, they weren't hidden. And yes, we found them. What do you think?"

My doorbell rang: Alicia had arrived with the bass and vegetables. In the front hall, Marla welcomed her and asked if she wanted some Amaretto. They laughed boisterously and then immediately suppressed it. This incongruous humor, plus Boyd's suspicions, plus the fact that it was now almost 4:00 on Monday, with still no sign of Tom, sent a wave of frustration surging in my voice. "Aren't you going to come and get these keys?" I demanded. "Aren't you going to arrest Bob Preston?"

"For what?" Boyd demanded.

I took the phone from my ear and stared at it.

Five inches away, Boyd's voice droned: "Should I arrest him for working on some volunteer project where you found some missing keys? A volunteer project that everyone who knows him knows he's working on? So if a suspect left the keys sitting out in full view, it sure would look like neurotically neat Bob Preston had just dropped them there?" The static distorting his words did not hide his sarcasm.

"I guess not," I mumbled.

Boyd said he'd be by tonight to pick up the keys. I told him I'd probably be finished at Hymnal House around ten.

"Then have Marla or your other cooking helper, Julian, pick you up. I don't want you to go around snooping after dark."

"Who, me?"

Boyd hung up.

Alicia left. Marla, with sighs that would have embarrassed a martyr, rinsed and divided the bass. We were in the middle of washing the new potatoes, baby carrots, and thin, delicate asparagus stalks when Julian and Arch arrived home. Their faces searched mine: *Any news?* When I shook my head, Julian placed a foil-covered glass casserole dish on the counter.

"A cow died so that you could have hamburger-noodle casserole tonight, courtesy of the Altar Guild. How's your back?"

"Don't start with the vegetarian agenda, I have enough problems. My back's doing a lot better. The examining board is starting their work early, and we're doing Chilean Sea Bass with Garlic, Basil, and Vegetables. Feel like chopping basil?" I did not ask him about the college acceptance situation; as with Schulz's disappearance, being asked for the latest news when there was none only served to remind you of what was missing. He would have told me if he'd heard anything.

"I'll butter the gratin dishes," Arch piped up as he scrubbed his hands. "I already scooped out cookies this morning. Did you bring them to the lunch?"

I told him that I had, and his work had been a hit. He beamed and measured out chilled unsalted butter. Julian washed his hands and expertly rolled layered leaves of basil, then sliced through them. Marla parboiled the new potatoes and baby carrots. I pressed pungent cloves of garlic, mixed them with the chopped basil leaves, and beat them into the butter. We formed an assembly line and artfully laid out the fish, vegetables, butter, and herbs on the buttered platters, then covered each tightly with aluminum foil. Our only interruption was a phone call from Lucille Boatwright. She wanted to know if I had donated the food from the wedding reception to Aspen Meadow Outreach yet.

"Yet?" I repeated.

"If you have not," she continued airily, "I wish you would consider sending it in for the funeral tomorrow, Goldy. We're going to have quite a few people in from out of town, I'm told. I can't get enough volunteers to make food, and I certainly can't let people go home hungry."

It was the least I could do for Father Olson, no matter what I thought of Lucille. I cupped my hand over the phone and asked Julian if he would mind schlepping the reception platters down to the church for the funeral. He nodded without looking at me. Julian seemed to be thinking that not keeping all that food was another way of tacitly admitting that our hopes for Tom Schulz were dimming. I put this thought out of my mind and assured Lucille my assistant would meet her at the church in an hour.

After hanging up, I asked Marla to pour a red wine vinaigrette over thick layered slices of navel orange and purple onion. Arch washed and packed heads of butter lettuce. Julian had taken a bag of Parkerhouse rolls from the freezer. We were ready.

With a herculean attempt to appear happy and hopeful, I said, "What would I do without my team?"

"Go out for pizza," muttered Julian darkly.

Julian insisted on driving the van with all the boxes for the night's meal over to the conference center. Marla chauffered me and my pile of exams in her Jaguar, with Arch in the back. She had told the boys she would take them out for pizza if they would explain the younger genera-

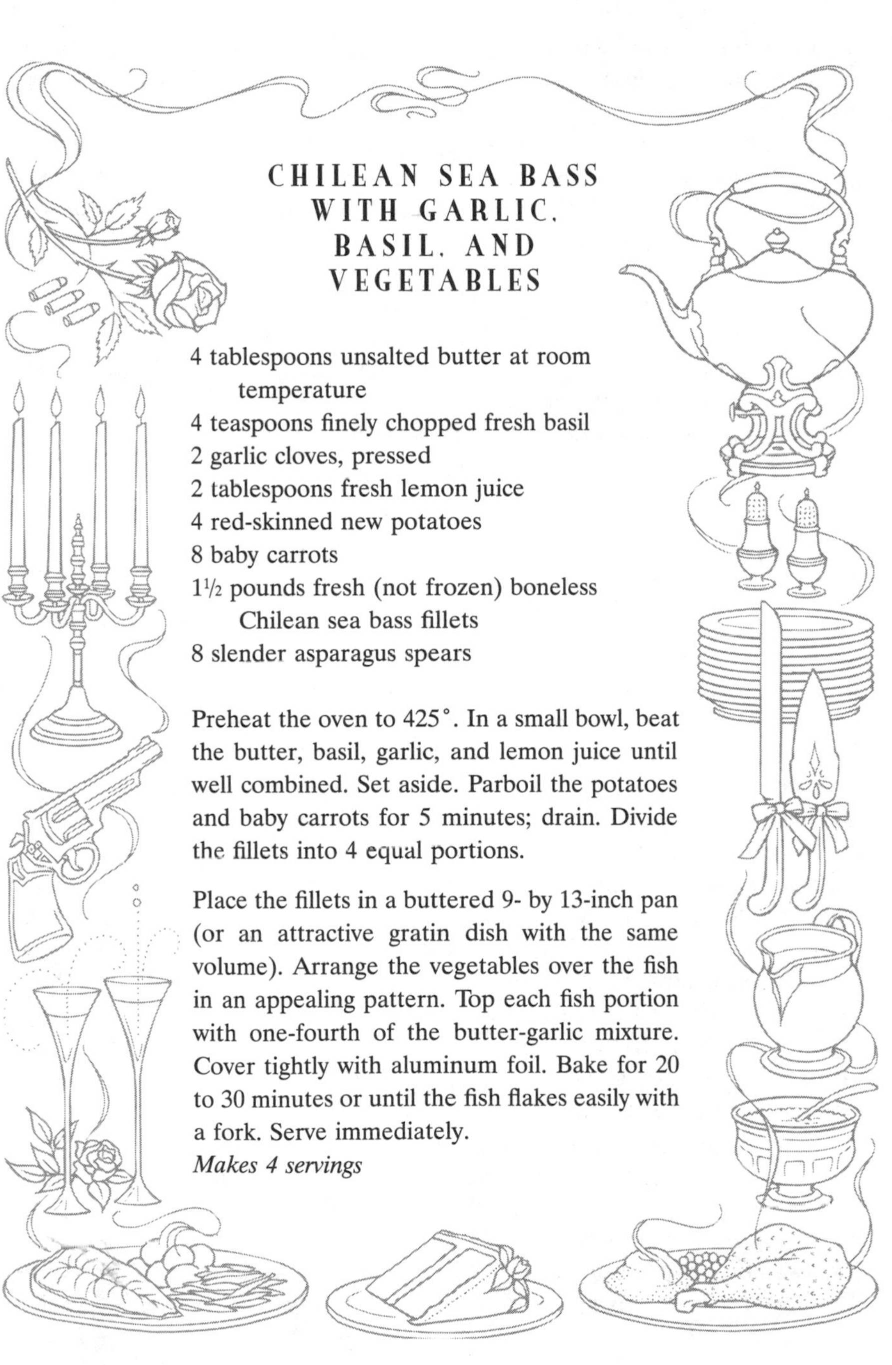

CHILEAN SEA BASS WITH GARLIC, BASIL, AND VEGETABLES

4 tablespoons unsalted butter at room temperature
4 teaspoons finely chopped fresh basil
2 garlic cloves, pressed
2 tablespoons fresh lemon juice
4 red-skinned new potatoes
8 baby carrots
1½ pounds fresh (not frozen) boneless Chilean sea bass fillets
8 slender asparagus spears

Preheat the oven to 425°. In a small bowl, beat the butter, basil, garlic, and lemon juice until well combined. Set aside. Parboil the potatoes and baby carrots for 5 minutes; drain. Divide the fillets into 4 equal portions.

Place the fillets in a buttered 9- by 13-inch pan (or an attractive gratin dish with the same volume). Arrange the vegetables over the fish in an appealing pattern. Top each fish portion with one-fourth of the butter-garlic mixture. Cover tightly with aluminum foil. Bake for 20 to 30 minutes or until the fish flakes easily with a fork. Serve immediately.

Makes 4 servings

tion's fascination with video games to her. I tucked a spiral notebook into my apron pocket and realized I did not have a single question prepared to ask the candidates.

"I'll be by to pick you up at Hymnal House at ten o'clock," Marla pronounced ominously once we'd arrived at the conference driveway. Julian was unloading and Arch was setting three tables for five in the old conference dining room. "Don't you dare go anywhere without me, Goldy, do you hear?"

I leaned against the Jaguar. "Since when do you tell me what to do?" I asked mildly.

"Since I helped you make lunch for the prayer group, and dinner for this pompous board, that's when."

"Ah-ha." Then I added, "I promise."

On the deck of Hymnal House, the three candidates for ordination, including Mitchell Hartley, and a dozen priests including Canon Montgomery, Doug Ramsey, and other men I knew from previous meetings, were sipping white wine and trying to look as if they all weren't terribly nervous. They hadn't asked for hors d'oeuvre, and they weren't getting any. But since the last thing I needed was for them to have a layer of alcohol on empty stomachs, I quickly preheated the ancient Hymnal House oven and popped the fish platters and rolls inside, then arranged the orange and onion on top of individual beds of butter lettuce.

Thirty minutes later, the platters emerged. The delicious aroma of basil and garlic that filled the air and the visual delight provided by the squares of fish, brilliant green asparagus, orange carrots, and pink new potatoes swimming in melted butter, gave the whole dinner a Christmasy sort of air, which is one of the things a caterer has to think of. When people don't know each other before a catered function, or have some particularly onerous interpersonal task to perform after the meal, it's usually a good idea to give them something to do at dinner, like opening a present of food. It helps to break the ice.

The conversation at dinner—how the new bishop in another diocese was faring, how some recent mass conversions to Anglicanism in Africa were going to affect the church worldwide—was light but somewhat forced. Canon Montgomery had said some volunteers from the Altar Guild were doing the dishes, and I was relieved when we could adjourn to the Hymnal House living room for Evening Prayer. This was followed by a brief, nonpoetic explanation of the meetings' mechanics from Montgomery: The end of our meeting tonight would be signaled by the old bell on the deck. We would go to the funeral tomorrow, then meet all the rest of Tuesday. The board would make its decisions Wednesday morning. The nervous candidates gulped and strained to look confident.

Doug Ramsey and I were assigned to an old upstairs parlor. The room had been the subject of unfortunate redecorations, and now boasted a bright green shag rug and two donated yellow-painted wood-frame couches with screaming pink cushions. It wasn't the best ambience to effect a reconciliation with Father Doug, to whom I hadn't spoken since our disastrous tête-à-tête at church on Sunday. He marched into the room in front of me, snapped open the latches on his briefcase, and took out a sheaf of papers with typewritten questions. To make things worse, he was acting inexplicably miffed.

"Hey, Doug," I said, "don't give me the ticked-off routine, okay? I did the dinner, didn't I? Now let's talk about how we're going to examine this guy."

"You didn't contact those newspapers, did you? Tell them I was the bishop's spy?"

"Of course not."

"Some woman reporter interrogated Montgomery. She wanted to know if he was jealous of Olson because Olson was an alleged miracle worker."

Good old Frances. "And did Montgomery agree with the allegations?"

At that moment, Mitchell Hartley entered the room. He coughed.

Doug Ramsey ignored him. He continued to me in a confidential tone, "There are *many* reasons why anyone would be jealous of the person in question, and not just for the monetary and . . . *other* reasons I mentioned to you on Sunday. He was attractive, he was smart. Why, I think he came through the ordination process in the *quickest* time on record, although I'd have to check that statistic—"

"Theodore Olson?" Mitchell Hartley's face contorted into an ugly smirk. Four inches of waved red hair hovered over his forehead. "Yes, your statistic is correct. He came through in three years." His eyes glittered feverishly.

"Please sit down, Mitchell," I said.

He obeyed, keeping his mad gaze disconcertingly on me.

Father Doug began by asking questions about the Archbishops of Canterbury, then moved on to what Tillich had said about this, what

Augustine had said about that, and what were the liturgical requirements for the laying on of hands. Mitchell stumbled and bumbled and most of the time said he didn't know. Doug was just getting revved up to do the Anglican Reformation when there was a rap on the door. It was Lucille Boatwright.

"Zelda and I finished the dishes," she said, glaring at me. *How dare you come up here to examine with the men when there is women's work to be done in the kitchen?* I said nothing; I was weary of Lucille Boatwright. She turned to Doug Ramsey. "We simply must talk to you about the liturgy for the memorial service tomorrow." It was not a request.

Doug lifted his chin: Duty called. He stood, tucked his sheaf of papers into his briefcase, snapped it shut, and marched out without another word. Guess it was up to me to finish with the candidate.

"Mitchell," I said as I reached to a dusty table and found a stub of pencil and piece of paper. "I found a photocopied page from one of your exams." I wrote 92-492 on the paper.

He glanced at it and raised one red eyebrow. "Where'd you find it?"

For better or worse, I decided to tell him the truth. "At Olson's house. Were you out there?"

At that moment, the outside bell gonged. Mitchell Hartley didn't seem to hear it, however. He had a dreamy look on his face.

"You were, weren't you?" I said to Mitchell. My voice was very quiet.

"I was not."

"Cut the crap, Mitchell. You know something."

"I do indeed," he said secretively. "Now." The bell gonged again. "You didn't turn the search over to the Lord, and now the Lord has revealed something to me."

"What? Please. It could be a matter of life or death."

He stood and sauntered to the door. "Everything," he said ponderously, "is a matter of life or death. Tonight's exams are over, and I don't want to talk to you anymore."

The door closed behind him.

I looked at my watch. 9:30. Despite the darkness of the night, there was a clear view of the conference grounds and driveway from the parlor windows. From where I sat, I could barely hear the voices and traffic from the front side of the conference building. And it was just as well. Mitchell Hartley wasn't being forthcoming, and I was in no mood to socialize with anyone else. I decided to wait right where I was and watch for Marla's car to come down the driveway. I would be grateful to get home, to get away from the swirling antagonisms and petty jealousies of this group.

I thought about Tom Schulz. Was he cold? Was he in pain? Had he given his kidnapper the desired information?

Then I remembered Father Olson's gentle compliment in our penultimate counseling session: "It's rare that I work with a couple so much in love." And yet tomorrow we were going to bury Father Olson, and no one knew if Tom Schulz was alive or dead. I let my head rest on the vibrant pink cushion. I was so tired.

I was not aware I'd fallen asleep until something jolted me awake. I felt as if I had climbed out of an avalanche, that I had heard a howl for help either in my sleep, or within the avalanche, or somewhere out on the road. I rubbed my eyes and looked out the window: Marla's Jag was there, its tailpipe sending clouds of steam up into the night sky. I lifted my cramped body off the couch and painfully made my way down the outside steps, which had dim lights every five feet. Shouts had awakened me. They came from the other side of Hymnal House, maybe from the deck, it was hard to tell. On the other hand, perhaps it was bikers partying down on Cottonwood Creek again.

Marla had the windows closed and the engine running; the Jag purred like a small airplane.

"Did you hear something?" I demanded when I opened the passenger side door and stuck my head inside.

"Nothing juicy, at least not in the last two hours."

I slid into the passenger seat, closed the door, and sighed. "Never mind."

She put the car into reverse and sent gravel spewing on her way out the driveway. Marla could never learn to drive cautiously.

"Did the police call?" I could hear the plea in my voice.

"Boyd did. I asked him, 'Boyd, do you have a first name?' He said, 'You can just call me Boyd.' Where'd they get that guy, *Dragnet*?"

"Marla."

"Okay, Bob Preston hasn't been at the Habitat house since Saturday, and he doesn't have a clue about those keys. How about you? How'd the exams go?"

We shot down the road that would lead us to Main Street and the front of the cliff by Hymnal House and Brio Barn.

"I agree with Ted Olson," I said, "in thinking Mitchell Hartley should fail. Montgomery said he'd probably pass this time, though—"

Without warning, when we were just below the conference center deck, the car screeched to a stop. Despite my seat belt, I went catapulting forward. When I had struggled upright, Marla cried, "Oh, God. Oh, Lord."

"What?" I said, but she didn't reply. I followed her gaze out the front of the car, along the line of blazing light cast by the headlight beams.

Mitchell Hartley wasn't going to fail his candidate's exam, and Mitchell Hartley wasn't going to pass. Mitchell Hartley was lying in the middle of Main Street.

He was dead.

20

Marla ran to a pay phone. Someone from a nearby gas station set out flares on the road. Within minutes, Boyd and his team had arrived. I sat in the Jaguar in a state of shock. I couldn't look out at the activity, although I occasionally glanced up at the conference center, perched as it was on that cliff overlooking both the road and the church. Then I gazed briefly at St. Luke's, on the other side of Main Street. I couldn't look at the sprawled corpse of Mitchell Hartley. Marla came back to the car. We sat silently in the front seat.

After more police and the EMT had arrived, Boyd approached us.

I slid down the window. "Is he—?" I choked.

Boyd didn't need to reply. His expression said it all.

"You don't think he's the one who killed Olson, do you? Do you think he knew where Tom Schulz is?" I demanded. My voice sounded shrill, and I was shivering uncontrollably. "Tell me. Do you think Hartley fell, committed suicide, what? Was he hit by a car?"

Boyd regarded me. Dark disks of shadow underneath his eyes showed his exhaustion. The past two days had been hard on him, too. "It doesn't look as if Hartley was hit by a car. I don't know about the rest. Need you to come and see something, though." I got out of the car and followed him to where a cluster of people surrounded the body. I recognized

Officer Calloway and other Furman County investigators. "Weren't you looking for this?" said Boyd. He pointed to a broken pearl choker lying near the center line of the road. In the circus-hued flashes from the police lights, it looked a child's bauble. But when I leaned close I could see the handwritten price tag: $2000.

"What in the . . . ?"

"It must have been in his pocket, or maybe he was holding it. Where do you suppose he got it?"

I repeated my theory that Olson had been keeping the chokers out at his house. There should be others, I added. Mitchell Hartley was poor, and he hated that, but he had never impressed me as a thief. Of course, I had not known him very well. Not very well at all.

"Okay," Boyd said. He didn't sound satisfied. "I told somebody to call your house. Julian Teller's waiting up for you, but he's not waking your son. Better not to upset him. You should get back into Marla's car. Are you cold?"

I was still shaking, but not from the weather. Mitchell Hartley had been in the upstairs parlor with Doug Ramsey and me less than an hour ago. *The Lord has revealed something to me.* What that was, of course, I had no idea. Briefly, I told Boyd about my last conversation with Hartley. Boyd said nothing.

Marla restarted the engine.

"Just a sec. Goldy, are you listening to me?" Boyd's face neared the open car window. I fastened my seat belt and tried to assume an attentive expression. "Don't go anywhere, okay? Don't try to figure this out. Somewhere along the line, whoever is doing this is going to make a mistake."

"So you don't think he fell from the conference deck."

Boyd pushed away from the car. He slipped a match into the side of his mouth. "I'll call you," he said laconically, and turned back to the group around Mitchell Hartley's body.

When we arrived home it was almost eleven. At my insistence, Marla left me off without coming inside and went home. All my supplies, cheesecake leftovers, platters, and bowls from the committee's supper were still in the Hymnal House kitchen, so there was not even anything to put away. Julian fixed me a cup of hot chocolate.

"I froze the wedding cake," he announced, apropos of nothing. "I just couldn't take it down to the church along with the other stuff."

I nodded and ran my hand over the gleaming enamel surface of Tom's stove. *Tell me what to do,* I mentally begged him. But there was no response. Whenever I was in a muddle, I cooked. But what did Tom Schulz do when he was faced with chaos, trying to sort things out? And then I remembered.

He took notes.

I poured out the hot chocolate and filled the espresso machine with water. Scout the cat made one of his noiseless appearances by the pantry, purring and arching his back. I fed him. Then I maneuvered the griddle attachment into Tom's convection oven, pulled out some fat russet potatoes, and got out a pen and the spiral notebook from my apron pocket.

Julian ran the fingers of one hand through his short blond strip of hair. "What in *the hell* are you doing? It's bedtime."

"I'm hungry," I answered him. "There's been too much going on, and I didn't have a bite of that fish. Plus I want some coffee."

"I see. So at eleven o'clock at night, you're going to drink some espresso, cook some potatoes, and then write about it."

"Julian, chill. I mean, I appreciate your staying up to make sure I got in okay. After all, there've been many meetings going on today—"

"Yeah, the tobacco church. Hazardous to your health."

"I just can't think about what happened tonight." I vigorously peeled potatoes. "Or at least I can't get any perspective on it."

"Now I get it. You're going to make Duchess Potatoes, and then serve them at the next church meeting."

"Julian, go to bed."

I grated the potatoes into a dishtowel and then wrung out their liquid over the sink. The chunk of butter I'd popped onto Tom's griddle began to melt into a golden pool; I swished it through a puddle of olive oil. Working carefully—a challenge with Scout rubbing insistently against my legs—I formed the grated potatoes into four pancakes on the griddle. There was no way I'd be taking these to any church meeting, but maybe I could make my contribution to Anglican cuisine.

"What do you think, Scout? *Bishop's Potato Pancakes*?"

Scout stayed still. Guess that meant no. Once again, my sanity seemed to be fraying, but I didn't care.

"Well, how about, *The First WASP Latkes*?"

Scout did one of his elaborate body rolls on the kitchen floor, ending with his stomach facing the ceiling and his paws curled. Clearly, this was a yes.

While the WASP Latkes sizzled, I picked up the pen and began to write.

1. The Reverend Theodore Olson. Smart, attractive, charismatic, "the magician." Went through ordination process fast. Protégé of

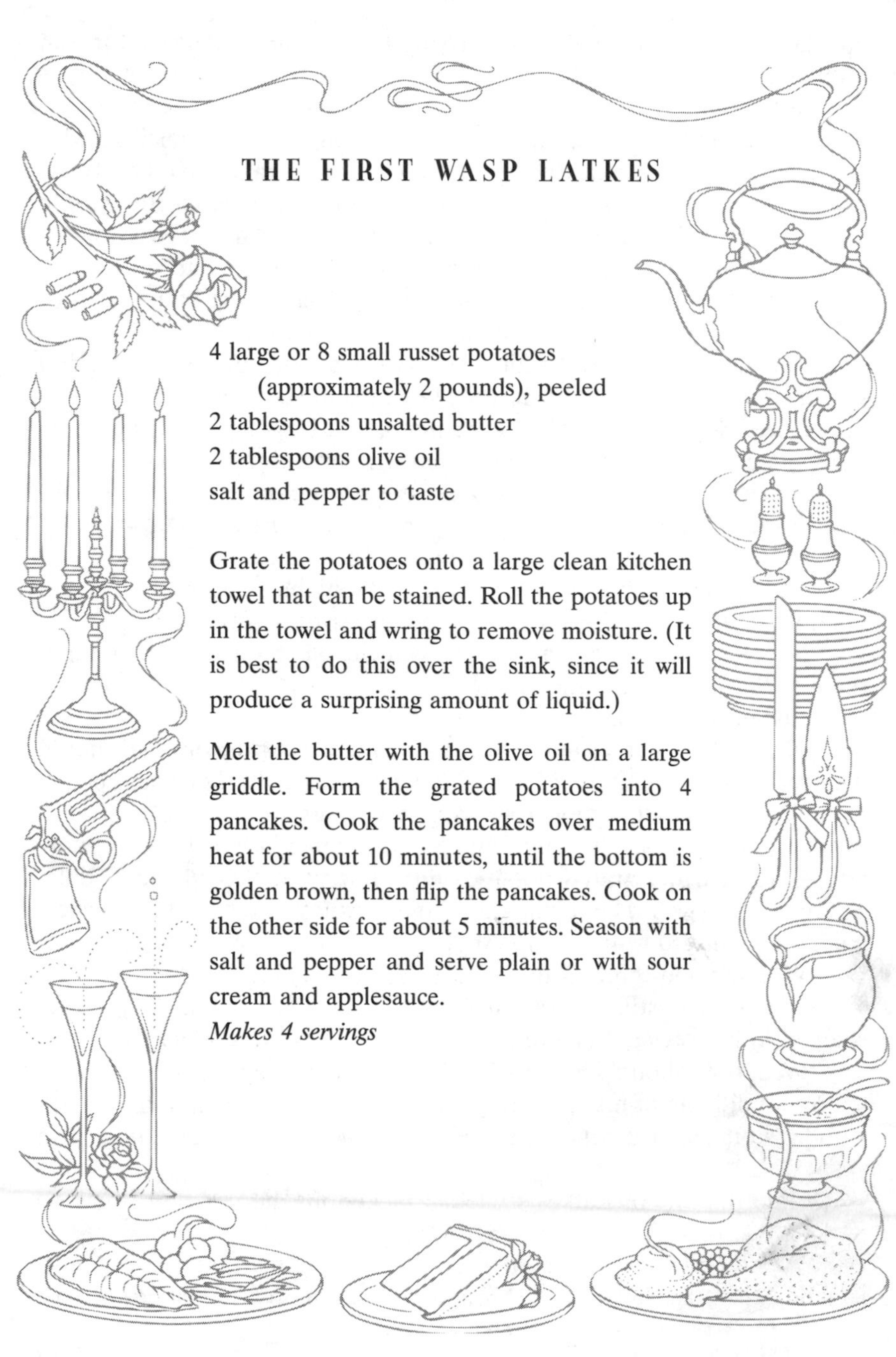

THE FIRST WASP LATKES

4 large or 8 small russet potatoes
(approximately 2 pounds), peeled
2 tablespoons unsalted butter
2 tablespoons olive oil
salt and pepper to taste

Grate the potatoes onto a large clean kitchen towel that can be stained. Roll the potatoes up in the towel and wring to remove moisture. (It is best to do this over the sink, since it will produce a surprising amount of liquid.)

Melt the butter with the olive oil on a large griddle. Form the grated potatoes into 4 pancakes. Cook the pancakes over medium heat for about 10 minutes, until the bottom is golden brown, then flip the pancakes. Cook on the other side for about 5 minutes. Season with salt and pepper and serve plain or with sour cream and applesauce.

Makes 4 servings

Montgomery. Fired the organist, to whom he preached reconciliation. Loved folk music and charismatic liturgies. Unloved by Pinckney crowd. Involved with miraculous healing of Roger Bampton? Involved with Agatha Preston? Dead.
2. *Mitchell Hartley.* Not smart, not attractive, not rich. Theologically conservative; charismatic. Worked at diocesan center. Going through ordination process slowly; flunked by Olson and Board of Theological Examiners once. Nobody's protégé. Knew something about exam paper at Olson's. Had pearls. Not at wedding. Dead.
3. *Zelda Preston.* Unreconciled about son's death from leukemia. Fired by Olson over music disagreement. Member of Altar Guild responsible for missing/found Hymnal House keys. Best friend Lucille thinks she might have killed Olson. Looking for letter from bishop about guitar music (Could Tom S. know where it is?). Not at wedding.
4. *Bob Preston.* Money problems, might have wanted pearls. Jealousy problems, might want letters from Agatha to Olson (Tom would know where?). Mother Zelda expects too much of him? Ego wrapped up in volunteer work; Olson causing problems with Habitat house? Vehicle keys found at Habitat house. Rifle-toting member of Sportsmen Against Hunger. Not at wedding.
5. *George Montgomery.* Thinks his protégé ran amok? Bad temper, bad preacher, *bad* poet. Jealous of Olson because of parish giving? Because of miracles? Is he the one Agatha referred to when she said, 'Someone demanding to see the blood tests?' At wedding, according to Father Doug Ramsey.
6. *Agatha Preston.* Loathes her mother-in-law, loathes her husband, loathes her life. Obsesses about hell but was deeply in love with Olson. Digging in columbarium area. At wedding.

I got up and flipped the latkes. The cooked sides were golden brown and crusty, and the delectable smell of potatoes crackling in melted butter made my mouth water.

I frowned at my notepad. What I had not written down was that Father Olson's office and house had been trashed and his death site vandalized. Not on my list were Lucille Boatwright, whom Arch had literally stumbled upon while she was surreptitiously snooping through church files, and Doug Ramsey, who, like Lucille, had wasted no love on Ted Olson. Father Doug Ramsey, also known as Father Hyperbole, Father Insensitive, Father Overtalkative. But I had seen him at the wedding as I had Lucille. You couldn't be kidnapping Tom Schulz if you were waiting for him to show up at the church.

And then there was Tom. I had felt his presence so clearly the night I had gone to Olson's. Now he felt absent to me, as if a phone were ringing, but no one was home.

You may feel God's presence or you may sense God's absence, Olson had said in a sermon once, *but God is still there, like the man who buys Halloween candy every year, yet no trick-or-treaters come.*

I gently removed the pancakes from the griddle and put them on a plate. I searched for applesauce and sour cream. Finding neither, I merely salted and peppered the potatoes and had a bite. They were hot, crunchy, and divine. *God is still there.* I lifted the phone from its cradle and dialed Tom Schulz's voice mail. His deep, rich voice filled my heart with hope.

Call me, Olson's voice said in my ear. I gasped. My mind had been working on the puzzle of Tom's note for two and a half days, and suddenly I'd figured it out. Or perhaps I'd gotten some kind of message from Olson on The Other Side. Better not ponder that one. With a shaking hand, I dialed the church's number.

"This is St. Luke's Episcopal Church," Ted Olson's voice happily announced, "on Main Street in Aspen Meadow next to Lower Cottonwood Creek. Services are . . ." And he went on to announce the two Sunday morning eucharist times. I tapped my foot. He continued, "If you would like to leave a general message, press one. If you have a confidential message for Father Ted Olson, please press two."

I stood in my kitchen, transfixed. Churchgoers, especially those going through a hard time, desperately desired confidentiality. I had found out the hard way just how elusive *please don't tell anyone* was. From as long ago as my divorce to as recently as the news about Tom Schulz, I had seen details of my personal life spread in the church like fire through a grove of dry aspens.

And it was in the note from Schulz that Olson had given a key to who his attacker had been. VM wasn't Victor Mancuso. And it wasn't Vestry Member. *VM,* I was willing to bet, was *Voice Mail.* But what was P.R.A.Y.? I stared at my phone, trying to remember Tom Schulz retrieving messages from his own voice mail. He waited for the message, and then pressed in a code. . . .

Four digits. Could P.R.A.Y. be a four-digit access code Olson had chosen? Unfortunately, I did not know how to use the code for the church's voice-mail system. *Think,* commanded Tom Schulz's voice inside my head.

"I am," I said out loud. I had already gone through Olson's files on the Board of Theological Examiners and the diocese twice. There had been no voice-mail instructions. And what if Olson had simply discarded his messages after he'd listened to them?

Are you kidding? Schulz's voice again. *That guy didn't throw away* anything.

I looked at my kitchen clock. Almost midnight. I called the Sheriff's Department and left a message for Boyd: Please call me A.S.A.P. He was probably getting tired of these messages.

I put the phone down. There was no way I could go to bed now. Besides, Tom Schulz, if he was still alive, probably wasn't asleep. I needed to concentrate. I covered the potato pancakes and put them in the walk-in, then scanned my kitchen.

By my own phone I had a list of numbers: Tom Schulz, Julian's and Arch's school, Marla, Alicia's supply company, Arch's friend Todd, the library. What had Olson had by his phone? The bulletin board in his office had all kinds of phone numbers on it; I remembered that from my time in there before the wedding was cancelled, and afterward, when I'd thrown the hymnal and notes had popped off the bulletin board.

And the answering machine at Olson's house had been destroyed. Could that have been the motivation for the mayhem out there: to destroy evidence, rather than steal anything? But why hit me and take the solitary exam paper from my hand? And what did *B.- Read - Judas* mean? I did not know. But I had no doubt that the phone messaging was key, and that was where I had to concentrate. Perhaps whoever had done the vandalism out at Olson's had not realized just how voice mail was stored. Maybe someone from a generation that did not like or understand developments in communications technology.

I looked out my kitchen window: A powdery, soft snow had begun to fall. I wanted to rush to the trashed church office, study the remains of Olson's bulletin board, and come up with an accessing phone number that would provide the answers to so many questions. As if in protest, my back contracted with pain—not enough for a pill, I told myself. I needed to stay sharp. On the other hand, I dared not go back to the church alone. Boyd would never forgive me. I hugged myself, angry with my own indecision.

Snow tends to muffle noise. That was why I waited to hear the faint stomping noise again. When it came, the fur on the back of Scout's neck ruffled. Someone was on my front porch.

I moved stealthily through the dining room and into the darkened living room. I heard more shuffling and stepping, even a small grunt. By the light from a street lamp, I could see yet another afghan hanging from my porch-swing hooks. The figure that hopped off the swing was Agatha Preston.

"Don't leave!" I shouted as I flung open my front door.

"Agh!" Agatha screamed as she reeled backward. "This was supposed to be a surprise! I've been so worried . . . and I just wanted you to have something . . . !"

On the deck railing was a mayonnaise jar filled with coffee. Or at least it looked like coffee.

I took a deep breath to steady myself. "Please, Agatha, come in."

She tossed her braids over her shoulders, reverently picked up the jar, and tiptoed inside my house. She was wearing a pink-and-white warm-up suit with matching pink boots. *Pocahantas as a candy cane.*

"Ooh, please don't get mad at me, Goldy. I told you I don't have a job, so I just crochet all the time, and I had these on hand, so I thought maybe . . ."

"Thanks, Agatha, I should have known they were from you. I saw one at Olson's house." She blushed the color of her suit. I wondered what color she was going to turn when I told her about the letters I'd found. I said, "What's in the jar?"

"Oh. Well you know, Ted really had the Power." Her eyes brightened. "Miraculous powers. And so I heard on television that if you dig up the dirt where the blood—"

"Don't go on, I know all about it. My son saw the same program. Come on out to the kitchen."

"But . . . I already poured some of this water around over at the church, because we have so much unhealing there—" She moved hesitantly into the kitchen, put her jar on the table, and sat down.

"At the columbarium site? I saw you—"

"—and I just thought," she turned to me breathlessly, "that since you'd had so many things going wrong in your life, you really needed healing, a supernatural kind that was sure to work—"

"Please. That is not miracle, Agatha. That is superstition."

She looked at me, her mouth open. "What's the difference? Don't you pray for things? Don't you think we need a childlike faith?" She stood and sidled over to Julian's mound of dirt. "What's this? Is it from Chimayó?"

"It belongs to somebody who works for me."

"Oh." She regarded me earnestly. "Didn't you ever in your life pray for something specific?"

"Of course." Agatha was, as I'd told Arch, part of the church family. I wanted to relate to her, I just didn't know how. I searched my memory for the kind of kindred experience she meant. "Let's see," I faltered. "Oh, yes. My parents sent me to a Roman Catholic school for first grade. I loved it because we made butter in the classroom."

"That's what you were praying for?" asked Agatha, confused. "Butter?"

"No, no. My mother had an unusually bad case of appendicitis. She was in the hospital for weeks. So I . . ." Suddenly I felt terribly foolish, but Agatha was leaning forward, expectantly. "So I wrote, 'Please make my Mommy well' on a piece of paper, rolled it up, and placed it between the stone fingers of a statue of the Virgin Mary in the school courtyard." I let out a tiny laugh of embarrassment.

"Wow. And was your mother healed?"

"Well . . . yes, but," I said, groping for words, "I think you have to test what you would call the *Weird* against church doctrine and tradition, maybe." My own words gave me pause. I sounded like a member of the Old Guard! I ought to believe in the *Weird* anyway. I certainly had experienced enough of it lately.

She pouted. "Your attitude is a cop-out. Ted had the Power."

"Great. What were you doing out at Ted Olson's? Did you steal a paper from him?"

She colored brilliantly. "I . . . I . . . was getting the dirt from the place where he fell. Is that a crime? What paper?"

I studied her carefully. For the moment, I was willing to believe she was telling the truth.

"I'm sorry, Agatha," I blurted out. "I found the letters you sent to Ted Olson. I gave them to the police."

The color drained from her face. "Oh, God," she said softly. "Oh, God . . . Well, at least Bob doesn't have them." She stared straight ahead, no longer wishing to discuss miracles, apparently.

And then I had an absolutely wonderful idea. It filled me with more lightness and excitement than I had felt since Tom's disappearance. "Agatha. Do you know how Ted accessed his voice mail?"

"Yeah, I think, I mean I don't know the code, but he had one. You see, first he had to call this number at U.S. West, and then he'd dial in the church number—"

Hallelujah. "Is there anybody at the church now, do you know?"

She looked at the kitchen clock, puzzled by my question. 12:30 A.M. "Now? I think they're having some kind of vigil until the funeral. The people at the ten o'clock Sunday service set it up."

Great. If Agatha accompanied me, then Boyd couldn't possibly get upset with me for wandering out. If there were people at the church, then it wasn't as if we were going into an empty place at night.

I could hear my heart beating. I whispered, "Do you know where Ted kept the number for U.S. West accessing?"

"Sure, somewhere on the bulletin board of his office. But why?"

"I'll tell you on the way to church," I promised her.

21

There were only two automobiles in the parking lot, not exactly a crowd for a vigil. I did not recognize either car, but then again, I didn't usually go to the later Sunday-morning service, and was unfamiliar with the charismatics and their vehicles.

"Does Bob have any idea where you are?" I asked when we disembarked from my van.

"He thinks I'm here. At the vigil."

"Ah. Do you know how to get into the office?" Around us, snowflakes continued to fall.

"The keys are on top of one of those log panels beside the office door," she replied promptly. "Lucille always teaches all of us how to get into the priest's office."

"Who's 'all of us'?"

"It's supposed to be just the Altar Guild, who are supposed to keep it confidential, but—"

"Never mind."

The lights were dim in the parish itself. Flickering light from the vigil candles played against the windows. I couldn't remember if it was liturgically advisable to have a vigil, much less a funeral, before Good Friday during Holy Week. But the charismatics in our parish loved vigils more than they cared about liturgical appropriateness. And people couldn't time their dying.

We stepped carefully over the yellow police ribbon. At the office entrance, Agatha reached up and snatched the key, then fumbled momentarily with it before unlocking the door. She pushed it open and reached in for the light, then wove her way over the illuminated mess. When we came into Olson's office, she pointed to the bulletin board on the floor, with its disheveled array of notes. Slowly, we pulled out thumbtacks and gathered up the notes with numbers that had landed on the floor. Diocesan Center. Altar Guild. Organist.

"Here's one," said Agatha. "Roger Bampton."

"I wonder why Ted would need to call him."

"Oh, you know, Roger was having copies of his blood tests framed for Ted. Roger called it 'his first miracle.' Ted was pretty excited about it. He told everybody. I don't know what happened to them, though. I know they were calling back and forth—"

"Eureka!" I read, "Alexander Graham, 555-6363."

Agatha wrinkled her nose. "That doesn't sound like anyone in our parish."

I said, "You don't have a son who loves codes. That's for Alexander Graham Bell, honey." I thought for a moment. Go to a pay phone, or try to plug in the phones here? Out at Olson's house, the vandal hadn't realized that just whacking a phone and pulling it out of the wall was not enough to destroy it. "Would you go see if you can plug in the secretary's extension? Then if you'll take notes on his messages, I'd appreciate it. I might miss something."

"But it's supposed to be confident—"

"Too late for that now."

Agatha clamped her mouth shut and minced into the outer office. She fussed with the secretary's extension while I plugged in Olson's smashed phone and got a dial tone. I sat down at the desk, whacked my foot on a pile of plumbing pipe, and cursed. I dialed first the 555 number, which was indeed the right US West messaging service, then dialed the church number, then pressed the buttons for P, R, A, and Y.

The first message came on. It was Agatha.

"Hi, it's me calling Thursday night. Sorry you have that society meeting tomorrow during the day. I'll miss you! Let's talk after the wedding on Saturday, plan something else. Love you."

In the outer room, I heard Agatha stifle a sob. I couldn't stop the electronic message and didn't want to. The voice mail beeped with another message.

"This is the diocesan office. Please pick up your photocopies of the General Ordination Examinations by Friday afternoon so that your committee can begin its work next week. Call if there's a problem."

Another beep. Lucille Boatwright said, "I just think it's terrible what you've done to Zelda. This never would have happened in Father *Pinckney's* time. In Father *Pinckney's* time, I never would have had to speak into one of these infernal machines, either!"

There was a long beep, as if Lucille had somehow messed up even while disconnecting from the infernal machine. The next voice was Bob Preston's.

"I know what you're doing." In the outer office, Agatha gasped. Her husband's voice was low and threatening. "I'm going to spill the beans on you to the bishop. You think they want to face another lawsuit in this diocese? You're dead in the Episcopal church, Olson. You're *finished.*"

Good God. There was another beep. "Sorry about the blowup at the meeting, old friend, especially after you'd brought that coconut last time, which was such fun. You are part of the communion, I didn't mean what I said, guess I just got carried away, you know how I do. Listen, you forgot to pick up your exams. I'll bring them out to your house to read Saturday morning before the wedding you're doing for that Goldy woman on the committee. Tomorrow then, nine o'clock?" Canon Montgomery disconnected.

In the outer office, Agatha shrieked. Then there was a dull thud.

"Agatha?" I said. There was no response. In my hand, the phone beeped again and another message, this one from Doug Ramsey, began playing back. I pressed the dial-tone button desperately. "Agatha?" I called. There was still silence from the outer office. I jiggled the button and prayed for a dial tone so I could call 911. Still the message from Ramsey droned on.

"Help!" I called. My voice sounded feeble.

"No one will hear you," said Canon Montgomery as he stepped into Olson's office. His white hair was askew. His face was scarlet. In his hand he was holding a collapsible baton, the kind available at police-supply stores. Only this one, I was fairly sure, was the one that had whacked me in the back by Olson's house, when I had discovered the one thing Olson's killer had left out there: a photocopied paper that was his excuse for being there in the first place. The one who would *Bring* the tests to *Read* was the *Judas.*

"They'll catch you," I said angrily. "You will never—"

"Shut up." He was dressed all in black, except for his snowy-white clerical collar, which didn't go with his flushed toadlike face and his hand gripping the weapon. "Where are the blood tests? You must know. I know he told someone—"

"What?"

"I know Olson was lying," he growled. "I—"

"Where's Tom Schulz, you son of a bitch?" I screeched. "Olson called Tom before the wedding because he was afraid of you. And well he should have been."

He laughed. It was a horrible gritty laugh that made my stomach turn. I glanced quickly around the ransacked office. From grimy windows to the shelves of books to the floor, where the tangle of pipes from the renovation lay in an unattractive heap, there was no way out.

"Where is Tom Schulz?" I demanded again.

Canon Montgomery shook his head. "You know, I could have destroyed Olson. I mean, fix it so he'd be defrocked. He had monkey business with that woman out there, he had questionable money transactions with the pearls and all this sudden giving. Driving a Mercedes. Pah!"

"But you killed him." Stall, I thought frantically. Do anything to keep him talking. So that someone will have a chance to see you or hear you. "And Mitchell Hartley, too. He must have found out something."

"No great loss, Hartley. He didn't even want to turn me in! He just wanted to tell me he knew I'd picked up Olson's exams, and that they'd found one page out at Olson's house. Hartley wanted to pass the exams in exchange for his information. We had a meeting last Friday. Olson and I fought over his idiotic miracle claims. He stomped out, and unfortunately I was seen by Mitchell Hartley picking up Olson's set of exams and the diocesan vehicle keys. Saturday, when I was out at Olson's, your cop friend was listening to Olson spill his guts. I know he told him where the blood tests are. Too bad."

He was insane. There was no doubt about it. I said, "You just couldn't stand him having that kind of power, could you? After he'd been your protégé?"

"People were worshiping him," Montgomery snapped fiercely. "I was trying to protect the church. And how fortunate he didn't give my name in that note. Then when the police find the bodies of you and that other woman, they'll suspect me even less. It'll just look like another burglary—"

I eased my hand under the desk, where one broken pipe was resting against the side of the file cabinet. "You'll never disprove the miracle, you know," I told him with as much aggression as I could muster.

"Oh?" He lifted his peaked white eyebrows and smiled sourly, as if we were discussing disputed theological points. "Why is that?"

"Because the blood tests are in the computer, you beast. Down at the pathology lab. Even if you destroy one set, there will be endless documentation. It's like the message you left. You can't get rid of it by axing the phone machine. The information is stored." I had a sudden vision of Lucille Boatwright complaining about the phone machine. "You couldn't operate the fax machine, and you couldn't destroy messages by breaking an answering machine. You and your generation just don't understand *technology*!"

With that I jumped up, pipe in hand, and slammed it into the window next to Olson's desk. Panes broke, but the frame held.

"Help!" I shrieked. "Help!"

Montgomery turned quickly and sprinted for the front door of the office.

"Hey!" I yelled after him. "Where's Tom Schulz?"

The office door banged closed. I leapt up and charged out to the secretary's office. My back shrieked with pain. Agatha was slumped over the desk, moaning. At least she was alive. I had to go after Montgomery.

By the time my eyes adjusted to the darkness and the swirling snow, Montgomery was on the flagstones. He was running toward the columbarium site. The parking lot and the road were just beyond it.

"Don't!" I yelled. Then I ran, faster than I had ever run before, damn my back. I was desperate to catch Montgomery. He could not get away. He could not disappear without telling me where Tom was.

Montgomery halted at the edge of the columbarium ditch. He couldn't seem to decide whether to go around the site or through it.

"Stop, stop, please stop," I howled, breathless from pain and exertion. I was twenty feet away from him.

He dropped to his knees and peered into the pit. I thought he was trying to figure out how deep the excavation was.

I gasped for breath and called out, "No matter what happens to the blood tests, some people are going to believe." I was at the bottom of the excavation. Montgomery jumped back up; his white hair looked eerily fluorescent. I yelled, "You can't stop people from wanting to think God was . . . working through Olson. Please. Please stop."

"You want a miracle?" he shrieked. "You're going to need one to find Schulz."

"Please don't, please wait," I pleaded as I started to scramble up the side of the hillock of dirt. Montgomery, watching me, backed away. "Wait!" I yelled. He spun around and looked again into the ditch, as if trying to judge if he could jump across. "This is an unstable spot," I begged. "Please don't . . ." He whirled back and stared at me, or at least in my direction. Snow fell softly all around him. His thin white hair and his clerical collar glinted in the light from passing cars.

"I'll never, I'll never . . ." his voice boomed before he fell backward, into the deep, dark pit.

"No!" I screamed. My feet sank into mud as I clambered to the top of the embankment. Below, I could see a blur of clothing, Montgomery jerking, off-balance in the frigid water of the ditch.

"Wait for me to help you," I yelled, already feeling helpless. I slid down the side of the bank. Damn Lucille Boatwright and her damn unapproved, uninspected columbarium project. I took a deep breath and waded into the water. It was like ice. I felt my legs for an instant, and then they were numb. I tugged at Montgomery's clothing, at his heavy body. He had gone limp. How was that possible? Above us, on the other side of the bank, a car stopped. Someone had come in from the road. People who had seen us fall from the top of the embankment were yelling down at us.

I rolled Montgomery over and cried at the sight of his face, which had gone from red to an ominous white. "Where's Schulz? *Where is he?*"

His eyes bulged, but there was no response. I shook him and tried to drag the water-logged body over to the side of the ditch, but he was too heavy. His hands gripped his chest. They were locked there. Damn it, I knew he'd had a heart attack. He needed CPR, and fast.

"Hey, lady, get out of that water. You're gonna die of hypothermia!" A fat man in a plaid wool jacket grabbed my shoulder and pulled me up. His friend tugged on Montgomery.

"Aaugh," I cried. I was so cold. Montgomery wasn't going to make it. And no clue as to where Tom Schulz was. My love, my Tom, would die, wherever he was. The police would never find him. I would never see him again.

"Gotta get you into some dry clothes, gotta get you a blanket!" the man who had rescued me insisted. "Hey, girl! What possessed you? I hate to tell you, but I think that religious guy is dead. At least he went fast."

When we came through the church doors, only Doug Ramsey and Roger Bampton were praying in the back pew. I hadn't seen Roger since the whole brouhaha over him had erupted. Now three people had died—

Olson, Hartley, and Montgomery, because no one could accept what appeared to be unexplained.

"My *heavens,* what in the *world,* did you fall into the *creek*?" cried Doug Ramsey as he scrambled out of the pew. "On your way to the vigil? Did you get lost?"

"Just get her some dry clothes from the Outreach box," ordered Roger Bampton, taking charge of me. He was a short bald man, with a wrinkled face and age spots on his hands. He seemed awfully ordinary looking to be the center of so much controversy. "Take those clothes off right away," he ordered, then handed me one of Agatha's afghans from the library couch. As he walked out of the library, he said, "They'll chill you to the bone."

I did as directed. I was shaking violently, too cold to cry. Doug Ramsey, whose inclination to exaggerate had thrown me off base ("The whole committee's here!" when Montgomery had not been, and "Women waited for Olson," when it was only Agatha), thrust his long, thin arm through the door of the library and dropped a man's sweatshirt and some bell-bottom jeans. When I'd put them on, I came out, and Roger Bampton offered me a cup of tea. My rescuer had just been informed by his friend that Montgomery was dead. Roger Bampton had called the police.

"Somebody needs to go check on Agatha Preston," I stammered. "She's hurt. In the St. Luke's office in back of the church." The man who had brought me into St. Luke's shook his head and took off in that direction.

"We were just here at the vigil, which I wanted to be sure was conducted in orthodox fashion," said Ramsey, who was incapable of keeping quiet in moments of crisis, "and we heard the racket in the parking lot, and then you came in, and then this news about Montgomery! Lord! I just don't know what to say, don't know what to do . . . In a way, you know, it's like the original Easter vigils, when the catechumens were kept underground, naked, until they could come up on Easter morning and be baptized and get their new clothes, although this is *hardly* the right time of year to be baptized in a *ditch,* much less the ditch beside a columbarium site, and of course you were christened long ago, I'm just saying—"

"What?" I yelled. I grabbed Father Doug Ramsey by the lapels of his black suit. *Kept underground.* Father Doug would know this, he was an expert on the liturgy, as was Canon Montgomery, who *always asked about the history of the Eucharist.* Montgomery, who'd just happened to be close by Agatha and me when we were dialing on the church office phone. The church office, where there was a whole underground space being dug out for new plumbing. "Quick!" I cried. "Help me."

Father Doug Ramsey pulled his chin into his neck. "*Now* what?"

"We have to go look at the church office, where they've been doing that renovation. Underground!" But I was already moving quickly, running to the hallway by the Sunday School rooms.

Doug Ramsey yelled after me, "Do we have to do it right *now*?"

Roger trotted along behind me as I dashed, barefoot, down the hallway past the choir room, through the side door, and up the icy steps to the bunkerlike office building. The man from the creek was helping Agatha up. She seemed to be stunned, but I didn't stop to determine her condition. Instead of turning left to go into the office, I darted right and flipped the switch of the dim bulb hanging in the area that was being renovated.

I swallowed. The large space was dark, stripped to the walls. I walked across a board that had been put down across the subfloor to the far side of the room, then turned on another dim bulb in a room that was torn out to its framing. Beyond that was only a small tunnellike space where the pipes had all been ripped out.

"Here," said a panting Roger Bampton behind me. Bless him, he seemed to be reading my mind. "You'll need this. I'll be right behind you."

I switched on the flashlight he thrust at me. My light flickered over a sleeping bag, and some provisions. I eased myself down to the entrance of the dirt tunnel. Earth fell on my face and got in my eyes. My clenched hands banged against the remaining shafts of pipe. I had heard that same noise when I was looking around Olson's trashed office. I flashed my light ahead. I rounded a turn and sent the beam as far in as it would go.

It was another tunnel. My beam reflected off of something. Coming closer, I saw that it was the missing chalice, paten, and ambry from Olson's house. I reached out to touch the cold metal, then lifted the lid on the ambry. But I already knew what I would see when I shone the light inside: the pearl chokers, glistening and lustrous in the narrow shaft of light. Only Montgomery would be able to figure out that Olson had kept the *pearls of great value* in something he valued equally: the sacramental vessels.

I slogged ahead into the blackness. There was another turn in the tunnel. I remembered placing my scrolled intercession in the hand of a statue. I prayed now, hard. *I believe; help thou my unbelief.* My flashlight beamed through the shadows.

There. At the end of the dark dirt cylinder, tied to a chair, was a motionless figure. Tom Schulz. Slowly, he lifted his head at the light and squinted. He was gagged.

I ran toward him and tugged the gag off.

"Goldy?" His voice was hoarse from disuse, and I could not see his eyes in the dim light. "Is it really you?"

"You bet," I told him, and then I grasped him in a wordless hug.

22

We were married the next afternoon, after the church emptied from Father Olson's funeral service. My parents flew in, joyful; Boyd and Armstrong met them at the airport. A small group from St. Luke's came, including a fussy Lucille Boatwright. I called Zelda and said I needed her to play the organ, would she? She said that of course she would, I didn't want that trash charismatic music, did I? No, just whatever she wanted; but I apologetically added that there was one condition to her playing. She had to let me invite her daughter-in-law, Sarah Preston Black, and her grandson, Ian Preston. "Just use me as an excuse," I told her. "I can't get married, and be happy, knowing you still have all that old pain."

Zelda gasped and then started to cry. "I guess I've been wanting to . . . in my heart. It's all felt so heavy there, like a dead weight. I think that's why I auditioned to play the organ at the Catholic church. Somehow, I really did want to see them . . ." She stopped, then said weakly, "All right. If you'll call them . . ."

Which I did. They would be happy to come. With much fussing and worry, Father Doug Ramsey agreed to perform the nuptials. I gave Marla the recipe for Stuffed Portobello Mushrooms, and she made them. Arch hauled the wedding cake out of the freezer.

Tom Schulz was weak, but he refused a wheelchair. His left ankle was broken; Boyd had driven us down to the hospital the night before and questioned him while Julian, Arch, and I had waited for Tom's cast to be applied. In nearly three days of captivity, Tom had only had some water. He hadn't known what Montgomery wanted with blood tests. But he'd bluffed him right along, though.

"Blood tests?" Tom protested. "Why would I know about them? But I pretended to know something, so the guy would keep me alive." I shook my head in disbelief.

Boyd swore none of it had made sense. The keys at the Habitat house seemed to implicate Preston; the pearls with Mitchell Hartley made it look as if robbery was the motive. All planted by Montgomery. Now *that* made sense. At Agatha's request, Boyd shredded her letters to Olson. Bob Preston would never see them. Agatha told me that she and Bob had decided to go into counseling; it was easier than divorce.

Back once more in their rented tuxedos, Arch and Julian beamed. With the morning mail, Julian had received his acceptance to Cornell. Marla added a wobbly *Congratulations* in frosting on the side of the thawed wedding cake.

The Prestons: Agatha, Bob, a wary Sarah, looking somewhat like a short Nefertiti in a silk pantsuit, and Ian, a compact swimmer like his deceased father, all came in to the church together. Ian brought an orchid corsage for his grandmother, whom he had not seen for five years. While Zelda and Ian were tearfully embracing, a triumphant Bob Preston told anyone who would listen, "Now *that's* a miracle."

At the part of the wedding where you say the vows, I said, ". . . for better for worse, for richer for poorer, in sickness and in health, to love and to cherish. We will not be parted by death. This is my solemn vow."

Father Doug Ramsey, who was flustered, seemed to be rethinking the sermon he'd given on the trinity. He didn't notice. Tom Schulz squeezed my hand. Then, carefully and distinctly, he repeated my vow. We exchanged the rings I'd been saving in my china cupboard.

"Now, finally, I'm Goldy Schulz," I declared happily as I hugged Tom's wide, wonderful body during our jovial reception in the narthex. "I'm so glad I finally was able to get rid of that last name Bear, you can't imagine."

Tom Schulz's large, beautiful green eyes seemed to be looking into my soul.

"God," he said softly. "Goldy, I missed you."

I kissed him. "You're not going to believe this," I told my husband truthfully, "but you were with me all the time."

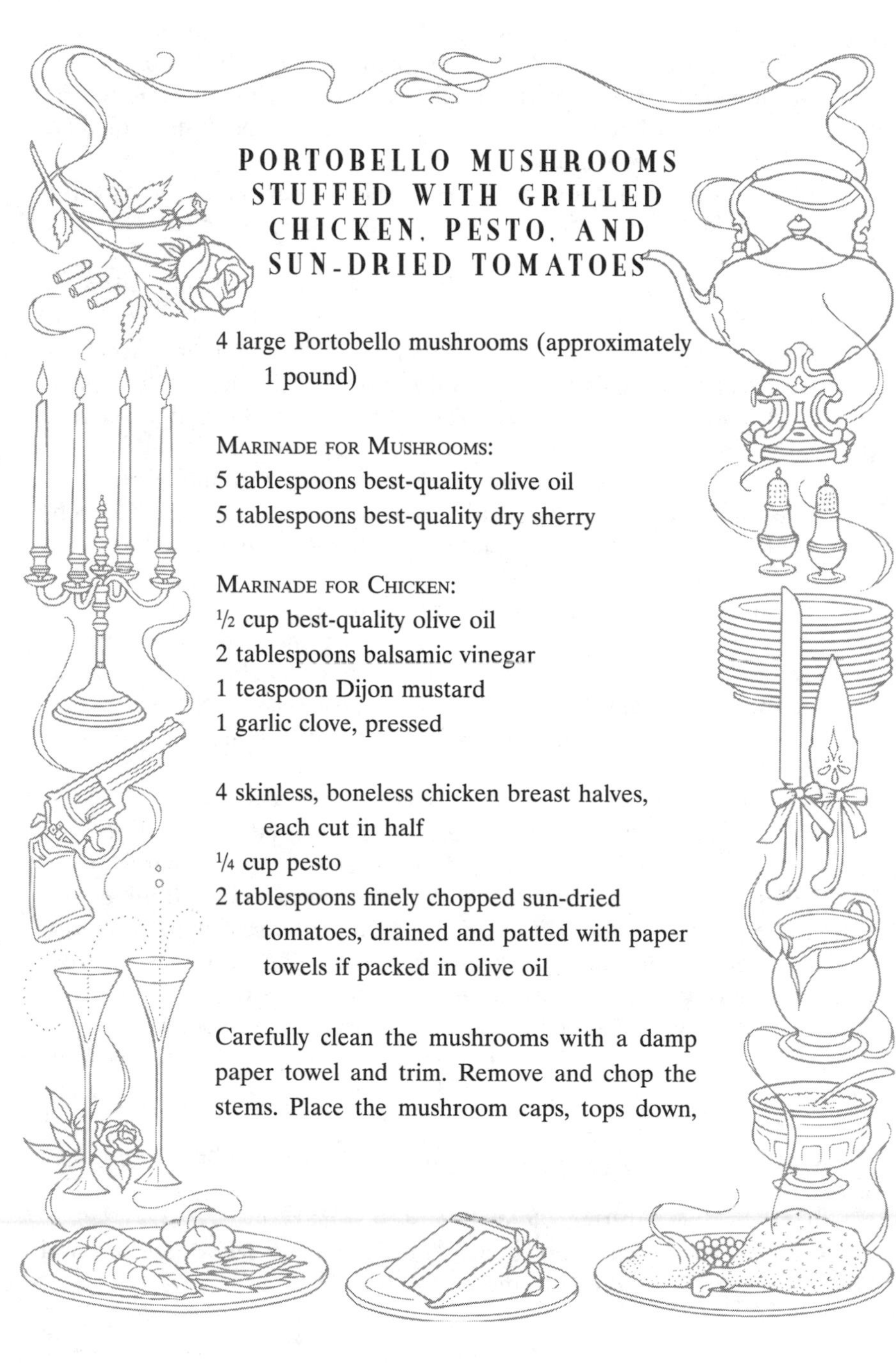

PORTOBELLO MUSHROOMS STUFFED WITH GRILLED CHICKEN, PESTO, AND SUN-DRIED TOMATOES

4 large Portobello mushrooms (approximately 1 pound)

Marinade for Mushrooms:
5 tablespoons best-quality olive oil
5 tablespoons best-quality dry sherry

Marinade for Chicken:
½ cup best-quality olive oil
2 tablespoons balsamic vinegar
1 teaspoon Dijon mustard
1 garlic clove, pressed

4 skinless, boneless chicken breast halves, each cut in half
¼ cup pesto
2 tablespoons finely chopped sun-dried tomatoes, drained and patted with paper towels if packed in olive oil

Carefully clean the mushrooms with a damp paper towel and trim. Remove and chop the stems. Place the mushroom caps, tops down,

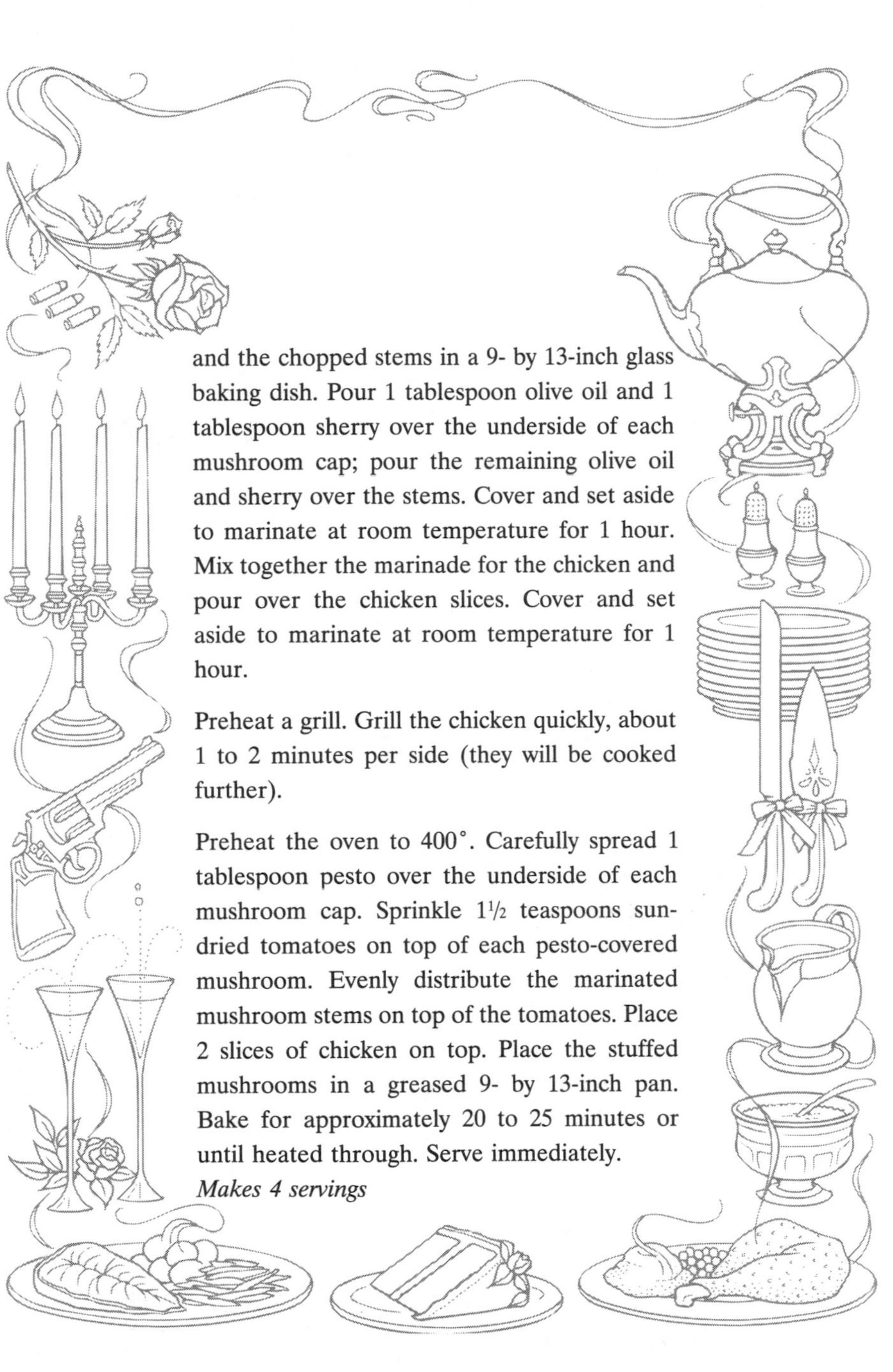

and the chopped stems in a 9- by 13-inch glass baking dish. Pour 1 tablespoon olive oil and 1 tablespoon sherry over the underside of each mushroom cap; pour the remaining olive oil and sherry over the stems. Cover and set aside to marinate at room temperature for 1 hour. Mix together the marinade for the chicken and pour over the chicken slices. Cover and set aside to marinate at room temperature for 1 hour.

Preheat a grill. Grill the chicken quickly, about 1 to 2 minutes per side (they will be cooked further).

Preheat the oven to 400°. Carefully spread 1 tablespoon pesto over the underside of each mushroom cap. Sprinkle 1½ teaspoons sun-dried tomatoes on top of each pesto-covered mushroom. Evenly distribute the marinated mushroom stems on top of the tomatoes. Place 2 slices of chicken on top. Place the stuffed mushrooms in a greased 9- by 13-inch pan. Bake for approximately 20 to 25 minutes or until heated through. Serve immediately.
Makes 4 servings

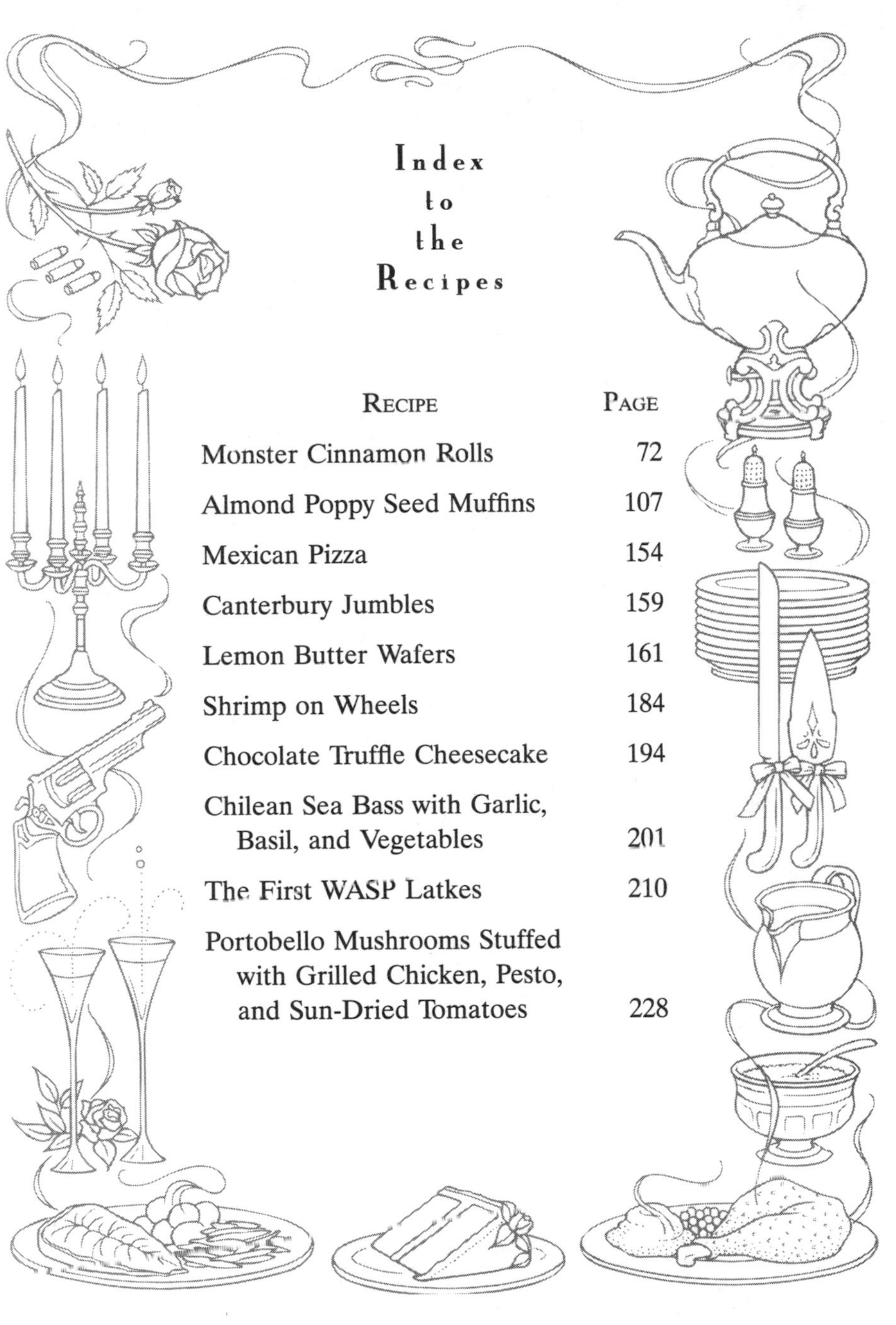

Index to the Recipes